THE
BLACK
SILENT

DAVID
DUN

PINNACLE BOOKS
Kensington Publishing Corp.
http://www.kensingtonbooks.com

Raves for David Dun and *The Black Silent:*

"Nonstop action that takes off from the very first page. David Dun knows how to keep the pages flying."

—*New York Times* bestselling author Tess Gerritsen

"Prepare to hold your breath!"

—*New York Times* bestselling author Lee Child

"Lock your doors and order in. *The Black Silent* by David Dun is a spellbinding adventure that's chilling, real, and unforgettable. With his unerring eye for detail and ballistic pace, Dun proves himself a master of intrigue and suspense. Watch out, Michael Crichton!"

—*New York Times* bestselling author Gayle Lynds, *The Coil* and *Masquerade*

"When you learn what's on the ocean's floor, you'll get the wits scared out of you. This terrific scientific thriller has a heart-pounding pace that never stops."

—*New York Times* bestselling author David Morrell

"Once you start reading *The Black Silent*, you won't come up for air until the very last page. Original, compelling, and, best of all, thought-provoking, it is a page-turner in the best sense of the word! I thoroughly enjoyed it."

—*New York Times* bestselling author Chris Reich

"David Dun combines cutting-edge science and classic suspense with superb results."

—Bestselling author Steve Alten, *Domain*

"David Dun delivers. You won't be done with Dun until the very last page."

—*New York Times* bestselling author Ridley Pearson

"Readers will delight in well-executed plot twists . . . escapist fiction of the first order."

—*New York Times* bestselling author Clive Cussler on *Necessary Evil*

ACKNOWLEDGMENTS

To Ed Stackler, my friend and editor, whose thoughtful comments are always invaluable and whose labors made a significant contribution to this novel; to Anthony Gardner, my agent, for being a great advocate, a terrific adviser, and a good friend.

To all the creative people at Kensington Books: to Publisher Laurie Parkin, for her book-savvy street smarts and for taking a chance on me, for her no-nonsense approach to the truth, and for having just the right dose of tact mixed in with her reality; to editor-in-chief, Michaela Hamilton, for keeping things on track and for our conversation about the essentials of compelling plots (and for privately editing my first book *Necessary Evil*); to my editor, Gary Goldstein, for his artful and efficient handling of the entire publication process, for keeping me informed and ensuring that I did not end up with mushroom status, for his great advice with regard to plotting and his enthusiastic support—every author wants this kind of thoughtful get-it-done editor.

To Stephanie Finnegan, a great copy editor whose inspiring devotion to all manner of factual and grammatical details is deeply appreciated.

To Dr. Michael Kinsella, Ph.D. (a fun guy with a great imagination), of Beneroia Research Institute, Seattle, Washington, for helping me understand the foundations of molecular biology and the evolution of the science of the human genome. Mike has been a major underpinning in my efforts to understand molecular genetic science in this and other plots.

To William Pendergrass, Ph.D., of the University of Washington Medical School, Department of Pathology, for his invaluable assistance with molecular biology as it pertains to aging.

To the University of Washington Marine Laboratory, for their generous hospitality and great assistance in showing me around the Friday Harbor, San Juan Island University Marine lab, and Bob Schwartzberg, who gave me a much appreciated personal guided tour.

To Professor Jerry Dickens Ph.D., professor of oceanography, Rice University, Texas, for his assistance in understanding the geology of methane deposits, possible mechanisms for methane release into the atmosphere, and the chemistry of undersea microbial life, as it pertains to food supply and energy consumption. He is one of the few people to have eaten gas hydrates from the sea floor (no lie).

To Professor Gregory Retallack, Ph.D., University of Oregon, Department of Geology, for his invaluable information concerning the accumulation of methane on the ocean floor and the various potential triggering mechanisms for catastrophic methane release that have been discussed among scientists.

To Sheriff Bill Cumming, the San Juan County sheriff, whose help was invaluable and whose professionalism and knowledge deeply impressed this author. His noteworthy honors, achievements, and activities in the community and Washington State are too numerous to mention, but no doubt account for his exceptionally long tenure. I want to particularly thank Sheriff Cumming for his help in understanding the sheriff's department, the chain of command, and the interplay between various law enforcement agencies, island culture, and the subtle permutations of law enforcement in an island community. My extrapolation from actual facts about the sheriff's department and the islands to construct a story was mine alone.

To Fred Wilson, BM3 United States Coast Guard, and Clinton Townsan, United States Coast Guard officer candidate, for their assistance in understanding Coast Guard command structure and activity in the region of Bellingham and the San Juan Islands.

To Jim and Kathy Crain, residents of San Juan, for showing me around the islands, for explaining island life and culture, and for Jim's tutelage in island geology.

To Anacortes Yacht Charters for supplying great boats with which to watch the whales and explore the San Juan Islands.

To Lauren Holden, resident of San Juan Island and the former proprietor of the bicycle rental shop on the landing above the ferry, for telling me about her life on the islands.

To the ever-enterprising oyster lady at the oyster bar on the veranda, and the oyster girls, who have learned how to feed the tourists and make a living cooking up great seafood and telling good stories.

To Ruth Johnson, for her extensive efforts in finding original research and articles, word processing, and logistical support; to Jo-Anne Stevens, in finding original research and articles, travel arrangements, word processing, and for logistical support.

To Justin Kirsch, for invaluable personal encouragement, helpful information concerning computer security, and insightful editorial suggestions.

To Richard Downs, of the Monday-night group, who, while sitting around the bar, told me of a fascinating article in *Discover* magazine concerning strange things in the deep sea, which provided the seminal idea for research on the subject.

To Mariana Krattiger, for creating the marvelous calligraphy map in front of the book.

To Miles Hay, for his technical assistance on the subject of weapons and firearms.

To all my friends, family, and coworkers from whom I have received a large measure of encouragement and inspiration, some who helped with a few words and some who devoted themselves to many hours, even days of thought and helpful editorial commentary. Not all of them are listed here. I thank you all for your generosity, support, and hard work. I will undertake the risk of naming a few of these fine folks (in alphabetical order): Nancy Andrew, Mark Emmerson, Russ Hanley, David Martinek, Missy McArthur, Bill Warne, and Donna Zenor.

To all of my friends at the Outback Steak House of Redding, California, who cook me up some great fish while I write into the night. Redding Outback knows my favorite recipe. You won't quite find it on the menu. These are fine people who give great service.

To Ritchie Phillips, proprietor of R&D, my network computer guru (and the ever-faithful Brian Small) who keeps the office connected.

To Steve and Mary McCaughey and Strange Birds, for their technical assistance in flying wounded airplanes.

To my wife, Laura, who is the love of my life, who unfailingly supports me, and who inspired parts of the Haley character when she piloted and flew me in a Lake amphibian around the San Juan Island chain.

Sunday morning, three days after Thanksgiving

PROLOGUE

The shock of no air hit him at the same instant someone pulled his mask loose from behind, filling it with icy water. Despite the shock, Ben's diver's mind instinctively began a countdown: he had two minutes.

Ben couldn't sense his attacker's location—the other diver had to be staying behind him, hovering at the edge of a forest of kelp, where Ben had been concentrating on a broken pump. Forcing himself to stay calm, he tried reaching up for his air hose, hoping to follow it with his fingers to the mouthpiece. But his assailant had looped his right wrist with a restraint. Ben struggled against the cuff, quickly realizing that his left wrist had also been fastened.

It had been perhaps fifteen seconds since his last breath. He pulled frantically on both the lines, but seemed only to tighten the restraints around his wrists. In the blur he saw that the material around his wrists led to some sort of white line around his torso and thighs. It was a simple but effective binding slipped on from behind in the distraction of work. Ben had no time to solve it. Compressed air pumped into the seawater behind his head, making a tantalizing bubbling sound. He wrenched his arms and reached for the air button on his buoyancy compensator to inflate and ascend. By hunching over he could barely push the valve. Instead of the comforting feeling of an inflated vest, a torrent of bubbles escaped the BC. The other diver had opened the release valve when Ben used the compressed air.

He tried hard kicks to propel himself to the surface, but his restraints seemed to be tied to the net wall of the octopus pen.

Panic set in. He forced himself to think of something else. Pumping air into his dry suit wouldn't work because his assailant had opened the heavy zipper on his back. Releasing his weight belt might help. Ben had enough leeway to unbuckle it, but when it fell away, he didn't ascend. It hung on him somehow, perhaps clipped to the lines at his thighs.

Almost unconsciously, Ben's fingers inched toward the backup mouthpiece velcroed to the BC at his chest. The lines at his wrists were too short; he couldn't bring it to his mouth. He hunched over, but his lips came just short of the mouthpiece.

Ben could feel the other diver's nonchalance, confidence born no doubt from days of preparation. His enemy would be agile and skilled, younger than Ben, waiting for him to tire, watching from behind while Ben drowned.

The man dropped to Ben's leg, wrapping him in kelp. They would blame Glaucus, the octopus that lived in the pen, or the kelp, or both for the drowning. It had all been choreographed. By Frick.

It has to be Frick.

The anger Ben felt couldn't compete with his growing fear. Ugly thoughts passed through his oxygen-starved head as the air in his blood dissipated.

Without thought he gave a mighty tug with his right arm and curled and hunched as far as he could. Miraculously, either the line gave a little or he hunched farther this time, because he was able to get his lips over the emergency mouthpiece. Sweet air bled into his mouth.

Through the saltwater murk Ben thought he saw the other diver now, still working below him and not looking up. The killer had made a mistake. Ben sucked deeply. The air gave him strength and hope. Ben forced himself to breathe regularly. And think. *Deep breaths, relax, relax, relax.*

Frick's face flashed again in his mind. With it came the solution: *Frick wants it to look like a fatal accident. To survive, play dead.*

Ben let his head dip as if he were losing consciousness. To add to the ploy he released the emergency mouthpiece. After an appropriate time he relaxed his body and listened to the vigorous bubbling from his equipment. Ben remained slack even as his lungs screamed once again for air. He felt the diver move up behind him, apparently satisfied that he had fouled his legs with enough kelp, so that he could unfasten the body from the mesh netting. He was probably watching him, waiting for the last exhalation of breath and bubbles.

Relax . . . be a dead man.

He felt the diver turning him to see his face. . . . Playing dead was becoming easier. Ben sensed his consciousness flickering, the freezing cold water feeling warmer. Through half-closed lids a blurry image appeared as the diver put his hands on Ben's face, peering at him.

The diver moved downward once again, fiddling with Ben's leg and the sidewall mesh. Oxygen-starved instincts overtook Ben's thoughts and he leaned to the emergency mouthpiece and sucked air. Consciousness bloomed again, along with the pain, the cold, and the fear.

The diver hadn't appeared to notice. A new thought occurred to Ben: on his dangling weight belt hung a knife, and he could reach farther down than up because the wrist restraints had been fixed low on his body and around his thighs. Ben managed to remove the knife and still the diver concentrated on fastening Ben's leg with kelp to the sidewall of the pen.

Ben quickly used his free hands to clear his mask. Through the strands of kelp he could just make out the diver's first-stage regulator below him, atop the tank. He gently took hold of the diver's hose and put his knife to it, waiting until the man released Ben's last leg restraint from the fence. Once freed, Ben cut the diver's primary air hose cleanly, then twisted behind him and cut the emergency air hose. As the diver flailed, himself now wound in the kelp, Ben slashed his BC so it would hold no air. The slice was so vigorous it opened the wet suit and drew blood.

Ben took more breaths from his emergency air. Thinking became easier, colors brighter. Ben inhaled deeply as he hung fast to the other diver's tank and weight belt. Predictably, the diver dropped his weights into Ben's hand, and Ben managed to cram the belt into the strap around his own thigh, where it hung with his own. They were going down together despite the kelp. Ben was heavy, his dry suit nearly full of water. The other diver was in serious trouble, struggling, and from the sounds of it, choking. He was becoming ineffective. Ben made him more so by removing the man's dive mask. He turned as the diver turned, staying behind him, just as the other diver had done to him, clinging to his tank.

Seconds later, the diver released his backpack. Ben put an arm around him from behind, keeping the man tightly against him. They hit the bottom, Ben on his knees, still behind the other diver, both of them swathed in kelp. In desperation the man shook himself and pried at Ben's fingers, but he was growing weak. The entire harness for the tank and backpack was loose. The man was still strong enough to get clear. Ben grabbed the diver's hood, pulled it off his head, and used it as a handle. They stayed down.

The man tried his BC again, but merely blew clouds of bubbles through the knife slit. Out came a knife. Ben saw it coming in time to bring his own knife up and slash the arm. Then he grabbed the diver's knife hand and the weakened attacker lost his grip on the knife.

In seconds all struggle went out of the man and he started to convulse. Ben cut loose the weight belts dangling from the lines, along with the pump clipped to his own belt, and hacked away at the kelp. They ascended with the buoyancy of the man's wet suit and the neoprene of Ben's own dry suit.

As they rose, a horrible thought came to Ben. If Frick were behind this, then he or another accomplice might be waiting at the surface. Or in Ben's office in the Sanker Foundation. Or outside. Ben would be no match for anyone on the dock. He slipped under his assailant and pushed him to the surface, remaining below his body the whole time. The mass of kelp should keep anyone on the dock from spotting Ben. He waited. Nobody came to the dying man's aid. If he'd had helpers, hopefully they'd fled when their part of the job was over.

At the dock Ben let go of the unconscious man and pulled himself onto an octopus-feeding platform at the edge of the water. Then he pulled him onto the planking and rolled him on his back.

Ben's assailant was the new lab tech. Surprise, surprise. Ben breathed into the man's mouth until the diver choked, spit up water, and began robust coughing.

Once it was clear that his assailant might survive if he didn't die of hypothermia, Ben ran into the building, went to the locker room, and grabbed towels and a blanket. With the large slash in the upper sleeve and body of the wet suit, water would have poured in around his assailant's chest. The cold would be overwhelming. Ben himself was shaking badly. Hurrying back out on the dock, he covered the still-gagging diver in an attempt to raise his body temperature or at least keep it from going lower. Significant quantities of heat are lost from out the head, so he pulled the hood back over the man's head. Ben was too weak to pull him up the steep incline and he had neither the time nor the inclination to get the man walking again. Wasting time would only set himself up for another murder attempt.

It did not surprise Ben that Frick had planned to murder him for the Sanker Corporation. Many men would murder to possess Ben's knowledge. Where they had erred was failing to realize that it was a secret not easily possessed.

CHAPTER 1

Ben stood on his carpeted office floor, dripping in his dive suit, his chest heaving and leg muscles cramping badly. But his mind was working fluidly.

It was a relief to find his workspace unoccupied. As dangerous as it had been to return, Ben simply couldn't leave things where they lay.

He had worked alone through the holiday weekend, feverishly setting flasks of nutrient broth inoculated with strains of genetically altered bacteria on an orbital mixer and watching three timers. He'd had no choice but to keep the manufacturing process moving at a frantic pace. Time was of the essence.

After growing the genetically altered bacteria, he had used the sonicator to break them up and then put the solution in the centrifuge to separate out the constituent protein of interest. He'd planned on completing the project by the wee hours of Monday morning, then leaving Sanker forever. The entire time he'd worked as if someone's life depended on it—in this case it was his own.

On the wood bench in front of him lay priceless tubes of

organic molecules; all of which had never previously been manufactured except by Ben. In fact, the last part of the process was using a new gene that promised to be even more effective. Nothing on earth existed like these particular organics, and in the future, men would study them with the devotion of acolytes.

An hour earlier, Ben had been working on the last phase when the Sunday-morning quiet had been pierced by the sound of a horn that sounded similar to the dive signal on a World War II submarine. It meant the lab's saltwater system was in some jeopardy. In minutes Ben had concluded the problem was in the octopus pen, and he'd left his work to don scuba gear and fix the malfunctioning pump. Just as Frick had planned.

Fortunately, as far as Ben could tell, Frick's people hadn't tampered with his lab. Perhaps they were waiting for confirmation of his "accident" and the death certificate before exercising the foundation's legal right to take possession of all Ben Anderson's research, materials, and lab work.

Ben wondered about Glaucus, the octopus that, in addition to the broken seawater pump, inhabited the marine pen. Glaucus was the world's largest-known North Pacific octopus. Ben had named him after a fisherman in Greek mythology who had eaten magic sea grass, becoming a sea god and gaining eternal life.

Ben admired the creature. Glaucus had a leg span of more than thirty-eight feet from tentacle tip to tentacle tip and weighed more than seven hundred pounds. Octopuses of Glaucus's species only had a five-year life span, Glaucus was now seven. That made him the rough equivalent of a ninety-two-year-old human with a thirty-year-old body. Only Ben Anderson knew how and why.

Before leaving, Ben had a few important things to do.

First, notify the police.

After a dozen or so rings someone answered at the sheriff's office.

Ben asked, "Is the sheriff in?"

"I'm sorry, he's on vacation."

Of course. Ben knew that. "Can I speak to a deputy?"

"This is the dispatcher. There are two cars on patrol, both at Roche Harbor."

"I have a situation over at the Sanker Foundation. This is Ben Anderson."

"Are you in trouble?" The dispatcher's tone had gone from bored to slightly concerned.

"Someone just tried to kill me," Ben said.

Real concern now. "Are you safe?"

"I don't know." Ben looked out his window and down the hillside. He couldn't see the walkway along Glaucus's pen. Somehow he doubted the diver was still there. Ben explained the events of the last few minutes as best he could.

"Okay," the dispatcher said. "Where are you in the compound?"

"In my office. Second floor in the Oaks Building."

"Just a minute."

Ben heard the dispatcher talking to a patrol car before returning to Ben's call. "Is your door locked?"

"No. But it will be." Ben went and locked the door, wondering what good it would do. "I need to go now."

"Okay, sir. Don't let anyone in. I'm calling Officer Frick at home."

"Wait. He's not a regular deputy," Ben said, heat rising into his neck and face. "Would you please send someone else."

"He's a special deputy with the rank of sergeant and fully empowered," the dispatcher said. "He's also chief of security there at Sanker. I'm going to call him now."

Ben hung up. It would be a waste of precious time to argue.

Frick had used the political power of Sanker and taken great pains to get himself fully integrated into local law enforcement. Frick had been brought in by Sanker almost a year previous, not coincidentally around the same time that Ben's research had started finally to become known in a general way to Sanker executives. In small communities retired cops could get special reserve commissions.

From what Ben had been told, the county sheriff didn't much like Frick and was trying to find a politically graceful way to get Frick out of his department or at least severely limit him.

From his closet Ben pulled out jeans and a shirt. People who swam in the ocean as part of their work tended to keep extra clothes. His morning's outfit remained in the dive room.

Now came the most important part. Ben ran back to the spacious lab and went to work destroying everything that mattered.

Next he took a wooden box full of 50mm freezer tubes bundled in five different lots, each lot with its own color, and removed it from a freezer, then ran with it down the stairs and a long hall to a workshop. There he pushed aside shelving that disguised a hidden door. He stepped into a secret study, most of it taken up with a Revco minus-eighty-degree freezer set to minus-twenty degrees. He put the box in the freezer and slammed the door.

Then he gathered his lab notes and took them to his office. There he added them to some other notes hidden in a large-scale replica of a blue whale affixed to the wall. He didn't touch the wall safe, even though he was supposed to be the only one with the combination.

A beep sounded; the light under his office's security camera was flashing. The foundation was rife with security measures that Ben had once considered excessive. It was a part of the corporate culture of this rich, private foundation that

Ben had always disliked—dislike that had turned darker after what they'd done to Haley.

Ben hurried to the video monitor and saw someone standing at the gate. He looked more closely. It looked like Haley. Panic filled him at the thought of someone hurting her. Adopted by Ben when she was nine, and raised by him and his now-deceased wife, she was his family.

He used the cell phone in his pocket, scrolled down to her name, and pushed the call button. "Haley, this is Ben"—the line had static—"Can you hear me?" It went dead. He hurried back to his desk, engaged the speaker phone, and called Haley's cell phone, hoping to warn her away. He got a steady beep that wasn't a busy signal and that usually meant the repeater was overcrowded. He tried again and got the voice mail. He muttered a curse.

"Haley, if you get this message, do not come inside the foundation. Get in your car and go to Sam. I'll call you as soon as I can."

With mounting frustration he watched her on the monitor just standing there ringing the bell. It occurred to him that she had never appeared to answer her cell phone. Without thinking about it much further, he pulled the spring-loaded handle that operated the front gate. A second camera followed Haley as she walked through. The image was grainy— probably the camera going bad. Something wasn't quite right. He pulled another lever that unlocked the main door to the facility. Then it hit him. That wasn't her walk. No wonder she didn't pick up her cell. It wasn't her.

The door opened and she disappeared. Then Ben watched in shock as two men ran through the camera's field of view, mere yards behind the Haley look-alike. They wore masks and moved with deadly purpose. Another thought occurred to him, horrifying and hopeful at once: if that wasn't Haley, then it was a decoy, and Haley was probably safe.

Ben heard heavy footsteps running on the stairs. He looked around the corner at the stairway landing. The two men were coming fast, both of them unrecognizable with nylons over their heads. If they were Frick's, why wouldn't he give them a key? He didn't have time to ponder that one.

Ben punched the silent-alarm button. Then he pulled back into his office, grabbed a knifelike letter opener, shoved it in his pocket, and ran to the window. He opened the window and put a foot onto the steep roof.

The roof dropped off for two stories at the gutter, a mere foot and a half from the window. He stepped through the window and onto the tiny section of steep roof. As carefully as possible, he moved along the face of the gable until he reached the corner. Then he began crawling toward the rooftop.

The roof was gray heavy composite shingle that looked much like slate. It was hard on the skin and slick from a light coating of moss. He heard nothing from below. The silence was anything but comforting. Then the window slid open and the intruders' voices became suddenly audible.

"There's no way out," one said. "They'd have told us."

"I think he went out on the roof," said the other.

Ben recognized neither voice.

"He's no athlete," said the first. "It's practically straight up."

Ben climbed as quietly as he could, trying not to look down at the lawn and stone work far below.

"I don't see anything." The second one again. "It's steeper than hell."

Ben could see nothing of them, but he could tell from the sound of the voice that the second man had stuck his head out the window. He crested the peak.

He had to escape. He looked around. There was the giant fir that grew up the two stories and a bit over the roof. Perhaps the uppermost branches would support him. Then his eye gauged the distance and he realized he'd need to be a monkey or a brave teenager.

There were gables on this side of the building as well. He slithered down the roof, but after having nearly rounded the gable, he heard the window open. A man's head appeared at the corner of the gable. Even with the nylon stocking the man's hair appeared short. From his arms Ben could tell that he was olive-skinned, with black hair to match. In his hand he held an ugly-looking pistol.

"Come on in before you hurt yourself," the man said.

Ben didn't respond.

"If you don't cooperate," the man said, coming closer, "we'll kill you pure and simple."

CHAPTER 2

Sam's chair sat on a large wooden veranda about one hundred feet above the ferry dock and overlooked the waterfront street on the hillside of Friday Harbor, San Juan Island, in the state of Washington. It was November, the Sunday after Thanksgiving. A cloud slid in front of the sun, turning the water more green than blue. In every direction beyond the small village, the abundance of trees and rough granite, of current-frothed deep waters, the land and sea presented a ruggedness that nourished Sam's soul. When the sun re-emerged from behind the small cloud, the water, as if by magic, took on a bluer hue, the whites of the boat hulls looked bleached, the seagulls contoured and gleaming like ornaments aloft.

It was a place of eagles and whales.

In the summer the harbor was like a carnival; in the winter it was more like a town of cousins going about their business. Those who thought of themselves as die-hard island people from way back tended to live inland, like their ancestors, the original settlers who saw beaches as weather-blown, joyless places where you couldn't grow a turnip.

The harbor, which was shaped somewhat like a bowl cut in half, with the hillside making the rim and the water making the bottom, bristled with houses and small business establishments, a haphazard road grid connecting it all.

To Sam's right stood a large, old home converted to a coffee shop, ironically named the "Doctor's Office," selling its wares to every caffeine-craving, nature-loving, ferry-riding, hippie dude on the island. And some of the moderate Republicans as well. To his left was a covered outdoor oyster bar that had dried up for the winter, leaving no oysters and no oyster girls to cook them. Some winter afternoons he missed the college girls as much as the oysters.

These days Sam made it a point to keep his life in time with the rhythms of the land. On San Juan, like the other islands, it was easy to be close to the land because they hadn't put concrete everywhere and the ocean kept things scrubbed of heavy civilization. Four-story buildings were rare to nonexistent. They had no malls, supermarkets of consequence, freeways, youth gangs, chain stores, doctors who specialized in something, multiplex movie theaters, or anything that amounted to much more than a village shop. There were no traffic lights, but there was a great farmers' market once a week in the more temperate months. And that was enough.

In abundance, San Juan featured pastures, forests, lakes, swamps, rolling hills, small farms, seals, seabirds, eagles, hawks, rabbits, deer, and peaceful places, all requiring little tending. It felt warmish two or three months a year and a bit chilly the rest, but not so damp or cloudy as Seattle. The places built by people felt quaint, homemade, handmade, and the places made by nature teeming with all but intelligent life-forms otherwise known as people.

In the old days you could smell the fish guts mingled with the beach, but these days there were far fewer fish and far fewer fishermen, so you mainly caught the natural sulphur smell of the beach at low tide.

The chill today would drive most inside, but in a wool shirt and medium parka, Sam felt comfortable for hours at a time, his big hands able to hold things even in a stiffening breeze without the usual ache from the cold. His body was accustomed to the outdoors and he spent most of his time there. He preferred to read in the light of the day even when it was cloaked in its mist-laden winter finery. If the cold did manage to work its way through the muscled layers of his torso or set his legs to being a bit numb, he would rise and walk as best he could with the injuries, and these days he did quite well. At the local San Juan physical therapy, he had even begun running on a treadmill.

There was a breeze over the harbor that kept Sam's long, dark hair slightly mussed. His carefully trimmed beard was black, with premature salt-and-pepper for a man of forty-two.

He sat and watched the harbor, as usual enjoying its unique harmony between man and nature. It was better here than most places. The people of San Juan Island were a similar breed, by and large, for they chose to live here, surrounded by water, separated from most of the twentieth century.

Sam came from a different world. A world of adrenaline and death, of great deeds, great fights, dark shadows, and deep secrets. He had run a form of private espionage business created by a newly dangerous world. Despite any number of close calls, that world had not killed him, but it had bitten him and bitten him hard. Now he'd left it behind, but he still felt the fangs, both in his body and in his mind. He hadn't decided what to do next in his life. He had enough money and plenty of time to figure it out. One thing he had decided on was putting an end to the killing business.

A bit sore from a hard workout, he rose and let his six-foot-two-inch body slowly uncoil. The intensive physical therapy had bulked his long and elegant musculature more than usual, making it all the more important for him to re-

main limber. His chest was big and well formed, built from
bench-pressing 350 pounds. His torturers hadn't gotten to
his upper body like they had his legs, so every curve remained as it should be above the thighs. From the thighs
down, Sam was the work of plastic surgeons.

The sound of loud, annoying voices came from behind
him. Sam pretty much stayed out of other people's trouble, but
he turned to look, more curious than anything else. Seemed
that an ugly-sounding man was giving the coffee girl a hard
time.

"You made a deal," he was saying in a raised voice. "I
need the money and I need it now."

"I don't owe you nothing," she said.

Obviously, they were discussing more than the price of
the coffee. The guy was big, a black man who looked like a
noseguard, and not friendly. Sam decided that his beard must
have stood for something other than tolerance. The fellow
had a friend who didn't look much better than a sheep turd.
Long Rastafarian hair glued with mud.

"I want what I bargained for," the black man said through
gritted teeth.

"You never said you wanted that. I was selling a stereo.
That's it."

"That was no thousand-dollar stereo and you understood
my meaning."

Sam figured that people took a long time to build character and usually they didn't change overnight. Sherry, the coffee girl, was solid and fair, good-hearted—she'd feed a stray
cat and pay respect to those that didn't deserve much. Sam
had seen that and knew what the woman was about. She hadn't
gotten that way overnight and would not behave unreason-
ably greedy with the stereo or money or anything else. What
this man apparently wanted, Sherry would never have knowingly sold.

Sam had walked up to within three feet of them. The big

fellow had a two-inch slab of belly fat that was probably un-
dergirded by a fair portion of muscle. The arms were big and
the man had obviously lifted. Maybe prison. From the shoes
and the pants it was obvious the man came from the city.
Maybe Seattle.

His fingers reached out to grab Sherry's upper arm.

Sam moved quickly and in a second or two his fingers
were buried at the base of the man's neck, to the brachial
nerve, just as he'd practiced a thousand times, and done
more times than he cared to remember.

"Jeeeeeeezzz!" the man screamed.

"It's a big nerve," Sam said. "It wouldn't hurt if you'd quit
with the girl."

The guy started struggling, and Sam's grip tightened, and
the fingers got right down on the nerve and took hold of it as
if it were a cobra's neck. To control the rest of him Sam got
the fingers of a hand and twisted the hand back at his side.
Screaming religion in the form of cuss words, the guy tried
to escape a second time. Sam let him come down to the side-
walk, as if laying his head on the concrete might bring some
comfort.

"This is a quiet place, but you aren't a quiet person. Calm
down."

The guy's buddy suddenly got active, seemingly over the
shock of Sam's attack, and actually took a swing at Sam's
torso. Without thinking about it, Sam knew this man had no
training. He blocked the punch and kicked him hard in the
ass so as not to hurt him. Not much for valor, the man held
his butt and backed off, while the big guy kept screaming.
Then he started begging. "Lemme go, lemme go." Next it
was back to the colorful cursing.

"Sam, don't hurt him. He looks like he's gonna die,"
Sherry said. "Even if he is a pig."

The man was on his knees with his nose about six inches
from the pavement, and Sam knew the man couldn't think

about anything but that big nerve near the base of his neck and the hand behind him that felt as if it were about to be wrenched off.

"Have we got your attention?" Sam said.

"Yes." He'd stopped cursing at least. Sam let go. His buddy was still rubbing his butt and keeping his distance.

"I oughta kill you," the black man began. Obviously, what had happened had not yet become a part of his reality. He was used to being the aggressor.

He took a good swing, pretty fast under the circumstances. Sam caught the fist as one might catch a fastball.

"You need to stop fighting and start—"

Before Sam could finish his sentence, the man grabbed for his throat. It was skilled, with fingers closed, and only his thumb open. Now the fellow was starting to act like he knew something about fighting. Before the man could close his grip, Sam stepped inside and delivered a moderate blow with his palm to the point of the chin. It stunned the man, and for a second the man lived in suspended animation. It was enough to force the man to relax his hands. Sam grabbed his little finger and held it as if it were a hot wing ready for the blue cheese.

"If I break the pinkie at the first knuckle, it will hurt a lot," Sam said. "You are not that good at pain."

"I give up. I give up," the man said.

Sam felt obligated to give the man a chance, though he knew that the guy's temptation to throw another punch would relapse like a disease. He dropped the pinkie and waited for the left hook. It came. Sam threw his head back, let it slide by, and then did a short strike, driving the points of three fingers right into the solar plexus. The strike hadn't even approached full power, but the man dropped and flopped like a fish.

Sam stepped back, disgusted with the whole matter. Nothing like this ordinarily happened in these islands. People were civilized and thoughtful. The old stench of unadorned aggression hung heavy over the scene. Sam reached over and tried to help the man up, but he was too badly incapacitated. Sam took off his coat and put it under the man's head. Men like this did not come to this island in winter, and Sam wondered at his wardrobe. Then another thought came to him: already today Sam had seen others like this guy, and it didn't leave him with an easy feeling.

"Who is he?" he asked Sherry.

"Just came a day or so ago. Calls himself Rafe something. Thinks I sold him my body just because he bought my stereo. I told him I didn't want to sell it. Told him it wasn't worth a thousand, but he insisted. And then after he took the stereo, he got real ugly when I wouldn't have dinner with him."

"That other one," she said, meaning the smaller man, who'd already disappeared, "I guess is trying to take up pimping."

"So he's not with the heavyweight champ here."

"Not regular, I don't think."

The insanity was starting to make a little more sense.

"What's this guy doing on the island?"

"I don't know, but he's got friends."

Sam nodded.

Rafe what's-his-name was coming around. When he got up, he kept his eyes pointedly away from Sam, brushed himself off, and walked straight away.

Sam went back and resumed his reading until he felt the weight of someone else's gaze. Without looking he knew that it was Haley, her brunette curls and eyes like bluish green silk, which were perceptive and inquisitive, and that once might have held just the proper mirth. Sam hadn't seen that light in her eyes in a long time, not since the Fourth of July, 1994.

She had missed the "Mud Head and Rafe Show" and that was just as well. She would have insisted on fighting.

Following his capture and torture and the death of his wife, Anna, Sam had decided on San Juan Island as the site of his convalescence. His relationship with his uncle Ben and Haley turned out to be the perfect balm. In his growing-up years, he on occasion came to visit Uncle Ben and now-deceased Aunt Helen, and quickly grew fond of them.

During the summer of his twelfth birthday, he had spent the entire three months working with Aunt Helen on the landscaping and Uncle Ben had taken time from work for a number of salmon fishing expeditions. There were various other visits and more salmon. For a time, when she was nineteen and he was twenty-nine, he and Haley had almost been an item. Over his recent months on the island, Sam had found this dormant bond with Ben was growing. Haley was more complicated.

Life had kicked Haley to the ground, but Sam admired her because she kept trying to get back up. The prestigious Sanker Corporation had thrown her out in disgrace, claiming she'd stolen the work and ideas of her fellow scientists. That was shocking because she was the adopted daughter of the eminent Dr. Ben Anderson, also at Sanker, known to be the straightest of the straight.

Sam knew that Haley's life had been a strange mixture of ups and downs. Before her adoption at age nine, life had been very tough. With Ben and Helen her intelligence flourished. By sixteen she could fly Ben's float plane and run any boat that floated.

Academically she excelled, obtaining a Ph.D. degree in marine biology at age twenty-seven.

Because of her success, Sam knew the last great fall was very hard.

For the present she had taken to operating a bicycle and motor scooter–rental business thirty feet from Sam's sitting spot. She owned it, and had part-time employees, but lately seemed to be showing up herself. Sam's return to the island had just followed Haley's expulsion from her job and concurrent ostracization from local scientific society. She hadn't wanted to talk about the scandal much. He glanced her way and waved. She used that iron will of hers to return a good smile left over from better days and waved back. Then she came closer.

"Can I interrupt your work a moment?" she asked.

He, of course, had no work during his recuperation but his learning, to which he was devoted. In response he put the book of early-island history aside. He was studying the history of the place, what grew in each microclimate, when it bloomed if it did, the resident birds, the migratory visitors, what was in the sea and what was beside it, the terrestrial life, the mammals, the invertebrates, the habits of each, and their place in the order of things. It was an ambition.

If Haley's face was looked at in an unguarded moment, the symmetry of it was pleasing, and the slight round of it and the softness in it had the look of caring. She was only thirty-two and beautiful. In her smile he saw the residue of pain. Lately she was always very welcoming, and when he looked at her, it was starting to feel like Irish cream in his coffee. That Fourth of July in 1994 passed through his mind again. He nodded.

"Of course," he said. "What's up?"

"It's about Ben," she said.

From the corner of his eye he saw Ben Anderson's lady friend and personal assistant, Sarah, approaching, the fourth member of their little family. Sarah was an attractive, forty-five-year-old redhead who looked in her late thirties and always had a good word at the right moment. She was sincere, soft-spoken, and liked corny jokes. Additionally, she was a fitness fanatic and had the strong elastic body to prove it.

"I assume Sarah's arrival is no coincidence," he said.

Ben, Haley, Sarah, Sam, and Haley's best friend, Rachael, had created something of an extended family.

Haley nodded. "I asked her to come."

It may have been Haley's tone, or Sarah's appearance here on a Sunday but Sam had suspected something was up. Also the bicycle-rental business was virtually shut down this time of year and Haley's appearance to repair a bike was a little thin. Sarah lived on Lopez Island, and on Saturdays she didn't typically cross San Juan Channel in her little runabout until later, about the time Ben typically quit his weekend work. Sarah worked for Ben, had for years, but Sam figured there was something growing between them.

Sam stood. Together he, Haley, and Sarah adjourned to the uphill side of the veranda in front of the sidewalk-servicing window of the local coffee shop.

They placed their orders, then retreated from the window to wait.

"Haley looks like a brunette version of Cameron Diaz in that hat," Sarah said, referring to Haley's tam-o'-shanter. Haley always wore a hat of some sort.

Haley gave a smile as if she didn't believe it.

"Haley wanted to talk," Sarah said, "and I did too. Although I have to admit that I'm feeling a little guilty because I didn't mention this talk to Ben. He and I are having dinner tonight after I, quote, 'finish some chores at home.'"

She had Sam's interest. He looked to Haley for an explanation.

"We're worried about Ben," Haley said.

"How so?"

"Well," she said, "he is not acting like himself. He's keeping things secret. Actually, he's keeping *everything* secret. From me, from Sarah. We want to know if he's told you anything he didn't tell us."

Sarah nodded in agreement.

"Ben doesn't talk much about his work," said Sam. "What do you think is going on?"

"I think he's got more on his mind than his work. Or leaving Sanker."

"You might be right," Sam told Haley. "You know the rumors—that Ben's discovered some sort of longevity secret."

"*You* heard that?"

"Only vaguely," Sam said. "From everything you *do* know, do *you* believe Ben discovered some kind of magic bullet to slow aging? I mean, for significant lengths of time?"

Sherry had their coffees ready, but no one moved to get them.

"Let me put it this way," Haley said in a lower voice. "If you conquered cancer in North America—I mean completely conquered it—you would only increase average life expectancy about 3.5 years. Heart disease is better, but still only about seven years. Isn't it shocking that by eliminating these two big killers, cancer and heart disease, we're only talking a little over a decade of extra life? The real miracle, if someone could pull it off, would be 'youth retention.'"

Sam raised his eyebrows in question.

"Youth retention," Haley explained, "would be truly slowing aging, not just extending life and being old for a heck of a long time."

Sam nodded.

"It's a hot area in biology these days, and the fundamental problem is that so many bodily systems deteriorate with age," Haley said.

"I think he's discovered something about energy, *and* something about aging," Sarah said. "But it's complicated—I don't understand it, and I'll feel very guilty if I speculate. I think he might have a secret lab and that's all I'm saying. Period." She sat back.

"That's a shocker. What on earth do you mean by a 'secret lab'?" Haley sighed, obviously frustrated that she hadn't gotten much out of Sarah, but Sarah had obviously zipped her lip.

"He's spending time with a lot of different people, I think," Sam said.

"What people?"

"Science people?" Sam speculated.

"Yeah. That's all I know as well. Strange goings-on—people coming into town at night, and Ben hustling off to meetings," Haley said. "He's mum as a mummy about it all."

"To me too," Sarah said.

"Well," said Sam, "we all agree that he's leaving Sanker. It's just a matter of time, right? Distance from Frick and the corporation has to be a good thing."

"Absolutely a good thing," Haley said. "If they *let* him leave."

CHAPTER 3

After Sarah left, Haley locked up the bikes, deep in thought. In the ocean when the fingerlings or the herring were jumping and roiling at the surface, you knew there was something having dinner down below. She couldn't shake the feeling that Sanker was having dinner. Her worry over Ben was incessant. As with Ben's work, she had questions about Sam. After a fashion she had known him for twenty-three years, since she was nine. At that time he was nineteen and an impressive college jock.

Sam's father—a difficult, macho-type guy, to hear Ben tell it—had all the empathy of a wooden wall, but he had a sister who was the opposite. Her name was Helen, and she married Ben. Because of the rogue-male lifestyle led by Sam's dad, Sam would sometimes come to stay with Ben and Helen. That was mostly before Haley's time, and then after her time, he came out of gratitude and affection for Ben and Helen. Sam had a little of that family feeling in him despite the tough upbringing.

As far as Haley and everybody else was concerned, Sam's life after graduate school had been mostly secret; so when he came to visit, it was as if he walked right out of a dark closet and into these idyllic islands. As far as his life and his persona in the islands, she knew a lot. He was very strong and athletic, a good listener, never bragged, and didn't mind going unnoticed, although it was hard not to notice him.

She looked down toward the water and saw a big black man and some white guys walking down the waterfront street. They did not have the look of people from the island. Then they were gone.

A few moments later, Sam came along, headed for his chair. She developed the familiar nervous knot in her belly whenever they were alone.

She smiled at Sam, hoping it wasn't brittle. He smiled. Although he had been here first with his chair, starting nine months ago, somehow she felt he should move, since she had taken over the shop.

Apparently he wasn't moving and neither was she. She glanced up. Sam had gone back to his book, sitting only about twenty feet away.

Her phone rang and she jumped, casting about for the cordless contraption.

"It's in your back pocket," Sam said without even looking up.

Seeing it was Ben calling, she came back around the building to get better reception, but the call died. Then it came again.

"Haley," came a staticky voice, "this is Ben. Can you hear me?"

"Hey, how's it going?" The static worsened, and then it sounded like they were disconnected. It happened all the time on the island. "Hello, hello . . ." She tried for a minute and gave up.

"Was it Ben?" Sam asked.

He must be on a Russian spy ship.

"Yeah, but he disappeared. I just caught a few words, but

he sounded stressed. Maybe things aren't going well in the lab. It's past lunch. I think I'll take him something to eat and see how he is. Maybe after, we can have a cup of coffee."

"I'll be here," Sam said, walking back to his chair.

Haley turned to leave.

"Say, Haley," he said as she left. She paused and turned. "Give me a call and let me know that everything's okay with Ben."

She nodded and left.

Haley parked in the lot behind Oaks, the building that housed Ben's office and lab. Clouds were now starting to blow across the sky and making intermittent showers in the distance. At the moment the rain clouds formed a dark band up Lopez and all the way to Orcas, maybe beyond. Over on the far side of San Juan Channel, it looked like heavy rain.

She wrapped her coat around herself and walked through blowing leaves. Down the way, at the main building, she saw much more activity than she would have expected on the Sunday morning after Thanksgiving. At the gate she held a plastic card that Ben had given her up to the electronic detector and passed through a heavy revolving gate. Months ago Garth Frick had taken her original key card with great fanfare. That had been the final humiliation.

Haley knew that she needed to be careful here. She didn't really like coming to Sanker. Those old feelings of self-doubt threatened her every time she walked in the place. Worse, if she were caught inside, Frick would seize the key card that Ben had loaned her for just such occasions. Fortunately, Ben's fellow scientists, although mostly against her, really weren't the sort of people to fight over entry privileges and they had ignored her on the few times that she had come. Their shunning only added to the pain.

She walked through some attractive gardens, with some artificial ponds and flowing water, and up to the glass revolving door, where she used the card again. Downstairs things appeared empty. As she mounted the stairs, she looked from a lower-floor lab's open door, through the window, and onto a small garden area. She saw a man running across the front of the building, apparently headed for the forest. That was strange.

Coming back down the stairs, she walked into the waterfront lab space and looked to the right, down the building. Sure enough, she saw a couple of men putting up yellow tape. Immediately she thought of the crime scenes seen on TV. She went back and ran up the stairs. The halls were half-dark, the labs all silent. Turning around, she looked for a sign of someone, anyone. Nothing. As she walked down the hall toward Ben's office and lab, shadows and dark corners and the occasional watchman making the rounds replaced her memories of cheery, collegial greetings and chats and the perpetual movement of people.

The lights were off in the organics lab too. She turned them on. What she saw was appalling, as if someone had gone on a rampage. Had something happened to Ben?

"Hello?"

She jumped, badly startled by a sound. It was Frick, behind her, leaning against the doorway.

Garth Frick looked the part of an unpleasant cop. He smoked small cigars and told jokes, but his cadaverously wiry body expressed menace that outweighed any efforts at geniality. Frick's hair was black, drawn back and tied in a small ponytail. His sallow skin matched the gaunt look of his frame and his crooked teeth—a man who looked fit, lethal, and unwell all at once.

"Where's Ben?" she asked.

"Come with me." He walked up to her and put his hand in

the small of her back, as if she were a girlfriend. She removed his hand, but he only chuckled. He led her to the storage room.

She followed a short distance behind. "Where are we going?"

"Relax," Frick said. "I want to show you something."

"No." She stopped at the door.

He turned around, grabbed her arm, and yanked her into the storage room, putting his face into hers.

"You're under arrest. Now quit moving and give me your purse."

"No." She tried to get out.

He punched her in the stomach, doubling her over in extreme pain. He slipped the purse strap off her shoulder and touched his mouth to her ear.

"I'm very busy at the moment, so I can't attend to you right now."

He took her hands and handcuffed them behind her back. Then he sat her on a box of glassware and stuffed a small towel in her mouth, using duct tape to keep it there.

It took Haley several minutes to recover from the punch. When she felt able, she rose, turned, and tried to open the door. Because there were radioactive isotopes in this storage room, the door had an extra bolt lock on the outside. Frick evidently had locked it. She returned and sat on the box and considered screaming, even with the towel. It didn't take her long to conclude that, yes, she should definitely scream. But the volume she generated was not impressive.

Then the lights went out.

While she sat in the storage room, Haley's anger and fear grew as she wondered what Frick might be doing to her adoptive father, Ben. The crime scene tape . . . she couldn't complete the thought.

CHAPTER 4

Frick paced while Rolf, the hacker, hunched over his computer keyboard and worked to break into the escrow at Boston International Escrow Services.

"This was supposed to be done two days ago," Frick said. "It was supposed to be solved. Now we have nothing. Nothing."

"Leave me alone and let me think" was all Rolf would say.

Frick knew he had little time. He couldn't leave Haley in the closet for more than twenty minutes without major complications, be it the arrival of her mysterious friend, Sam, or some sort of mutiny among the county deputies.

They were in an office off the IT department especially set up for data transfers by visiting scientists. Rolf had converted it for his purposes over the weekend. It had been a simple task to make his PC look like Ben's from a data transfer standpoint, imitating the range of IP numbers used by Ben's office and his personal computer's Mac address. He had Ben's password and so had a much easier time breaking into the escrow than would a cold-calling hacker. Frick had just learned that the man also liked to work in semidarkness.

Ben Anderson and the Sanker Foundation had signed a contract that provided for an escrow service of national repute to hold electronic copies of all Ben Anderson's scientific research papers. Rolf had managed to break through the firewalls and get inside the escrow to examine those documents. Even though Ben could deposit files in the escrow account, he could not remove documents that had been on file more than sixty days without special authority. Nor could Sanker; hence the need for the hacker.

Rolf was a heavy fellow with puffy cheeks, a wispy beard, heavy glasses, and food-spotted clothes. Since he made plenty of money, obviously he had simply given up on his appearance as a lost cause. Frick detested the unkempt nature of the man and his body odor. Killing him would be an act of purity. Frick fantasized extensively about hanging him by one foot and slitting his throat. Rolf was a pig and Frick had experience in killing pigs.

On the first pass through the first set of files, they had found nothing that explained how to build five genetically engineered bacteria that would produce certain critical proteins and peptide hormones. They had one set of files left to go. Unless it contained the vital information, the old man had snookered them.

Then there was the mystery gene—something else they didn't understand, something not used in the organics lab to make products from transgenic bacteria. "How long now?" he asked.

"A while," Rolf answered. "Longer if you stand around looking over my shoulder."

"I gotta have something short typed out and printed fast."

"Will you leave me alone if I do it?"

"Just do it."

Rolf apparently decided not to defend his dignity and typed for Frick:

> *I, Haley Walther, hereby admit that on this date I was trespassing at Sanker, having entered the premises unescorted by Ben Anderson and in violation of my agreement with Sanker; and that I was hiding in the radioisotope storeroom to avoid detection when someone locked the exterior bolt, inadvertently locking me inside. I was thereafter discovered by Deputy Frick. I am freely and voluntarily agreeing to answer questions posed by officers in their investigation, have been read my rights, and hereby waive my rights, including my right to remain silent. I have requested that I be allowed to remain on the premises during a portion of the investigation. I agree to answer all questions and to remain with a police officer at all times while on the premises, and I agree to surrender myself for arrest and booking for trespass upon request by any officer of the San Juan Island Sheriff's Department and I understand that a formal citation will be issued.*
>
> *Acknowledged by Haley Walther*

Rolf printed the document. "Now if I'm through with my secretarial duties, perhaps you can go entertain the lady while I work."

Smart-ass. Frick hurried back to the Oaks Building and to Ben's office, where he had the safecracker working on Ben's wall safe. The moment he saw the pissed-off expression on the man's face, he knew he had a problem.

"How long?" Frick asked.

"I gotta do invasive stuff. I just can't do this in a few minutes with a stethoscope, like in old movies."

"You can have ten more minutes," Frick said. "If you

can't get it open in ten, I'll have to bring you back. I've got deputies out there—this is a crime scene—and there's no way I can hold people off much longer. It's already looking strange."

Old man Henry Gardner Sanker sat in the bar off the grand-gathering room, which in smaller homes would be akin to the formal living room.

His bar was nice, even by billionaire standards: gleaming hardwood and brass, with gorgeous mirrors to reflect the tawny colors of the various libations. He'd reserved the gold leaf for other areas. Sanker liked the warmth of all the fine wood—it spoke of comfort and class—and this was the place he chose to sit and hold court.

He kept a small desk in the corner with a phone, for business was never far from his mind, and tonight he wore an old tweed sport coat and sipped a glass of 1927 Fonseca port.

Sanker had a full head of silver gray hair and a long face that he thought looked like shattered safety glass, for all the wrinkles. His eyes, though, remained bright as new pennies, and his mind, in contrast to his body, was robust.

Stu Rossitter, the president of Sanker, had come in the other entry, let in by the help.

"I am concerned," Sanker said when Stu Rossitter approached the bar.

"I share your concern. Shocked, actually. I was sure we'd find the goods in the escrow. We're lucky to have our Judas."

The old man's eyes moved over Rossitter, noting that the shoes had just been shined. He wore a speckled gray cardigan and gray wool slacks—a little formal for Rossitter this time of night. Sometimes Rossitter didn't keep his shoes perfectly shined, but the old man had noticed that when Rossitter was worried, a new shine could be expected, sometimes even a new pair.

Garth Frick, by contrast, let scuff marks accumulate on the toes of his shoes. It was no wonder he was a murderer.

"Your Judas wanted a lot more than thirty pieces of silver, and even then I worry he'll stay bought," the old man said.

"I'm counting on it," said Rossitter.

"You're damn right you are. It's our families, the *world*, we're talking about."

Rossitter wisely kept his counsel.

"We all have a lot to lose." Sanker pressed the point. "Does Frick know the papers weren't left in the escrow yet?"

"Maybe. If he doesn't, should we figure a way to tell him so he won't waste time?"

"We don't dare," the old man said. "You don't tell a pigeon he's a pigeon. Let him think he's our eagle. What went wrong?"

"I don't know. The way Frick evidently had it planned the old man should have drowned, and we should have had the stuff out of escrow. It obviously was never there for any of us to find."

"I knew Anderson was double-crossing us. I had to swallow my bile just to make the deal, and I've never begged a man in my life. But he wouldn't breathe a word about his discovery, and it's half mine! Arrogant bastard goes behind my back, cheats his way out of the escrow. . . ."

"He'll be dealt with," Rossitter said.

"We have to find him before anybody else does. And quick. Any hint that we have anything to do with his disappearance, never mind his death, and we'll be swinging in Wall Street's wind."

"Frick will catch him," Rossitter said. "But we may have to help. We could pass tips from Judas. . . ."

"You think I want to hear any of this?"

"I'm sorry. I—"

"You know I would never stoop to this if I didn't have to," Sanker growled. "Never."

"Of course," Rossitter said.

"See that it's solved, my friend. Just see to it. It's more than what we own. It's the very balls of our existence. Our pride. I never should have gone down this path, never even thought about the merger with American Bayou. But that prick forced me and I will see his soul in hell."

Rossitter waited the few moments it took to make sure the old man wasn't changing his mind. Sanker nodded at last, the signal that Rossitter could leave.

The ferry coming in reminded Sam of the time. Haley had been gone twenty minutes. He called her cell number but got no answer. That was a little strange because normally one could get reception over on that side of the harbor. Of course, she could be in the bowels of the lab, but she had promised to call, and Haley didn't forget things like a promised phone call. Perhaps he would take a ride over there and see what was happening. He had taken a break from the history of the islands and was reading about the whales. He couldn't concentrate on the narrative or the pictures, though. He put the book back in his leather pouch.

Sam could walk with no discernible limp, usually trying to keep his full weight off the bad knee. He eased his bulk into the Ford Taurus and turned his mind to Frick. When Haley had begun pouring out her soul about Sanker, Frick had figured prominently in her theories about who had stolen data from her computer and framed her.

Sam had done a little checking, getting most of his information from Ernie, his longtime FBI contact. Ernie called Frick "very bad news," but he wouldn't give Sam any details beyond the basics: Frick was a former homicide detective. He had been suspected, but never accused, of murdering a police commissioner. The sudden disappearance and presumptive death of the commissioner and two investigating officers had abruptly ended an investigation into the activities of a large corporate client of Frick's.

Sam had first met Frick at a local charity fund-raiser, and from the way Frick watched him, he had supposed that Frick was running a check on him as well.

It took only a couple of minutes to get to the wooded road into Sanker. Inside the front gate were parked three San Juan County police cars and one plain vehicle with a portable police light.

Already a yellow tape marked a crime scene. Sam went slowly, taking the measure of the place and the people as he got out of the car. He knew a lot about crime scenes and rule number one was that they didn't allow visitors.

A very intimidating fence, a more artful version of something that would enclose a high-security industrial complex, surrounded the place. Near the entrance, long steel staves rose about ten feet and then turned at a forty-five toward a potential intruder, and each was tipped with a leaf-shaped razor-sharp end piece. Away from the entry it gave way to a wall with razor wire on top.

A single uniformed deputy stood just inside the gate, although that hardly seemed necessary, given that it was electronic and didn't open without a card. As he watched, a sturdy-looking plainclothes officer, with a mustache and thinning hair, approached the gate and began talking with the uniformed officer.

Sam walked over to the men. "Hello, gentlemen. What's going on?"

"It's a crime scene," the uniformed officer said.

"I'm Detective Ranken," the plainclothes man said.

"Is the undersheriff or the Orcas sergeant available?" Sam asked. No response from Ranken. "Maybe the San Juan sergeant?"

Sam had socialized a bit with the sheriff, and had taken mental notes regarding the chain of command. He also knew the sheriff was in Europe. On this little island a lot of people knew about the trip. Fewer knew that the Orcas sergeant took command after the undersheriff. This was Sam's subtle method of pointing it out. Even in an emergency, to get down to Frick in the chain of command, the sheriff, the undersheriff, and both the Orcas sergeant and the San Juan sergeant would have to be unavailable. But he wasn't sure if that held true for crimes only involving Sanker, where Frick had special jurisdiction. A potential murder or kidnap, though, would clearly be viewed as involving much more than just Sanker.

Ranken hesitated at Sam's familiarity with the department.

"Do I get to see Haley Walther or not?" Sam asked.

"I'll have to clear it with Special Sergeant Frick."

Ranken got on his cell phone. He walked away a few paces. Sam couldn't hear what he was saying. Then he came back.

"Sergeant Frick says to wait here and he'll see you in a few minutes," Ranken said. "You got a badge of some sort?"

"I have a driver's license."

"Let me see it."

Officer Ranken glanced at the license and handed it back.

"You know the sheriff?" Ranken asked.

"Yes, I do. We have a mutual friend in the FBI."

Ranken registered surprise. "How would I know that?"

Sam took out his cell phone.

"What are you doing?"

"Calling our friend in the FBI," Sam said. "That's easier than getting Sheriff Larson in the Swiss Alps."

"You don't need to do that. It doesn't matter if you and the sheriff have a friend in the FBI. This is still a crime scene."

But, of course, it mattered. Ranken didn't need the sheriff pissed-off because they wouldn't call someone out of a building for an important message. Small towns ran on mutual understandings, give-and-take, neighborliness—small islands even more so.

"Look, I don't know that Haley Walther is in that building," Ranken said. "I'm just waiting for Sergeant Frick, so I appreciate your patience."

"She's in Ben Anderson's lab," said Sam. "I believe the organics lab. I know where it is. It would be a great personal favor to me if you'd take me into the organics lab for just a couple minutes."

"You want me to escort you in there?"

"If it wouldn't be too much to ask."

"All right. I don't know what's taking Frick so long."

"I really appreciate this," Sam said. "I have no doubt you're a busy man."

"You don't have to butter me up. I'm already taking you."

Officer Ranken then got a radio call, the timing uncanny. It was Frick telling Ranken to bring Sam in.

Haley guessed she had been locked up for around thirty minutes. The fabric in her mouth and at the top of her throat made breathing more difficult, and felt suffocating, requiring her to concentrate on remaining calm and forcing down the panic. The cuffs on her wrists were clamped way too tight and imposed a physical torment. Time plodded along slowly.

She cheered herself with the thought that Sam would wonder why she hadn't called. He was very thorough and a detail like this would not go unnoticed. He would come over and start asking a lot of questions and he was not a man that you could easily ignore.

The lights came on, blinding Haley momentarily. She smelled Frick's aftershave before seeing him. He always looked the same, anyway, his hair never varying, never soft or loose, always pulled back. Casual clothes, clean, but never anything colorful, always a stainless-steel watch, always the plain gray shirt buttoned to the neck, always perfectly shined shoes except at the toes, which were slightly scuffed as if for some reason he couldn't quite finish polishing them.

"I want to talk to you—a few questions," he said as he took the gag off.

"You have no right to do this, you son of a bitch! Where's Sam?"

"He's signing a release for Detective Ranken and answering a few questions. In the meantime you and I will talk."

When he removed the cuffs, she shrank back from him. He moved closer, but only to hand her the purse he had taken earlier.

"I regret to inform you that Ben is dead," Frick began. "We're trying to find the body." He regarded her with lifeless gray eyes that matched his shirt. "This is your doing, you know. You should have taken my deal. It may not be too late to make a new one."

In spite of her shock she responded with heat. "I won't lie for you, for Sanker, or for anybody else."

"Did your drunk mother teach you that? I know all about you, Haley Walther. The sorority stunts—streaking naked, passing out drunk. You're a loser."

Haley felt sick. The thought of Ben dead was more than she could bear. "You're in a lot of trouble," he said. "We have a video of you bringing assailants into the building. We came over here in response to a call from Ben and found you snooping around his laboratory. A lab tech is dead—somebody killed him."

"Where's Ben's body?"

"You should think about your alibi, about now. You're not supposed to be in this building. Isn't that right?"

"Ben invited me."

He grabbed her hair and pulled her head back.

"What's the rule?" The pain was intense. "What's the rule?"

"He has to be with me."

"So where is he?"

"I asked *you*," she said through clenched teeth. "I don't know."

"I can jail you until we have a bail hearing next week," Frick said. "But I'm willing to deal if you'll cooperate."

"I don't believe this. Where's Sam?"

He ignored her question. "Your choice. You wanna give me a hard time; then I'm taking you in. Otherwise sign this."

She read it. There was little doubt that if she didn't sign it, he would take her to jail and her lawyer could ask her questions later.

"As usual you're working hard to manipulate the situation." She crumpled the paper and tossed it at his feet.

"All right. That half-crippled friend of yours just arrived out front. I'm gonna kill that big buck bastard and you can have that on your conscience. You and that half-breed get it on, don't you? He'll be dead ten minutes from now and you won't be far behind him."

In that moment, looking at those dead eyes, Haley knew that Frick would find a way to do it.

Picking up and straightening the paper, she took his pen and signed.

"This may get you out of grabbing me, but not anything else."

"You worry about your legal problems," Frick said with a dead, flat stare, "and I'll take care of mine."

Sam and Detective Ranken found Garth Frick at the top of the stairs inside the building.

"So, Mr. Robert Chase, more commonly known as Sam. What brings you here?"

"Where's Haley Walther?"

"Recently you don't seem confined to a wheelchair. Is the limp real or is that fake too?"

"Are you trying to make some point?"

"The point is, if you're gonna walk around my crime scene, I need to confirm your real identity."

Sam handed him his Robert Chase driver's license.

"You can't even keep the same beard," Frick said. "Around here they call you Sam. Then I hear Robert Chase. Why the bullshit?"

"Sam's a nickname. The FBI and the states of California and Washington use Robert Chase."

"I traced Robert Chase and it's a real deep ID." Frick gave him back the license. "Somebody went to a lot of trouble. What last name you got to go with Sam?"

"If you need a last name, you get Robert Chase."

"Let me see a credit card."

Sam still had a couple on him and showed him one in the name of Robert Chase. "Why don't you take me to Haley; then we can look for Ben."

"Why don't you tell me what you know first."

"I know I haven't killed any police commissioners."

Ranken, who had been standing quietly, stared at the floor on that one.

Frick actually smiled, but his eyes showed pure malevolence.

"No, I don't imagine. You don't have that kind of talent." Frick delivered the line easily. "What kind of weapon are you carrying?"

"Ten-millimeter Glock."

"I'll take it. You won't need it on my crime scene."

Sam drew it and handed it to Frick, butt first.

Frick racked the slide. "It's empty."

"That way it won't hurt anybody."

"Gimme your ammo."

Sam reached into his back pocket, pulled out the clip, and handed it to Frick.

"You'll need to sign some papers, a release, and answer some questions for Detective Ranken," Frick said.

"Questions?" Ranken asked.

"A witness statement," Frick responded as if Ranken were slightly dull. "When you come in, you touch nothing. Understand?"

Sam nodded. "Right."

"There's a videotape of the break-in."

"I'd appreciate seeing it."

"I'm sure you would," Frick said. "It's confidential police business, so I'll just tell you: A brunette woman and two masked men enter the place. The brunette appears to be Haley Walther. Without her, there would have been no entry because the equipment demonstrates that Ben Anderson let them in. And, of course, she was here looting the place when we found her. Up to her old tricks—stealing secrets."

"You went to quite a little trouble to arrange that for the record, did you?" Sam said.

"What did you say?"

"Why don't we cut to the chase. Somewhere along the line you went from a bad cop to a common criminal. We both know that. You want something and only you know about it. If what you want hurts Ben Anderson or Haley Walther, you can overlook it. Well, I can't."

Sam watched Frick's gun hand. Frick kept it and his glare steady.

Ranken cleared his throat. "You want me to interview Mr. Chase, then?"

CHAPTER 5

After Ranken was finished taking his statement, he walked Sam to Ben's office. Frick had no doubt ordered Ranken to delay him, for reasons he was sure he would soon discover. Ranken didn't much like being a stooge, but he was going along with Frick for the moment.

The building that housed Ben's office was impressive: the walls were of some rough-surfaced, stonelike concrete block; the ceilings were tall, about twelve feet; great care had been taken in making moldings of natural wood; the floors appeared to be acid-stained concrete made to look mottled in gold and rust. The money behind Sanker was evident.

A couple of officers stood in Ben Anderson's large office. There was no sign of Frick, and Ranken seemed interested in leaving upon arrival.

"You stay here with Officer Wentworth and Ms. Walthers. Officer Frick will be by with more questions," Ranken said.

Haley stood near one of the officers, looking a combination of angry and discouraged. Sam went to her immediately, searching for any evidence of harm.

She gave him a look that said she was all right. "This is

'Crew' Wentworth." She indicated a handsome officer with a blond buzz cut. Sam had seen him around and had observed Haley talking with him when the squad car was curbside near the coffee shop.

"She's been telling me a little about Ben's work," Crew said.

Sam raised his eyebrows. Haley nodded quickly—Crew was okay.

"Basic molecular biology," she said. "One of the things Ben did was compare long-lived species with similar but shorter-lived species. Like the tortoise that lives maybe one hundred fifty years versus a sea turtle with a much more modest life span. Bottom line: he studied the DNA of sea creatures as it pertained to longevity. I think he was looking at over two hundred or so genes of interest."

"I'm supposed to find Ben's most current work," Crew said. "How the hell I'm supposed to tell, I haven't figured out yet. A Dr. McStott is really in charge of the technical stuff. Haley here is my best hope. I'm supposed to be looking for papers about DNA. About genes."

"What about DNA?" Sam asked.

"Something that would slow aging."

"I'd like to talk to Haley a moment," Sam said to Crew. "If that's okay with you."

Crew nodded. "Just don't touch anything, and don't take long. I need her help."

Sam moved with Haley a little farther away from the deputies, near an open window.

"Are you all right?" Sam whispered.

She nodded. "He cuffed me, gagged me, and threw me in a room."

"Frick did that?"

She nodded.

"He must be desperate to take that kind of risk."

Another nod.

"He won't be in charge for long," Sam said. "Soon the undersheriff or the regular sergeant will probably show up and I have a hunch things will change. He let me in only because he thought he might get more information that way."

"Frick says Ben's dead," Haley said. "He said I was part of the murder. He's going to put me in jail for something, maybe murder, maybe some kind of unlawful entry pending a bail hearing. He even said he'd kill you. Unless I cooperated."

"Wait, now. What did he say you did?"

"Let in the killers. A lab tech is dead as well."

"And he threatened to kill me?"

She nodded. "And he was serious. So I signed the paper and he totally changed his tune."

"Yeah, he's playing his own version of good cop/bad cop. He's using Crew to get you to lead him to Ben's work. They're onto Ben's aging stuff?"

Another nod.

"Maybe he doesn't know any more about what Ben was doing than we do."

"Sam—I'm scared. Do you think Ben's really dead?"

"I don't know. It seems unlikely if Frick's got no body." Sam looked out the open window and studied the drop to the ground. "Does this building have balconies?"

Haley nodded and explained where it was located. They walked back over to Crew and his huge stack of papers.

"Crew . . . may I call you that?"

"Everybody else does."

"Did Officer Frick tell you to get Haley to tell you what Ben was doing?"

Crew nodded. "That obvious, huh?"

"Ben just disappeared, as far as you know?" Sam asked.

"He called the department. Said somebody tried to murder him. We found footprints below the balcony at the end of the building. We suspect they're Ben's."

"Does Frick know about them?"

"Oh yeah. They're pretty obvious. Deep in the mud. We do have a dead lab tech, though. Found him in the bushes."

"So Frick says Ben's dead, when he's not," Sam said. "And he wants you to talk your old friend into getting him Ben's secrets, right?"

Crew didn't answer.

"Aggravating, isn't it?" Sam asked. "Makes you wonder what he's really doing."

Crew pretty much maintained a poker face, but he was an unhappy young officer.

"You may want to have someone make a plaster cast of Ben Anderson's footprints."

"If Frick says so."

Sam moved to Ben's desk and began looking over the papers.

Crew made another half-hearted stab at being Frick's errand boy. "Haley, what do you think Ben was actually doing in the lab?"

"If you mean the organics lab," she said, "probably growing bacteria, then breaking them down and separating out the critical proteins, pro hormones or whatever he was making."

"I mean, what was he trying to create?"

"I don't know."

"You're a scientist," Crew said. "You might be able to guess."

"Ben didn't tell anyone what was going on." Sam could hear the bite in her tone.

Crew didn't seem to have the heart to keep doing Frick's dirty work.

Sam moved away from the desk and looked around the office. In the large photo cabinet and on a few of the shelves, Ben Anderson had displayed something of his life. Sam looked it over to see if anything had changed since his last visit. A fairly recent picture of Haley, taken by Sarah, showed her at the Special Olympics with each arm around the shoulders of a kid. The way the kids gazed at her had touched him the first time he had seen the photo.

Aside from pictures of Haley, which were numerous, Sam saw pictures of Helen, Ben's deceased wife, and shots of various San Juan festivities, the sheriff and his family, and Ben with other friends. There were a number of more recent photos of Sarah in which she looked fond of whoever was taking the picture. Sam knew it was Ben.

The place was neat and tidy, if crammed, and Sam knew the orderliness was Sarah's doing.

Another photo showed a group of men and Haley standing in front of a house with the ocean in the background.

It was Ben's beach house on Lopez Island, where Sam had been a frequent visitor. In the photo older scientists were standing around and Sam suspected these were some of the fellows participating in all the private meetings.

Ben had also tacked a series of quotations on the wall. A couple of them were new.

It's not that I'm afraid to die, I just don't want to be there when it happens.

—Woody Allen

I can do anything now at age ninety that I could do when I was eighteen, which shows you how pathetic I was at eighteen.

—George Burns

The term Haley had mentioned—"youth retention"—came immediately to mind.

* * *

"Nothing. Nothing." Frick screamed at Rolf as he walked out the door to the IT room. The escrow was full of meaningless documents that told them nothing of Ben Anderson's secrets. There was only the slightest consolation and that was the geek's assurance that he might figure what Ben was doing by studying the memory of Sanker Foundation's server computer.

Frick was always cautious and he had backup plans to the backup plans. He was supposed to have twenty men from Las Vegas in Friday Harbor waiting. It had cost $100,000 in Sanker money to have them on standby, but it was worth it. It took only seconds on his cell phone to make sure they were in place.

When he arrived at his office, he considered the unsavory next step: calling Sanker. Sanker was in a tough spot. They had entered a merger agreement with American Bayou and, after signing, Sanker stock value had plunged because Haley Walther refused to tell a few white lies. They got rid of her, but that didn't help the stock. If Sanker stock did not rise, then old man Sanker and all his executives would be out in the street taken over by the American Bayou people. The way to save the old man's skinny ass was to make sure that Sanker got Ben Anderson's aging discovery and announced this new molecular magic to the world.

Frick's mission was simple: Ben Anderson had to die—after Sanker understood all the ramifications of his discovery. As long as Ben Anderson lived, he controlled the invention and chose the manufacturer, with Sanker controlling nothing and getting half the profits.

The phone call to his contact at the Sanker Corporation would have to be oblique because no one, least of all Sanker, would be willing to discuss the real issues.

"I've been negotiating with Ben Anderson," Frick began. "It's just a hunch, but I think he may not have been complying with the terms of the escrow. And now he seems to have disappeared. Of course, we're looking for the details of his work." Frick kept the wording as vague as his contact, a Mr. Nash, would likely want it.

"What?" That single word expressed Nash's shock.

What followed was a short conversation that went badly. Frick repeated to Nash the same general bad news, but in more detail, and with a few hints at his knowledge.

"That's your issue," Nash said. "It's your job. We need you to find Ben Anderson. Big-name scientists don't just disappear. If he did, you make sure you get the relevant details and make arrangements to acquire his discovery. And I tell you again: break no laws."

Nash was a pompous hypocrite, but he controlled the six-figure payments due Frick upon completion of his tasks.

"Understood."

Frick now realized how lucky he was that his inside man had failed to kill Ben Anderson. According to the plan, several days previous they were to have looted the escrow and obtained all the secrets.

Frick made one more call, this one to a man called Griffith, also on the Sanker payroll. Frick had brought Griffith and one other man in much earlier than the rest. Griffith was already in place on the island, and he knew the plan.

"Is Zebra Three still there?" Frick asked without prelude.

"Yeah. Hasn't moved. Seems oblivious."

"Pull the wire on the house phone."

"It's gone that far?"

"Just do as I say," Frick said. "Call me the instant he leaves the house. I'm still Zebra One as long as the undersheriff doesn't show up or call in."

"Two-oh-one is taken care of?" Griffith asked.

"Don't worry about two-oh-one. Worry about containing Zebra Three and finding Ben Anderson."

Frick hung up the phone and sighed.

Ben Anderson was supposed to be discovered in the sea pen—a victim of a diving mishap. Certain death and a prompt discovery of the body would enable Sanker to acquire Anderson's research, perfectly legally, in short order. Now there was the need for a middle step and that was learning the secret before dispensing with its founder.

Frick swept the phone off the desk and onto the floor. He stood, his temples pounding, mind spinning.

Things were rapidly turning to absolute shit. Frick was self-aware enough to admit that he was headed down a path that might result in his having to flee the country.

Frick entered Ben Anderson's office with a spring in his step and a knowing look on his face. Sam's eyes followed Frick's right hand, which held an iron crowbar.

Frick stepped to Ben's desk drawers, tested them, and found them locked.

Frick looked at Haley, then Sam, then shoved the pry bar above the top drawer. The wood splintered with an ugly crack. Sam knew Frick was baiting them; he made no motion to stop him.

"It's a consensual search," Frick said. "I checked and the desk was purchased by the foundation and I just gave myself permission to tear it apart."

Behind Frick's jaunty air Sam detected tension, anger. Whatever Frick was up to was not going well.

With the top drawer out, Frick was able to pull the others open.

"Well, look at this." It was a gift box complete with a ribbon and a card reading: *To Haley, on her birthday*.

"My birthday's in April," she said quietly.

"That's obviously Haley's and belongs to her," Sam said. "What you're doing is illegal."

"It's evidence," Frick said. "You can argue about it in court during Haley's trial a year from now."

"Hey, wait a minute—" Crew began.

"You," Frick cut in, throwing Crew the box. "Open it up."

Crew carefully removed the wrap. Inside was a lacquered box, hand-painted with a scene showing beach and sea. He opened the box, revealing a strand of pearls at least eighteen inches long. Under the pearls lay another small card. It had a line drawing of a house and garden on one side and writing on the other.

"Give me those," Frick said, nodding at some greatly oversize tweezers in front of Sam. Sam slid them across the desk within Frick's reach. "By moving the tweezers I'm not suggesting that Haley consents to this search of her property. It's absolutely not consensual."

"I forbid you to touch what is obviously a gift to me," Haley said, getting Sam's drift.

"I'm a witness," Crew said quietly.

"Whatever." Frick used the tweezers to pull out a card that read:

> To my treasure, my child, my student, more than my
> flesh: They live in the Black Silent on less than they
> consume and are not killed by their excess. Swimming
> above them the mastodons of the deep don't even pos-
> sess such fantastic secrets. But they do have a few. Follow
> the logic. ARCLES

Frick looked at Haley, then Sam. "Do you know what that means?"

Haley shrugged.

"How about the picture. Surely it's here for a reason?"

"I don't recognize the picture at all."

"I'd say the mastodons are the whales," Frick said. "I only see one whale in this room." He walked over to a large model of a blue whale mounted on the wall. He fingered the outside of the whale, apparently looking for entry into a hidden compartment. "Know what ARCLES means?"

"I have no idea," Haley said.

Sam shook his head.

Frick touched the polished model with the heavy pry bar and nicked it.

"That's Ben's," she said.

"Wrong again." He knocked on the whale again. "Foundation property, no matter how Ben modified it."

Without warning, Frick slammed the crowbar into the side of the whale at the seam. He did it again, then began to pry. The wood shrieked as he tore into it like a man possessed.

Crew looked sick but said nothing.

"Seems hollow. Made to open," Frick said.

"It is nevertheless empty." Sam hoped that needling Frick might cause him to make a significant mistake.

"Maybe you'd like to dust this for prints and then use your latex to pull up on the bottom," Frick said to Crew, pointedly ignoring Sam.

Crew nodded and signaled to a tall fellow with a fingerprint kit, who came over to the whale. There were plenty of prints, probably all Ben's. When they were done, Frick probed the bottom of the compartment. In moments he had it open, exposing a deep belly cavity. Papers lay inside. The deputies picked them out with tweezers.

"What are these papers?" Frick asked.

"I'm assuming you can read," Haley said. "You tell us."

Frick thumbed through the pages. "Does he ever have these lab notes typed up?" He looked up at Haley. "Probably has Sarah type them, I expect," he answered his own question.

Crew was spreading the papers over the large desk so they could be seen. Haley came closer and moved them around with a pencil eraser. Sam knew it was strange of Frick to let them stand watching and concluded Frick was in a very big hurry and wanted instant reaction. The man's desire for information outweighed the normal concern an officer would have about keeping important information confidential so that it could be doled out in a useful manner.

"And where would the legible notes be?" Frick asked.

"I don't know," Haley said. "This is in Ben's shorthand."

"Sarah can read this, right?"

Haley set her jaw.

"Take her to the station," Frick said to Crew.

"I suppose that's obvious," Haley said at last.

"We'll need to take these notes for evidence," Frick said.

"Evidence of what?" Sam asked. "If you take that property you're looting, pure and simple. You need a warrant."

"Go to hell. This is a crime scene. That's evidence. Period. Now, what is this house drawing?"

"I have no idea," she said.

Sam suspected that Haley was sincere and wondered what the drawing might mean.

Crew tensed but kept silent when Frick gave him a cautionary stare.

"You'll need a warrant, anyway," Sam said, pushing Frick again.

The tension was palpable; Frick looked lethal even if under control.

"They stay here until we get the court order," Frick said. "You men don't let those papers leave this desk. And you two," he said to Haley and Sam, "touch nothing. I'll be right back." Then he walked out of the office.

Sam wondered what Frick was doing and figured they wouldn't like it. One of the papers that came out of the whale was stuck under another, and from the little that Sam could see, it appeared particularly interesting. Along its bottom edge was scrawled *ARCLES*.

"Next, I suppose, he'll be opening the wall safe," Sam said.

Crew looked around.

"Behind the picture over there," Sam explained.

Crew walked over to the picture to take a look, giving Sam the opportunity to snatch and secrete the ARCLES page.

Frick walked back in without warning. Dr. McStott, the man who had gotten Haley kicked out of Sanker, walked in with him and commenced looking at the papers for himself. Frick was folding up his cell phone. "I need some more information before we take you down to the station," he said to Haley. "Why don't you just run me through where you were today."

"Hold it," Sam said. "You've implied that she's a target of your investigation. You've imprisoned her without her consent and made her sign a phony confession. Now you're taking her into custody. You haven't even read her Miranda rights to her. She may want to exercise her right to remain silent."

"Get him out of here. He's under arrest for interfering with an investigation."

Crew couldn't cover his shock.

"Cuff him and remove him," Frick said.

Sam saw Frick's hand move to the semiautomatic holstered on his belt.

"If you'd just go out and wait by the car, I'll stay here with Haley," Crew said to Sam. "I'd like to have a word with Officer Frick."

As the tension between Crew and Frick grew, Sam nodded to Haley. Sam walked through the door and waited just around the corner, in the hall. Being out of sight would work in his favor. It was always better to enter a fight on your own terms. More important, he figured he was about to learn more about Frick and Crew.

CHAPTER 6

It had taken some doing for Ben Anderson to make it to his boat. He'd had to stab a man with a letter opener on the roof of the Sanker Foundation and watch him plunge to the ground, then use the balcony at the far end of the building to get himself down to safety. Now Ben was to meet his friend Lattimer Gibbons here at the marina at the far south end of Friday Harbor at 1:00 P.M. sharp, and there was nothing he could do until Gibbons showed.

From his position low in the cockpit of the boat, he glanced at his watch, impatient to cast off before he was caught. In recent months, Ben had taken many precautions, to avoid the detection of all of his activities. One of the things he'd done was to "sell" this boat. In reality, he had simply moved it to the far end of Friday Harbor and signed it over to the Arc Foundation, changing its name to *Alice B.*, apropos of nothing in particular. Documentation was now in the name of a corporation owned by a friend. They changed the canvas colors on the flybridge and the dinghy, scuffed up her sides, and made her look like any other badly used Carver.

He had dive gear aboard and the keys in the ignition. H

started the motors to let them warm, centered the rudders, watched the oil pressure, and glanced back at the exhaust. Then he turned on the electronics, including a sophisticated graphic display depth sounder and forward-looking sonar uncommon on most private yachts. He switched on the GPS and chart plotter and pulled up the Nobeltec bathyscaphe chart for the sometimes treacherous President Channel. One of his biggest concerns remained that he could not reach Haley. As he imagined her anxiety, the pain of it was almost more than he could bear. Soon he would find a way to make contact. Another call on her cell produced only the voice mail. With his cell phone nearly out of battery power, he called Sarah and got no answer. It was too dangerous to tell her how to meet him by voice mail. There wasn't another phone that he dared use until he reached his destination.

It was of some comfort to him that Haley had a friend like Sam. Sam had been into very heavy things in life. Ben didn't know the details, but he understood the general gist. Without ever having had a terribly explicit discussion, Ben knew that Sam would protect Haley with his life.

But where is Lattimer?

Ben made another check of the dock. Two men were walking toward him in heavy parkas and casual slacks—odd wear for a November afternoon on this part of the dock. There weren't that many sizable boats and these guys didn't look quite dressed for a wintertime ride in a runabout. Furthermore, they seemed fixed on the *Alice B.* and that made him nervous. He hadn't time to cast off the lines and motor out; moreover, he needed Lattimer to drop him off.

The men invited themselves right up and into the cockpit. One man was broad and heavy, like an NFL linebacker. The other seemed more wiry but still oversize and broad-shouldered, plenty big enough to enforce his will. There would be no wrestling match between them and Ben Anderson that lasted longer than ten seconds.

"Hello there," said the big man. "You Ben Anderson?"

"Yes."

"I'm Special Agent Stu Farley and this is Special Agent Len Morrison. We'd like a word with you."

Ben went weak in the knees. He wasn't liking this, and right after being a near murder victim, he trusted no one unless he knew for certain whom he was talking with. Climbing down from the bridge, he kept his cool and shook hands affably.

They showed him badges that said *Federal Bureau of Investigation.* It would be illegal to impersonate a federal officer, but that wouldn't stop someone who was onto Ben's research.

"What can I do for you fellas?"

The bigger one, Farley, continued to do the talking. "We understand that you have some insight into some things that concern the United States government."

"You'll have to be more specific, I'm afraid. That statement would apply to just about anyone, wouldn't it?"

"Not everyone's a molecular biologist whose work has national-security implications."

Government or not, they knew what they were talking about. Ben chose a direct approach. "Well, my work doesn't concern the government very much or else the government would be responding to my requests."

"From what we understand," said Farley, "the government was corresponding with you about your research and hit kind of a sticking point. We'd like to talk to you about that."

"My research or your hypothetical sticking point?"

"Both, I'd say."

"Are you officially investigating me?"

"Investigating. Negotiating. Following up. Call it what you want."

"I want a lawyer."

"What we're asking for, Dr. Anderson, is your help."

"I gave my stipulations for a discussion of our information," said Ben, "and so far the government can't seem to comply."

"We understand that you're into all sorts of things that could affect national security. The government can't merely 'comply' in such a case. You were asked to meet with the director of Homeland Security. And the assistant director of the FBI and the head of NOAA. And if that weren't enough, you were promised a meeting with the National Security Advisor—if it were determined that you knew what you were talking about."

"I gave my conditions."

"Your conditions might take an act of congress." Farley's voice remained calm. "We are a government of laws. The executive branch can't just issue proclamations."

Ben knew he should just shut up, but he couldn't resist giving them a piece of his mind, now that he had government representatives in person. "The government didn't just want a talk. They wanted me to give them hard information. Facts, figures, the substance of my work. I'm not signing over my half of the research and all my rights until I have certain assurances, for the benefit of the public."

"You're playing poker with the government, Dr. Anderson, and we've got all the chips. With everything you're into, you must have broken some law someplace." Farley's voice deepened subtly. "We don't want to negotiate that way, but if you force us, we'll have to."

"Gentlemen," Ben said with finality, "I know you've got a job to do and I appreciate the government's concern. I'm sure we'll work it out and build a consensus, but it will take time. I'm not ready to talk until the government meets my terms or equivalent terms that provide the same protections."

At that, Morrison, the smaller agent, who still stood over six feet tall, spoke with the authority of the person really in charge. "I'm afraid we're going to have to insist. We want you to take us to your gathering place over on Orcas. We understand you have some work to do over there."

Ben's gut tightened at the information contained in that statement. He thought for a moment, and he didn't like the conclusion.

"You're not from the government."

"We are," said Phillips. "It's just that the government is concerned, and we're not exactly going to play by the rule book on this one."

"You're impersonating federal officers. Now, both of you, get off the boat."

Morrison stepped back, in order to let Farley advance in the cramped quarters. The tall man's face was a mask of sympathy and regret. "Well, Dr. Anderson, I'm afraid I have to decline. We have some handcuffs here and we're going to put them on you, one way or another."

"I told you to go after Sam." Frick's veins were bulging in his neck, but Crew refused to budge.

Sam had disappeared out the door seconds ago.

"Follow him, Officer, and put him in the car," Frick said to Crew. "That's an order."

"Please stay," Haley said.

"With all respect I think I should stay here," Crew said to Frick.

"With all respect," Frick mocked, "get your ass after him. Your career is dead if you refuse a direct order from the officer in charge."

At that moment Detective Ranken came in.

"Ranken here will stay with me and Ms. Walther until Crew gets 'Mr. Multiple Names' handcuffed and in his cruiser."

Crew looked worried. "I'll go check on him."

"You go with him and make sure he does it," Frick said to Ranken. "And run a check on Mr. Robert Chase."

"I thought you already did that," Ranken said. "And I thought I was staying here."

"I ran the NCIC database, not WATCH. Run the state. That's an order."

Ranken didn't hide his resentment, but he walked out the door.

The instant Ranken was gone, Frick turned to Haley, who took an instinctive step away from him.

"We have this little rubber room over at the jail and tonight, in the middle of the night, it's gonna be just you and me in that room," Frick whispered. "You don't want to be in that room with me."

"I don't want to be anywhere with you."

"That smart mouth won't last the night."

Frick grabbed Haley's wrist, threw her to the ground, and twisted her arm behind her back. As she knelt in incredible pain, he got down on his haunches behind her, close to her ear, and applied more pressure on her arm. With his other hand on the back of her head, he shoved her face into the carpet. Pain turned to bursts of electrical agony from her twisting nerves and burning skin.

Suddenly Frick released her and she heard an animal groan. Haley flipped to the side and saw Sam with his right hand like a claw burrowing into Frick's shoulder at the base of his neck. Frick contorted his face, unable to make a sound now, merely gasping as Sam pinned his gun in its holster with his left hand. Frick managed to take a swing and connect with Sam's jaw, prompting Sam to pull Frick's gun.

"I'm gonna have to ask you to stop that," Crew said, back in the room, his gun aimed at Sam.

"Sure." Sam stood down while Frick, looking crippled in the right arm, began swearing in long strings and massaging his clavicle area.

"You're under arrest for assault," Frick said through gritted teeth. "Both of you."

Haley scrambled to her feet, her arm still in pain.

"Your fellow officer is abusing Haley," Sam said to Crew. "He's violating her rights and hurting her. What are you going to do about it?"

"Stay right here," Crew said, sounding determined.

"I will resume my questioning." Frick began trying to speak through the pain as if nothing had happened. "Take Mr. Chase here to the car. He's under arrest."

"I'm not saying a word," Haley said.

Crew lowered his gun. "I believe that ends the questioning."

CHAPTER 7

Ben rode on the flybridge of the *Alice B.* with his hands cuffed behind his back. Farley, the bigger fellow, and Morrison wore equally grim expressions, saying nothing.

Although this was a drab morning that had brought dire circumstances, the small islands in this inland sea had not lost their unending charm. They had an aura of the wild and the naturally beautiful; the churning, flowing blue salt water running with the tides; the sheer, angled rocks plunging nearly vertically into the sea; the gnarled, old Rocky Mountain junipers and tall stately firs; the incomparable wildflowers and marvelous creatures both in the sea and out; all of it magnificent for Ben.

With the ease of a practiced mariner, Farley activated the next waypoint on a route that would take them past the Wasp Islands. In the distance the isles looked like a flotilla of dark boats on opening day of yachting season.

If he kept them on this route, they would travel on the inside of Jones Island and in about thirty-five minutes arrive in President Channel. Their apparent knowledge of Ben's secret world was eerie, and Ben had no explanation for it.

Ditto his dealings with the government. He wondered what else these men knew, and who might have told them.

After a moment's private discussion they turned to him.

"We want you to tell us two things: First, exactly where is the gathering place? Second, where are the ARCLES files, including the formulas for the Arc regimen?"

It shook him to the core that they even knew enough to ask the second question. These were no more government men than Frick was an archangel. Ben wondered why they'd even bothered with the lie.

"I'm not going to answer," Ben said. "Question one or two."

Morrison turned around, muttered something, and pulled out a semiautomatic pistol. With matter-of-fact assurance he put the cold steel barrel to Ben's forehead.

"If you don't answer the question, you're of no use to us."

Ben closed his eyes and pondered the implications of any disclosure. They could actually be agents—agents of a foreign government. More likely they were with Sanker. Or, God help him, American Bayou Technologies. Or they could represent someone else altogether.

"Shoot me."

Crew escorted Sam and Haley to the patrol car.

"I have to put handcuffs on you," Crew said, "and to advise you of your rights. But I promise I won't leave you alone until we find the undersheriff."

"Get real," Haley said, as if she were chiding a brother.

"Do you really think Haley conspired to kill Ben Anderson?" Sam asked.

"I don't have a choice," Crew said. "I'm doing what Sergeant Frick ordered."

"You might ask him what his probable cause is," Sam responded. "And then you might ask him about the crime he's here to commit."

Crew sighed. "Here's how I'm trying to think about it: I'm asking for your cooperation to assist us in an investigation."

Neither Sam nor Haley bothered to respond.

Crew fingered the cuffs. "Let me try the undersheriff again."

Sam heard something behind them. He turned and saw Frick walking up the path. Sam supposed he'd never been far behind. Frick had his own pistol holstered and Sam's gun in his hand.

"This is not a tea party, Deputy. Cuff them."

"That's not a good idea," Sam said. "It's an illegal arrest."

"It's a simple job," Frick said quickly. "Taking the suspects to the station. Can you handle that job, Crew?"

Crew looked ready to cry. "I was wondering about probable cause, because—"

"She attacked me when you were out of the room," Frick cut in, "and he's obstructing the investigation. She got the criminals in the building. Is that enough for you? *I'm* the one arresting them, Crew; you're just taking them in. Stop tormenting yourself."

"That's a lie," Haley said. "You attacked *me*." She looked like she might attack Frick for real. Sam grabbed her arm. "I would never hurt Ben," she said more quietly.

When Sam nodded, she set her jaw and stopped talking.

"I can handle it," Crew said.

"See that you do."

Crew asked Sam to turn around and place his hands on the car. Instead of complying, Sam turned and walked toward Frick.

"Floating a badge on a cesspool is unseemly," Sam said, deliberately provoking Frick.

Frick squared on him and raised Sam's gun slightly. "I don't need to listen to—"

In a fluid motion Sam grabbed Frick's gun hand and struck a palm-up blow to Frick's nose, staggering him. At the instant of the blow Frick discharged Sam's Glock, the direction of the shot, which went wild, controlled by Sam's hand on the wrist. They struggled a moment and Sam twisted Frick's hand so that the gun dropped to the ground.

From the corner of his eye Sam saw Haley struggling with Crew, who was trying to enter the fray. Sam saw Crew's hand go for his pepper spray and Haley grab it and pull frantically.

Frick, still suffering from the blow, teetered, took a step back, and caught himself. Blood poured from his nose, but he was tough and ready to fight.

As Frick tried to unholster his own gun, Sam gut-punched him and reached inside, closing his hand over the top of it. Frick doubled over, and Sam pulled the semiautomatic from its holster and threw it deep into the trees. Sinking to his knees, Frick managed to pick up Sam's Glock. Lightning fast, Sam grabbed Frick's gun hand, pulling it toward himself and pulling the barrel past his body. Incredibly, Frick seemed to let Sam do this. Using Sam's momentum, Frick directed the gun at Crew and fired.

The bullet hit Crew just above the groin and below the protection of his Kevlar vest. Crew fell with a cry, then lay still in shocked silence.

Haley screamed and went for Crew's middle as if trying to stop the blood, but it was pouring out behind him through what Sam knew would be a gruesome exit wound.

Frick seemed to pause, perhaps shocked by his own success. Sam broke the pistol free and hammered Frick across the face, knocking him unconscious.

Haley was wailing and Crew was calling for his mother. For Sam it was one of the sadder moments in a life that had seen many such incidents. Crew arched his back, rolled his eyes, and died.

Gregory Taula, called "Khan" by everyone who knew him, sat behind a lifeless seafood bar and empty veranda overlooking the ferry terminal at Friday Harbor. He got the nickname when as a cop he killed a houseful of crack dealers after charging the place. Another officer, a history buff, said he had the grit of Genghis Khan.

He'd been to the coffee shop next door and heard Sam's name a few times and various recitations of the story of Sam's gun and other stories about this quiet "man of mystery," including his "miracle recovery from the wheelchair" saga. Khan watched the few people coming and going to the coffee shop, most of them hippie types. He wondered where the Republicans went for coffee in this place. In his mind's eye he pictured this Sam sitting in the wooden chair, reading the paper or a book or God-knew-what-else, and he tried to imagine what he might be looking for up on this veranda. The more Khan heard about this man, the less he liked it.

After a time Khan saw Rafe Black walk into the coffee shop. He knew Rafe was following him, hoping to strike up a conversation and learn more about the job. All the men were curious. Seventeen of them had been flown in on two prop jets from Vegas, and that was a real happening. It said something very big was coming down. Only Khan knew Frick, and knew they were merely on standby.

Khan had issues with Rafe Black. Their mutual employer, Saber Strope, ran a string of Las Vegas strip clubs, some casinos with shabby interiors but a good return for the gamblers, and a small herd of escorts that were nothing more than careful prostitutes. Rafe got involved with the girls on company time.

With a large mocha in hand, Rafe leaned against the railing on the front porch of the coffee shop—no doubt trying to get up the nerve to come over—trying to be cool. Rafe reminded Khan of Frick, but he was definitely "Frick lite." They were both taken by their own strange needs, which made them weak and sometimes irrational. Frick had a raw cunning that saved him, whereas Rafe just became obsessed with things. Still, Khan could use Rafe's old rage to get things done, and so he took the good with the bad.

Khan hadn't yet figured out what had fed the flames of Frick's madness. If it weren't for the extraordinary payday Frick was extracting from his corporate masters, Khan wouldn't have risked working on such a remote, large-scale operation under Frick's direction.

Suddenly Rafe sat bolt upright. He thought he'd seen a slight hand signal from Khan beckoning him over. He stared. Khan's eyes appeared veiled, even at fifty feet. Then he saw it again. The trigger finger was beckoning. Rafe walked down the stairs and over to the veranda.

Khan's shoes were stylish in a big-city way. The man always wore handmade shoes, Armani suits, fine jewelry, and drove a nice clean Mercedes instead of some pimpmobile. Today he wore a black T-shirt under a casual suit and a leather topcoat. It was completely out of place on this island, but Khan paid no mind to that. That was Khan.

"We got a nice little job here on this island," Khan said. "I need you to remember, Rafe, that you're a Strope man. If we get activated, you're gonna get a ton of money for this one, and so you gonna give it all you got, just like a good Strope man would."

Rafe nodded, knowing better than to smile.

"I've known the guy running this job, name of Frick, for quite a while. Tough son of a bitch. Pro. We gettin' top money for this, so we're gonna do it right. We have been on standby, but I figure we're gonna boogie soon."

"How do you know that?"

"I can smell it. Listen to me, Rafe."

Rafe looked him in the eye.

"Can't be too human, Rafe. Not this time. You gotta be cold and disciplined for this job."

The look on Khan's face made Rafe nervous, but he nodded. "If I gotta, I can eat a baby's eyes."

Khan smiled. "Bring your fork."

CHAPTER 8

Haley was screaming, but not quite hysterical. In a second or two, Sam had made a calculated decision. He wouldn't kill Frick in cold blood or kidnap him. But since Sam's own pistol was now a murder weapon, it was time to go.

Haley was still shrieking. Taking her by the arm, he led her to her car.

"Wait here," he said, putting Frick's own cuffs on him. The keys to the cuffs were on Frick's key ring and he promptly hurled all the keys into the trees. Then he half-ran, half-hobbled, his bad leg aching, to the building as best he could. Right at the door he met Detective Ranken. For a second the officer stared, obviously trying to determine why Sam was headed toward the building. Sam punched him to double him over, grabbed his hand in a disabling hold, and drew his pepper spray.

"No," the officer choked as the noxious stuff went in his eyes and down his throat.

It was an unusually bad reaction; Ranken curled up in a ball, focusing on nothing but the next breath and the fire in his eyes. It was an unfortunate way for Sam to continue the afternoon, but the worsening situation required that he access Ben's office. It took only seconds to gather up all the whale papers on Ben's desk, then a minute or more to get back to Haley's car.

Haley was talking to herself softly, asking why Frick did it. Tears were running down her face.

"Haley, I need you to focus on saving Ben and put everything else out of your mind until that job is done."

She managed to stop rambling and accepted a tissue.

"Crew was my friend," she said after a moment.

"When we get done with this, we will mourn your friend."

"How many times have you had to do this?"

Sam started the car and accelerated rapidly.

"Too many. I'm calling a friend in the FBI." Sam flipped open his cell phone and called Special Agent Ernie Sanders's personal cell phone.

Ernie answered on the first ring. "What the hell are you doing not calling through the office?"

"I have a real problem."

"You're supposed to be resting on a quiet island and learning about nature."

"Supposed to, yeah."

"So you took on another job?"

"Actually, the job is taking me."

"What's up?" Ernie sounded concerned.

"A bad cop, the guy you looked up for me, one Garth Frick, just fatally shot a good cop, a local deputy. Frick's trying to frame me and a young lady." Sam went carefully through the part of the story Ernie had not yet heard, ending with his best guess at the situation: Haley, Ben, and he were now serious threats to Frick and the Sanker Corporation, and Ben's valuable research was the motivating item.

As he spoke to Ernie, Sam decided on a destination: Haley's house, which was an easy walk to Ben's.

"How the hell can you get into something like this just kicking back?" Ernie asked.

"Trouble always finds me, I guess."

"Sanker is a legitimate business, isn't it?"

"Don't know," Sam said. "But Garth Frick's as bent as you hinted."

"How much does it look like you did it?"

"Superficially, a lot."

"But forensics will support you?"

"Forensics may or may not help, but the truth is the truth."

Ernie sighed. "You know I can't jump in and take over a local murder investigation, especially in a matter of hours. Let's see . . . to get federal involvement, you could file a civil rights complaint. Even then we'd have to follow procedures."

"You can call the local dispatcher and get one of the sheriff's deputies on the phone. Tell him it's crucial not to let Frick control the evidence," Sam proposed.

"I'll try, but I'm afraid it's a long shot. Had you considered just turning yourself in to the staties?"

"I'm on an island, Ernie. There are no state police, and Frick's running the locals. Sheriff's gone, undersheriff too. I'm guessing the timing's no coincidence. That's why they took Ben Anderson this weekend."

Ernie said nothing for a moment. "That could be a problem."

Frick's head hurt, and his face had taken some serious damage. His jaw was swelling out of control, but his mind was clear despite the pain. He made his way down the hall of the main office building and lab complex, hands still cuffed, headed for Ben Anderson's office. Jim Ranken walked along, helping to steady him, his pepper-sprayed face red, his eyes looking horrible and still runny. Frick's hands were still cuffed behind his back and he swore unremittingly about the whereabouts of the bolt cutters. Supposedly there was a spare set of keys to the cuffs in the glove box of Frick's car, but they weren't there. An officer finally arrived with bolt cutters large enough to cut the tempered steel.

It had been almost thirty minutes; Ranken seemed to be breathing again.

"Make sure every available man's out looking for Haley Walther's car," Frick said.

"They are. I think maybe . . ."

Ranken seemed to be struggling for words and it irritated Frick.

"Spit it out."

"Maybe we should call the state attorney general."

"What the hell is the AG gonna do on a holiday weekend? Nothing. We've got two detectives working and about a dozen deputies."

"The AG could give us advice," Ranken said. "They could bring in the state police."

"I'm not gonna have the state police screwing up this investigation before I get the foundation laid."

"But we always—"

"I know what we always do," Frick said. "And I know why we're gonna wait until Monday to do it. In the meantime I can round up a bunch of cops from the mainland and some off-duty state police to help out."

"I—I don't think the sheriff ever conceived of a situation w-where you would be in charge of full-time regular deputies," Ranken stammered.

"Let's review." Frick's words came out like bullets. "A special deputy has whatever powers the sheriff confers. In my case I have full powers. This is logical because I'm an ex–homicide detective. Further, all Sanker matters are assigned to me. This involves a Sanker scientist disappearing from the Sanker facility. Two-oh-one would be next in charge after the undersheriff. He called dispatch and said I was in charge until he returns. So what don't you understand?"

"But you were involved in a shooting," Ranken said. "Crew's dead, for God's sake. And how are you getting off-duty cops in here that fast?"

Frick stopped cold, realizing he was going to have serious trouble with Ranken. "What the hell are you saying?"

"I'm saying you . . . we are parties to this shooting. You're a material witness. We can't just continue to pursue this case alone. Another jurisdiction should be keeping the evidence, not us. That's procedure. Bringing in outsiders to work for us is not."

Frick got directly in Ranken's face. "Robert Chase killed a San Juan deputy! You want me to stop pursuit of a murder suspect?"

"I'm just saying—"

"You heard Sergeant Finley on the phone. It's my investigation and that's an order. Go outside and help get it done."

"You're not going to take those papers from Anderson's desk without a warrant, are you?"

"I'm gonna take any damn thing we need." Frick realized he was losing it. He stepped back. He needed to be careful. "I'm going to follow the law, Detective. Now get the hell outside and help."

Ranken did as he was told, but he had Frick worried. Frick was pretty sure Ranken had questions about who had really shot Crew. He might have even seen part of the scuffle.

Frick began looking for the papers from the model blue whale. It took about ten seconds to realize that they were gone.

He closed his eyes and tried to breathe. Sparks, like fireworks, streaked across the inside of his eyelids. He felt a sort of anger like he hadn't felt since the day he'd beaten the commissioner with a baseball bat. As the commissioner writhed on the floor, in his bloody gray suit, Frick had turned him into a bag of broken bones.

Frick heard himself cursing, then bit his tongue to stop himself. He realized he was becoming incoherent in his rage. His eyes were wide open, but only now was he seeing. He'd moved down the hall from Anderson's office. For a moment he had to remind himself that he was a person very much in control. He was deliberate. He was strong. He was intelligent. He had been a detective. He was the most formidable industry security man in the country. He could put it all back together.

Christ, his face hurt.

Just then Ranken walked back in and came up the stairs.

"I want to register an objection here," the detective started. "I don't think you should be leading the hunt for Chase and Walther, and I don't think we should be searching the doctor's office or wall safe without a warrant. The whole thing looks bad. We don't even know that Ben Anderson's—"

Ranken stopped as Frick's eyes sank into him. "What exactly are your concerns?"

"I just told you. And this Chase or Sam fellow or whatever? He *apologized* to me on the way back out after spraying me. I mean, I'd like to kick his ass personally, but he wasn't acting like a cold-blooded murderer. Maybe we're talking about manslaughter here." Ranken fidgeted under Frick's cold stare. "I don't know. Maybe we're pushing this thing too hard. We don't want more people getting killed needlessly."

"Robert Chase made an ass of you. He went right around you and stole the papers that were in the whale."

Ranken didn't respond.

Still holding Ranken with his gaze, Frick swept up the

giant tweezers from the surface of Ben's desk. His hand was gloved. "I need to show you something else. It's down in the workshop in the basement."

Fifteen minutes later, Frick walked back to the conference room near his office in the Sanker Main Building. The expansive conference room, which overlooked Friday Harbor from the northern rim, had the best water-view seats in the house.

Frick dialed the phone.

"This is Doris," came the familiar voice from Vegas.

"Garth Frick. Give me Strope."

"Just a minute."

It took her about thirty seconds.

"Give me a number where Strope can call you," she said.

A few moments later, the phone rang.

"You must have a problem."

Typical Strope—already starting to gloat.

"I do," said Frick. "I want them now. Khan, Rafe, and the others, like we talked—ten crude, ten smooth."

"Yeah, yeah. I got eight crude, nine smooth for you. They're on your island as of yesterday. I'll call Khan and—"

"That wasn't our deal," Frick interrupted.

"Take it or leave it. I can't control when guys get sick or leave town. You're only down three. I'll make the price thirty grand less."

"Get me Khan now," Frick said, "and we're good."

"He'll be there within the hour," Strope said. "Two days max on location, right?"

"That's right."

Frick hung up, thinking about the total price. He would need more money. Except for Rafe Black and Khan himself, Strope's people didn't whack anybody as part of the plan. The deal was that Khan could kill and Rafe could kill, but he had to make a separate deal for that with Khan. The only exception was self-defense and, of course Frick would label any inadvertent gunplay as just that: self-defense.

In addition to the basic fee of $350,000, actual dead bodies were $100,000 per head for the first two and $50,000 thereafter, regardless of who killed them or why. Any dead body that made it into the press added to the fee. He'd have to raise the price with Nash. Frick shook his head. That meant another call to Sanker Corporation.

"I need more money," Frick opened with Nash. All negotiations regarding the project went through Nash.

"I'm afraid that's not possible," Nash said.

"Making sure Ben Anderson is safe is costly. Finding a kidnap victim is always costly. I don't have time to argue. Either you're with me or I have to resign." Frick reminded himself that it was necessary to maintain the fiction that any kidnapping that might occur would be done by someone else—certainly not Frick and certainly not Sanker.

"We already paid one hundred thousand to protect Ben Anderson."

Frick knew that saying nothing was the quickest way to end this session. He rubbed his sore jaw, but didn't speak. After a long pause he heard a sigh.

"All right," Nash said. "I suppose the one hundred grand was just to get people in place. How much?"

"One million." Frick said it as if there were no room for negotiation. He wanted plenty for dead bodies, if it came to that. Already there were two—thankfully not on Khan's bill—and more were likely on the way.

This time the sigh was bigger.

Frick placed his next call to Griffith, one of two men already on Frick's personal payroll. Grif had no formal connection to the sheriff's department except that he'd been arrested plenty in his life.

"Go to Ben Anderson's. Wait there for me. If the fellow

Sam or the woman Haley shows up, call me immediately and stay out of sight. Got it?"

"I got it."

Frick slammed the handset down. All the talking had his jaw throbbing and the job had turned bad. His life was on the line and there wasn't enough money in Nash's coffers for that kind of risk.

There was no way this would end cleanly. His only hope of ending it quickly was finding Ben Anderson's secret in the safe—and then finding Ben Anderson.

Sam made his way toward Haley's place by a circuitous route, starting on Beaverton and then cutting down to San Juan Valley.

Haley had stopped crying, but she hadn't said a word for several minutes.

"If you're ready to look at this," he said, handing her a piece of paper, "I found something interesting that Frick and his men never saw."

The message, in Ben's writing, was cryptic:

> *Together they make more than they consume and they waste very little. We do the opposite and we are inefficient to boot. It's the by-products of inefficiency that they avoid and that we do not.*
>
> *There is a reason Mother Nature has not given us the same gift and in due course I will reveal it. If we take a lesson and get the gift for ourselves, we'll have a rain check on individual deaths, save ourselves collectively, and solve the biggest problem of our discovery.*
>
> *Perhaps the second phase of "creation," if you will, is for intelligent life to make choices that supercede natural selection. Intellectual life wants to preserve*

consciousness as an end in itself. Now there's a thought.
Check where the ocean cleanses itself.

"I think he wrote it for you," Sam said. "Someone he trusts and who knows something about science. At the end he seems to be telling us where to look. Does it mean anything to you?"

Haley thought for a moment. "He's discovered a creature, something amazing, apparently. The 'cleansing' thing rings a bell."

Sam was glad her mind was off Crew's death, for the moment at least. "How so?" he asked.

Haley explained that deep in the sea, oceanologists had discovered that the oceans did have a sort of self-cleansing mechanism. Miles below the surface, fracture lines occurred on the ocean floor, where the earth's crust's tectonic plates rammed each other like slow-motion bumper cars. The collision of the plates created geographic features like the mid-Atlantic ridge. They also created cracks, which allowed seawater to flow down into the earth's crust. Water forced into the crust was superheated to seven hundred degrees or more, then returned, under great pressure, back into the ocean through vents. Over the course of 6 to 8 million years, every molecule of seawater would have traveled, at least once, down into the earth and back out into the oceans.

"Okay," Sam said. "Where would that mean he's leading us?"

"I don't know. Vent sites are found a mile beneath the sea and lower. We won't be seeing them any time soon, so he must either be referring to studies or photos of the fissures or vents. He has plenty of pictures."

"Where?"

Haley took a moment to think about it. "One of his friends was on the team that took the deep-diving submersible *Alvin* down to the Snake Pit. A couple of miles deep, if I recall. The pictures would be in his house."

"We've got two things to do," Sam said. "Ditch this car, and send Frick some place other than Ben's house. Did Ben have a safe-deposit box or any place a person might logically keep papers?"

"He had a box at the local bank," Haley said.

"We need to talk with Sarah. She'll be frantic about Ben." He thought for a moment. "Maybe we can tell Sarah to let Frick know about the bank."

Haley grasped the idea immediately. "Okay."

Sam hastily outlined a plan. They would have Sarah call on the phone and ask Frick about Ben's disappearance. When Frick asked the obvious questions, she would tell him about the safe-deposit box. Then she would disappear to ensure her safety.

CHAPTER 9

They were proceeding along the water on the south side of the island while Haley called Sarah on her cell. Sam's own cell rang in the middle of the conversation. It was Ernie, of the FBI.

"I have a new boss and he's not real into meddling in your situation," Ernie began. "I guess he's impressed that Frick's an eyewitness to the murder of Officer Crew Wentworth. I told him that was bunk and that you would murder no one, and that sort of moved him back to center on the thing. Just to let you know the situation, I still can't be real aggressive on this like I could if the boss really believed your side of this. I gotta work with it, you know. I called the state police and it's a damn holiday, but they will get an assistant attorney general, they say. By Monday they'll be in full swing. They've called deputies on the island that they know and they say you killed Wentworth. And uh . . ."

"What?"

"You met my boss once in New York," Ernie said. "I guess you were trying to get some movement by the bureau on something. Anyway, you'd recall him as Special Agent Arnold Cross."

"Say no more. I understand," Sam said. "Does he still go around with a telephone pole up his alimentary canal?"

"Pretty much. And his daddy is a senator, so that doesn't hurt. If you were still in business, you'd be using 'Big Brain,' I suspect."

"I suspect you're right," Sam said. Ernie was talking about a supercomputer that Sam had used frequently in his previous life.

"So I, ah," Ernie's voice went quieter, "sort of ignored the boss . . . insubordination really . . . and got Grogg on a conference call. He connected to Big Brain remotely and we did a lot of checking real fast."

"I'm impressed," Sam said, smiling for the first time since this ordeal began. "And grateful." For a moment the sun burst through the clouds.

"It seems that Sanker Corp is in a merger deal with American Bayou Technologies," said Ernie. "They're both heavyweights, and the deal started friendly, but it couldn't stay that way because they're both predatory. Management of one won't live with the management of the other. Someone is going to win and someone is going to lose. Up until recently, Sanker thought they were certain to win. Maybe American Bayou knew something Sanker didn't. Now Sanker desperately needs a bump up in its stock price. Stock price will decide who ends up with the controlling interest in the conglomerate. Does anything you're dealing with have the potential to affect Sanker's stock price?"

"Yes. To say the least. In fact, one press release could do it." Sam gave Ernie a thumbnail description of the possible range and impact of Ben's work. "Of course, we don't know if this 'fountain of youth' discovery is all that potent. Or even real," he added.

"But just a good story would do it," Ernie completed the

thought. "I get it. I wish I could call Cross on this, but, of course, I can't, because officially I don't know what you just told me, about the fountain of youth–thing. We never had this call. Somehow, though, I'll find a way to run across the information, and when I do, then I'll tell him."

"You're a good man, Ernie. You make me feel lucky."

"I'm touched by your compliment."

"Good. I have one more favor."

"Uh-oh. With you it's always the second favor that costs me."

Sam asked Haley if she had a home fax; fortunately, she did.

"Please fax me the memo about Frick."

"Are you out of your mind? That's FBI property."

"It could be critical in trying to bring in the Washington State Police."

In the long silence that followed, Sam could sense Ernie's stress.

"I must be losing my mind."

"Thanks, Ernie. I'll be careful with it. I wish I had a choice, but they want to put me in jail. We do have a dead officer."

Haley had ended her call with Sarah, so Sam filled her in.

"Sanker is merging with American Bayou, as you know."

"I don't really understand it."

"It means the strongest guy wins. The old man and all his henchmen could completely lose control of Sanker because their stock price tanked."

"When I told the truth about my new strain of sea grass, they screamed about the stock price. I just didn't know it was such a big deal for Sanker."

"They tell me the work you did was brilliant, coming up with the new strain of sea grass. What all does it do that's good?"

"Makes cheap protein. Feeds people. Has a lot of pharmaceutical applications like so many things from the sea. Immune-system drugs." Haley sighed as if wistfully remembering when she was at the height of her glory. "The issue was that the sea grass is host to a whole little universe of life. When I genetically altered it, you know, you change the house, you could change the inhabitants. I wasn't saying we couldn't use it, for God's sake. I'm not like one of these nuts who says we can't use genetically improved corn. I said we need to study it before going hog-wild on production. The seaweed seemed to be functioning differently after the genetic change. The single-celled organisms weren't acting the same. I wanted time to study it. Evidently Sanker was desperate about their stock price and wanted a big announcement."

"So McStott and Frick concocted the scheme to make it look like it was mostly his work, and that you stole it."

"That's it. Of course, McStott had no concern about the sea grass's effect on the environment. Frick and McStott saw to it that my article with the warnings was never published. Instead, they published an article touting the discovery. But they had no credibility because some university people cried foul. And see, that also hurt my credibility. It was a mess."

"You couldn't show it was your discovery and that these guys were jumping the gun with it?"

"Well, it's long and complicated, but McStott and I shared the same file-server computer. We did collaborate. He just had nothing to do with the creation of this strain of sea grass. They switched our lab notes. Hell, there are all kinds of things going on that only the scientists involved really understand when it comes to knowing who does what." She let out a long breath. "And there was one other problem. Like an idiot, I trusted McStott and against the rules I gave him my computer pass code. You're never supposed to do that. So when I started saying he stole and that I gave him my pass code . . . well, that was considered stupid, and on and on."

"I'm sorry," Sam said. "He betrayed you."

"In a very personal way."

"The merger also explains why they'd go after Ben now," Sam said. "Especially since he was getting ready to leave the foundation."

Sam pulled over about one hundred yards from her drive.

"Where can we hide the car?" he asked.

"Up ahead on the left there's an overgrown orchard and a shack. Nobody lives there. It's actually on Ben's forty acres."

Sam pulled into the orchard. Trees were old and gnarled, with twisted bark and old wounds.

"Hopefully, they're not here yet," she said, speaking of the police.

"A man as pissed off as Frick? You'd be amazed how fast he might get somebody here."

They hurried through the forest as fast as Sam could manage, back across the road, and into the forest again. As they approached Haley's house, they went more slowly. When they saw no one and no police cruisers, Sam hoped it was only moderately dangerous to duck in the back door.

Haley's fax had the FBI memo from Ernie. Actually, it was an excerpt from an FBI memo and parts had obviously been redacted. But it was better than nothing.

They searched through Haley's garage until they found a tarp, then took it back to the car and covered it completely. People would come by the house and there might soon be planes and helicopters flying overhead.

Haley called the dispatcher on her cell phone and explained that Crew had been shot by Frick, not Sam; that the FBI had been notified; and that the FBI would be making a formal request to keep the evidence pristine and out of Frick's hands.

She asked the dispatcher whether the FBI had called, but the dispatcher refused to confirm or deny such a call. When the dispatcher made the obligatory request that Haley and Sam surrender themselves to a deputy, Haley disconnected.

None of it was surprising, since the dispatcher was following normal police procedure. They weren't in the habit of collaborating with murder suspects.

Minutes later, they arrived on foot at Ben's house, some two hundred yards from Haley's. Sam had Haley hunker down with him in the trees while he checked for company. It was a large, sprawling home, gray with lap siding and white trim, appearing all the more stylish for the rustic nature of its setting. From his own experience during summertime work, he knew that the gardens had been Helen's inspiration and he was reminded of the sweat and the creative eye in all the curves and the shapes in the various plantings and rows. It was a bit blustery and looking like another shower. The breezes made it anything but quiet. Sam let his eye wander carefully by every leaf and every decorative boulder hauled from the beach. He saw nothing moving, save that which could be moved by the wind, but he remembered Crew and worried for Haley. How could he be sure that there was no one lying in wait? Ben's house was an obvious destination.

Sam could see the back patio from this position, but not the front porch. He first moved to the left, checking out the front-yard area and the gardens and the long drive, which approached up a gradual hill. A large porch sat under an overhang. Nothing there.

Now he moved back to the right and circled behind the house, remaining inside a small patch of trees. On the back patio stood two barbecues and flower boxes with a multitude of plants in full color, maintained by hired help. It would be impossible to completely verify that no one was watching.

They would have to take a chance.

Sam motioned to stay low and led Haley as quickly as his leg would allow over the last open ground between them and the house.

* * *

Frick had the safecracker back at work on the wall safe in Ben's office. He had regained his composure and now felt calm and confident. When they had the safe open, it would become simple. With Ben's research in hand, he'd be free to find and kill Ben Anderson—still difficult, but doable—and that would end the matter.

The safe expert had electronic listening devices splayed across the metal surface. Numbers had been flashing across a laptop on the desk for at least ten minutes. As Frick watched, the man slowly turned the dial through the sequence for the twentieth time. Suddenly the numbers on the computer stopped at eighty-seven.

"Uh-huh." The safecracker turned the handle and the safe opened.

Inside stood a handmade sign: *Fools rush in where angels dare to tread*.

As the technician leaned in, an explosion sent sticky black soot everywhere. The technician took the main force of the blast, covered by a harmless but nasty substance. Frick was largely unscathed, but that was little comfort. They had bet everything on the escrow; if Ben had fudged that, the research would be in the wall safe.

The safe held nothing else, and the clock was ticking on Frick's life.

CHAPTER 10

This time Rossitter contacted him by phone. Sanker wondered if he had the new shoes on yet.

"We haven't located Ben. Neither has Frick."

"What does Judas say?" Sanker felt as if he'd already had a bellyful of uncertainty.

"He says he doesn't know."

"Has he got his hands on the formula?" Sanker asked.

"Not yet. He says there's only one place and he has to get there. He's not even sure about that."

"Where does he think it is?"

"Like before, he said that's not part of our deal," Rossitter said.

"It's our deal for him to deliver it as a backup."

"He says as long as we have Frick trying, we don't need the backup. He says he'll tell us, though, the minute he has it."

"I have a question," Sanker said, pondering even as he spoke.

"What's that?"

"Are we sure that Judas is a he and not a she?"

There was a long pause. Obviously this hadn't occurred to Rossitter.

"It's a male voice, disguised, but still male. You're thinking Judas could be more than one person?"

"There are a number of possibilities. How do we know for sure that Judas is even a Judas?"

"He told us what Anderson was planning," Rossitter said, while still not sounding certain.

"Judas could be a man, woman, or a group," the old man began. "He could be working both sides, like a double agent, ours and American Bayou's. And Ben Anderson could have been afraid we'd find out he was leaving, anyway, so he devised some kind of test and he's playing us. Keep in mind, the information may not always be true. Remember Judas learns things from us just as we learn from him. Judas could be working with Frick, American Bayou, or some other third party. Who is feeding who, here?"

"I still think it's as it appears. Judas wants money, and we're the biggest source."

"You're right, I suppose, if it's all true. You tell him next time he calls that we demand to know Ben Anderson's whereabouts. Even the manner of his response may tell us something."

"I'll do that. For now, I recommend that we stick with the plan."

"Do we have a choice?" Sanker sounded as irritated as he felt. He wanted to be proactive, not reactive, and he couldn't find a way to get complete control and drive events. It was an unaccustomed subservience to history in the making.

Sanker clicked the receiver in Rossitter's ear without saying good-bye in order to signal his dissatisfaction.

Rossitter was typically good under pressure. Maybe he would come up with something.

* * *

Twenty minutes later, Frick sat in a small grove of Douglas
fir and watched the undersheriff, Roy Knauff, through the
branches. In preparing for the weekend, Frick had made a
special point of learning the undersheriff's likely whereabouts. The undersheriff, Frick discovered, was tight with his
cousin, an electrical contractor on the island. Sure enough,
Frick's hired man had followed the undersheriff to his cousin's
house and he was here kicking back just as his man had
promised.

Meanwhile, Frick had the department working on a new
front. They were close to obtaining a search warrant for a
safe-deposit box that Ben Anderson rented. Anderson's secretary, Sarah James, had told Frick about the box when she
called looking for Anderson. He doubted the search would
be fruitful. She had given up the story a little too easily.

There was no cell signal at the undersheriff's cousin's
place, here on Wescott Bay. The pager would work, but the
undersheriff's was broken. Frick had seen to that. The dispatcher had left a message on the undersheriff's cell and sent
someone around to the undersheriff's place. Frick knew it
was only a question of time before the undersheriff called in
or the dispatcher found him, so he had to work fast. He had
known all along that if the papers weren't where they were
supposed to be, things would unravel and he would need to
handle the undersheriff. When the time was right, Frick
wanted to be the one to tell him about Crew's murder.

Through the window of the house, a pretty redhead was
laughing and the undersheriff was giving her his undivided
attention. Had to be the cousin's wife. In Frick's world no
man ever paid that much attention to his own wife. While he
watched them, he used an encoded police radio to call Khan,
who'd arrived shortly before Frick left. Khan had set up base
in the Sanker conference room.

"Khan."

"What have our eggheads found?" Frick asked.

"I'm no scientist. Your guy McStott calls it a lot of basic genetic research. Probably not what you're after. Then again, it stands to reason, though, that a man can't completely cover his tracks. We have mounds of paper and printouts from his office and lab, and McStott says he's piecing it together. But nothing exactly on point."

"We have this weekend," Frick said. "That's it. By Monday this place will be raining state cops and feds. Chase is not going to sit still. He must know people."

"We're trying to pull it together."

Frick clicked off. Khan and McStott didn't seem to get it. Mounds of irrelevant paperwork was Ben Anderson covering his tracks to perfection.

Frick would need to improvise. He called the Strope man he had at Ben Anderson's place.

"Seen anything?"

"I was about to call you. Someone just got here. I saw a faint light go on inside the house. Earlier I saw movement outside."

"Who is it?"

"They must've come on foot—sneaking. It's got to be them."

"If they try to leave, stop 'em any way you can. I don't care if you shoot Robert Chase, but don't kill Haley Walther."

"I'm not looking to kill anybody."

"Do your damn job. They're dangerous fugitives, for God's sake."

Frick dialed the undersheriff's cousin, on a satellite phone watching through the window as the redhead started at the sound of the house phone.

"May I speak with the undersheriff, please."

He could see the man take the phone.

"Hello?"

"We have a situation," Frick began. He told him his version of the whole story.

"The guy who used to be in the wheelchair shot Crew?"

"Yeah. But you know he's not in a wheelchair now. The wheelchair was a fraud all along. I don't think he was ever hurt at all."

"No lie?"

Frick patiently outlined the events of the afternoon in more detail, with some important omissions and additions.

"We think they're looking for Ben Anderson's research papers," Frick concluded.

"Why would they want those?" the undersheriff asked.

"Haley Walther has a history of stealing research. Anderson's papers are apparently valuable."

"You're at the facility?"

"Just heading out to Anderson's house now."

"I'll meet you there. Haley Walther's no violent criminal." The undersheriff waited for a response. "You understand that, don't you?"

"Why don't you let me make sure the place is clear. Meet me at three twenty-five."

Frick knew the undersheriff would be reluctant to see Haley as a violent criminal. The undersheriff was a good man—short, well-built, and strong. Frick supposed it was a shame that he'd have to die. He watched as the man slid into his leather coat. Then the undersheriff shook the host's hand and kissed the redhead quickly on the cheek. It was happening fast, but it seemed slow to Frick. Probably because it was the last few minutes the man would have on this earth.

Better thee than me.

CHAPTER 11

Sam and Haley entered Ben's house through the side garage door. They emerged from the garage into a hallway that led into the kitchen and a family room area. To the left another hallway accessed a library and beyond that a living room. Off the grand entry to the living room was a short hall to the master bedroom. Haley went into the library first. She selected a set of tall mahogany bookshelves and began pulling down albums.

"Look for anything that says 'Snake Pit' or *'Alvin'* on it," Haley said.

In moments she had an *Alvin* photo album that featured the deep-diving submersible. She began flipping through it and Sam did the same with an adjacent album. They found one undersea shot after another.

"We've got ten or fifteen minutes at best," said Sam.

"I'm surprised Frick's people aren't here. If it weren't Thanksgiving weekend, deputies would be shouting through a megaphone at us."

"Yup."

Sam didn't tell her that the one reason Frick might not do

any shouting with a bullhorn is if he wanted to kill one or both of them.

Haley reached the end of the album and looked up. "This will take forever. We can't do this. His library's only the beginning; there are more bookshelves downstairs. Which one do we choose? Could he have narrowed the field for us and we're just missing it?"

"The bathroom," Sam said.

"What? Why?"

"Because he's talking about the ocean cleansing itself, and there might be a sort of crude parallel to people. And because it's unlikely."

Haley looked willing if unconvinced. "Okay, there are four. Let's try the master bath."

They exited double-wide doors into the large entry hall, crossed it, and went into the master bedroom. The master bath was spacious and decorated with small watercolors of tropical islands and one stunning photo of an undersea coral reef. They found no other photos of the sea, let alone any that involved undersea vents.

"Maybe it's downstairs," Haley said. "Or back at the office. Or even over on Lopez Island at the beach house. Oh God . . ."

"Try the other three bathrooms," Sam said.

He followed her back through the large entry hall, past the library, past the back door to the garage and down another short hall to a back bedroom. Just outside the bedroom was her old bathroom. On the wall of Haley's old bathroom hung pictures of characters from famous children's stories, like Winnie the Pooh, supplemented by sweaty, screaming rock musicians of twenty years previous. She had been a precocious kid and had grown up fast.

"Two bathrooms left and then we're sunk," she said.

"Let's look in your old bedrooms. The first bedroom first."

It was around the corner. She led the way.

It was still decorated like a girl's room: part kid, part teenybopper—the latter before she moved downstairs.

"Did you have a hope chest or a special place?" Sam asked. "Maybe a place for, I don't know . . ."

"A diary," she said excitedly. "My right-hand desk drawer."

Her white dresser stood against the wall at the foot of the bed and next to a desk. She pulled open the drawer. No diary, but a *National Geographic*. The February 2003 edition.

"Say," Haley said, "you're good."

"Not that good. It wasn't in the bathroom."

She flipped through it until she reached the section on an *Alvin* deep dive. It was the Snake Pit Vent. Scrawled in pen across the bottom of the picture were the words:

> *One sigh and we're all dead. Feed them so we can breathe and it kills us, anyway. We must learn to empower the lungs of the earth and get more than breath. Let us not breathe only to watch us suffocate or roast.*

Under the magazine lay an envelope full of papers. Across the bottom of each page was the word *ARCLES*.

"I've been meaning to ask," Sam said. "What's ARCLES mean?"

"I don't know, but I do think I know where we're supposed to go next."

A sound from outside interrupted them. It sounded like tires on gravel.

Sam drew back the drape a half-inch.

A car was nearing the end of the long driveway.

"It's a patrol car," Haley said.

"Do we need anything else here?"

"I don't know," she said. "I'll tell you in a couple hours, when it will be too late."

As Sam dropped the drape, a boom shattered the silence. Haley jumped and grabbed him. It was a deep, concussive roar that Sam associated with his 10mm Glock or some other similar weapon. Most 10mm gun models could not handle what was considered the optimum powder charge. The Glock packed the full wallop and sounded like it.

"I think that might be Frick framing me." Sam hobbled on his bad leg in a weird sort of run to the front door. From the gravel driveway, only about fifty feet from the house, a patrol car had run off into the grass, lights on and its engine running. Sam could almost picture the neat round hole in the windshield.

Opening the front door a crack, he listened and watched. The fields and yard had the still quiet of a chilly winter afternoon interrupted only by the faint sound of a beginning rain and the swirling breezes. There was no movement in the car and only a quiet hum from its engine. Sam was certain now: He and Haley were being set up. Again. Frick would be wearing surgeon's gloves and would leave no sign of his passing. Even the shoes on his feet would be discarded.

"Someone's shot a deputy," Haley whispered frantically. "We have to help him."

"Yes," Sam said. "And we will. Stay where you are. Call the dispatcher. Tell them to send an ambulance. Officer down."

Sam went to a door in the family room that opened onto the patio. There was a small, glassed alcove, which protruded from the side of the house, that framed the door. If he stepped forward, he could see to the left and right through angled wing windows. Ahead, through the glass doors, against the perimeter railings of the patio, he saw flower boxes and billowing plants. Not wanting to show his body or his whole face, he peeked around the corner of the left wing's window. To his immediate left were barbecues along the wall of the house. To his right, steps led off the patio to a garden. He could not immediately discern any shooters waiting in the shadows.

To the left an outline stood against the wall behind the barbecues. It was perhaps the top of a person's head, although he couldn't be sure. He watched quietly for a good two minutes before he saw movement. Someone had turned to look down the wall toward the alcove. Probably there were at least two men at the house, one in front and a second in the back. There was no easy way out the back—no easy way to stalk the shooter in front. Maybe they could make it through the side garage door again. But maybe not.

He wondered how Haley was doing, imagining her standing in the gray light of the hallway, shivering in fear, and wanting to go to the fallen deputy.

He hobbled as quickly as he could back to Haley at the front door. A fire truck emergency-aid vehicle was coming up the road and turning in.

"Call the station," he whispered. "Tell them that we need more ambulances."

"They'll think I'm nuts."

"The truth grows on people. Tell them to send the fire department and ambulances. Tell them there's a chimney fire and that Frick has us pinned down inside the house. Tell them it won't be long before he burns down the house."

"There's no chimney fire," Haley said.

"There will be."

While she made the call, Sam went to the garage, where he remembered seeing some paint thinner. Using sheets, towels, paint thinner, and furniture cushions, he built a fire in the living-room fireplace until the roaring flames indeed looked like they might burn the house down.

Sam shuffled through the kitchen, grabbed Haley, and headed back to the garage. On their way there someone broke through one of the back doors. By that time Haley had run and Sam had limped at a half-run to the door to the garage. They went through it as quietly as they could. Sam imagined that the intruder came in through the dining room and headed into the living room. That would put him on the far side of the house.

That left someone, probably Frick, at the front. He considered the odds. A lot of dead men in Sam's life had played the odds. Hopefully, the man inside the house would check the garage last.

Sam found lawn mower gasoline and filled a canning jar with it. He screwed the lid down over a rag. He didn't have a match, but there was an acetylene torch in the garage and it had a barbecue lighter hanging from a string.

Timing would be everything.

Ben had a Jeep in the garage; they hid behind it.

The sound of fire engines came through the walls, and hopefully the ambulance. Sam was pretty sure that with the paint thinner in the fireplace, flames were spewing out the top of the chimney. There was no sound from the house and now it had been three minutes. Any second the garage door could open and they would have a problem.

When it happened, there was no time for thought. Slamming open the inside garage door to the house, a man jumped through and stood behind a hot-water heater for cover. Sam lit the rag and tossed the jar. For a split second the masked shooter stepped out with two hands on the gun, taut, braced, ready to shoot. He wore a police officer's uniform.

The bullets started at about the same time the jar struck the wall over the door. Between the conflagration and the muzzle flash, the deputy was lost to sight.

Bullets punched the wall where Sam's head had been, and then the firing stopped. From the concrete floor Sam saw the door and the shooter were burning. Flames rose from the man's arms and back, where gasoline had drenched him. His screams filled the air with his agony. Walking crazily, he reentered the house. Frick would come around to the garage, probably from the outside.

Sam motioned Haley to run for the flaming door through

which the shooter had disappeared. They found the man rolling in the hall, ripping off his jacket as he fought the flames.

"Extinguisher," Sam said. He remembered one in the kitchen.

Sam grabbed it from the wall, hurried back to the man, kicked the pistol far away, and blasted the burning man with fire suppressant.

Haley came with a small bucket of water and a blanket to smother the flame.

Sam grabbed the groaning man by the shirt.

He screamed. He was burned badly over his back.

"Who'd you shoot?" Sam asked.

"I didn't shoot anybody," the man said in great pain. "Frick probably did."

"Does Frick have any idea where Ben Anderson is?" asked Haley.

"No."

"Are you really a deputy?" Sam asked.

The wounded man hesitated. "Not normally. I'm from Las Vegas."

Sam knew it was past time to leave. They left the burned man and the shot officer in the car to the medics that no doubt were in the front yard. He took a risk and led Haley, crouching low, through the back door and into the trees.

They heard more fire engines in the distance as they went. Sam ran as fast as he could. It took a little over three minutes to make it back to the forest edge near Haley's. They both puffed a bit, Sam more from the pain than anything else. They stayed low in a swale, but Sam worried about the open forest and the fact that they had already put a man at Ben's. He considered their options. Other than Haley's car, which was hidden in the orchard, they had nothing but one of her rental motor scooters.

"You stay put. I'll go get your motor scooter out of the garage and we'll get out of here," Sam said.

"I'm supposed to stay here while you get shot? I'm coming."

"So you can get shot too?" Sam sighed, exasperated that she wouldn't just do as he said. "You stay here." He said it as if he were a fighter on the verge of a brawl. For some reason it worked. She nodded but glared.

He and Haley were going to have to come to an understanding.

Under the circumstances the motor scooter was the best choice. Haley had concluded the same thing. She handed Ben's papers over to Sam and devoted herself to starting the scooter. Unfortunately, with every cop on the island looking for them, the odds of making it on the scooter were not good. They climbed on and it was a tight fit, like two big men on a burro. Haley drove because Sam grudgingly had to admit that he was more accustomed to Harleys. As they ran down the highway, moving away from Ben's, he hoped they wouldn't run into a cop before they could turn off Beaverton. Once they got onto Boyce and other back roads, he breathed a little easier. It was hard to think about motor scooters and traveling after having just read the startling words of a very serious man, a man who seemed to think that a relatively ordinary event—comparable, at least in metaphor, to a sigh—would precipitate a catastrophe—roasting or asphyxiating.

Dr. Ben Anderson *had* said, "*All* dead."

CHAPTER 12

Sam directed Haley to turn the motor scooter right onto Bailer Hill Road and then back to the southeast to a gravel drive that meandered past a house and led to an old barn.

"Why are we going to Rachael's?" Haley said over her shoulder, obviously surprised at their destination.

They dismounted and Sam pushed the motor scooter into the barn. Inside, he closed the doors and flipped on a set of fluorescent lights. As Haley watched, he pulled the tarp off his 1967 Corvette. Even without natural light it had a sheen that appeared three-dimensional, like the deep blue of the ocean.

"That's yours?"

Sam smiled. He put both piles of Ben's papers on the car hood.

"Oh, I get it," Haley said. "You didn't say anything because that would actually give us information about you. I'd have died thinking you drove a two-year-old Taurus. And Rachael was a perfect choice for you. She is one of the few people I know that can really keep a secret. How did you figure that out?"

"Ben told me. We discussed where to hide my car."

"Ben told you?" she asked.

Again the surprise was evident. More like shock, Sam thought.

"I feel a little left out," Haley said. "She's my best friend."

"Believe me, you weren't left out of much. Most of the time I've spent with Rachael was because you invited her to dinner at Ben's. Now let's talk about Ben's message in the *National Geographic*. Deadly sighs?"

"I have no idea what that means," Haley said, her face still fallen. "The rest I think I understand. You've heard that the rain forests are the lungs of the earth? Well, plankton use photosynthesis and they're equal to all the forests of the world as a major source of oxygen. Given that Ben's talking about the sea, I'd call plankton the lungs of the earth. Some scientists have even suggested fertilizing the ocean to create more plankton to reduce CO_2 and slow global warming. But it sounds like Ben's saying that's dangerous, that if we make more plankton, we could have a big problem. I don't get that part."

"Are you sure Ben was familiar with this plankton-feeding idea?"

"For sure. He and his friend Lattimer Gibbons argued about the effectiveness of the idea all the time."

"He seems to be leading us somewhere. Where do you think?" Sam asked.

"Three possibilities: Lattimer Gibbons's place, Ben's office, or his beach house on Lopez."

Sam nodded and signaled for her to continue.

"Ben was part of a joint invertebrate project with the University of Washington lab. The committee he was on published a series of articles that used the subtitle: 'The Ocean Breathes for the Earth.' So I'd look for his copies of those articles. He used to have them all in a bunch of binders in his office. We can't get back in there."

"Maybe we can, maybe we can't. Tell me more about Lattimer," Sam said. "The few times I met him, he seemed odd. Anxious maybe, sort of fussy, but thoroughly devoted to Ben. Ben has always been patient."

"You know what I know. He's a retired engineer. He and Ben used to argue about fertilizing the ocean. I don't know if you were around for any of those arguments. Lattimer loved the idea and used to torture Ben with articles from other scientists who were touting it."

"Could Lattimer have the binders? Or copies?"

"Yeah," she said, "he definitely could have some of it. Maybe some copies. He could have a lot of things."

"And the same for Ben's old family beach house on Lopez?"

"There's deep-ocean stuff there, but that's actually related to the plankton because they die and rain down on the bottom."

"So back to the sigh and everybody dies," he said.

"I'm not following that part. At least not in relation to the plankton thing. But maybe Ben figured something out about that."

"Lattimer strikes me as the type that might hide things for Ben," he said.

"Yeah. And since his association with Ben is totally informal, I don't think anyone would think to look there. I could definitely see Ben hiding his *real* research with Lattimer. You know that nonconformist streak of his."

"Or hiding with Lattimer himself," Sam said. "Let's go see Mr. Gibbons."

Haley moved back toward the scooter, but Sam wasn't following her. Instead, he opened the trunk of the Corvette and removed and opened a small suitcase full of makeup.

Haley raised her eyebrows at the sight.

"This is pretty much what's left of my old life."

"I wish you'd tell me about your old life."

Inside the case was foundation makeup, skin-whitening cream, blush, prosthetic plastic, spirit gum, fake hair, and a host of other fillers and toners that you'd find on a typical movie set. Sam began placing the items on the hood of the Vette.

Next he removed a heavy lockbox. It contained documents that he rifled through carefully. He found a car registration form that said *Frederick Raimes* and pulled out the corresponding license plates.

"I really don't get this bit with the license plates," Haley said.

"It's okay. All legal."

It took him a minute or two to change the plates.

"I'm going to call for a tow truck," he said.

"Why?" Haley asked.

Sam took out his cell phone and dialed 411.

"State of Washington. San Juan Towing, on San Juan Island, please."

The operator rang him through.

"Hi," Sam told the mechanic. "My name is Fred Raimes. I'm a Triple A member. I was here visiting and I need to get my car back to Anacortes. What would you charge to take my car on the eight P.M. ferry tonight?"

"Is it broke down?"

"Yes. Blown head gasket."

"You could have it fixed on the island."

"Yeah, but I'm a mechanic and I want to get it home."

A pause. "Uh, it comes out to be about two hundred fifty bucks, including the cost of the ferry."

"Great." Sam read him the number off the AAA card in the name of Fred Raimes.

They confirmed a time and place, and Sam hung up.

"Frick's gonna be disappointed," Haley said. "You said you were Robert Chase."

Sam put a hand on her shoulder and squeezed. "Now you're catching on."

"It's none of my business, but is Raimes the name you used in your life away from the islands?"

"Sometimes. Now I go only by Sam Wintripp. I was born Samuel H. Browning."

"The name we knew," Haley said.

"You know about Helen's ancestry?"

"Helen and your father were originally descended from the Scottish Highlanders," Haley said. "Originally they were named Broun. Then their ancestors emigrated to England and changed it to Browning, right?"

"Right."

She stopped. He could tell she wanted to ask more, but there was a quiet reserve about her—a stubborn resolve. Sam nodded. He was pretty certain he knew what was really on her mind. The summer of 1994 still hung in the air between them. Instinctively, though, he felt now was not the time to break open the old scab and try to clean out the underneath.

"I took the name Wintripp when I discovered that Mother was alive and not what my father claimed—a dead mestizo woman with a bad history."

"I'm sorry about that. Everyone in the family was told the same story about your mother. Maybe that's why I identified with you. God knows my mother had her own problems." She was quiet again. "You would show up now and then, to visit, like an apparition out of the mist, saying nothing about yourself or your life. You were in the 'export business'? Give me a break. Even now," she said, "today, I wonder who you *were* back then, I mean as a person. Around 1992 they said you went into the computer business and then as a person with a life, you mostly disappeared." There was a hint of frustration in her voice and he knew she was getting nearer the source of her feelings.

Sam began shaving his beard away with a portable electric razor, using a mirror to watch his progress. There were things he had to work out in himself and they needed more time to talk if he were ever to bring up the past.

"People who knew me, and there weren't many of those, called me Sam back then. No last name."

"When did you find out that your mother was a Tilok Indian?" Haley asked.

"When I was twenty-one."

"I think I was eleven when you told us. Your father hid it from you then, as long as he lived?"

"Yes. He was a shrill, bigoted, stubborn, macho Englishman—or actually Scotsman, if you will —emphasis on the macho. He was dead for a year when you came to live with Ben and Helen in '81. When I found my mother's family in '83, the Tiloks, I was given a new name: Kalok. Kids called me Kai and I liked it better. Anyway, fast-forward to nearly a year ago. After some tough circumstances—all these injuries and some worse things— I chose a new path in life. I decided, though, that Kai was too unusual for most folks and I was used to Sam; so outside the Tiloks, I'm still Sam."

"We've always known you as Sam. Who picked Sam?"

"Actually, my mother, before they told her I died. She liked Samuel Clemens. That's the story, or as much of it as I can tell you right now." He looked away from his small mirror and into her eyes. "I'm trusting you to tell no one."

She nodded, perhaps slightly happier now.

"Were you a spy?"

Sam thought for a moment.

"I was chasing the worst form of sophisticated criminals and terrorists, and there were plenty of them to chase. For now, that's all I can tell you."

She seemed, reluctantly, to accept this and went back to reading Ben's documents while Sam finished shaving. Sam liked to face things fair and square, but his relationship with Haley was not like most things.

"I'm always amazed at how fast you read," he said, glancing at her while he began applying makeup.

"Uh-huh," she said, oblivious now to everything but what was in front of her. The intense look of concentration heightened his curiosity.

When she was done, she put down the papers and looked up. She took a long look at his disguise-in-progress and gave him a thumbs-up. "Ready to hear about the papers?"

"You bet." Sam continued working while he listened.

"The papers from the whale are in Ben's miserable shorthand, which I can barely read. I think he's making four peptide hormones with different protein expressions, using genetically altered bacteria at least for three of them. But I can't tell more than that. They're working notes—notes he wouldn't even type up."

After a few minutes she spoke again. "This is pretty interesting."

"What?"

"Ben started with about two hundred eighty genes of the twenty-five thousand or so found in humans and other higher mammals."

"Okay . . ."

"To get down to six genes or so," Haley said, "is a major step. He clearly was onto something, but I can't see what that something was. Nothing here tells me that he was on the verge of solving the problem of aging."

"Could six genes really solve a problem like aging?" Sam asked. "To get youth retention would be tough, like you said."

"Exactly. Aging is a diffuse process. It's brain, it's body . . . it's widespread. How are you supposed to fix that with six genes? Add to this that when your body's cells divide to replenish themselves, they have a built-in clock. . . . Well, you read *Nature*, you know about telomeres. You're stuck with old cells when you get old."

"You still don't believe in this discovery, do you?" Sam asked.

"Do I really believe that Ben has something that will allow people to live decades longer or hundreds of years? I haven't changed my mind. That would be hard to swallow."

Sam had finished with the skin whitener and had gone on to the foundation. "You're a good teacher. Keep going, but hurry." He now applied the foundation makeup in layers of slightly different colors to give the mottled appearance of real skin. Because of time constraints he had opted for only a small bit of prosthetic plastic, so he had to do some contouring with nothing more than heavy makeup.

"Oh, my God," Haley said.

"What?"

"Listen to this." She read aloud:

"Microbial life in the deep seafloor is widespread, to depths of at least eight hundred meters into the bottom sediments. Samples indicate that methanogenesis occurs at the deepest sediment layers where carbon dioxide and hydrogen are converted to methane. The depth limit of anaerobic life in deep-sea sediments is not known. Most striking we have discovered that methane-producing Archaea divide every few thousand years, maybe one hundred thousand years. Their life span, if we could call it that, is unparalleled, indicating a DNA stability unknown in terrestrial life. Notably we have discovered a gene isolate in one species of methanogenic Archaea that differs by twenty-four percent from its nearest relative.

"Then he goes on," and Haley continued to read:

"Popular magazines have picked up on the longevity of Arcs and put it in much more poetic terms describing them as living in time with the slowest rhythms of the earth or as living in 'geologic time.' Interesting that the basic truth is not obscure.

"He actually mentions *Discover* magazine instead of a science journal. There's a little tongue in cheek there."

Sam was silent a moment. "Archaea, it says?"

"Ben wrote his own comment on the article. '*Archaea* are the longest–lived life-forms on the earth. And they are closer to humans, DNA-wise, than are bacteria. The truth is under our nose in popular magazines and in numerous more serious journal articles.

"'They live in geologic time,'" she quoted again. "That would mean these microbes are thousands and thousands of years old. At least. Geologic time implies *millions* of years old."

Sam could see Haley's mind was spinning. She was determined not to be overly dramatic, but she knew better than anyone that Ben Anderson always chose his words carefully.

"What is it?" Sam asked.

"I think I get the concept of what Ben was doing, if not the details."

"Tell me."

"If a gene releases a protein that, say, translates to a peptide hormone that performs a vital function, and we can duplicate the protein or its function in medication, then maybe we affect aging. But how do you use a gene from a deep-sea microbe to help a human being?"

Sam shrugged.

"Here. We need to give you a wig, make you blonde, and put some age on you," Sam said.

Haley was still concentrating on her discovery.

"The answer is you don't use the gene. But Ben seems to be replicating gene functions with organic molecule products. In Ben's case he's allowing bacteria infused with the gene of interest to make the organic molecules that become the medicine. Yet he's still talking about a microbe and you would think its gene would not produce human-compatible proteins."

"So," Sam said, "to know what Ben's doing, we'd have to know something about how certain of the microbe's genes function?"

"To understand it, we would. I suspect what he is doing is letting genes express their products, which would be proteins and then using them as medicine with the caveat that the proteins may ultimately be broken down into pro-hormones, hormones, enzymes, or the like." She explained how that worked.

Then Haley referred back to the notes while Sam splotched her face. "He calls these microbes 'Archaea.' He does have these two hundred eighty other genes he was studying. So maybe he found homologous genes in microbes, animals, and humans."

Sam nodded. His makeup job looked nearly completed. Hers had a ways to go. "It would be astonishing if we could use ancient microbes to lengthen our life spans." He applied a finishing touch. "People might kill for that."

"I just realized something else that makes sense," Haley said, trying to work on her makeup and talk at the same time. "Archaea microbes live in the bottom of the sea, down where the ocean cleanses itself. How about that?"

*   *   *

They hadn't shot him.

Ben didn't expect that they would until they got their information. They seemed unsure of themselves, which gave him the advantage, since he was completely sure of himself. No one was going to get a whiff of ARCLES, unless and until proper safeguards for the public were in place.

They could try torture, but he had a glass capsule up beside his molars and it was filled with enough ricin to kill ten people almost instantly, and there was no known antidote. Game, set, match—or checkmate, if one preferred chess to tennis.

Ben should have been grateful to be tied up in a chair and not tortured for what he knew. Instead, he sat there wondering why they weren't hurting him, or at least shouting questions at him.

There has to be a reason.

They already have the information? Impossible.

The drugs and torture were still to come? Most likely. And soon.

His heart beat faster and he could hear it and didn't like it. He listened for sounds but heard nothing except the faint blare of bluegrass music in the distance. It sounded obscene in the face of his impending doom.

He needed to urinate, and that bothered him as well. It had been many decades since he'd peed his britches and he was probably about due for diapers in another decade or two, but he hadn't been planning on it this weekend. Sons of bitches were being downright uncivilized.

His sole comfort was that old man Sanker would by now be hysterical with frustration. Unless Sanker himself was behind Ben's current imprisonment. If so, it wouldn't take long to discover that Ben's secrets would not be easily won.

Despite the jocular thought of Sanker, Ben was seriously frightened. If Sanker weren't behind this abduction, then at least two well-resourced parties were after him and ARCLES. At this point he had lost control of his life except to end it, which was not the sort of choice he wanted.

For mental exercise he went through the possible identities of his captors: Sanker; Frick independently; federal agents, renegade or not; foreign oil interests or other nationals; even American Bayou, which could have gone around Nelson Gempshorn and taken him. Then the chilling thought occurred to him that Nelson could be in on it. Nelson was a bit of an odd man and never completely revealed himself, or so it seemed. The possibilities were nearly endless and there was no use speculating.

All the while, Ben had been working hard on the arm restraints and intermittent effort seemed to be loosening the duct tape. He began twisting an arm, and although it was painful, he continued in the effort, stripping the hair from his skin and no doubt turning them lobster red. He figured he was now stretching the tape and getting his arms a good half-inch from the leather of the chair. Now he rolled his arms and rocked them, to and fro.

The music grew suddenly louder, as if someone had opened a door. Ben heard someone fiddling with a lock. He wished he weren't wearing the damned blindfold.

"I don't understand why we have to move him," someone was saying. It sounded like Stu.

The door swung open.

"Okay, old man, we gotta go." Definitely Stu Farley.

"Before we go, I want you to listen to me." This was another voice entirely, with a heavy accent. Ben imagined an Arabic speaker. His gut tightened down as he realized he really did not want to die. "If you would answer the questions thoroughly"—the voice was measured and calm, but there was not the slightest hint of humanity in it—"we would not need to strap you to a table and jolt your body with electricity with large probes in your rectum and smaller probes in your bladder. And if that does not loosen your tongue, to inject you with a paralytic and slowly dissect you while you watch in mirrors and feel the pain. I do not need to dramatize this kind of agony. Consider what I've said while we move you. Consider whether you will talk."

Ben felt the glass capsule with his tongue.

A heavy hand grabbed his jaw and someone shoved rubber between his teeth. In a panic he tried to feel for the glass. Pliers grabbed his tongue and the pain was excruciating. Fingers slipped inside his mouth and suddenly the glass capsule was gone.

The Arabic speaker grunted. "He thinks we're amateurs."

Ben realized why they had left him alone. They had been watching on video, noting the slight movements of his jaw and tongue as he played with the capsule. Now even that choice had been taken from him.

Sam kept a Kevlar vest in the Corvette and after a brief argument, convinced Haley to put it on. She thought he should wear it because, so far, he'd taken most of the physical risks. They climbed in the Corvette, ready to visit Lattimer Gibbons.

First, though, Sam intended to stop at Rachael's house.

"She'll freak," Haley said. "I thought the next stop was Lattimer Gibbons's."

"It is, but we have to remember that we're on a small island that Frick pretty much controls at the moment. We could use a convincing messenger to get to the state attorney general and the state police. Remember the FBI memo?"

"Okay. But what's Rachael going to do?"

"We need someone to go to a main state police office, like in Seattle. That's where Rachael can help. There is nothing like someone in the flesh pleading for justice. Rachael's family is connected. The rich always know people."

"I can hardly wait to hear this," said Haley.

"You're about to," he said.

"Maybe you should call first. You know how she is. She doesn't always wear clothes," Haley said.

"No time."

It was 4:50 P.M. and Ben had been missing for over six hours.

Rachael answered her door in a somewhat sheer bathrobe, seemingly unself-conscious about her obvious nudity beneath.

Rachael was blond, beautiful, and fit. Her even teeth and Nordic face, with the astonishingly blue-green eyes, would normally leave an impression. Sam made it a point not to notice the slim threads or the natural beauty. For all the effect it had on his demeanor, she could have been a seventy-year-old farmer in overalls.

Naturally she didn't recognize Sam in the makeup, but she squinted at Haley and figured it out. Then she gestured for them to enter.

"Come in quick," she said, looking over their shoulders. "The news says you're wanted for the murder of a police officer and that you're armed and dangerous. They say you killed a lab tech—slit his throat. They say —Ben's missing too, in case you don't know."

"We know," Haley said. "We know."

"We also have some huge favors to ask of you," Sam said.

"Will I be an accessory to murder?"

"Eventually no. Initially maybe," Sam said. "You will be risking your life to do the right thing. But you'll be running to the police, not away from them—"

"Please believe me," Haley cut in. "A deputy named Frick is framing us. He's working for the Sanker Corporation, which is trying to steal Ben's work the way they stole mine."

Rachael looked from one to the other as the gravity of their request sank in.

Haley explained in short hand what they knew and suspected about Frick. She told Rachael about their fears for Ben and about the shooting of the second officer.

"That was the undersheriff," Rachael said. "They'll think you tried to murder him as well, won't they?"

"You mean he's not dead?" Haley asked.

Rachael explained that the news said that he had been taken by medivac helicopter to the Harborview trauma center on the mainland and was expected to recover.

"To answer your question, yes, that's Frick's plan," said Sam. "He's using my gun and covering his tracks."

Rachael nodded, still uncertain.

"This won't get sorted out quickly," he said.

Rachael put on a brave smile. "I suppose I always wanted to be a hero. What can I do?"

Sam explained his plan to use her as a messenger.

"This may help you." Sam held out the fax from Ernie. "It's an internal memo of the FBI. Parts of it have been excised, but you can see for yourself, they are suspicious that Mr. Frick has done bad things. When you get to the mainland, drive all the way to Seattle or Olympia. Find the highest-level state police officer you can find. Ask him to talk with someone from the attorney general's office. Show him this paper." Sam went on to explain what she should say and how to get Ernie on the phone. "But remember that Ernie could be bureaucratically castrated for this. There's only so much he can do."

"I got it. He's a bureaucrat."

"With big cojones, big heart, good brain, but yeah he's still a G-man."

"Okay, I'll try."

"I need some tools," Sam said. "And I need a dress for Haley, and a stocking cap."

"That's easy."

It took only a couple minutes to get the things together and put them in a large duffel bag that Sam put in the trunk of the car.

"I'm recalling that you have relatives on Orcas," Sam said to Rachael. "If we got you there, could you make it to Anacortes from there without the ferry?"

"Tonight?"

Sam nodded.

"Yeah. I believe I could. My uncle has a boat at a private dock."

"Where?"

"Near Poll Pass."

Sam thought for a minute.

"Is it a fast boat?"

"Yeah, the *Inevitable*. A custom express cruiser. But why not the ferry?"

"They may try to stop the ferry. You wait for our call. We'll figure how to get you to Orcas. It'll probably be an experience you won't forget."

"This will help you?" Rachael asked.

"Trust me," Haley said. "It's to save Ben's life. And ours."

CHAPTER 13

Sam drove the Vette down Cattle Point, hoping to get to Argyle without a roadblock on Mullis, one of four main thoroughfares into town.

"Are we gonna walk?" she asked.

"No. We're gonna make like baby kangaroos." They stopped next to a dilapidated barbed-wire fence in a second-growth forest. Sam called and talked Don, the tow truck mechanic, into coming over to Cattle Point to pick up the Vette. Don arrived in only six minutes. He looked like a fullback but acted about as cheerful and friendly as anyone Sam could recall, a lot like a big black Lab puppy.

It was tough to get Don started hooking up and towing because he was dying to look under the hood. Sam promised Don could play with it when he got them back to the service station in Friday Harbor.

They joined Don in the cab of his tow truck, and when they turned onto Mullis, just as Sam feared, they found a police cruiser waiting.

Don pulled up slowly and saluted.

"How goes it, Deke? What the hell you doin'?"

"Don't you watch the news?"

"Not if there's football, I don't. What do you think, I'm metrosexual?"

"Who are your friends here?" the officer asked.

"This is Mr. and Mrs. Raimes."

The officer nodded and moved on to the next car.

At the service station Don got out, and Haley whispered to Sam. "How are we going to get Rachael to Orcas any time soon?"

"I have some ideas. Before we get into that, I need to know: any reason you can't fly Ben's plane tonight?"

"His plane's in the shop for its annual tune-up. Other than that, if I can get to it, I can fly like hell. I fly more than Ben does. You know that."

"Is Grant working on it?"

"Yeah."

"You got his number?"

"Yes."

"Does he like you?" Sam asked. "I mean, a lot?"

"Yeah. Known me most of my life."

"Did he believe Sanker's story about you?"

"Hell no. I'm sure Ben told him I'm innocent."

"Can we trust him?"

"As much as anybody," she said.

Haley got Grant Landon on the line and approached him in the same way that they had approached Rachael. Then she put Sam on the phone.

"You can make that plane fly this evening?"

"For Ben Anderson? Maybe. It won't be according to the book."

"That'll be just fine."

When he got off the line, Sam told Haley what he had in mind. Haley looked shocked about the danger but pleased with his trust. Before they made a final decision to risk both their lives, they would talk to Lattimer and see what they could learn.

Sam got his duffel out of the Vette's trunk, and Haley joined him.

Don was giving the car a close look.

"I see why you don't mind paying for a tow truck," he said. "This is beautiful. But there's nothing stock on it. You've even done a lot to the body."

Sam didn't tell him about the Kevlar. "I'd let you drive it, but I think she's got a blown head gasket. Small leak. It's got a bored-out four twenty-seven with an adjustable boost twin turbo L eighty-eight that brings it up to seven-fifty to-the-wheel horsepower. We put in a six-speed transmission and reworked the suspension with hardened axels, Eibach springs, and Bilstein adjustable shocks. We added the roll bar and put in the Brembo brakes. There were some other goodies too."

"I'm gonna go over this thing with a fine-tooth comb." Don knew instinctively to look for a custom pull knob on the driver's side and opened the hood.

"Go ahead," said Sam, "just be sure you're on the eight P.M. ferry with my car hooked to your tow truck. I'll be a walk-on. I don't want to wait in the vehicle line."

Sam gave Haley a wink, and together they walked away.

Nervous about leaving Haley alone, even for a few minutes, Sam picked up his duffel bag and beckoned Haley to follow him into the men's room of the service station. She watched as he changed his disguise entirely. He began by applying women's cosmetics over the existing base with an extremely heavy hand.

"Let's talk about long life," Sam said.

Haley shrugged. "Okay."

"I've been thinking about the concept, and I see some problems with it. Do you think Ben's figured out what a mess it would be if all of a sudden, people lived an extra twenty or thirty years or longer?"

"Ben is meticulous. He thinks of everything. The question is whether he would have solutions."

Then he took off his trousers and heard Haley suck in her breath.

"The legs aren't as bad as they look," he said. His boxer shorts covered most of the thighs, but the calf area was well-tattooed with suture lines. "They'll try some more plastic surgery soon."

She looked away. "What happened to you?"

Sam didn't answer.

Silent, she looked as though she wanted to hug him but didn't dare.

Removing a pair of black tights from the bag, Sam pulled them on, then reclaimed his jeans. He worked fast, knowing they still had to get to Lattimer's.

She looked at the overall effect of the disguise. "Well, you look almost like a 'she,'" Haley said. "It's close. Especially with the blond wig. It's your size that's the problem. Can't disguise that."

Next he shuffled through the bag and found heavy boxing tape and a couple towels. Taking the towels and putting them on his back all bunched up, he had her apply the tape liberally to hold them in place. Then he once again put on the trench coat and stooped way over drawing his shoulders in.

"You look like a bag lady."

Next he pulled out the dress for Haley that he had borrowed from Rachael and had her put on the dress over her jeans. It fit well and she rolled up her jeans just as Sam had done.

"I hope Ben is at Lattimer's," Haley said.

"Me too."

They exited the rest room and walked away around the back.

As they emerged, a patrol car came around the corner.

Sam was hunched and deliberately turned his face to the

car. It was a half hour or so after sunset and nearly pitch black. He could imagine the squint of concentration on the officer's face, the car passing slowly as if making an appearance in a lonely parade. The street was quiet and the buildings without life. The dark clouds had begun wringing themselves out. Misty rain fell along with the big drops and everything was wet, water beading on Sam's stocking cap and running down his face. It poured off the rooftop eaves and gushed out of down spouts. Few cops would get out of their patrol car without cause. There was certainly no point in stopping for a stooped old woman with her daughter.

Sam's leg hurt, but it helped him feign an old woman's walk. In the officer's spotlight and with no other foot traffic, Sam hoped the cop would have little perspective to measure the scale of his bulk. The humped back and the tights and the womanly face hidden behind too much makeup all looked pretty normal. He knew the officer's own expectations would slant the man's perception. After all, they were walking along the street in plain view, moving slowly. What fugitive would do that?

"You're good," Haley whispered. "You're really good."

Lattimer Gibbons lived on the hill on Harrison in the south part of Friday Harbor, only a few minutes' walk. Gibbons's house stood at the far side of a small, circular, concrete drive. The place looked old but in good condition.

They looked up and down the street for any sign of a parked police car. The rain had gone as fast as it came leaving only a dark night and swirling clouds that made the weather uncertain like everything else. Perhaps the clouds would open and allow the islands a little reflected light from the moon.

Haley called Lattimer Gibbons on Sam's cell.

"Are you alone?" she said.

Sam hoped Gibbons would recognize her voice. After a moment she hung up.

"We're on."

"All right. I guess we take a chance."

The driveway was steep; they felt exposed even inside the hedges and so they hurried to the front door, hoping the police were not inside. Quickly Sam removed the towels, the stocking cap, the wig, and dropped his pant legs. After putting the discarded part of the disguise in his duffel bag, he tossed it in the corner on the porch.

Haley knocked while he wiped off as much makeup as he could. A bespectacled man with a neat white mustache opened the door. He appeared fit for his age. Perhaps fifty-five, he had a flat stomach under his starched dress shirt and gray slacks. He wore dress shoes that were carefully shined but well-worn, with deep creases in the leather. Sam supposed the guy would drive a ten-year-old Caddy in mint condition.

Gibbons gave Haley a kiss, while keeping his distance from the drenched clothing, and ushered them inside. "I've been watching the television. They're looking for you."

Sam decided that if Gibbons were Ben's friend, then he was acting strangely serene under the circumstances.

Gibbons's house was meticulously appointed and arranged. Small brass light and coat-hanging fixtures gleamed, as did an antique brass ship's compass on a stand next to a stub wall that partially separated the living room from the entry. It was apparent that Gibbons paid attention to every detail of his life. They hung their coats.

The entryway led to an ornately furnished living room on the left and to a kitchen straight ahead, where Sam glimpsed a large wood-burning stove that was definitely an antique.

"Gibbons, you look really good," Haley said.

"Thank you. Come on in. Get warm." Gibbons led them toward the kitchen.

"We'd love to stay, but we're afraid Frick's trying to steal

Ben's work," she said. "It's only a matter of time before he comes here—for Ben or his work. Do you have any idea where Ben is?"

Gibbons just kept walking. "Do I have any idea where he is?" he repeated over his shoulder.

Sam always mistrusted people who repeated a question rather than answering.

As if pondering an answer, Gibbons turned and asked, "You're sure no time for coffee?"

"We are really in a hurry," Haley said. "We don't have time. Do you know where Ben is?"

Sam saw something in his eyes. They glanced quickly and looked especially alert for a man acting so casually. Despite his demeanor, Gibbons was nervous.

"If I talk to you, I won't be charged with helping fugitives?"

"We've committed no crime," Sam said. "You're an accessory to nothing."

"Well," Gibbons said, "I also know nothing—"

"Tell me this," Haley cut in. "What do you know about Ben's research on aging?"

"As far as I know, that was strictly confidential stuff."

"This is Ben's life," she said. "I need you to tell me."

"I would, but he didn't tell me. Look, I know you wouldn't hurt Ben," he said as if rethinking his conclusion. "I'm not trying to make this harder. Really."

"What do you know about the microbe Archaea?" Haley said.

Lattimer's physical response told Sam that he knew plenty.

"Well, let's see. I actually went on a trip with Ben that involved Archaea. Arcs, he calls them for short. Ben wanted to look at mud from the bottom of the Black Sea. He wanted to measure the quantity of Archaea microbes."

"What did you find?" she asked.

"We didn't find mud—it was solid microbes. Solid living mass on the bottom of the ocean."

"What did he do with the microbes?"

"Studied their DNA." Gibbons responded so quickly it sounded rehearsed.

"How did they help Ben understand aging?" Haley tried again.

"I haven't the faintest idea."

"Does he use Arc DNA in any way?"

"I can't imagine that he does," Gibbons said. "But he studied Arc DNA from all over the world."

Sam signaled to Haley by pointing at the papers tucked in his pants.

"Do you have any of Ben's research papers or lab records?" Haley asked.

Lattimer shook his head no, as if he didn't want to actually say the words.

"But, Lattimer, I know you and Ben talked about this kind of stuff. I think you even helped him in his work." Haley tried to soften her voice. "Please tell us."

"You'll have to be more specific." Gibbons wouldn't give up his maddening act.

"Okay," Haley said. "What about long-lived people? Didn't you help Ben study long-lived people?"

"We found a French family. Ben used them."

"Any relation to the family of Madame Jeanne Clement?"

Gibbons smiled. "Very good. You must have been following the subject."

"Let me in on this," Sam said.

"She was the longest-lived person in the world. Died at one hundred twenty-two. She's well-documented. Others are not," Gibbons said. "We didn't use her family. In another family, same region but seemingly no near-term genetic ties, the average age was actually higher, although the eldest was only one hundred eight."

"What exactly did Ben do?" Haley asked. "Did he take DNA from these people?"

"He grew skin fibroblasts."

"So he got their genome. Did he isolate genes?"

"I don't know, and even if I did, I would feel uncomfortable telling. I was sworn to secrecy."

"About what?"

"About everything!"

It seemed to Sam that Gibbons was close to losing his cool.

"He was dead serious about it," Gibbons said. "And excited. I was excited too. Who wouldn't be? Gout, low-back pain, can't pee right, have to do it two times a night, arteries going to hell, moles all over the place, hair growing out my ears." He paused again as if the weight of the world were on his shoulders. He looked at Sam, then at Haley.

"Death lies in the weeds. It's always there when you pass by. As the years overtake you, it creeps ever closer to the path. You start to sense it at first, hiding there, but you brush it off, banish it from your mind; then you start to smell it; eventually you begin to see it; at first just snatches of it as it follows you along. It's a demon. It's the universal truth and the great equalizer. I think of it as black as the blackest silk, and with eyes that shine. As you grow old, it slithers beside you and makes only the slightest rustle like a stalking cat. Death is everywhere, it's in everything, it comes too soon, and it is relentless." He looked up at them as if he'd been having a dream.

Sam looked at Haley. Much passed between them in that glance.

"Lattimer," she said, "you don't look old at all."

"As if it cares."

Haley sighed audibly, frustrated at Gibbons's evasiveness, annoyed that the frustration was getting the better of her. Ben had been at peace with death as much as anyone she knew. He understood the order of things and he had always told her that she could find peace in the inevitable. Death did not slither for Ben. It was ordinary, Mother Nature's tax collector.

Gibbons was a different story entirely. Something was happening that Haley didn't understand, something she did not recognize from her earlier encounters with the man. Something was happening inside Gibbons.

"Tell me this, then," she began. "You remember your arguments with Ben about the ocean being the lungs of the earth? You thought it would be great to attack the greenhouse effect by fertilizing the plankton in the ocean with iron particles in order to increase photosynthesis."

"Mm-hmm. I've been following that. It's not working very well. Seems that not enough sequestered carbons actually make it into the bottom sediments to be stored, which is the whole idea."

"Do you still have the articles?"

"They're over here."

Gibbons walked into the living room and pulled a binder off a shelf. He paused for a moment.

"I thought you didn't have anything," Sam said.

"I forgot about these."

Another three-ring volume stood beside it.

"What's this binder?" Sam asked.

"Things I was involved with for Ben," said Gibbons. "I wouldn't call them research papers."

"I see the word *ARCLES*," Sam said. "What does that mean? I assume it has to do with Archaea."

"I have no idea." Gibbons stiffened at Sam's questioning.

Haley gave it a try. "These are in your house, all bound up, you've obviously looked at them, and you really have no idea?"

"None."

"These are all the materials you have?" she asked.

"Please understand," Gibbons said. "I can't betray Ben's confidence."

"Oh baloney!" Haley cried. "His life is in danger. Stop screwing around!"

Gibbons set down the binder and sat on a window seat. "All right. Ben deliberately spread his research materials around. He didn't want them all in one place. For safety, you see."

Sam and Haley nodded.

"So I got this binder. It's part genetic work and part microbe work. It's all related."

"Related how, exactly?" she asked.

"Ben never told anybody, so how could I tell you?"

Sam stepped forward. "We want to take the volumes."

"I'm not big enough to stop you." Gibbons handed them over.

"You have more," Haley said. "Ben said you did."

"I don't understand."

"What don't you understand?" she said, her voice rising again. "We want the other binders. He said you have them hidden and that you'd give them to me."

"He didn't tell you that," Gibbons snapped.

"You can level with us," Sam said, "or you can tell your story to Frick. We've seen him in action. He doesn't take no for an answer."

Gibbons shrugged like a petulant child.

Sam picked up Gibbons's telephone and dialed a long-distance number, then put it to Gibbons's ear.

"Federal Bureau of Investigation."

"Agent Chase, for Ernie Sanders, please," Sam said into the mouthpiece.

"Hang up," Gibbons said. "I want nothing to do with this. It was all Ben's doing."

CHAPTER 14

As tough as she was, Haley had looked worried when he placed a call to Ernie. Sam made a mental note to ask her why.

"What *was* Ben doing? The experiments. Aging."

Gibbons pursed his lips, as if holding them together would keep him safe. "I'm not telling you a thing, and really I don't know much, anyway."

"Just give us the rest of the documents," Haley said, "and I promise we'll leave."

"Ben really told you that I had other documents?" asked Gibbons. "Because I don't know what he's talking about."

Sam picked up the phone again.

"Wait. There were some . . . irrelevant things."

"Get them," Sam said. "We all need to leave this place."

"I'll get the papers." Gibbons started up the stairs.

As he did, the doorbell rang. Sam saw a large figure through the curtains. Loud knocking followed.

"Go out the back door and hide," Sam told Haley as he moved to the stairs. With his bad leg he had to avoid the temptation to try to climb them too quickly. At the top of the stairs came the second-floor landing; then the stairs continued. Gibbons was moving more rapidly than Sam.

Sam ignored the pain and the fear of reigniting his partial paralysis. He entered the attic just behind Gibbons. Everything here bore the marks of age. Mold, rough woodwork, knob-and-tube electrical wiring, and single-pane windows that would almost let the breeze blow through.

"Over here." Gibbons crouched at the far end of the room before a set of bookcases. From one he drew a brown envelope.

Sam was taken aback at the pedestrian nature of the hiding place. Immediately he wondered if this was really everything or a trademark red herring left by Ben Anderson.

"Police," came a voice from below. "Anybody home?"

Gibbons jumped.

"I have to hand this to Haley." Gibbons indicated the envelope in his hands.

"I can hold it for you while you get rid of the officer. Then you can give it to her."

Gibbons ignored him and turned to the stairs, taking the envelope and putting it under his shirt and down the back of his pants.

Sam hurried to the top of the stairs, reached under Gibbons's shirt, and grabbed the envelope as he started down. Gibbons turned, but footsteps were already sounding on the stairs below.

"Good day there, Mr. Gibbons," came a voice from down the stairs.

Gibbons turned back to the officer on the stairs, obviously in a state of consternation.

"You know, I know most of the deputies, but I don't recognize you."

"I'm a special deputy appointed for this emergency. As

you may or may not know, we're looking for Haley Walther, Ben Anderson, and a Robert Chase. Chase is also known by the first name Sam."

"Haley's out back and Chase is upstairs."

"What?"

Sam prepared himself for one all-or-nothing attack.

"Hey, I'm just kidding." Gibbons forced an almost-credible laugh. "Just a joke."

"You could get in a world of hurt with smart-ass remarks like that."

Sam knew this man was no cop.

"I try to see Ben all I can, but I haven't seen him in two weeks, Haley longer, and I don't know any Robert Chase. Ben won't admit it, but he can only stand so much of me. I'm a little intense for his taste. What did you say your name was?"

"I'm Officer Black." The fake cop's voice had subtly returned to professional-polite mode.

"Like I said, I haven't seen them and wouldn't know this Chase character if he was standing right in front of me." Now Gibbons sounded quite convincing.

"I hear he spent a lot of time in a wheelchair above the ferry on the veranda there by the doctor's office," said Black.

"Don't recollect anybody like that."

"He's walking around now," Black continued. "Big, slightly dark-looking fellow. Probably bearded. Maybe a little Indian or Spanish. Quiet sort."

"Like I said, nobody like that."

"You call nine-one-one the minute you see any of them."

"Will do."

The footsteps started back down the stairs.

The front door opened and closed and Sam hoped Rafe had actually left. He hoped the pile of discarded clothes in the duffel didn't catch the man's attention.

In a moment Sam heard Gibbons's footfalls as he climbed the stairs.

"Just a minute, Mr. Gibbons."

Sam froze. It was Frick's voice, coming from downstairs. He had almost surely slipped in through the back door. Sam hoped he hadn't seen Haley.

Gibbons didn't respond.

"Come on down. We're gonna have a talk."

Sam could feel the demon in Frick's voice; Gibbons would sense it too and be frightened.

"What do you want?" Gibbons's voice had turned into a nervous squeak.

Sam had to do something fast.

Another door slammed open. Sounded like the back door.

"Get your hands off me!" Haley screamed.

Black grunted. "Stop fighting."

Sam had to act immediately or not at all. After stuffing the envelope under his belt, he went to the third-floor window, opened it, and contemplated the drop. His bad leg could be completely ruined by this drop—ruined beyond even the surgical repair that he planned. His spine could be reinjured. At the very least the pain would be excruciating. He heard footsteps on the inside stairwell, slid through the window, hung, and dropped. It was about a twelve-foot fall from the third-story window to the porch roof below and a little over four feet from Sam's soles when he let go.

Using the roof to break his fall, he didn't try to land and remain. Instead, he hit feetfirst, came down, tried not to overbend the knee, and rolled. With his shoulders and arms burning from abrasions, from the shingles, he rolled off the edge and dropped another twelve feet or so during which he managed to get his feet mostly beneath him so that they could break his fall before another roll, this time in the soft grass. His body hit the ground with a tooth-jarring thud and a terrible pain raged from knee to thigh on the bad leg. Almost as critical, the blow knocked the wind out of him. For a second he could not rise. It felt like asphyxiating. Finally he could suck in some air.

Although stunned, he struggled up and had the presence of mind to dive into some bushes and crawl to the concrete footing of the house. He caught himself groaning from the agony in his knee. The back door opened and Frick came out.

"He hit the roof," Rafe Black called out from inside.

"Sure he did, but he didn't stop there," Frick said.

Frick looked around and, in the dark, evidently couldn't see the impressions in the grass. Sam could hear him moving across the yard, through the shrubbery, probably pulling himself up to peer over the six-foot fence.

Frick cursed. "I need a flashlight."

"I'll get one from the house," called Black.

Sam lay on the ground, his face pressed into the earth, his body still on fire with pain. He was pretty sure nothing was broken. Sam knew how to fall and had dropped from much greater distances when he wasn't busted up.

He caught the sound of Frick pulling aside the bushes.

"Oh hell . . ." Frick cursed a stream of expletives that would have done the Devil proud.

The door slammed again.

Sam heard Rafe yelling about a flashlight. Forcing himself, he crawled out of the bushes, went around the corner of the house, and saw what looked to be a stump that he could use to climb over the fence. Using his hands, he felt the vague shadow in the darkness confirming what his eyes could barely detect. Before he stepped on the stump, he drove the heel of his shoe deep into the ground and then ripped up the grass so that even a city boy wouldn't miss it. Over the fence he landed in a neighbor's backyard, heavy with brush. He retreated from the fence several paces, then hobbled down toward the street. Once he got to the street, he went as fast as he could and climbed the stairs to the front door of Gibbons's house. Inside, Frick stood on the stairs with a large flashlight. He had apparently already been upstairs, surveying the roof. He was trying to determine his next move.

Rafe Black, the heavily muscled somewhat fat black man with a wide face and a large flat nose, had his arm around Haley's neck and was fondling her, obviously enjoying his job while Frick did the work. By concentrating on her, Rafe was taking his brain away from his job. He'd be relatively easy to dispatch, given the opportunity. Sam had a slow burn going for the man, ever since he'd accosted the coffee lady earlier in the day, but he knew that at this point keeping Haley alive outweighed the rest of it.

"Quit playing with her and get your worthless ass out in the yard and help me find this guy," Frick said, holding out handcuffs. "He already had bad legs; with a fall off that roof he won't go far. Cuff her to the stair railing."

Sam could hear the loud talking and realized one of the living-room windows must have been open. Staying low, he went across the porch and was not surprised to find the first window open a crack. He put his ear to it.

"I wouldn't leave her by herself or him either."

"Do as I say, damn it."

Sam peered through the window.

Frick had Gibbons by the neck. "You stay glued to this spot or I will come back and cut your nuts off before I kill you. You understand?"

Still muttering his disagreement about leaving them, Rafe handcuffed Haley to the handrail. It was stout; Frick had judged correctly that she wouldn't be able to pull free.

They both walked out the back door, leaving it open. Sam waited a minute for them to get around to the side yard and find his shoe print by the stump in the light of the flashlight. Sam opened the front door a crack. In the moment that he hesitated, Frick reappeared, his flashlight casting about as he walked in through the back door.

"Oh God," Gibbons breathed at the return of what must have seemed to him like the Devil incarnate.

"Take him outside, Rafe," Frick ordered.

"I wanna watch this," Rafe said.

"You're trying my patience." Frick turned to Rafe and sucker punched him in the solar plexus. Then he grabbed his little finger and bent it back as if to break it.

"Ah, shit, don't." Rafe could barely talk.

"I'll break all five of 'em. You understand?"

Rafe was grunting.

"Do you understand?"

"Yes." It came out in a gasp.

Frick let go and addressed Haley. "You've got ten seconds; then I'm really gonna hurt you. I want to know where those papers are that you took from the whale. And I want to know why you came here. What were you looking for and what did you and your friend find?"

Rafe struggled to his feet, held his gut with one hand, and grabbed Gibbons's elbow with the other. When he had taken the older man out in back, Frick put his lips close to Haley's ear as he seemed to like to do but spoke at normal volume.

"I know your kind. You give yourself to every guy that comes through. You're a worthless whore. Do you understand what I could do to you?"

Haley was silent. Sam couldn't tell whether Frick was playing a deliberate mind game or truly deranged. Or both.

With his gun to her abdomen, Frick grabbed her hair, jerking her head back.

"Do you know what we do with pigs like you?"

She didn't answer.

"Do you?" He pulled her head back again. Sam got ready to break through the window, all the time staring at the gun pressed into her belly. Frick's finger was on the trigger. It was too great a risk.

"No."

"We hang them up and we bleed them slow into a barrel. Do you want that?"

"No."

"Your boyfriend is keeping me from my work. Can you call him on a cell phone?"

Haley didn't answer.

"Then you deserve what I'm gonna give you. Right here. Right now."

Haley's eyes were wide, but she kept her wits. "And if I tell you, then you'll kill me, anyway. 'Cause after what I've seen you do, you'd rot in jail."

"Rafe," Frick yelled. The man returned with Gibbons. "You can have her now for a while. I'll be back in a half hour to an hour, as fast as I can, for the real work. See if you can get her talking. What you do to loosen her tongue is your business, but I don't want any mute psychos."

"Wait," Haley said.

"What? You wanna talk now?"

"What do you want?"

"Where are the papers from the whale?"

"Sam has them."

"Call your boyfriend. I wanna talk to him about your health."

"Take off the cuffs."

"Tell me the number first."

She gave it to him. Sam already had his phone on silent and let it ring.

"The prick doesn't answer. That really pisses me off." Frick shoved the phone in his pocket. "Where's Ben Anderson?"

"I don't know," she said.

"Where'd your boyfriend go?"

"Somewhere nearby. We're on an island, remember?"

Frick gave her a backhanded slap so hard, her knees sagged.

Sam forced himself to wait.

"Where would he go?" Frick asked.

"I don't know."

Frick's cell rang.

"Yeah?" Pause. "Yeah. Be right there. We got Haley Walther." Pause. "I'm taking care of it. I gotta go."

Sam tensed up, knowing he could surprise Frick as he came through the front door. Instead, Frick turned on his heel and headed for the back door.

Sam groaned inwardly. Frick was going to take one last look around the yard.

"This is gonna be real good," Rafe was saying as he cuffed Gibbons to the stair railing and released Haley so that he had her, hands cuffed behind her back.

"Upstairs. We're gonna need a bed and a lighter. I ain't got any condoms, so I guess we'll just do without."

Sam went to the side of the house, looking for signs of Frick. He didn't want Frick behind him with a gun. On the far side of the fence, he heard someone walking through the brush, then saw flickers of light through the boards. At the end of the fence was the street and Frick's car.

Haley was probably near the top of the stairs by now. Soon Rafe would start. Sam fought the impulse to go inside. Quickly he made his way down toward the end of the fence. Suddenly Frick sped up and began crashing through the brush and then onto the road. He jumped in his car. Sam waited for Frick to start the engine. Seconds went by like slow thuds in his head. *Start the car. Start the car. . . .* Frick must have been on his cell phone again.

Sam went ahead, deciding to forget Frick. What was Rafe doing? He tried not to let his imagination start. A desperate sadness came over him. Just what he'd wanted to avoid . . .

another fellow traveler. Sam wondered if he was in love with Haley and then put the thought away like a jewel in its case.

He slowly moved up the hill under the cover of darkness, wanting to get to the porch so that he could get to Haley. As he neared the porch, another car pulled up, a man got out and spoke to Frick. As they talked, Sam slipped up on the porch and went through the front door.

At last the car started and Frick peeled out. The second man was no doubt coming to the house.

One more problem.

Gibbons looked at Sam and nodded upstairs.

With a painful effort Sam yanked off his shoes. He had seconds at best.

CHAPTER 15

On the way back to the foundation, Frick made a quick call to the hog farm, explaining that he would need the grinder by the next day or the day after. He would land at a private strip. After what Rafe and he would do to Haley Walther, she had to disappear. Ground up with grain and turned into hog feed. The public would learn of a tragic boating accident as the suspect sought to escape justice, after which Walther's body fell victim to strong tides and/or marine predators.

It took him about four minutes, driving at reckless speeds, to get back to the foundation. He needed to get on the phone with Nash, but Nash didn't like cell phones. At the conference room he found eight men waiting and decided to put off the phone call.

These were crude men—the ones with lengthy criminal records—and they were here for a pep talk and the dos and don'ts of the job. Calm and baritone, Khan's voice carried the certainty of authority. As he spoke, he strode in front of a blackboard on which he had made some notes and taped large photos of Robert Chase and Ben Anderson. Khan sounded as calm as a college professor, but everyone knew he was as ruthless as any thug. Consequently, he did well leading rabble, staying above the fray, while at the same time letting them know he was serious. When Khan did lose his cool, it was part of a very effective act.

Some of the men worked as hard money collectors, some as personal bodyguards for some very tough people, who ran meth labs and worse. Three were bouncers in the seediest Vegas strip clubs, places that were little more than fronts for prostitution. Many had personally been beaten senseless by Khan, which engendered a respectful attitude. Using these types worried Frick, but the thought of an out-of-control operation headed for failure worried him more.

Khan abruptly ended the lecture. "You've been entertaining Haley Walther?"

"Not yet," Frick said. "We need to talk."

They walked into the hallway outside the conference room.

"You must be pretty desperate, having me use this crew," Khan said.

"You got that right. So what?"

"Is there extra if I deliver?"

"You know it."

"How much extra?" Khan said.

"Fifty K for good measure," said Frick. "Additional fifty K per head if you or Rafe have to waste somebody. You work it out with Rafe."

"That'll do it. How are we gonna solve your problem by Monday?"

"It's a small island. We're hitting everybody Ben Anderson knows and watching all the harbors. Rafe has Haley Walther. She may be able single-handedly to solve the problem."

"He'll rape her."

Frick just stared at Khan.

"I'm telling you 'cause Rafe tends to get distracted by his own pleasure," Khan said. "You need to know that."

"Yeah, well, he was all I had at the moment. We've got eight more men to dispatch."

"Give her to me, instead."

Frick thought about that. "Maybe later. Right now, I need you running these guys."

"I'm a professional. I'm not looking for conjugal rights. I'll get the information."

"Just manage your boys. If I need your help with her, I'll ask."

Frick then laid out the places they needed to search and watch. After Khan had his questions answered, they got down to the specific assignments.

That took a few minutes. Khan had one last comment.

"With what's going on inside that house between Rafe and the girl? That boyfriend of hers will come back. In his gut he knows."

"He would if he could, but he's hurt. Ran off the property. I left another guy with Rafe. I don't expect the boyfriend will be back all that soon. We need to discuss the most important job you got. I need you to supervise personally."

"Okay."

One of the things Frick liked about Khan was that he listened. And he was smart.

"You caught up on what McStott's pulling out of Anderson's research?" Frick asked.

"Octopuses, genes, and proteins. Crazy shit, but I followed."

"McStott's nothing more than a dirty scientist; he's got a couple lab tech helpers that are greedy bastards to help out. You supervise and try to tell the pony from the horseshit."

Khan simply nodded.

"I'm putting you in charge of the gold mine," Frick said. "I want results, and I don't want McStott getting any ideas about hiding what he finds. It's a little after six. I figure we have sixteen hours, maybe even until Monday evening, but no more, and by then, somebody will blow the whistle. Somebody will ask why Sergeant Frick is still in charge. Then the state comes in and we're done."

"McStott won't steal anything or turn us in," Khan said. "But I want to tell you something. Strope knows a man in the government. This government man heard a little about a guy named Sam who has a lot of names." Khan smiled, but it had the look of derision. "You made a big mistake not killing him when you could. And a bigger one leaving Rafe with his woman friend."

Sam heard Haley say something unintelligible as he climbed the stairs. Occasionally his feet made a creak on the old hardwood, but Sam knew that a man in Rafe's frame of mind wouldn't be likely to hear.

When he reached the landing, he went to the first door and listened.

Nothing.

"No."

The word came out muffled. The bed creaked. Quickly he stepped to the next door, where he heard her more clearly. He put his hand on the knob and concentrated on moving the latching tongue out of the door frame without a sound. Once he had the knob all the way turned, he slowly opened the door. They were on the bed. Her hands were tied and her feet, so she was spread-eagled, gagged in a bra and panties.

Rafe had his knife under her chin.

It was time to move. Sam passed through the doorway and stood quietly, worried about the knife so near her carotid.

"Just talk to me and I'll stop," Rafe said.

On a dresser stood a large, glass snow globe. In one smooth motion Sam picked up the globe and hurled it at the back of Rafe s head from a few feet away. The ball exploded on Rafe's skull; Rafe fell on top of her, quivering. Sam checked his pupils and determined he was out cold.

He grabbed Rafe's knife and quickly cut Haley loose. Once she spit out the gag, she grabbed him and held him tightly. He wrapped himself around her. He knew they had to leave and did his best to calm her as fast as he could.

"I was so scared," she cried.

He murmured assurances as he helped her dress. Together they went back to the stairs. Gibbons, at the bottom, gave a nod with his head. The second man was in the living room, no doubt assuming the crash upstairs was part of the torture program.

"Listen," Sam whispered. "I need you to run down those stairs hysterical, with me chasing you. The guy in the living room will go after you. I'll be right behind."

"That's risky," she said. "What if I get too far ahead?"

"You won't."

They looked at each other one more time and without hesitation she ran down the stairs screaming.

"Help me! Help!" She sounded terrified.

Sam limped after her with Rafe's knife. The man came running out of the living room and intercepted her in the hallway.

He never saw Sam come around the corner. With his knife hand Sam punched the side of the man's head. He whirled. In a fluid motion Sam switched the knife to his left hand and struck with the palm of his hand into the man's nose, then smashed an elbow into floating ribs. The man dropped in a state of semiconsciousness, bleeding badly from the face.

Sam grabbed the railing, put his foot against the wall, and, despite new pain in his knees and back, heaved with all his might. The bottom of the railing broke away, leaving Gibbons with his hands free.

"Frick probably has the key to those cuffs," Sam said. "You got any bolt cutters?"

"I'll get them," Gibbons said. He went to the basement door and disappeared with his hands still cuffed in front of him. Sam checked the guy on the floor. He wore blue jeans and a flannel shirt with a Kevlar vest beneath the shirt and cuffs in his back pocket. In seconds Sam had the guy chained to the radiator pipe in the living room. He wouldn't go anywhere, even if he regained full consciousness, any time soon. Sam hoped he hadn't overdone it when he hit him. He checked his pupils and his pulse, worrying about intracranial bleeding. There was no emergency room on the island, although there were paramedics and rapid helicopter evacuation to a trauma center.

Gibbons returned with a large pair of bolt cutters. Sam quickly snipped the cuffs.

"Come with us," Sam said.

"I'm not leaving," Gibbons said. "I'll hide in my basement. They'll never find me."

"They may, and if they do, they'll kill you."

"Believe me, they won't."

Sam realized that arguing was a waste of time that they couldn't afford. "You need your car?"

Gibbons thought for a minute. "Better you take it; that way they'll think I've left. And one more thing."

The way he said it, Sam knew it was big.

"I think Ben might be hiding at the foundation."

"Why didn't you say so before?" Haley cried.

Sam took Haley gently by the arm, kept her back, and worked on getting Gibbons talking.

"Why do you say that?" Sam asked.

"A hunch."

"Tell me. You can see these guys aren't screwing around."

"In the workshop there's a small study. It's hidden behind some shelves that move. You might find him in there. And I think you'll find more of his research too. Maybe you would be interested in those volumes, even if you don't find Ben." He paused. "But you might indeed find Ben. It's a good bet."

Just when he thought Gibbons was done with the revelations, the older man cleared his throat.

"There is also a small storage room that you access with a door that's behind some lumber racks."

"Anything there?"

"I don't know. I just mention it because it's out of the way."

They moved to leave, but on second thought Sam stopped and grabbed Gibbons's bolt cutters.

Outside in Gibbons's car Haley seemed lost in thought. Sam wondered if she was reliving whatever had happened upstairs.

"Are you okay?" he asked.

"I'm fine. Just wondering how we get back into the foundation. Now we have two reasons to go there. The plankton volumes and Ben."

"Once we get in, we still have to get out. Since you told me about the volumes in his office, I've been giving some thought to it." Sam looked at her more closely. "Are you sure you're fine?" She seemed to be putting effort into not crying.

"You didn't come any too soon," she said. "The bastard. He was all over me. I hate him. I hate him. I want him rotting in jail."

Sam started the motor and clicked the electronic garage door opener. In seconds they were on the street. As he drove, he saw her hands clenched so tight they were turning white.

The tears were coming now.

On a back street Sam pulled over and faced her. Touching her seemed different, but he chanced it and put his arm around her. Perhaps it was becoming more natural. At first she resisted; then she came close.

"Lattimer was lying," she said.

"What do you mean?"

"He has an ax to grind. An agenda," she said. Sam drove.

"How?"

"It's just a hunch," Haley said.

"He acted like his evasiveness was all about being loyal to Ben."

"I think he is paranoid," she said.

"His agenda is certainly not our agenda."

"Well, at least he gave us the documents he had." She began flipping through the computer printouts. "Every one of these pages has ARCLES at the bottom of it."

They entered the parking lot above the Friday Harbor Marina, where boat owners parked. It was well-lit, with few cars and quiet—a typical off-season night in Friday Harbor.

"It's time to call Rachael," Sam said. It took the punch of a button because he had her number in memory. "Are you ready?"

"As I'll ever be," Rachael said.

"Meet us at the marina parking lot."

"I'll be there in about twenty minutes. Maybe just a little more."

"Here's a section about Arcs," Haley said. "Ben apparently has other scientists working on this. I recognize Jacob Krevitz, a retired fellow from UW. Oh, and Miles Knoff, retired from Cornell. Ben's really been putting brainpower into this."

She read on. "Here are some calculations regarding a methane/sulfate cycle. Not that I know what that has to do with anything."

"What's it mean generally?" Sam asked.

"It's a cycle that doesn't use oxygen," she said. "By comparison we breathe oxygen, we exhale CO_2; vegetation does the opposite. You know?"

"Sure."

"According to this, some Arcs live on a methane/sulfate

cycle like we live on an oxygen/CO_2 cycle. Methane-producing Arcs take in CO_2 and hydrogen and make methane. The point is, if you calculate the available energy in their various chemical cycles, factoring in the normal amounts of energy required to maintain an organism, then Archaea cannot possibly live. None of them. That means that by our standards these Arcs are energy efficient beyond comprehension. It would be equivalent to discovering a race of people that could live for a year on a slice of pizza." She returned to the pages. "Somebody actually did the pizza calculation." She was quiet for a while. Sam watched a couple men coming up Water Front Street—mere shadows passing through the streetlamp halos. He studied them. Not in a hurry, relaxed, nothing in their hands, they looked like people accustomed to the island.

"Wow," she said.

"What?"

"The ramifications of what I just told you—they're enormous."

"Tell me," Sam said.

"Aside from the fact that these things appear to live on practically nothing, the methane makers produce much more methane than the methane eaters consume. Ben did a mass calculation for methane production by Arcs. He says there's more methane stored in the bottom of the sea than all the oil, coal, and gas reserves put together."

Sam whistled long and low.

"Not so hard to believe," Haley said, "when you consider what Ben says here: 'Arcs comprise one-third of all the living stuff on earth.' Unbelievable! And to think Nelson Gempshorn worked on this."

"Who is Gempshorn?"

"He's a vice president of American Bayou Technologies."

"The company that's merging with Sanker?"

"Yeah." Haley looked surprised that Sam knew this. "That's right. And you know, I don't think I ever mentioned it to you, but I walked in on Ben and Nelson one day at Ben's place. They had some kind of a model of something and they sort of seemed to panic when I came in. The model had something to do with the seafloor and ships. Now that I think about it, American Bayou Technologies is in the energy business. Offshore oil, mainly."

"You see where this is leading?" Sam said. "American Bayou would have a huge stake in what we're looking at here. In the merger Ben may not only have the key for Sanker with aging, he may also have the key for American Bayou. If American Bayou obtains a big energy discovery, that would enable them to win in this merger struggle."

"But who says you can use this methane?"

"That's a good point," Sam said. "Gempshorn might know something about that."

"It's probably not relevant, but Gempshorn had cancer."

"What do you mean *had*?"

The windows were fogging, reducing visibility. Sam started the motor and turned on the defrost. Twenty minutes was forever.

"I don't know. He's still alive. In fact, that day I saw them, Nelson had an IV plugged into his arm. Said it was for the cancer, but said not to tell anyone because his family didn't know. He didn't want to worry them."

"Do you know for a fact he was treating cancer?" Sam asked. "Doesn't that seem odd, doing chemotherapy at a friend's home?"

"Ben's a biologist, but, yeah, I suppose it does."

"What if they were panicking in part because you saw the IV?"

"God, you have a suspicious mind. On the other hand . . ." She stopped.

"They told you nothing about the IV?"

"They said it was doing good things, working, whatever, and they asked that I keep it confidential."

"And, of course, this cries out for the possible conclusion that they were giving him some kind of antiaging formulation. Would that be a huge leap?"

"I think it would," Haley said. "I never knew Ben to experiment with people. It's completely unethical without an approved trial, and he had no approved drug trials that I know about."

"At any rate this document is amazing," Sam said. "And Gibbons was just sitting on it."

"The question's whether it has anything to do with long life."

"I see more pages," Sam said.

Haley read for a minute, while Sam studied a couple men parking a car in the marina. They had a big anchor in the back of their pickup. He doubted Frick would do anything that subtle, but he wished Rachael would hurry.

"Oh, my God." Her voice startled him. "Here's something else altogether. One of Ben's colleagues shows that this methane could explode up from the ocean floor." Sam looked around, watching for Rachael, watching for deputies.

"They think methane explosions have caused catastrophes a number of times already. Some of this looks like a literature review to substantiate the calculations," she said as she flipped through the pages.

"According to this, it could have caused the mass extinction at the end of the Permian Era. Ninety-five percent of the marine species and seventy percent of land animals and plants. Gone."

"That's scary, but it's just a guess."

"It says, 'Methane was also involved in precipitating a giant underwater slide off Norway. . . .' Man, we're talking a massive one, Sam. It was eight thousand years ago, but it created tsunamis sixty-five feet high. Compare that to Indonesia. An earthquake triggered the methane release, and that caused the landslide."

Sam nodded, his eyes still on the parking lot.

"Oh, my God. They think that in prehistoric times the atmosphere itself lit on fire as a result of a methane release. Or even if there wasn't enough to burn, this says, oxygen could get so thin it would be like living on top of a sixteen-thousand-foot mountain."

That one Sam could imagine, having climbed Mt. McKinley as a teenager with his father. Sixteen thousand feet was substantial. He could imagine someone sitting in their living room unable to breathe except in gasps, nauseated, head aching . . . incapacitated.

"Listen to this conclusion," she continued. "'The world slumbers not realizing the great peril of an unstoppable chain reaction methane release.'

"'The seafloor methane cycle is part of earth's carbon cycle and exercises a great influence over climate shifts that has not been sufficiently studied. Vast quantities of methane have been stored in ocean sediments and there are various potential mechanisms for catastrophic release.' But there is a note here that Ben wonders if this would happen over time, threatening a crisis round of global warming, rather than asphyxiation in your living room."

"Astounding, perhaps deadly either way," Sam said. "I get Ben's meaning now. 'One sigh and we all die.'"

He checked his watch. "It's time."

CHAPTER 16

After what Gibbons said, Sam had altered the escape and diversion plan to allow for a return into the Sanker Foundation facility. It was worth taking one last look inside to find Ben or more of his research. Then, depending on what he found, or didn't find, they'd leave the island and go to Lopez Island across the channel, per the original plan.

Haley appeared as stunned on the review of the plan as she had the first time. She bore a significant responsibility in the scheme to keep Sam alive while they went after Ben. Sam could see that she appreciated being trusted to this degree. The problem was, though, that what she would be doing was very dangerous, and he wasn't sure she could do it and survive. A bond had been growing between them, and Sam realized that he was probably more concerned about Haley's safety than she was worried about herself.

The parking lot was well-lit, but the mist blowing through left halos everywhere, the fog sending an extra chill down the backbone, especially when one contemplated extreme boat maneuvers in the black of the night.

Sam turned to her. "There's something I need to tell you. It's about the work I've done."

"I know it's been ugly. You've told me enough to know that."

"It's not just that. I've lost a lot of people. Some were people I loved. So far, I haven't lost me. But what works for me doesn't always work for my fellow travelers. And here's the thing, Haley: I might be able to hit Sanker and do the rest without you. Would you consider walking to a friend's house and just hiding until this is over?"

"Absolutely not," she said. "Your plan depends on diversion, on rattling Frick and making him look weak in front of the deputies. I see how it works—Ben's life, our lives, depend on it—and I'm going to do it."

"I know how important Ben is to you. And stopping Frick."

"That's right. Thanks to Ben, I'm an experienced pilot, and thanks to growing up in these islands—and my ex-boyfriend and Ben—I know a lot about fast boats.

"I need to live long enough to see my heel on Frick's neck," she said. "If I die, I swear I won't hold it against you."

At that, he struggled to smile but couldn't quite pull it off.

"We can't let Frick hurt Ben," she continued. "You just need to trust yourself. I don't know what those people did to you, to your legs, but I know you're here, and so one way or another you beat them."

He looked at his watch. Rachael was due.

"If we assume that Ben discovered something that would slow aging, or prolong youth, how long ago do you suppose he did it?" Sam said.

"I'd say quite a while. Frick came to Sanker nine months ago, so it was probably at least three months previous that Ben somehow tipped his hand to Sanker that he had something of value working. It must have been years in the making."

"So Ben has kept his work to himself a long time."

"Yeah," she said. "And let's not forget Glaucus, the youngest old octopus in the world."

"Right. How old's he?"

"Now I have figured out that he is probably seven. And it seems like Ben could have had something five years ago, if that's the case. Or maybe even seven if he genetically altered Glaucus at conception."

"There she is," Sam said. A car had pulled in behind them.

"What now?"

"I've got to go down to the dock with her and help her find a hiding place until you come by with Frick's boat. I'll get a portable VHF radio from a friend's boat. I'll leave her there and she'll get ready. Then we've got to go park her car."

"Was this sort of thing routine for you during the great silent period?" Haley asked.

Sam opened the door. "Regrettably, it was."

It had come to Frick at a moment of frustration. McStott was droning on, taking a long time to say nothing, and something triggered a memory of Sarah James. Her mention of the safe-deposit box had seemed choreographed—another of Ben Anderson's precautions. She lived on Lopez Island and commuted daily to Friday Harbor on her speedboat. As his assistant she knew Anderson's comings and goings, and she was also his close friend. Frick suspected that they had become lovers, or at least that they thought about it.

He needed Sarah under his control. Now.

Frick sent men to fetch her and authorized them to soften her up on the way. He started to think of a cover story for her abduction, then stopped. At the moment it was a waste of his time. If things flew much more out of control, or took much longer, his deal with Sanker would be history, anyway. If that happened, it would be every man for himself, and cover stories and disappearing bodies would start to lose their importance.

He realized that Khan was talking to him.

"McStott thinks his guys found something."

"So in plain English," Frick said, "what did they find?"

"Anderson was making something he called an Arc regimen. And he thinks it was like a production deal, maybe for animal experiments."

"So he called it an Arc regimen. Big deal. How's it work? What's it do?"

"Well, if McStott knew *that,* he'd probably be here instead of in the lab. Right?"

Frick tolerated the sarcasm, waiting for Khan, who seemed to have something to say.

"What?" Frick said.

"It seems to me that what we're doing is nearly impossible. But if we *could* pull it off, we'd be in the catbird seat and it would be worth a hell of a lot more than whatever you're getting paid to retrieve it."

Funny how Khan's mind worked like Frick's own. "What's your point?"

"Maybe we're both working for the wrong people," Khan said. "Maybe we should be working for ourselves. Could be a chance of a lifetime if there's anything to this bullshit."

"I'll think about it. Get that weasel McStott in here."

It took a few minutes for McStott to arrive.

"Dr. McStott," Frick said in mock-grandiose tones, "how would you and some of your colleagues like to win the Nobel?"

"Only if I earned it."

Liar. McStott's beady rat eyes shifted and looked away. Truly, the man had led a despicable existence, Frick thought.

Working in the church, he hummed Satan's tune. As for himself, at least Frick didn't question which choir practice to attend.

It was quiet, cold, and overcast and the northwest winter damp was pervasive. Most people were off the streets and the few who were out had their necks pulled down inside their heavy coats and their hands shoved deep in their pockets. Sam had a great tolerance for cold, but the moldy damp of this wet fall had him on the verge of shivering.

"Let's leave it here in the shadows," Sam said of Rachael's car. Other automobiles lined Warbass Street; one more wouldn't be a standout. "Leave your cell phone in it with the dry clothes and take Lattimer's car. Stay on the back streets and I'll meet you off Guard Street on Marguerite, in twenty minutes. Rachael and I will walk back to the docks. Good luck." He kissed Haley on the cheek.

Sam looked at his watch. It was 6:45 P.M. Rachael walked beside him, obviously succumbing, bit by bit, to the shivers. They took their time and Sam made it a point to be somewhat aimless in his movements, stopping now and then to look at anything that gave an excuse. At the Coldwell Banker's offices he looked at the properties on the outside wall neatly arranged in a glass display case.

Sam's mind kept returning to Ben's research. He supposed that whatever the discovery was, it would be like most new things—not as good as initially thought. Perhaps it would add a few years to a person's life or identify a new energy source that wasn't cost-effective to mine.

For a moment, though, Sam let himself imagine something that would add hundreds of years to a human life span. Administering the elixir to large groups would be expensive because there would probably be scarcity, at least initially. That would mean rules about allocation. Who would choose who gets a long life? Literally everyone had the aging disease. Once a cure appeared, age would be *the* dread killer on the planet.

It didn't take much for Sam to imagine the envy, even violence, between the haves and the have-nots.

Would everybody with money get the stuff? Would the government try to make sure that it wasn't available to terrorists or people with violent propensities—or people who supported "evil" endeavors? Would there be some sort of test to qualify applicants? Would the test have a moral component? Would you give it to people on welfare?

The more he thought about it, the more he realized how treacherous such a discovery would be.

Ben's research had turned up more than the fountain of youth–issue, though. He was also concerned about people dying in a methane disaster, and Sam wondered exactly how imminent such a thing might be. Big meteors and asteroids would eventually strike the earth, but one hoped it wouldn't be any time soon. Underwater lava flows were not that unusual and neither were landslides and volcanoes. It was puzzling how the same scientist seemed to be obsessed by two such different research tracks. One idea was living and the other dying. Sam guessed that one could view both notions as the problem of staying alive. That and the Arc microbe seemed to connect the two. There had to be more, something they weren't yet seeing.

As he and Rachael walked down the waterfront road, Sam realized he'd lost track of his surroundings for a minute or more. He never allowed that on the job, instead striving to live keenly in the moment, aware of everything in his environment. It was how he had remained alive. This daydreaming was completely out of character. It struck him then that the notion of extreme longevity was a beguiling mistress.

He saw a sheriff's boat sitting with its running lights on at the outer entrance to the moorages, where a deputy could see any passing vessel. Sam wondered whether it would be a real deputy or some Frick stooge, like the fellow who'd gotten burned at Ben's.

Geisha, a beautiful Swan sailboat, was moored close to shore on the sprawling docks of Friday Harbor. It belonged to Sam's friend.

"Don't look up," Sam told Rachael, watching a patrol car moving slowly up the street toward them. That meant the police were watching the harbor from the boat and an onshore lookout. Sheriff's Boat 2, usually stationed at Orcas Island, was also available at the dock. No doubt Frick had brought in mercenaries and was manpower rich. He recalled the man at Ben's who claimed to be from Las Vegas.

He and Rachael climbed up the slight incline of Front Street toward the wharfinger's office, entering into a well-lit area. There they were spotted by a cruising patrol car.

"They're curious about us," she whispered.

"Just stay cool. You're not Haley and I'm not a big, dark-haired, scraggly-bearded guy who's maybe Mexican or Indian."

"Your makeup may be noticeable."

"Yeah. In good light, if you're looking for it."

They kept walking to the large ramp at the head of the dock, where the cop car was now waiting.

Sam walked right toward it, as if curious.

"You head into the ladies' room," he said, "wait two minutes, no more, then come out."

Sam went and stood under the streetlight near the squad car. As the officer studied him, Sam pulled out his cell phone and pretended to talk. The deputy backed up until the car was ten feet away. Deliberately Sam kept his face in shadow, using the brow of the cowboy hat, and waved as he continued talking to the imaginary caller.

"Darling, I said you've got to do your homework before you can watch some reality show. Reality is homework.

That's reality." Sam droned on like a weary father with a teenager.

"How are you this evening, sir?" The officer had gotten tired of waiting and didn't hesitate to interrupt Sam's phone call.

"I gotta go, you mind your aunt." Sam turned to the officer. "Pretty good. We're picking up a VHF radio on one of the boats."

"What boat would that be?"

"Geisha."

"Your boat?"

"Belongs to a friend."

Just then Rachael came out.

"They're interested in our travels," Sam said.

One look at the beautiful blond Rachael in the incandescent light and recognition flashed in the officer's eyes.

"You seen a big Indian guy and Haley, the scientist from the bike shop?"

"Neither," Rachael said. "Is something wrong?"

"Say, why don't you go get the radio and meet your friend." Sam made a show of shivering and hugging his coat around him. "I'll beg the deputy here for a ride back to your place."

The deputy looked surprised. "I'm on patrol."

"I thought you were a public servant," Sam said playfully, and winked.

"Good night, now, folks. Call us if you see either of them." The deputy rolled up his window and left them in a hurry.

CHAPTER 17

Frick addressed the nine men seated around the table.
These were the smooth ones, all of them private detectives
and none with any significant criminal record. This was a
different group from the first and they looked it, both in the
face and in the way they dressed.

In the midst of his talk about their goals, the assistant interrupted. Her name was Delia and Khan had pulled her in
from Las Vegas, along with the others, just for this occasion.
She had a talent for keeping her mouth shut and knew most
of these men at least enough to match a name with a face.
She was fast, efficient, and smart, and Frick was happy to
have her.

"Khan's on the line and said to interrupt," Delia said.

Frick had let Khan go over to check on Rafe's progress
with Haley Walther.

Angry at the delay, Frick walked out of the room and took
the call in his office.

"Yeah?"

"We have a problem. This Sam character came and
sprang the woman."

"Damn it. How did it happen?"

Khan told him what he'd found.

"Lattimer Gibbons is gone too," Khan said. "The garage is empty. If he had a car, they probably took it."

"Have men tear the house apart for anything like lab papers or documents, anything else of interest. When you get men started there, do the same at Ben Anderson's. You make sure *you* decide what is pertinent. We've got all four roads out of Friday Harbor blocked so they can't get far."

"This happened early enough that the roadblocks probably weren't in place."

"I understand," Frick said. "Now get to it."

He slammed the phone down, wanting to kill Rafe.

But in his gut he felt cold fear. Other than Haley, he considered who might know something. Then it occurred to him that they hadn't yet brought him Ben's secretary, Sarah James. The safe-deposit box had been a bust, just as he'd expected. Frick cursed himself for being stupid. He should have started with Sarah at the very beginning.

He went and got a picture of Haley Walther to put alongside the pictures of Robert Chase and Ben Anderson, then walked back into the room, where the men were waiting. He forced himself to keep his cool. Utter confidence was important.

"We've just had an escape. Add Haley Walther to the list. Anyone asks, you're plainclothes detectives over from the mainland to help out. You've already been deputized. Be polite unless you actually see Ben Anderson, Haley Walther, or this Sam character. You should all have pictures with you. Once you have positive ID, do whatever you have to do in order to follow the suspects. First, though, if you see any of them, you get on the radio and tell everybody where you are and that you've seen them. Give GPS coordinates just to make sure. Khan or I will make the arrest. Questions?"

None.

"From this moment on, your base of operations will be my home," Frick said. "You will not be returning here."

One guy raised a hand; Frick anticipated the question.

"If fired upon, you may fire back. Do not fire first unless you are directly threatened. We'd like them alive, but that is not absolutely necessary with Sam, aka Robert Chase. Anderson we need and Walther as well. Delia here will give you each a list of addresses where we might find Ben Anderson or the other two."

Sure enough, the guy with the question didn't raise his hand again.

"Let's go," Frick said, and they all headed for their rental cars.

"FBI is on the phone," Delia called out.

Frick came back and took it.

"This is Ernie Sanders again. FBI, Washington, DC."

"I know who you are," Frick said, "and I'm busy."

"We don't want to interrupt you, but we do want to caution you."

"Yeah, you are the guys who take calls from the cop killer and expect me to listen while you talk about civil rights."

"No need to be hostile," Ernie said. "I'm just calling to tell you that it would be good if there were no more dead or wounded citizens."

"Yeah, well, that's not necessarily up to me," said Frick. "You go back to your job and let me do mine."

"I understand the frustration of local law enforcement when two of their number have been shot. I'm telling you that we know Robert Chase, and our experience is much different from yours. So we're not jumping to any conclusions. Under the law we have no authority to tell you to halt a murder investigation. What I *can* tell you," Ernie said, "is not to tread on the United States Constitution."

* * *

Ben sat in what appeared to be a veterinary doctors' surgical suite consisting of one sparse room with off-yellow walls and an attached alcove on the far side of a pass-through area, where the surgical packs were kept. The room had a stainless-steel hydraulic operating table about five feet long by 2½ feet wide. There was a stainless-steel extension to the table to gain over six feet in total length and they apparently intended to use that for him; a monitor cart to track the various vital signs; a rolling surgical tray, where the surgical packs were opened and kept during the surgery; overhead lights of the sort common in hospitals; an anesthetic machine; and a second monitor sitting on a separate rolling cart, which looked as if it had come from a hospital. Somewhat depressing, there was also an electro-cautery machine. They tended to use electro-cautery on dogs to stop the bleeders in lieu of hemostats where possible, and he wondered if he would be treated more like a dog or more like a human.

Ben had been around medical establishments, both human and animal, and was pretty familiar with everything. It all looked impressively businesslike.

They were rigging the IV that would run the paralytic drug succinylcholine into his arm. It had no painkilling properties whatsoever and would serve only to leave him staring at the ceiling, able to hear, feel, and see the world around him, but unable to so much as spit over his chin. The man with the Arabic accent—who, Ben could now see, was tall and had long black hair—was showing him a stainless-steel bowl that looked rather like a large salad bowl.

"This is the bowl into which we will put your intestines. We will open your belly, tie off the bleeders, carefully lift out your innards from just below the duodenum to the middle of the large bowel, everything pretty much remaining intact and still connected, and then we will put them in here. We are putting on these straps because when we give you the antidote to the sux, you will be able to move, and we don't want you moving around and opening up bleeders. Once we have neutralized the succinylcholine, you will be able to talk, and if you start talking about important things, we will initiate a spinal block to dull the pain. Realize, please, that if you tell us everything, we will immediately anesthetize you, carefully put your intestines back inside your abdomen, and sew you up. However, I'm sure with your education, that you have determined that this is not a surgical suite designed for humans and there is a real risk of infection even if I do good work."

Ben could barely comprehend what they intended. It was clearly worse than anything he might have imagined.

"Would you like to speak now and spare all of us the surgery?" the man asked.

"Why don't you fry them," Ben said. "Tripe's actually quite good, I understand."

The man looked at him with amusement in his eyes. He knew who would win, and Ben now believed that they would disembowel him. Suddenly his joke didn't seem so clever.

"We'll have you take off your shirt and the rest of your clothes and lie down there. We'll begin a sterile prep, start the IV, and get you on the ventilator."

Ben stood feeling like the next few steps were the death walk. He glanced at Stu.

"Hey, man, you don't want to do this," Stu said.

"Gas pains worse than green apples?" With that, Ben now believed himself to be clinically insane, laughing at his own demise.

Stu, Ben, and the Arab watched while Ben removed all his clothes.

"Get on the table," the Arab said. Ben just stood there staring at the gleaming stainless steel and the round holes in the perforated surface that would allow his blood to run down inside the table. He wondered where the blood went.

"We can do it the hard way," Len said.

"Go to hell," Ben said.

Someone threw open the door to the exam room.

"Wait a minute!" another man said. "We're going to get Sarah James. The boss says to use her for the rough stuff. Anderson won't be able to take it and he'll be more coherent that way than with his guts in a bowl."

The Arab man sighed and turned away. "That is a complete change of plans."

Ben felt a new level of fear at the mention of Sarah's name. Was this true? Was it a choreographed act? A bluff?

"We'll be taking Dr. Anderson to her location," the new man said. "You can do it there. She's by herself in her house. We'll have her in minutes. Unless, of course, Dr. Anderson wants us to stop, wants to spare her the terror."

"We may take out her uterus first. See how he likes that," the self-styled surgeon said.

"Animals," Ben said.

Ben took a closer look at the newly arrived man. He carried a small automatic rifle and wore a camouflage suit. His face triggered a faint glimmer in Ben's memory.

CHAPTER 18

Sarah James sat in the kitchen of her cedar home in a wooden chair that was not as comfortable as the chairs or sofa in the great room. But she had no interest in relaxing or watching more of Frick's manufactured history on the evening news. She had turned out the lights, believing it was safer. She worried about Ben.

The great room off the kitchen had a high-prow point that looked out into the second-growth forest, but it did not provide a view up the driveway. For that, she would need to stand and look out the kitchen window. In the dark, though, the lights of any approaching vehicle did illuminate the interior of the kitchen, turning the cedar golden. So she waited for the tiny photons to arrive in their inexplicable waves.

She wore a dress for Ben; he was old-fashioned enough to like them, although on her he never seemed to notice—at least until recently and then she wasn't sure. It was painful but true and she didn't believe in kidding herself. Her romantic interest in Ben had been relatively recent and very secret and frankly had surprised her. He was twenty years her senior and she hadn't known that she could feel such physical love for an older man until one day she was looking at him and wanted to go crazy on his desktop.

Tonight, under her dress, she wore a bathing suit—not for flirtation but as a necessary part of the next step in their journey. She glanced at her watch: about fifteen minutes left.

She used memories of Ben to stave off the anxiety. One of her favorites had occurred on a Friday afternoon several months previous. It had been time to go back home to gardening, tennis, maybe a little golf.

She and Ben were discussing lab supplies and new summer interns from the university. They were standing close and, for some reason after all those years, she had felt so familiar that she inexplicably put her hand on Ben's belly and sort of patted it. There had been some conversation about whether he was getting fat. He wasn't.

Then he took hold of her hand and looked down at her and Sarah knew he was going to kiss her. But he didn't. He hesitated, obviously wanting to—about to—but somehow conflicted. No doubt it was all those years with his sweet Helen. She had been his soul mate. When he had disengaged, he kissed her forehead. It was sweet, but not what she had in mind. When she returned to her desk, she had allowed her imagination to roam free about what might have happened. Lately, however, he took every opportunity to be with her and wasn't at all above making up reasons. Getting together "as friends" was becoming a regular habit.

Although she wanted to come clean about her feelings for Ben, she knew she didn't dare. It was for Ben to validate them, and so far he had not. Ben had become no less charming, but he had become very secretive about his work. He had told Haley little for her own protection and hadn't told Sarah much more for the same reason. His leaving Sanker and avoiding other, greater threats was a thicket, and only Ben could negotiate the passage.

It was time to leave. She gathered up her things, and her

packed bag, and called Betty Horngrave. Of course, her friend of many years would be happy to check the place and feed the cat. The dog was already in the kennels. Then the phone rang. She picked it up and there was a click. Something about that seemed ominous.

She grabbed her small bag and her laptop computer, looked around, and walked out the door.

She was nervous and was unable to imagine what might happen when she arrived at the dive site.

Ben had explained to her that all of the San Juan Islands were created at the end of the Ice Age and were composed of glacial till. Most of the islands had thin topsoil, less than twenty feet, and in many places the leftover giant chunks of rock were at the surface. Near Orcas Nob and at various points along the edge of Orcas, some very large rock chunks the size of stadiums were at the surface and the beach face was composed of hard-rock cliffs. Near here sat an experimental area operated by Ben some years ago, and Sarah had a hunch that perhaps that was where he was taking her tonight. It was a hunch based on something Nelson Gempshorn had said about a picnic she and Ben had enjoyed a long time ago. She couldn't imagine why she would be diving in that area; it was a steep drop-off to water ninety to three hundred feet deep. But if not there on President Channel, then where? And why Gempshorn's mention of the picnic, if not to clue her in?

She couldn't guess.

Sarah did think it odd that Ben had not called her himself. But the explanation that he was on the run and headed for a safe place had to suffice. She did not know Nelson Gempshorn well, but she knew that Ben did, even though he had tried to disguise the relationship and never spoke much of the man.

Some years previous, Ben had sometimes taken his small research submarine out there. The area was about one mile north of an intriguing abandoned lime kiln from the early

1900s, with a standing chimney and underground passages that surfaced at the bank near the water's edge. There were no houses along that stretch of waterfront, although there were homes to the north and to the south. Now the area took on added interest and she tried to consider what could be going on and how she could have missed it.

When she was about to leave, she once again tried Haley's phone and received no answer.

As she was walking to the garage to get in her car for the drive to the Fisherman's Bay docks, a sedan pulled in. It wasn't a police car. Quickly she stepped back next to a large tree. A man jumped out of the car. Suddenly Sarah had a sick feeling in the pit of her stomach.

Sam left Rachael on the *Geisha* with the lights off, but for a small reading light. They had turned the heater on. Rachael waited by the VHF radio for their call, where she would sit, read, and try to relax until the appointed time.

With the *Geisha*'s portable VHF radio in hand, Sam met Haley, and she drove them in Gibbons's car to the university compound immediately to the east of the Sanker Foundation, where there were various university dormitories and dwellings. Traveling to the marine lab would require only a brief inland deviation from a straight line.

Once in the university compound, Sam felt safer. Haley seemed to as well. It was dark, there were few lights, and the main administration building had been shut down for the holiday. When he climbed out of the car, he thought hard about taking the bolt cutters. They were large and awkward, but would cut through a fence in seconds. The alternative would be a pair of needle-nosed pliers that might make a simple job excruciating. He used some loose twine in the trunk to tie the bolt cutters to his belt.

Venturing into dark woodland, they slowly felt their way

along under the fir and madrona down through the undergrowth alongside of the main building until they reached the beach.

For just a moment Sam thought about their chances of dying and it made him turn to her. As if she'd been thinking the same thing, Haley quickly kissed him on the lips. Once started, the kiss became deeper, stirring the repressed desire in each of them. It wasn't quite what Sam intended, but there was a sincerity to it that made it something to receive rather than reject. Or so he told himself. Too suddenly she stopped. It wasn't a normal ending to a good kiss.

Next came an awkward moment and then they hugged and pulled each other close. Neither spoke. Neither wanted to try to define the moment.

"If you die, I'm going to be really pissed and you'll never hear the end of it," Haley said. "And if I die because you die, I'll be twice as pissed."

"We need to discuss exactly how you are going to get Rachael to her uncle's dock on Orcas."

"Okay."

"My thought would be to take the way to Crane Island through the rock pile, going off the ferry route. Just like the smugglers used to do. You should go as fast as you can and survive."

"I'll go fifty at least."

"Turn off your running lights before you're even with the outer marker; then when you're almost past Crane Island, turn hard right back, double back through Poll Pass, stop at the dock before they can see you. Come on back by Crane Island, this time on the safe side, and lead them on a chase. Then do it just like we discussed."

"You're thinking this crazy-ass route will stop them, confuse them?"

"Would you follow somebody into those rocks at night? Or would you wait and see what the hell they're doing?"

"Effectively, I'm making a circle around Crane Island."

"Yes. I realize I'm suggesting that you run fifty knots at night through the narrowest navigable passage in the world."

She looked at Sam without blinking. "I can do it," she said simply.

"At night you can't run this like you're in a race," Sam cautioned.

"I guess we'll find out, won't we? I *am* in a race for our lives. Don't kid yourself."

Sam didn't have a quick answer to that one. As a practiced sailor, he knew that when these boats operated at one hundred miles per hour plus, absolute attention had to be paid to the throttle. If the boat went airborne and the props came out of the water, the engines would overrev and burn themselves to a crisp. The antidote was to back off the throttle as the propellers left the water. But if the throttle was off too long and the props were resubmerged without power, they would be ripped off the boat with the entire drive assembly. There were plenty of race boat drivers who had learned the hard way not to push the speed in chop and lose control of the throttle.

Together they crossed to a thin rivulet of a creek that came down to the beach. It reflected a bit of the light from the lab parking area and some from the lights of Friday Harbor across the bay. Except for that dark mirror on the sand, the beach was indistinct, like the bottom of a freshly used coal bin. Moving slowly down the beach, they were careful to keep the crunch of the gravel to a minimum. With so much life at the boundary between the land and sea, things were constantly dying and their decay left an odor that mixed with the salt air in a kind of olfactory stew unique to beaches. Soon the beach turned to steep, slick, solid rock. This portion was very slow going with Sam's bad knee.

Frick's boat, the *Opus Magnum,* was completely tarped down. It was a customized 46 Rider XP with twin 1050-

horsepower MerCruiser engines and ostentatious for its speed. Sam knew the engines weren't winterized because he'd seen Frick use it on sunny days to travel around the islands and over to Anacortes and Bellingham. On calm days he sometimes went to lunch at one hundred miles per hour over to Lopez. There was too much wood in waters surrounding these islands to sustain those speeds without great care. Even then it was a death wish to travel at high speeds for sustained periods because of so called dead heads—logs nearly full with absorbed water that float one end up with the top end barely visible or just under the surface. If it rained, Frick took a more conventional foundation boat, and if it was particularly choppy, he did not exceed about sixty. The boat was the talk of the island, and it was no secret that it really belonged to old man Sanker.

Getting to the moorage dock would be a trick. It was gated and the ramp leading to it was high above the steep rock cliffs that substituted for a beach. The tide was close to high. Unless he wanted to swim in fifty-something-degree water, and he didn't, their only option was either to climb over the six-foot barbed-wire-topped gate at the head of the ramp, or climb up underneath the ramp on various cables and braces and then scale the cage along the side of the ramp and over the top of it. Add to all that the significant risk that someone watching might see them.

Their best bet was making the climb near the head of the ramp, where they would be visible from fewer angles. There still wasn't a lot of activity around the Foundation, but if Sam was right about Sanker's intentions, then that condition would not last. He scrambled over the rocks as best he could, frustrated with his bad knee. Haley had an easier time, half-walking, half-crawling.

When they reached the ramp to the floating docks, Haley stayed on the beach while he climbed vertical supports and the cross members to reach a thick cable. Stabilizing himself with his hands on the underside of the walkway, he was able to walk the cable, and as he did so, his body gained elevation until he reached the attachment point of the cable to the walkway and began climbing the sidewall fence.

The entire ramp was lit and he knew he presented a clear silhouette, so a shooter with a high-powered rifle could kill him with ease. He was happy he had put Haley in body armor. Using the bolt cutters, he made a hole in the bottom of the fence. The metal gave way like noodles. In less than sixty seconds he had two sides of a square hole cut. Then the door near the gate at the top of the ramp swung open.

Somebody was coming. He froze like a spider caught in a gust. A man in overalls stood in the doorway staring out into the night. Any second Sam expected the fellow to call out and he readied himself to flee back down the cables. With his bad leg and no gun he knew his chances of surviving were slim. Frick would kill him this time. The man yawned and took out a smoke. Now, at least, he knew why the fellow had opened the door. Cupping his hands, he lit up. Sam was amazed that the man hadn't seen him exposed as he was beside the fence. He figured he dare not move or the man's eyes would seize on the motion. In the squat by the fence things got tough in the legs and lower back, and he remembered the days when he'd have felt no pain.

"Jack," someone called out.

The man quickly put out the cigarette and closed the door. Sam breathed deeply, suddenly realizing the fear. Quickly he went back to work and cut the remainder in seconds. He crawled through the break in the wire and lay flat. Now he beckoned to Haley, and she began a fast climb to the ramp and through the hole. In less than a minute she lay beside him.

With his duffel slung on his arm, Sam hobbled down the dock in the glare of the lights, feeling like a sitting duck. Haley ran ahead. He arrived at the *Opus Magnum* and followed Haley under the canvas. It was an exquisite piece of machinery, and it took someone like Sanker to afford it. As he expected, there were keys in the ignition. It was a locked and guarded facility, after all.

They turned on the dash lights; then Haley found a chart light at the helm. Having owned his own ocean-cruising sailboat and chartered many so-called bare-boat-power cruisers, Sam was familiar with the electronics, as was Haley. Normally, these racing boats didn't carry radar, but as a concession to the fickle fog of the Pacific Northwest, this boat had a custom-made radar arch. The screen was specially mounted between the two consoles. He turned on the radar and let it warm up on standby. Crawling outside, he took the canvas off the top of the dash but decided to leave the rest in place for the moment. These boats did not have windshields unless they were a completely enclosed canopy with fighter jet-grade Lexan. If one of these boats went upside down at over one hundred miles per hour, any normal sort of windshield would separate from the hull and decapitate driver and navigator.

Haley turned on the chart plotter, the GPS, autopilot, the depth sounders, and the rest of the electronics. The most significant custom feature was a gas pedal integrated to override the hand throttles. Old man Sanker had customized the boat so that he could control the power without a navigator and keep two hands on the wheel.

"You know that you shouldn't go over seventy in chop," Sam said.

"I can if I let off the gas when I become airborne and reapply the throttle when I hit."

Sam looked at her askance. He knew that her last serious boyfriend had been a wealthy race boat aficionado from California. According to Haley, the man had a boat with three 1000 hp Paul Phaff–built engines, with MerCruiser number six outdrives in a forty-two-foot hull. It was a few years ago, but having driven that, she might drive this speed machine.

He noticed a tremor in her hand. She zeroed the chart plotter in on Friday Harbor and Brown Island. Keeping the volume down, Sam tuned the VHF to channel 16, knowing that she was likely to hear a lot of yelling from the foundation over the hailing channel. That brought a brief smile.

Quickly he went below and rummaged through the cabinets looking for Frick's personal items. It didn't take him long to find what he needed.

When everything was ready, he pulled back a good section of canvas making an easy escape hatch. He clicked the radar off standby, making sure it was set to one-quarter mile, and that the gain gave her a sharp image. It would be critical.

Taking a deep breath, he jumped back on the dock, cast off the stern, and tossed the line in the boat, then the midships and last the bowline. She was drifting backward when he saluted her and half-ran, half-hobbled as best he could up the dock to the Sanker Building. The knee was hurting him bad. At the building he waited on the hinge side of the door to the foundation labs.

Wasting no more time, she fired up the engines, gave them a goose on the throttle once, didn't bother with a warm-up, and then popped them in gear. Then she stepped on the gas and the turbo diesels whirled the props, causing the fifteen-thousand-pound boat to leap out of the water.

Haley switched on the running lights and the rear deck lights as well as the spotlight up front. Now she was lit up like a Christmas angel atop the tree.

"Hey!" someone shouted as she literally roared away from the docks.

Sarah pressed herself against the wall of the house, hoping that the man would go to the front door and not the back.

He walked forward slowly, seemingly uncertain. He was large in every respect. No doubt he was a thug who worked for Frick. He wore a trench coat and something bulky beneath it that protruded from under the sleeves. For some reason he was looking back at the county road and then looking around 360 degrees.

She was afraid to think about why he might be doing that. Then he opened the trunk of the car. She shivered despite herself. These days car trunks were supposed to have internal latches. She wondered if this car had one.

She was frightened, more frightened than she could recall. She tried to be absolutely still but found herself breathing more heavily and she had the terrible urge to run.

Instead, she ducked low and went down the three stairs of the back porch to the ground level and got on the far side of another tree. Then she moved down the side of the house toward the forest. She lived on five mostly forested acres, typical of the island, and she was going to get away from the house where no one would find her. When she glanced back, she saw him coming forward, obviously approaching the back door. Perhaps he had heard her. Then she was around the corner of the house, her shoes full of mud, scrunching her toes to keep them on as she ran.

"Roxy, Roxy." She barely heard the calls. Suddenly it came clear to her. The man was Ted Henry, her neighbor, looking for their cat, Roxy. The bulky thing under the trench coat was his pajama top. His pants had looked baggy. They were the pajama bottoms. *Darn*. She looked down at her mud-spattered nylons and her ruined shoes. She marched back across the mucky grassland and walked around the corner. Then she froze. There was a second car behind Ted's, who was now a shadow lying on the ground under a man's boot. The boot was on Ted's neck and Ted was swearing to the man that he didn't know anything. The man was saying something about a Peeping Tom. Instantly she got it. The thugs were pretending to have something on Ted so that they could rough him up, rattle him, get him to talk about Sarah and Ben. Lately Ben had visited often and Ted had noticed the comings and goings and, of course, had remarked upon his observations.

"Hey, you," the man with the foot on Ted's neck shouted.

Sarah ran hard, straight for the forest, and did her best to keep her shoes on her feet. Nelson hadn't told her much, but he'd made one thing clear: these people would kill her when they were finished getting what they wanted. She clutched her laptop computer and ran without her bag.

CHAPTER 19

Frick sat in the conference room in the main building at Sanker with Khan, waiting for the arrival of Sarah James and also for reports from the checkpoints and from men going house to house. The two men after Sarah hadn't found her at her home, but they had just minutes previously seen somebody running and they were searching now through the forested area, hopeful that they'd capture her. Although the Orcas sergeant, officer 201, was still sedated in his own basement, the canine unit he handled could be brought to Lopez if they didn't find her soon.

On the wall was a map with pins showing the various places from which private boats might leave San Juan Island, the locations of known friends of Ben Anderson, and the locations of four private airstrips. They would see to it that all the planes at the private strips were inoperable for the night. None of the air services out of the main airport would run a charter tonight. No one was leaving on public transportation by his order. Frick wasn't only worried about the fugitives or Ben Anderson, he was also worried about someone telling stories and bringing in the feds or the state.

Rolf, the hacker, was trying to tell him something. Frick gave him his attention.

"We have something really weird," Rolf was saying.

"What's that?"

"Long story short, Ben's computer is set up to pass certain e-mails through to his home and it automatically double-deletes them on the Sanker computer. There are numbers of retired scientists that he corresponds with, and now that we look at the phone bills, he's been calling all over the place. He's working with a lot of people besides Sanker scientists and contractor labs."

"How many?"

"More than twenty. Probably more than thirty."

"Why in the hell didn't McStott know about this?" Frick asked. "Never mind. I guess you wouldn't know that."

"The e-mails from a dozen or so men are automatically forwarded and deleted," Rolf said. "Clever, right? But the e-mails of their secretaries, assistants, or spouses are not. I gather that they meet over on Orcas. Lots of credit card activity in the West Sound retail area."

At that moment McStott showed up and plopped himself down in one of the conference room's swivel spring-back conference chairs. No doubt he was worried about being upstaged by Rolf. McStott had on a bright pink shirt that irritated Frick.

"Any relation between all this collaboration and Anderson's aging research?" Frick asked McStott.

"We don't know," said McStott. "But we do have an idea of one topic under discussion."

"What's that?"

"Natural disasters, millions dead, due to sudden methane release. Tsunamis, climate change. Some of it's hypothetical, some based on the geological record. Pretty compelling stuff."

"Like what?"

"Do you really want me to bore you with the details?"

"Bore me with killing millions of people? With more than twenty damn scientists we don't know anything about? With secret meetings on Orcas? Risk it and bore me!"

"We found this file folder full of articles, journals, and magazine stuff," said McStott. "It all related to the danger of methane deposits. Listen to some of these quotes.

"'Prehistoric oceans could have had releases with energy up to ten thousand times the entire nuclear arsenal in the world today,'" McStott read.

"'Similar, smaller-scale eruptions of methane over time could account for other events and climatic changes, including the biblical flood.'

"They cite an article from the *American Journal of Physics* postulating that methane bubbles from the seafloor could be sinking ships in areas like the Bermuda Triangle.

"Apparently there's a huge methane deposit just off the coast of Oregon—there's a map here that shows it and all the other methane pockets along the continental shelf. Potential time bombs, they say. And all the methane's made by tiny undersea microbes. One of the articles says: 'Unfortunately, they make so much methane that if even a tiny portion of it were released, we would be faced with gigantic tsunamis from underwater landslides, runaway global warming from methane in the atmosphere, and resulting extraordinary extinctions.'"

"Impressive," said Frick. "But nothing about aging?"

"Nothing direct or concrete, but we found a note that said this methane release could start happening at any time but most likely within about four hundred years in the Arctic because of warming trends affecting permafrost and shallow water. Get this: one of these scientists noted that with 'Arc,' something they're apparently working on, some people alive today could be alive when a cataclysmic methane release begins."

"Four hundred years?" Frick asked.

"Uh-huh. Bingo."

"Seriously?"

"They obviously believe it," said McStott. "One more thing: one of the twelve main collaborators is Nelson Gempshorn, of American Bayou Technologies."

Frick held up a hand to stop McStott so he could think. The job had just become more complicated than killing an old scientist and stealing his secrets.

Frick puzzled it out silently for a few minutes. American Bayou's retiring vice president met with Haley Walther. What the hell did that mean? A disaster for Sanker if Ben was dealing with American Bayou too. And why was Anderson studying doomsday scenarios? Were the twenty or thirty other scientists in on the secret of aging? There had to be answers and he needed them now.

"The ferry is coming, running a little ahead of schedule. I'll call the deputy." Khan picked up a second phone that had been plugged in temporarily and set it on the conference table. "That ferry is huge; must be all kinds of places to hide."

"It doesn't matter about hiding," Frick said. "That ferry doesn't leave."

"How you gonna do that?"

"We're gonna tell them they probably have a cold-blooded killer on board." Frick turned to McStott and Rolf.

"Find out why Ben is studying doomsday, if it's really four hundred years that people might live, and get me the names of all of those scientists that he's working with. Find out where they meet on Orcas."

Frick dismissed them and told Khan to assign a couple of the smartest and least thuglike men to assist McStott and Rolf. Khan nodded yes while listening to somebody on the phone. Frick's mind was spinning. Khan pushed the button on the speaker phone and Frick heard one of his deputies at the ferry trying to reassure Khan that he had searched the ferry traffic as it waited in line.

"They have to get on the boat to escape," the deputy said, obviously referring to the fugitives.

"All they need is a friend's truck, and a deputy that isn't too thorough," Frick said. "We don't have that long. We . . ."

Frick paused, not believing what he was seeing. "What the hell is *that*?" he heard himself shouting as the scene outside the window gelled in his mind. "My boat's lit up." Frick picked up the radio. "Down on the dock, fast! They're stealing my boat!"

Haley had felt power like this in her former boyfriend's boat, but she had never felt such stark fear. It displaced her anger at Frick as the lump in her gut. When she approached the outer dock of the Friday Harbor marina, she saw Rachael, slowed, and came alongside, allowing Rachael to leap in the boat. It was a gutsy maneuver and they were lucky Rachael wasn't hurt. As she once again invoked the awesome power of the big engines, Rachael hugged her and kissed her on the cheek. In seconds the danger in what she was doing overtook her and she couldn't even take a perverse pleasure in stealing Frick's precious toy, not at this speed.

She knew that driving the eight-foot-beam boat at over one hundred miles per hour would feel like driving a motorcycle on rough ice. The connection between fingertips and the throttle pedal and the ocean's surface would be highly sensitive when she couldn't see, and any misstep potentially disastrous.

Glancing at the radar while trying to feel the water through her hands on the wheel, she tried to keep the boat headed just off the tip of Brown Island so that she would pass close by it as she headed into the San Juan Channel. For a couple of seconds she spied a radar target in the bay a quarter of a mile to her starboard, knowing that she would see it again in a short time. It was a log raft used as a tie-up for some derelict sailing yacht occupied by a fellow of little means that had no doubt been kicked out of the harbor, leaving behind only what had been his floating front porch.

It was smooth in the harbor and so she was able to go full out. The noise was all-encompassing, like standing beside Niagara Falls. The vibrations of the first little wind waves came hard. Rachael was gripping a handhold in front of her, watching the electronics.

Only the slightest touch of the wheel was required to control the boat. As she passed through the entrance out of Friday Harbor into San Juan Channel, the turbo-charged diesels were screaming in a high-pitched whine, and when she looked back, she saw the sheriff's safe boat accelerate quickly from the mouth of the main marina, its twin custom-installed 325-horsepower turbo-charged diesels pushing it to sixty miles per hour.

She heard shouting on channel 16, something like, "Get them." Only nobody could get this water rocket because there wasn't a boat north of Seattle, short of a hydroplane, that could catch Frick's ocean racer.

Out in the channel near the shore of Brown Island, she encountered moderate chop. It did not bode well for the next leg of their trip to Wasp Islands. For the moment they would circle Brown Island to increase their lead on the sheriff's boat and to reconnoiter the planned finale of her boat ride. *Opus Magnum* began to pound and some of the smacks on the water hurt their teeth if they didn't clench. Rachael looked grim. Sometimes the boat wanted to ricochet off the small lumpy waves, and at those moments she felt out of control. Wind whipped over her head and then was catching the loosened canvas boat cover that had never been removed. Glancing at the speedometer, she noticed that she was at one hundred miles per hour when the canvas pulled off the grommets and disappeared behind the boat.

Even at night the sensation of speed at 106 miles per hour was incredible. The skin on their faces was molded back by the wind and their ears literally vibrated. At these speeds the wind came at hurricane force.

Blips on the radar screen held their eyes and Rachael's unending concentration. Every bird on the water, every decent-size chunk of wood, even waves with unusual crests, could make a blip, and a blip dead ahead could mean disaster.

In less than two minutes they had run the entire length of the outside of Brown Island and slowed to about seventy miles per hour to round the southernmost tip of the island, now heading back into Friday Harbor.

"*Opus Magnum, Opus Magnum*, this is the sheriff."

The sheriff's boat with its sirens and lights was hailing her. And it was gaining on her, having made a much tighter corner around Brown Island still at top speed. She swung wide and went very close to San Juan Island, so close she was afraid of hitting the docks. There was much more to this game than making it around the island. She had to worry about the longest of the docks. Using the radar, she lined up the tips of the yacht docks that came out into the channel like a series of fingers. She let her eye fall on the most prominent that reached out much farther into the water than the rest. Without increasing her speed she set the autopilot for dead ahead. Autopilots were not normal equipment for these boats and the placard said not to use it when traveling in excess of thirty-five knots, which was almost always. Ignoring the placard, she lined up perfectly on the Sanker Foundation docks and the small floating log raft in the channel between Brown Island and San Juan. At night the raft was visible only on the radar.

"Slow down, slow down," the deputy yelled. "You'll hit something. Dead ahead on the radar; dead ahead, turn!"

CHAPTER 20

Sam went through the Sanker Labs Oaks Building door. After the third security guard had come running out onto the docks, the man stupidly aimed his service revolver toward the bay and the speeding boat. Sixty seconds later, Haley picked up Rachael and was halfway to Brown Island, breaking one hundred miles per hour.

Sam went in the door to the first hallway running parallel to the water and skipped the first lab, going to the second lab area from the outer door. All the labs on the waterside had a good waterfront view and this was no exception. Ben's office and labs were on the floor above, however the shop described by Lattimer was on this floor. He made his way past the paper cluttered desks and the many plastic tanks with their circulating salt water and myriad tiny creatures. After Haley disappeared behind Brown Island, he put the portable VHF to his lips.

"Hello, Frick," Sam said into the radio.

"Go ahead," Frick answered.

"Twenty-two alpha." He deliberately picked the coast guard working channel for the conversation and changed over from channel 16.

"Frick?"

"I'm here."

"This is Robert Chase," Sam said. "Nice boat you have here. Foot pedal for the gas is nice for two-handed driving—excellent custom addition. I like the singing bass on the wall plaque belowdecks. I also found your collection of pornographic torture magazines. They certainly are windows into your soul. Of course, we knew what you were; this will just help during your trial for the rest of the world to understand."

With that, Sam ended the call, got on the lab phone, and called the police dispatcher.

"Sheriff."

"I understand you're looking for Robert Chase," Sam said.

"Yes, we are." The dispatcher's voice crackled with tension.

"I think a tow truck just took him and his 1967 Corvette and put them on the eight o'clock ferry that's motoring past Brown Island on the way to Anacortes. Only he gave the tow driver the name Fred Raimes."

"I'm showing a caller ID that matches the Sanker Foundation."

"I work security here, and I don't want any hassles with Frick. All right?"

"Okay. How do you have this information?" asked the dispatcher.

"I stopped to get gas at the Chevron and there was this hopped-up '67 Corvette, and I went over and talked to the tow truck driver, who was checking out the running gear and the engine. That's it. Good luck."

Sam hung up. The story sounded plausible enough.

Sam got on VHF channel 68 and said one word: "Go."

"Copy that." Rachael replied from the navigator's seat.

* * *

"Hey, there goes the ferry," Khan said. From the conference room they looked out over Friday Harbor and the ferry dock in the distance.

"The ferry pulled out when we were screwing around," said Frick. "We don't know where Robert Chase is. He could be using a VHF from anywhere."

"So he's looking at your porn and you don't know which boat Chase was in?"

They watched as *Opus Magnum* swerved to miss the log raft and then turned sharply back out toward San Juan Channel.

"Get boat two after them," Frick snapped. "Boat one is already being outrun. Out in the rough of the channel, the police boats may keep up."

"Boat two has my guys in it," Khan said. "We won't have anyone to watch the marina."

"I know who will be in it. They'll never catch *Opus* if it gets a big start. They used the loop around Brown Island to leave boat one behind. Boat two goes about fifty-five miles per hour with no fat asses and light on fuel."

"What about the Coast Guard?" Khan asked.

"That's liable to bring in the feds," said Frick. "Get your guys after it. Now!"

Frick's cell rang.

"This is dispatch," said the female voice.

"I know," Frick said wearily.

The dispatcher explained the anonymous call from Sanker Foundation.

"Damn it to hell," Frick muttered as he hung up.

Khan ended his call with the newly deputized men just getting into the second boat.

"They're getting the engines started and trying to get away from the dock."

"Now I've got to stop the ferry," Frick said. "You've got to interview the security people in this building and anyone else in the building. Someone called from here. I'll explain in a minute."

"We're being played like fish," Khan said.

"Yeah, well, he's got Moby Dick on the line. We've got forty men and it's a small island."

Frick got on the phone and called the deputy sheriff who had been at the ferry lineup when they loaded the ferry. In sixty seconds the deputy had him livid. After a brief bit of cursing, Frick got off the phone and turned to Khan.

"The moron checked every trunk on every car and every truck except the trunk of the Corvette on the tow truck. Says that is because he just never thought a tow truck driver would allow someone in the trunk of a towed vehicle. Why in the hell does he think Robert Chase is gonna ask permission?"

"It's not likely he's on the ferry."

"I can't take a chance," Frick said. "We need those papers. And call the men after Sarah James. I need her more than ever."

Four hundred years. Four hundred years! It was so fantastic he couldn't get it out of his head.

"Go see how they're doing on the list of scientists," Frick said. "Let's start calling them and asking them if they've seen Ben. You never know what an egghead will say."

Although Ben had been blindfolded again, he could tell that he was in another dark room and it had a familiar musty smell. His mind flooded with thoughts of Sarah: the way she smelled; the look of her in clingy silk dresses, her leaf green eyes watching him. Leaning against a tree, playing with children, dancing in an empty ballroom when only he was there to spy. Now that they both faced death, he knew he'd made a big mistake in not asking her to be his wife. It was something he would remedy if he ever got out of this mess.

He tried to focus on his environment. The complete silence made him think he couldn't be in a home or otherwise occupied building. Heating in the winter and refrigeration, among other things, would be audible in the quiet. He was pretty certain the floor was concrete. Was it a cellar? A warehouse? A garage?

He strained to listen for voices or road noise but heard nothing. This time his captors had been much more cautious about escape. He wore manacles fastened to something that seemed to be a table or a heavy desk. The chair was hard and felt cool like metal. The temperature was probably below sixty, but Ben still wore his windbreaker, so he was okay. They had fastened him to a stretcher when they transported him, but he was sure he had been lowered a considerable vertical distance, also puzzling. Suddenly he heard a creak, then someone walking on concrete. They stopped and again there was silence.

"Who is it?" he asked.

"Your worst nightmare," came the answer.

Sam went back to the doorway of the lab from which he had come and glanced up and down the hall. The place was quiet. The concrete floors, although not the quietest walking surface, were the most practical and aesthetically pleasing in a building honeycombed, in a work environment with large tanks and flowing salt water. He waited and after a moment heard the security people returning from the dock, their voices and radios chattering away.

"Did you see that? Stole the boat right from under Frick's nose."

"Our noses too. Don't forget that. There'll be hell to pay."

Their radios crackled. "Garrity? Khan."

"Yes, sir. Right here on the first floor."

"Keep your eyes open inside your building. We don't know what's going on right now."

"Yes, sir, we're watching."

They clicked off the radio.

"Why the hell would somebody steal a boat and then break in here? He's nuts," the man called Garrity said.

"It was Frick's boat," said the other. "It's like a dog who pisses on your tree."

"Everybody is trying to figure out what Ben Anderson was up to," Garrity said. "And I know, but do you think they'd ask me?"

"What was he doing?" the other guard asked.

"He was up to something really good," said Garrity. "I guess I better look around down here."

The two others evidently walked away up the stairs. Sam looked around and saw no obvious hiding place. Opening cupboards would prove noisy. The best he could do was move behind the door and cram himself next to a bookcase. He waited. Garrity was moving down the hall and by the sound of it went in the lab next door. There were occasional sounds as though the man was actually checking closets and the like. Moving as fast as his stiff-legged gait would allow, Sam went to the edge of the door to the small lab and flattened himself against the wall. The night had taken a toll on his bad leg, and he was stiffening badly in the knee. Worse yet, he felt stiffening in the spine where he'd had surgery. In the back of his mind he began wondering about the return of paralysis.

Hearing something that sounded like the opening and closing of cabinets, Sam stepped past the doorway, and went as fast as he could down the main hall. Halfway he ducked in a lab, amazed at his luck. Any second Garrity might exit the one lab and move on to the next.

"Hey, Garrity," a voice said. "You seen any big, dark-haired-lookin' guys down here?"

Another guard had come back downstairs. His manner sounded easy and relaxed.

"Frick's all in an uproar and has us checking the building. The guys he's hunting just stole his boat and told him so and he's so paranoid he's got private dicks crawling all over this place. Our new fearless leader, you know . . ."

"Khan," Garrity said.

Second mention of Khan. Sam made it a point to remember the name.

"Yeah, he's more even-keeled."

"Don't kid yourself, that's one mean dude," Garrity said. "Damn, I'm probably just jumpy, but out of the corner of my eye when I was on the dock, I thought I saw the door closing and somebody going through it."

Sam knew he was in trouble. They might be dumb and slow, but they would start searching the place.

"Well, hell, why didn't you say so? We're down here by ourselves."

The new guy got on the radio. "Jack, Garrity thinks he might have seen something."

"But I'm not sure," Garrity said in the background.

"Garrity's scared to say anything because if he's wrong and we bring people over here from the main office, then Frick will have one of his fits."

"Yeah, I know," the fellow on the radio said. Sam gathered it was Jack. "Well, let's get started, but let's stick together."

"Then you better pull your gun out, man," the other guard ribbed Garrity.

They were spooking each other and that was both good and bad.

Sam had no gun and he was about to be cornered. He

would have to move very fast. Sam found a seat and removed the cushion.

He went to a double-pane slider window, opened it, and
breathed a sigh of relief when no alarm sounded. The trouble
was they could be silent alarms. He climbed out to the steep
rocks next to the building. Hobbling on the uneven ground,
he made his way down the building, carrying his bag and his
cushion.

There was more activity at the main building. The Sanker
main building was connected to the Oaks extension by a
breezeway and he was now headed to the end of Oaks—the
end opposite the balcony where Ben had escaped. All the
lights were blazing in the main building—probably where
Frick was working when he wasn't at the sheriff's office.

The workshop Gibbons had mentioned was supposedly at
the very end of the Oaks Building by the breezeway on the
upland side. The waterside of the building was taken up by
another small marine lab. When Sam got to the end of the
building and there was only a breezeway to the main building beyond, he took the cushion, placed it against a lab window, and smashed the window through the cushion. It required
repeated strikes to clear out both panes. Worried about the
loud clinking and shattering sounds, Sam sidled in as fast as
he could.

It was some distance from where he had heard the two
men. He'd entered a lab with numerous tanks and benches.
Light came in from the hallway, but the room was dark, and
he passed through it in seconds. When he arrived at the door,
he checked the breezeway to the left and the hall to the right,
saw no one, and shuffled across to the workshop.

He opened the door to the workshop, looking for the
shelves that would hide the small office. His eyes stopped
casting about when he saw the small door into the storage
area Gibbons had described. The boards and plywood were
pulled aside, and the passage was already open and not hid-

den. Although it was dark, Sam could just make out something hanging from the ceiling. He looked more closely. It appeared to be a large side of half a beef. He flicked on the light and gasped.

Detective Ranken hung by a foot from a block and tackle, suspended over a barrel. Embedded in his throat were the large tweezers from upstairs.

The tweezers Sam had handled without gloves.

Another nice setup, Frick.

Frick must have watched Ranken bleed into the barrel as he hung, gagged and struggling. Sam's heart pounded. He was being beaten at his own game.

Haley had her hands on the wheel and was using the foot pedal for gas. Engine temperature was 180 degrees. If she was particularly afraid of dying in a boat crash, she was even more afraid of being shot. Guns scared her. As a child, before she came to Ben and Helen, an uncle had taken her with him on a deer hunt when he was supposed to be baby-sitting. As he drove through the forest, he came to an enticing meadow and a hillside turned green from fall rains. There was a deer on the slope, beautiful gray among the green, and her uncle shot the animal through the open truck window.

Forever afterward, the vision of a gut-shot deer was frozen in her mind; she couldn't shake it, and she never wanted to be shot. Being hurtled free of the boat, through the air at over one hundred miles per hour, after colliding with a deadhead log, sounded like a quick and merciful way to die.

The boat skipped across the water, and sometimes when it came down, and cracked the back of a nasty little swell, the jarring could put a tooth through her tongue if she didn't keep it sucked down in her mouth. It was punishing work, fraught with the worry of flipping the boat or tearing off the power drives to the propellers and sinking the boat. Coming off a particularly bad wave, the boat seemed to float and was dangerously bow up. There was a horrible sickening fear as they balanced on the head of a pin. They nearly flipped. She heard the speed of the overrevving engines and she slowed down. At sixty she found she could keep the propellers in the water and the boat more stable in the building sea.

Haley looked over her shoulder. There were two sheriff's boats, both falling behind, but not by much. Rachael shook her head, realizing the need to get a big lead in order to hide the drop-off at Orcas. The near boat had come straight out of the harbor and hadn't been slowed by the run around Brown Island. The water was pitch black outside the shaft of light created by the spotlight near the boat's bow. Above they heard an airplane, and the moment Haley got an inkling that it was staying above them, she doused every light and they disappeared into the blackness and plunged into their worst fears.

Once established on a heading, they were at Wasp Islands in seconds and Haley went over in her mind Sam's instructions for getting Rachael deposited at her uncle's without detection. The Wasp Islands were a bit of a maze for those not familiar with them. There were all manner of rocks near the surface sprinkled amid a bevy of small islands. Out in the channel she made a sharp turn to starboard and lined up on the ferry route, a narrow passage between Neck Point and Cliff Island. The interisland ferry route was narrow, but at least it was a straight line and was the traditional route used by yachtsmen. The line taken by the ferry was 1.69 nautical miles in length, beginning right beside the rocks off Neck Point and ending a hundred feet short of the rocks at tiny Bell Island. The route was ultimately pinched between Shaw Island and Crane Island. On her chart plotter the ferry route line showed crisp and clear, and even at a hundred miles per hour, the boat could pass safely, so long as it remained exactly on course.

But the route outlined by Sam was much more difficult and much more dangerous. Its advantage was that it would slow the sheriff's boat for a moment and allow her to disappear from their radar. Now that there were two boats that was especially important.

She decided to slow to thirty knots and eased back on the throttles. One slip and she would crash into the rocks. It all depended on a Global Positioning System that could easily hiccup. She set the radar to one-sixteenth mile per ring. Never had she gone this fast through such a narrow, treacherous area. She glanced at the radar and noticed that the distance to the police boat was closing. Without hesitation she leaned on the throttle and upped the speed to fifty knots.

"Oh, my God," Rachael shouted, looking at the chart plotter radar overlay. "How are you going to do this?"

The sweat popped out of Haley's pores. Rachael touched her arm. It would be the only time in her life that Haley would do anything this stupid.

Clenching the wheel and saying a prayer, she went from San Juan Channel to the start of the rocky gauntlet in sixty seconds. During that minute she left off all her lights but for the instrument panel and the screen in front of her. It was now a life-and-death exercise. Instead of heading sixty-nine degrees true through a narrow straight passage, as would the ferries and any sane yachtsman, she held eighteen degrees true north and went to what would be considered the wrong side of Cliff Island. Magnetic variation in this area was 19.1 degrees east. Her heart was pounding as she shot between the rocks. She held the heading for just over three-tenths of a mile, less than twenty seconds. On the chart plotter screen she watched the progress of the *Opus Magnum* as shown by the GPS. Thirty or forty yards distant to her right were rocks that would rip the bottom out, an island on her left.

Her mind focused without distraction, knowing that the least error would make a very dangerous situation more dangerous. This thing had no seat belt. The beacon lights over on the ferry channel moved by with mind-numbing speed. After about twenty seconds Rachael called out, "Turn sixteen degrees to a heading of two degrees true." She would hold the heading for only 325 yards. That took a second or two. At the next waypoint the boat had to turn very sharply. She turned hard over to the right. Her eyes flashed from compass to screen. She thought she had the turn and Rachael activated the waypoint. She stared, every muscle in her body taut, wondering if she'd gotten the heading exactly right.

"Right on," Rachael called out. She glanced at the compass, then at the plot line.

"You're off the course!" Rachael shouted suddenly.

Haley flashed to the depth sounder and saw sixty feet, fifty-two feet; she was outside the channel route, forty feet. She wanted to scream.

"Stop," Rachael shouted. Haley let her foot off the throttle. Fifty feet. Fifty-five feet. She came to the left a few degrees.

"Good," Rachael shouted. Back in the channel she slammed her foot down. Crane Island was just under six-tenths of a mile distant and she was flying toward it at a mile a minute and accelerating. She got ready to slow and make a left turn before she hit the rocks. Quickly she glanced over her shoulder. The lights of the first sheriff's boat were clearly visible. They were slowing, obviously confused. Behind them the second boat was barely visible.

No time to ponder. She went left along the shore of Crane Island at fifty knots, now completely out of sight of the sheriff's boats, and more important out of radar range in the shadow of Crane Island.

Then a green line on the radar—dead ahead—out of nowhere.

"Look out!" Rachael screamed.

Haley got off the gas and twisted the leather-covered

wheel. Her wake slammed into *Opus's* stern lifting it crazily. She managed to resume course and then she tried to get oriented. The boat was askew in the passage but rapidly straightening. She told Rachael to goose the starboard engine with the hand throttle and that brought it square. Then in a giant gamble, Haley hit the foot pedal, opening the throttle on both engines full out.

She glanced and saw the sheriff's boat following at speed evidently having overcome their fear. *Opus Magnum* heaved its mass out of the water as it rose up on the plane. She reset the course more than ninety degrees to the next electronic way station lined up with Poll Pass. Scared, she held the wheel—as if by gripping it, she could will the yacht through the passage.

The distance between the small boat piers on her left and the shore on her right was less than one hundred yards at low tide. But there was considerable kelp choking the area. It was now about low tide and she probably had an unobstructed passage about thirty yards wide. It was the narrowest navigable passage in the world's oceans.

If she found one log in Poll Pass, she would be out of luck. Maneuvering would be impossible even if the radar picked it up. She had a few seconds to think this thought; then she was aligned, using the wheel, locking the autopilot, and approaching full speed. Her left hand hovered over the wheel and her right was on the off switch for the autopilot. Given the very narrow passage and the near-zero visibility, she thought the autopilot might do better than she could. She had to get through Poll Pass before the police boat saw what she was doing. She was in the pass itself for a couple seconds, then in the still inner channel beyond.

She spun the wheel and nearly flung Rachael out of the boat. She popped on the spotlight and radiated the dock and the big express yacht that she knew to be *Inevitable*, belonging to Rachael's uncle. She pulled up beside the dock, Rachael touched her shoulder and leaped. Rachael waved as Haley doused the spotlight and raced away. It was lonely and the fear was even worse. Once in the middle of the converging passages, she stopped amid the swirling white water of her own incredible wake. If one of the police boats had proceeded on the ferry route, they would be popping up directly in front of her. What she expected was that one of the sheriff's boats would follow her route and the other would approach Crane Island, cautiously sticking with the ferry route and avoiding the S turn, and then depart the ferry route and follow the shore around Crane Island as she had done. From there, she didn't know what they would do.

She poked her nose out into the ferry lane and watched the radar for oncoming traffic. There was no police boat. They had both gone behind Crane Island trying to follow, but no doubt at a slower speed. She waited a minute more and then reversed direction at full speed, breaking one hundred miles per hour on the ferry route along the south side of Crane Island. When she reached the middle of the island, she glanced at the radar. The absence of the police boat from the radar picture made her suppose they had to be near the opposite end of Crane Island, near Poll Pass. Hopefully, they were confused, doubting their radar. There were three routes to Anacortes or to Bellingham. Worse yet, each of the various starting points had multiple possibilities the further you traveled, so it would get confusing, quickly, if they lost her.

She kept the power full on and headed back out to San Juan Channel, trying to remain in the shadow of Crane Island for as long as possible. As she passed the western end of Crane Island, the night was pierced by flashing lights. One sheriff's boat had waited right by shore in case she made another circle as she had done at Brown Island. There was a boom and she knew a bullet had just ripped through the hull. Fear coursed through her like electrical energy.

CHAPTER 21

Khan was tapping Frick's shoulder, but Frick was staring at the ferry disappearing in the distance.

"Don't let that ferry go!" Frick shouted at the deputy.

"How can I stop it?" the deputy shouted back. "You gotta call the department of transportation."

But Frick knew that the captains of the ferries made those decisions. Nobody told the captain of a ferry where he had to go when under way. They could ask. The ferry could be hailed on 16, but that was a public channel. They also monitored channel 9 and that was used by the public much less often. However, there was also a special channel used only by the ferries. He called the dispatcher, who had the special channel in a file, and he used that method. Instantly the captain was on, Frick explained and got his wish. It had been easy. The captain agreed to return.

Although decisions while under way were the captain's, it might be different once he was docked. To keep the ferry there all night, Frick might actually need the department of transportation. There was no way he was going to devote the manpower required to search the boat in a couple hours. He knew that Chase would not stay cooped up on a ferry tied to the dock, even in the unlikely event that he was on it. Delia put through an employee of the transportation department, whom Frick had been trying to get on the line for fifteen minutes.

"This is Roy Nageler."

"This is the sheriff of San Juan County," Frick lied, "and I have asked the captain of the ferry to stop and return to Friday Harbor. He's coming back to the dock."

"The ferry's coming back to Friday Harbor, you say?"

"Yeah, and I want to keep it here as long as it takes. Maybe all night."

"All night?"

"I think that's what I said," Frick said.

"This will have to go up the line. I doubt that all night's gonna fly."

Frick hung up, waiting for the next call.

"Our men at the scene think *Opus* could have dropped someone off at Orcas," Khan said.

"We can't worry about that."

"Earlier, a deputy saw a big blond guy down at the docks. He was with a blond woman named Rachael Sullivan." Khan consulted a set of notes. "Her uncle has a place on Orcas and her parents have a big place in Anacortes."

"I know who they are," Frick said. "That's bad if *Opus* dropped her off."

Frick put out a call on the radio to the deputies chasing *Opus Magnum*.

"*Opus* is going full out," Khan's men explained over the radio from the boat. "We nearly hold our own in the rough water on the way to Wasp Islands, in the San Juan Channel. We're barely keeping her in sight on the radar when it's smooth. She looks like she's headed for Lopez." Frick clicked off, disgusted.

"They've gone to great effort to convince us they're leaving, and to spread us thin," Frick told Khan. "I think they're staying."

"So what's your suggestion?"

"The woman— Rachael's uncle owns *Inevitable*. It's the fastest express cruiser around. Custom-made. Let's have someone waiting in Anacortes at her folks' in the event she goes there. We're running out of time, and if we want different results, we're going to have to use different methods."

"What are you suggesting?" Khan asked.

"We forget about Monday and the state police and the FBI and we concentrate on now. We get results. Then you and I get out of here with the goods. I want Sarah James found, strapped down, and made to talk. She must know more than she's saying. I want to know about these scientists he's been talking with. I want to know what the hell is going on." His mouth went dry with anticipation. "Actually, if they find her, I'll handle her myself."

"If we make people disappear, rough 'em up, we're gonna pay."

"I'm planning on leaving the country," Frick said. "Too much has gone wrong."

"That takes money," Khan replied.

"You'll have plenty," said Frick. "Like you said, we're working for ourselves now."

Khan's cell rang. He listened and smiled. "They caught Sarah James coming out of the woods, going for the neighbor's place."

The guns had missed her and anything vital. There was a hole right in front of her knees where the fiberglass was blown in. Haley was sure that there were more such holes behind her, but everything still ran for the moment. Turning down San Juan Channel, she headed for Lopez Island. Concentrating was difficult and at times Haley's eyes felt

like they were being sandpapered. Green blips came and
went as waves tossed the objects in and out of visibility and
even seabirds sometimes appeared as unknowable, disappearing phantoms. Eventually it was a game that she would
lose—unless she was lucky enough to make the planned finale before she hit the log with her name on it. Out in the
San Juan channel heading south, there was a good chop and
a rising breeze. Winds were at twenty-five knots on her nose
and there were small craft advisories.

She slowed to seventy to maintain control. In the after-
math of the warm front, winds were blustery and seas were
still building.

She was headed dead on toward the Fisherman's Bay nav-
igation lights. With no lights on the boat she had taken off
into the black abyss. She squinted trying to see the outlines
of land, looking for something other than electronic security,
but she could see nothing. There was a plane flying low,
probably looking for her. She decided to take a chance on a
burst of speed. Her foot went to the floor. The wind blasted
her face. The boat rocketed and then the props screamed. Off
on the throttle, she told herself, then hard on it just before
she scuffed the next wave. The boat landed so hard it hurt,
but she kept on it to one hundred miles per hour. Any second
she expected to lose control and die. Off on the throttle when
she flew, back on it before she hit. She did it four times and
then could stand it no more.

She cut to seventy, keeping the boat down. She could
only hope that her wake would not phosphoresce. And that
she didn't hit a log.

It was 3.1 nautical miles from inside Friday Harbor to the
entrance of Fisherman's Bay on Lopez Island, but she had
taken a substantial detour to Orcas. It took just over four
minutes to get from the Wasp Islands back to calm water
near the outer marker of Fisherman's Bay. Instead of slowing
down in the calm water near the entrance, she punched it to

one hundred miles per hour again, hurtling toward the channel and aiming for the marker like a rifleman lines his sights. Indeed she was traveling faster than a hardball pitch.

Ideas and images sped through her mind as if they were detritus on the sea—words moving on to the next words: *Colored lights reflecting. Gauges. Heading. Swell. Bad bounce. Flash, flash, flash. Things on the water. Line up. Line up. The channel. The buoy. The reef. Throttle back. Line up. Okay. Hit the throttle.*

The boat came into the narrow passage at fifty knots. It might as well have been an F15 breaking the sound barrier for the grand entrance. The trick was not to kill somebody else with this outrageous nighttime helmsmanship. Even at fifty knots, in this narrow channel, nearby boats would be split-second images in the night. Fortunately, she had been in through the snaky entry to Fisherman's Bay many more times than she could count—it was still the boat-driving challenge of a lifetime. More difficult in some ways than the run through the Wasp Islands.

The police boat was far out in the San Juan Channel looking for the disappearing race boat when she sped into the twisting ribbon of water. Close proximity to the land would mask her presence on their radar. The steep beach on one side and mudflats, a stone's throw away on the other, made it impossibly treacherous. Her hands gripped the wheel and fingernails sank into rubber. Brain and boat were fused. Entire yachts riding anchor passed in eye blinks.

The slightest deviation from the required course would send her hurtling to her death. Her hands made every minute correction and her mind willed it past the inner buoys.

She had been inside the harbor only a couple seconds when she dropped the power. Her wake washed up on the beach and the sound of her homicidal engines was calmed. Without a doubt she had brought shadows to the windows of the houses that lined the entrance. She glided toward the

dock with frightening speed, throwing a massive wake as the
stern settled. In seconds she had motored stern first into a
slip with the finesse of the most seasoned of skippers. With
the boat still completely dark she waited in the glow of the
dock lights behind the only sizable yacht in the first dock
complex of the bay.

The point was to make sure the deputies realized that she
could have dropped a passenger.

After a moment she was distracted by shoes on the dock
ramp and saw two men escorting a woman down to the floats.
Something about them gave her pause and then she saw the
woman turn and try to run. They grabbed her, obviously
manhandling her. Instantly she knew it had to be some of
Frick's thugs. And she knew the woman was Sarah James.

Dear God, she thought. Watching her friend was agony.
Sarah was an attractive woman, the kind who, by no effort of
her own, would stir men like these. Like Rafe Black. One
man held Sarah around the middle while they dragged her to
the boat. There was something on Sarah's face, over her
mouth. Probably tape. As she watched the pathetic spectacle,
Haley gasped and bit her knuckles to keep from shouting.
Somehow she needed to help Sarah, but she didn't have a
gun—they did. And even if they didn't, she couldn't over-
power them. It was hopeless.

Then she remembered the flare pistol.

Virtually every boat had one. Haley looked for the orange
container under the dash and found it. Quickly she unscrewed
the top from the bottom. It was roughly football-shaped but
flattened on the ends. She found the pistol and loaded a shell.

The men had dragged Sarah near their boat and were trying to force her in. Haley looked toward the channel and saw
the chase boat streaking into Fisherman's Bay. She had to
decide. She watched them struggling with Sarah and she
began to weep. One flare shell with two men would not
work. If she stayed, she would not get *Opus Magnum* out of

the slip. With two boats she could be pinned. If they got desperate, they might start shooting. It boiled down to Sam's life, to Ben's life. The whole plan was at risk if she abandoned *Opus*. It was a horrible weighing of desperate circumstances. If it were just her own life at risk, the choice would be easy.

Now the police boat was coming fast toward the docks. The men on the dock, seeing the deputies' boat, seemed to hunch and shrink as they finally struggled to put Sarah in their boat. Obviously, regular deputies manned the sheriff's boat and Frick's ploy would be blown if they observed the crime Haley had just witnessed.

If real deputies saw it, she knew they would immediately rebel and Frick would lose control. She could only hope.

Haley remembered Sam's hand on hers and his quiet insistence that she follow the plan, no matter what. But Haley could not help herself. She had to try to free Sarah. Sam's words haunted her. He was counting on her.

Try to save her now or later?

"Oh God." She whispered her anguish.

Fortunately, the police boat was going for the second dock in front of the big resort, having missed her hiding place entirely. She shot the flare over their heads so they would know they were seen; then she fired the engines and actually screamed her anguish. The men with Sarah jerked their heads in surprise. Then she put a heavy foot on the throttle and the boat leaped out from beside the sleek yacht lying quiet in the night. Like a cheetah it accelerated with shocking force that threw her back against the seat. Turning hard over, she heeled the boat on its side and raced behind the startled deputies in the chase boat.

One of them reached for his gun and her heart went cold.

*   *   *

"We have a situation over at Lopez," Khan said.

"What the hell now?"

Frick took the phone. The deputies fetching Sarah James were on their cell. They had her securely in their custody, but there was other news.

"*Opus Magnum* went into Fisherman's Bay at the dock. It hid and got past one of the sheriff's boats. We saw it leave, but we can't be sure someone didn't get off."

"Are you telling me they could have unloaded someone there?"

"Yes, sir, on the docks at Lopez. Do we bring the woman now or search the boats at the dock? We don't think anybody got up the gangplank."

Frick sighed his disgust and thought for a moment. "How many boats to search?"

"Maybe ten, fifteen."

"I think it's a ploy. Bring the James woman here now."

There was a burst of white light streaking across the sky right over their heads. For a second Sarah thought the police had arrived. Then it was black, but for the halogen dock lights, and she could barely discern the outlines of Frick's well-known ocean racer among the boats at dockside. *Frick.*

"Walrus Face," with the mustache, twisted her arm behind her back. They had been abusing her ever since they caught her coming out of the forest. She cursed herself for not remaining in the forest, but she had wanted to make it to the rendezvous point set by Nelson Gempshorn.

Walrus Face also had garlic breath, and it was hot on her neck, smelling like the leftovers from an Italian restaurant. He moved her body around like it was a twig. His weight and strength, the size of his viselike hands, made her feel helpless. Something from a television show flashed through her mind and she acted on it, stomping on his instep, throwing an elbow into his gut.

"Uhhh," he grunted, favoring the foot; the elbow to the stomach was like hitting rubber-coated concrete. Limping and the pain of it put a fury in him and she could feel it, palpable, as if it were an aura. He grabbed her neck and she felt as if he might snap it. Then he wrenched her arm and the pain shot up her shoulder, exploding in her head.

"You bitch," he said in a whispered rage, still favoring the foot she had wounded.

She was vaguely aware that Frick's boat was roaring away from the dock.

He let up. "Say anything and I'll kill you." She saw the flashing lights of a sheriff's boat and wondered how long they'd been there. Then it took off after Frick's boat.

Immediately he went back to twisting her arm.

"Okay. Okay," she muttered in response to the pain. She relaxed, unable to take the torque on her arm. "I'll go."

"Bitch," he muttered, still twisting her arm. "Tell me where Ben Anderson is or I'll break it off before we even get to Frick."

"I don't know. I don't know. I haven't talked to him."

"Have you talked to anyone?"

"Yes. They said they would meet me at my house," she lied. "And then you people came."

"Lying bitch. Your bags were packed."

"I thought they would take me away to Ben. I swear I did. But I saw Ben's boat. In the bay here. If you'll let go of my arm, I'll tell you where."

He let the pressure off.

"Who said they'd take you to Ben?"

"I don't know. A voice."

Instinctively she had known that the man with the walrus mustache was way over the line and he was convincing her that brutality was a viable option as a strategy to break her down and get her talking. And that confirmed that they would murder her when they were finished, and that had made her desperate.

Now they were on the radio and it was apparent that they were going to take her to Friday Harbor and Frick.

She couldn't let that happen.

Walrus Face had a layer of fat over most of him, especially in the belly, and he was round in the face with a bull neck. She guessed he was in his forties, had led a worthless life, and didn't know where he was going or just what he wanted, except enough ale and enough women. Worst of all, he seemed to have a nasty, cunning sense of what she loathed and what she feared.

The thin man had odd angles about his face. Things seemed as if they had been knocked askew: His Adam's apple stood out and his nose was long and a bit crooked. His hair was dark and starting to gray. She suspected that long ago someone had taught him right from wrong, but he was willing to forget it for enough cash. There was a maddening resignation about him that obviously allowed him to partake in things with which he had no agreement.

Now "Thin Man" held her while Walrus Face tried to get some kind of a charley horse out of his foot.

"Where is the boat?" Walrus Face muttered, sounding like he was ready for another round of brutality once he took care of the foot.

"You want to go to it?"

"Whatever the hell gave you that idea?" Walrus Face said.

"No, go ahead, tell us where it is," Thin Man asked her. He had held on to her by the arms, but didn't put his hands on her body. It was Walrus Face who had the obvious propensity for degrading women.

"Driving down the road, I believe I saw Ben's boat near one of the docks," she said.

"You wouldn't be bullshitting us now, would you?" Walrus Face said.

"No, I wouldn't. It's a twenty-seven-foot boat. A Sea Ray with an open bow. There aren't many around here."

Sarah hoped that Ben's boat had been left there many hours earlier and that Ben had been sending a different boat to fetch her.

They got on the radio and spoke with Frick a second time and received the go-ahead to check out Ben's boat.

"So you gonna be cooperative with the authorities?" Walrus Face asked as Thin Man untied the boat.

"You're thugs," she said. "Not the law."

Walrus Face stared at her with beady eyes and ran his hand over his mustache.

Thin Man jumped back in the boat and started the motors.

"You wouldn't dare turn me over to a real deputy," she said.

"No, ma'am, we wouldn't."

His forthright answer frightened her more than anything else.

CHAPTER 22

Haley could barely keep the boat on a course as it skipped through the blackness. To the eye, it was like hurtling through an abyss; to the stomach, it was a pounding free-for-all. There was no anticipating the jarring. The waves were a blur in the spotlight and the mind was taxed to the max trying to control the foot throttle. Weary, she had backed off to seventy again in order to maintain some semblance of control and to minimize going airborne.

When she was almost across the San Juan Channel, near to Shaw Island, she glanced back and saw one set of deputies just exiting the Fisherman's Bay. The other sheriff's boat was in the middle of San Juan Channel coming in her direction. Using the GPS and the radar, she headed right for Point Gregory on Shaw Island. Behind the point was Parks Bay, rimmed in rock to the sides with a nice flat beach at the bottom of the boot. On sunny days the rock and the trees surrounding the sheltered bay relaxed her mind. It was away from the busyness of Friday Harbor and it was nice to lunch at anchor. Tonight she intended to hide in it and to get near enough the rocks that, again, her pursuers couldn't discount the fact that passengers may have landed on the island. The other more important factor was that Sam might not yet be through in Sanker and she was a major distraction for Frick.

Suddenly there was a loud bang and a jolt, and a split second later, she knew she had hit a small piece of wood. *The engines are still running. No vibration. RPM's good. Rudder indicator okay. Trim tabs fine.* If she'd hit a prop, the damage wasn't bad; the drive units were still straight. No sooner had she assimilated that information than she had covered another half-mile.

She slowed to about fifty, and flashed by Point Gregory less than two hundred yards off the rocks. Her chart plotter indicated that the water was only about thirty feet deep. The shore was but a shadow in the night. After she dropped the power a bit more, she lay the boat over in a turn so tight it threw her into the side of the seat. She sped around the point and into the bay, then went in close behind the point and killed the power. At idle the engines made a throaty rumble. She waited—her gut in a knot. The thought of guns gripped her. She was shaking. This time she didn't want to pass close enough for the sheriffs to shoot.

After waiting for just a couple minutes, she stomped the pedal and the engines came to life. Then she heard a sound that was a cross between a lip smack and a quiet tap on a bass drum. She glanced at the temperature and saw that the starboard engine was overheating. Kelp leaves or sea grass on the cold water intake. She prayed that it hadn't gone into the sea strainer. She watched in horror as the temperature climbed toward 220 degrees. Once she was back out in the channel, she headed toward Friday Harbor. As she applied power, the wind blurred her eyes; the skin on her face was smoothed back and she became engulfed in the feel of an unremitting hurricane. One sheriff's boat was coming at her, the other was in the distance moving away from Fisherman's Bay at Lopez. In the lee of Shaw Island the water was relatively calm. Going over one hundred miles an hour, she came to port twenty degrees with a barely perceptible nudge of the wheel and headed right at her adversaries.

They were more worried about living than she was. They kept coming, their closing speed over 150 miles per hour now, less than a few seconds to collision.

Temperature 190. Steam was venting. She took the flare pistol and tried aiming dead on at the sheriff's boat, but the jostling and pounding made it ridiculous. She pulled the trigger and it burned brilliantly. The deputies did a panic turn, heeled to the starboard, throwing a wall of water. She was literally screaming her frustration as she bore down on them, aiming to convince them that she would slice them clean through—missed them by less than fifty feet traveling a full one hundred miles per hour plus. When she hit their wake, *Opus Magnum* slammed explosively through the top of the wave, sending her airborne like a javelin in the wind. Instantly she got her foot off the throttle, trying to guess when she would slam down. It was surreal. She hit the throttle and hit the water at almost the same moment. Nothing came apart, but it was a neck-snapping crash. It felt like she needed to get her stomach back above her guts.

Haley imagined the panicked curses and shaking hands. Desperation for their lives would help them concentrate on getting off her tail.

Temperature two hundred degrees. The seawater pump would burn. She killed the power and a huge following wake slammed into the stern, pushing the boats ass high into the air and throwing water everywhere. She waited a moment, backed up hard, then stood on the gas once again. The temperature began to drop. She had shaken off the seaweed.

She didn't want the deputies to die and she needed to live long enough to find Ben—the beauty was that they wouldn't know about any desire of hers to live. If they shot at her, she didn't hear it. Aiming would have been nearly impossible.

Glancing over her shoulder, she saw them turning around at what was probably full throttle. Safe boats could do that. The other boat was coming at her, but with her incredible speed, it would not intersect her course.

Brown Island was coming up fast.

Haley's mind raced; she felt barely able to hold it together. She knew she was shaking, and that things were happening too fast and overwhelming her. No way could she think ahead of the boat. Instead, she was just hanging on, trying to aim this fiendish rocket that seemed any second ready to fling itself and her into space. When she came to the tip of Brown Island, she slowed to sixty and the terror ride became more manageable. She made the turn, able now on the calm water to plot mentally her course in front of the docks and through the anchored boats. The first time had been a practice run. She waited until she was about opposite the first dock in the series to punch the autopilot.

The boat was probably going sixty when she leaped overboard and hit the water very near the most prominent dock. The impact of her body on the water was bad and she actually rolled across the water, skipping like a stone before she slowed down. It stung like a beating with willow branches. Then the cold rushed over her, crushing and aching to the bone. Like many marine biologists, she was an avid diver and water person, and around the San Juans she wore a protective suit for warmth. Tonight she had nothing.

In water like this, in the low fifties, the average man could survive only about twenty minutes before losing consciousness—the average woman a little longer.

She had locked the autopilot of the *Opus Magnum* onto the floating log raft. She heard a great explosion when the boat reached its destination—another crime added to their collection. Apparently in calm water the autopilot worked fine at over thirty-five.

She found she was no more than forty feet from the ladder at dock's end. It took less than two minutes and she was out of the water and running. The sheriff's boat was two hundred yards down bay, near the burning hulk, looking for bodies; the other just coming around Brown Island.

Perhaps by this time Sam had found the answer to Ben's puzzle, or maybe even Ben himself.

Now the toughest part of her job had come.

Sam glanced around, expecting Frick to step out from behind a cabinet at any moment. When that didn't happen, he looked back out the door and saw an empty hallway. The odds were now with Frick. He probably had thirty, maybe forty, trained men. It was a small island and he was right under the man's nose. There was no doubt in his mind that the deputies would see Ranken or a digital photo, and Frick would have a suggestion as to how they should feel about it.

After a last look at Ranken's corpse, Sam turned and saw the supply shelves that Gibbons had described and moved them. Behind was a simple door with a wooden sort of twist handle that was flush with the wall. Sam opened the door and inside was an amazing little office with a very large freezer. *Alice in Wonderland* came to mind.

Sam could picture Ben working undisturbed here on his ARCLES files, but he couldn't imagine what was in the freezer. Immediately Sam spotted notebooks matching those at Gibbons's and his heart raced. He felt like a plunderer of pyramids who just found the pharaoh's vault. His vision of reality shifted again. Maybe Gibbons wasn't lying, after all.

All three volumes had the word *ARCLES* at the bottom of the page. He grabbed them and put them in his duffel.

He opened the freezer and looked inside. It contained a wooden box lined with Styrofoam. Inside it were what looked like test tubes with caps. They were color coded with paper bands and there appeared to be six different colors. One grouping of vials, the red, appeared to be empty.

Curiosity burned in him. Why was Ben hiding vials in a freezer? There were six different kinds of something, judging from the color code. *Probably the product of at least six different genes. Some of the liquids could be mixtures. Expressed proteins or their products*, the documents had indicated. Alongside the vials lay a brown manila envelope.

With eager hands he picked up the envelope, certain he was about to find something. Four-digit numbers ran down the left-hand margin of the page. Each four-digit entry down the side seemed to correspond to a row across the page. The four digits probably referred to the animals that were receiving the injections, substitutes for names.

What if they aren't animals?

He told himself that was a giant leap. There could be thirty-six mice or rats or octopuses. There was no reason to think Ben had already turned to people. He left the vials but kept the volumes, envelope, and papers; then he closed the freezer and returned to the outer workshop area.

Frick had left Ranken with his weapon, so Sam took it off the body and an extra speedloader with six bullets. Ranken carried a rather lightweight firearm, a Smith & Wesson model 10 thirty-eight special. It was economical and better than throwing rocks.

Sam also took the pepper spray. He wanted to take Ranken's body down and treat it with respect, but he knew he would be destroying forensic evidence.

Taking the weapon was the worst form of manufacturing circumstantial evidence, but Sam needed it. Even with the revolver, his odds were little better than nil. Standing again, his knee felt as if it were punctured by a hot needle and muscle cramps were beginning in his thigh, along with the increasing stiffness in his lower back. Moving around was now an ordeal. Carefully planned exercise was so different from racing around with an adrenaline-filled body. He didn't know what would happen if he tried to fight again.

He took one last look around the room before leaving. After a moment his eye went to three wooden boxes identical to the one in the freezer. Sam took a closer peek, trying to make out the small print on the wooden box. Surprisingly, it said *American Bayou Technologies*.

That was food for thought.

Sam crawled out of the little room and heard footsteps coming down the hall. After dousing the lights he pulled the .38 and stood behind the door. This could be the end of it. Thank God for the gun.

The door pushed open slowly. Probably someone was using his foot and had a gun in his hand as well.

In fact, the gun came next, a semiautomatic visible in the light from the hall. This was not a trained individual.

"Hey," came a voice from behind the figure. "We're doing this organized. We're down at the other end. You don't just go off by yourself."

"I've seen Dr. Anderson slip in here in the evening. I thought it would be a good place to look."

"We're doing this by the numbers. We're all down at the other end."

"Okay," the man sighed.

Sam waited about two minutes, then opened the door.

Surprisingly, the hall was empty. They were in rooms at the far end. He decided to take a chance and hurry down the hall to the stairs. It seemed to take an eternity and any moment he was sure he would be stopped. As he approached the stairs that would take him to the second floor and Ben's office, he heard voices. He ducked in a room and discovered it was the dive room. It was near both the door to the docks, where Sam had entered, and the stairwell to the second story.

Right away he noticed a pile of clothing. He checked the

wallet in the jeans and it was Ben's. Very interesting. Ben had left his credit cards and driver's license. Amazingly, no one had thought to check the dive room yet. Sam fished through the pants pockets and found a piece of paper. He pocketed it, returned to the door, flipped off the light, and listened. When he opened the door, it was plain that a group of three or four men was searching the lower floor, one room at a time. They had started at the far end and still had a distance to go.

Exiting the dive room, he rushed up the stairs to the first landing. He was able to see the top. A man sat on a stool, flipping through a magazine. Obviously he was permanently stationed. Sam doubted that he could bluff his way through, despite his fraying disguise. He would need to try another way. Feeling exposed, he went back down the stairs and managed to cross the hall to the outside door without being seen. Once again he went down the outside of the building, only this time he remained low, and traveled in the opposite direction, heading for the balcony from which Ben had originally jumped.

He found the balcony and climbed one of the small trees at the southern end. It was a fir and it sagged terribly under his weight, but he managed to make it to the edge of the balcony and climb over. The door to the interior was locked. There was a window and he looked inside. Someone was turning on all the lights during the search for him. He waited. In a couple of minutes someone made his way to the end of the hall, turning on lights in the various labs and offices.

When he reached the end of the hall, Sam tapped on the glass. Instead of panicking, as Sam expected, or calling for help, as Sam also expected, the man decided to be a hero, drew his gun, and approached the door. Sam lay on his back beside the door. The door opened and he could see the tip of the man's gun. Throwing the door open, the man stepped through, looking everywhere but down. His mouth was open and Sam shot a stream of pepper spray right at his partially opened mouth. Before the man could comprehend what had happened to him, he dropped the gun and grabbed for his throat.

In an impressive display of total surrender, the man fell to the ground with his eyes open wide.

"You'll be okay, it's just pepper spray," Sam said. He could empathize because he was suffering badly enough just from the residue.

Working quickly, he got the man's pants and shirt off and put them on over his own. Fortunately, he was a big guy. Sam found a badge indicating he was a special deputy, no doubt one of the newly deputized. Another play in Frick's game.

Unfortunately, the clothes reeked of pepper spray and the residue continued to burn his eyes. Using the man's own cuffs, he locked his hands behind his back; then he quickly closed the door, leaving the man gasping in his underwear.

This man carried a SIG-Sauer P229, standard fare for the FBI and a better weapon than Ranken's Smith & Wesson, if the criteria for "better" was the efficient killing of people. Sam hobbled down the hall dressed in the uniform of a security guard.

A loud boom came from outside—strong enough to rattle the windows.

"Check that out!" someone hollered. "*Opus Magnum* just went off like a firecracker."

Sam appreciated the timing but worried about Haley.

He made it all the way to Ben's office without being stopped. Those who saw him were evidently too busy looking out the window at Frick's barbecued boat to pay attention. Inside half an hour Sam hoped he would be reading documents that without a doubt would blow his mind.

Ben Anderson had not disappointed him yet.

* * *

It was evening, and Sanker was in a mood.

Rossitter walked in wearing new shoes.

"That bad, huh?" Sanker said.

"What do you mean?" Rossitter didn't get his meaning.

"You're wearing new shoes."

Rossitter still appeared confused by the comment, which was troubling because it meant the man didn't understand his own eccentricities. Sanker knew it was one thing to have them and another to lack any self-awareness of them. The old man sighed, suddenly feeling weary.

"Did you talk to our Judas?" he asked Rossitter.

"I tried calling him back. He won't return calls. Something is happening, I can feel it," Rossitter said. "I think it's like you said: Judas is two people, and I have a good idea who one of them is."

Suddenly the old man felt a welcome shot of adrenaline. "Well, who?"

"Sarah James—Ben's assistant." Rossitter said it as if trying to convince himself.

"How did you and your minions come to this conclusion?"

"Judas said we should follow Sarah to find Ben," Rossitter said. "Even said tell Frick to let her go."

"That's inconsistent, isn't it? First he says we don't need to find Ben, that's not part of the deal. It's a backup in case Frick doesn't get him. Then he tells us to find Ben? By following Sarah?"

"What do we do?" Rossitter looked more and more worried as their control of the situation grew thinner.

"One thing Judas likes doing is talking. Let him talk. You listen. Act cooperative, but don't agree to anything. Then report back to me."

"I see," Rossitter said. "He really could be on anybody's side."

"He's on his own side. We just have to figure out what he

really wants. I'm tending to believe he wants something that Sarah has," Sanker said.

"Sarah James is close to Ben Anderson. I hear she fancied him and he her. Ben took obvious precautions, hiding his work, et cetera. It's logical that she might know something. Or have something. Judas can't get to her if Frick has her. And Judas is supposed to deliver Ben's secret to us if he wants his reward."

"I still wonder why deliver it to us."

"That's easy," the old man said, growing more sure of himself. "Judas wants the Arc regimen. It's a complicated recipe, apparently. Judas says it has six primary components. He knows so much about it that I think he's seen it, maybe used or taken it. So he's desperate. What if he can't get any more of it? If he can't get it from Ben, he hedges his bets. He knows we would have the means to produce it, if only we knew how. Can't you see it?"

"Isn't that a lot of conjecture?"

"I made my fortune being good at conjecture," Sanker snapped back.

"So you think this Sarah knows the Arc regimen?"

"Not necessarily. She knows something that Judas wants to know, or has something he wants to have."

Rossitter looked down at those new shoes, clearly at sea.

It didn't matter. Sanker knew Judas's need intimately, because Judas's need was his own.

"There is nothing in here," Walrus Face said.

"What do you know about this?" Thin Man asked.

Sarah sat huddled in the back of Sheriff's Boat 3. Like Boat 2 it was a twenty-seven-foot Boston Whaler, but this one had a pair of 225-horsepower Suzuki outboards, and a tiny cabin. It was unusually aggressive for Thin Man to make the inquiries.

"I don't know a thing, other than what I told you," Sarah said. "I just saw the boat from the road."

Thin Man: "In the dark?"

"I wasn't sure this was the boat. But he usually ties up to that dock."

"That sounds like bullshit to me, designed to waste our time," Walrus Face said.

A breeze on the bay made sizable ripples that rocked the boats. The sheriff's boat tapped the gunnel of Ben's when they pitched.

"I'm sure you'd enjoy a stint with Frick," said Thin Man. "He's a charmer."

Walrus Face climbed back in the boat. "I think it's time for some candor lessons."

Walrus came toward her, and Sarah eyed his gun without staring. She had to get to it. Once she did, she was good enough to use it effectively. He pulled her to her feet and pushed her toward the cabin.

She opened the cabin door and stepped in front of the opening. Down inside the cuddy cabin there was a bunk. She knew that what she had in mind could get her brutalized, but given her options, it was worth the risk.

He came toward her and pushed her back inside. "I'd love to hump the hell out of you," Walrus Face said as if considering it, but not planning on it.

He reached for her coat and grabbed the zipper. She struggled and he slapped her across the face. Without further significant struggle she let him unzip the coat. He ripped open her blouse.

"I know what you want. Let's get it over with," she said.

She didn't have to work at making her hands tremble as she began unfastening his belt.

"You first," he said, obviously surprised and uncertain. She had called his bluff.

She didn't step back but made as if to open her blouse.

Walrus Face started feeling around for a light switch. At the same time she reached for his groin, again surprising and distracting him. His mouth came open slightly and he gasped. For those few seconds she had no scruples. It was a job and she aimed to get it done. Using her left hand, she reached for his gun, releasing the holster snap and pulling it free, while he tried to adjust to what he thought she was doing. In a split second he was looking down the barrel of his own gun.

Shock was apparent on Walrus Face. It was as if he'd looked into the future and seen his end.

She couldn't quite see his eyes. He could try to grab it. At that moment she wished he would. In the movies they grabbed guns. In real life people usually got shot when they tried it. Her father had been a cop before he was a contractor and they had discussed such things. They had also fired hundreds of rounds from various weapons and she still remembered how to do it, and she knew that on a night such as this, a thug would carry the gun with the safety off and a round in the chamber.

She watched him swallow hard and slid by him out of the cuddy cabin.

Thin Man hesitated, trying to comprehend what was happening. She backed to the corner stern of the boat, where she held the gun aimed in their direction.

"Jump over," she shouted at Thin Man. She lowered the gun and fired, missing his leg by inches. The gun boomed up the bay. "Next one blows your leg off," she said. "Ten-millimeter round, I think." Thin Man jumped. "You're next, Walrus Face."

"You bitch . . ."

She fired. The near miss rocked him back. "Next one's in your chest," she said, her hands shaking more than before. "It'll knock the crap out of you even with your flak jacket."

He jumped at her and she fired, knocking him back against the wheel. He looked like he was all done. Then he shook himself and somehow regained his faculties. Again he came at her, stumbling, and again she shot, this time two rounds. They knocked him down, the bullets' force incredible. She guessed she had hit the steel breastplate in the vest. It didn't matter. She knew it would incapacitate him, for the moment.

"You just couldn't stand that you were bested by a woman. So like an idiot you kept coming," she said, amazed and shaken at his bullheaded tenacity.

In the dash lights she could see his eyes rolled back, spittle running down his chin. He was shaking himself, trying to recover.

"Get up, you bastard."

No blood, so she knew the injuries were internal only. She was shaking and barely able to aim the gun. She fought hysteria and, oddly, guilt that she had actually shot a man three times. Struggling, he managed to get to his knees, holding his ribs in terrible pain.

"My ribs are broken."

"Good," she said. "I'll shoot some more if you don't crawl over the side."

"Please, I can't," Walrus Face groaned.

She couldn't help herself. She was starting to feel sorry for him. Seeing him wounded made a difference, somehow. "Get up or, so help me, I'll kill you." She put the gun a foot from his head, knowing that she didn't mean a word of what she said.

"I can't. I swear, I can't move. It feels like I got ribs in my lungs."

He was in real pain. What she saw couldn't be faked and there were those holes in the clothing over his chest. She reached down and felt a dented steel breastplate in the Kevlar. Another big dent in the Kevlar wasn't over the breastplate. It must have hurt him bad. Her daddy had talked about vests as well. In fact, Walrus Face probably felt as if he couldn't move.

On his belt she found handcuffs. Based on what she'd seen in the movies and on watching her nephew play with real cuffs, she clamped one end of a cuff on tight to his wrist, then cuffed the wrist to the outboard-motor bracket. It was more than stout. She turned on the ignition and left Thin Man to flounder through the mud to the private dock. In seconds she was going forty-four knots back toward the main marinas. Riding over the small waves, the boat and motor vibrated and Walrus Face screamed in pain.

Sarah had to get to Ben quick. She was already thirty minutes late.

CHAPTER 23

Once on Warbass Street, it had taken Haley only a few seconds to put her soggy backside on the soft leather of Rachael's BMW. She started it, begging aloud for the heat. Her clothes stuck to her skin, her body felt like rubber, and her teeth literally rattled with the shivering. Never had she been so cold. She checked her pocket with trembling hands to make sure she had the keys to Ben's airplane. God, it was hard to think when your body felt so cold. Her thoughts were a jumble of genes, longevity, the end of the world, and a desperate determination that neither Sam nor Ben should die.

Get to the plane and get to Sam, she reminded herself. She could come in second in this race. She struggled with the old feeling that her mother's loser's karma was trying to take her down. This time she fought it like she had never fought it before, and the fight was part of the antidote to giving up.

Already near panic, she gasped at what she saw in the rearview mirror. Headlights were coming down the street and a spotlight was moving side to side. Looked like another sheriff's deputy. There was no time to put on the dry clothes in the backseat.

She stepped on the gas, careful not to spin the rear tires. The deputy was traveling slowly, probably looking for someone on foot. She continued down Warbass, then noticed that the deputy was speeding up and had doused the spotlight. She exited Warbass near the top of the ferry landing and took a quick, sharp left back up the hill, accelerating hard now that the patrol car was out of sight. In seconds she found herself back on Gibbons's street.

It gave her an idea. She pulled into Gibbons's garage, jumped out, grabbed the bag with her dry clothes, and pushed the garage door button as the deputy's car went careening past. It was a shock when the garage light automatically turned on at the push of the button. It was like a neon sign.

Down the block the brake lights of the deputy's car shone bright.

Without waiting, Haley hit the button, stopped the garage door from closing, grabbed the clothes, and sprinted out into the night. As the police car was backing, she turned into the thick hedge next to the garage, forced her way through, and began climbing the hill at a frantic pace.

Flames were still skyrocketing from *Opus Magnum* three minutes after the crash. Frick was still waiting for the ferry search to commence and trying to figure a way to keep the ferry stationary all night. He would use his men for something more productive than a full-scale search of the ferry. It smelled like a ruse and he couldn't follow every one of this bastard's feints. The deputies were starting to look for survivors at the wreck site. That would have to end quickly.

Frick had just yelled at the assistant to the CEO for the ferry system when, amazingly, the transportation secretary called. Obviously he had already been briefed.

"I'm sorry," the secretary said, "but we just don't keep ferries all night at Friday Harbor. We have a boatload of passengers. We'll call the state police and have them search as people get off in Anacortes. They'll search the vehicles, I'm told."

"I'm calling from the Sanker Foundation," Frick replied. "Mr. Sanker, of the Sanker Corporation and this foundation, and the governor's friend, does not want to call the governor on the Thanksgiving holiday. We believe scientific papers of the utmost importance, so valuable that they might have national-security implications, have been stolen. An informant claims that the thief—who's already shot two police officers, one to death, and killed one employee of Sanker—is on that ferry. We want to keep this confidential and there is no way to do that if that ferry heads back to Anacortes and you bring in the state police. Furthermore, that ferry is due to stop at Lopez and there is no security there whatsoever."

There was a long pause. Frick knew that the last thing the secretary would want would be to disturb the governor on the holiday weekend with a problem from his department. Old man Sanker had probably contributed a lot of money to various political causes at the governor's suggestion. Although it was doubtful the secretary knew the amount, or even the order of magnitude of the contributions, he could imagine the general level of Sanker's influence by reputation alone. Guys like the secretary got their jobs because they understood politics.

"Mr. Secretary?"

"I'll call right now and ask the CEO to suggest to the captain that he remain at the Friday Harbor dock for repairs to the electronics. It's still much closer than Anacortes and it's dark. We'll do it for safety. The search will be incidental. I don't want to set a precedent here."

"Understood." Frick breathed a sigh of relief and signed off, expressing more gratitude than he felt.

"We have something suspicious on Warbass," Khan said as Frick hung up the phone. "I'm sending in a bunch of cars."

"Do it," Frick said.

Then it hit him. The so-called Sam was a professional with an agenda. It was the only reasonable explanation for all that was happening. This was the moment when Sam had worked the maximum distraction, and if that was true, this was the moment of maximum danger for Sam and his plan. So what was the most dangerous thing Sam might be doing?

It was obvious, now that he thought about it. Frick grabbed his radio and advised everyone that Sam, aka Robert Chase, might be in the building or in the Oaks Building next door. Soon they'd search the workshop, which was fine with Frick. It was time the world find out about the brutal slaying of Detective Ranken.

Sam took from Ben's office the volumes Haley had described—four thick three-ring binders—and moved toward the window. He stopped for a moment. With the volumes he'd already gathered, he now had a sizable burden. Too much to carry onto the roof. He needed to narrow it down.

Taking what he could, he opened the window and spread four new volumes down the roof, along with the two he had brought from the shop, the bases of all six binders resting in the gutter. He turned off the office lights and then in agony forced his bad leg through the window and crawled onto the narrow wisp of a ledge. He closed the window and moved down the ledge until he reached the side of the dormer. Here he half-reached and half-crawled to pull each volume to his sorting spot.

Risking the giveaway of the beam from his penlight, he skimmed as fast as he could. What would normally take minutes or hours had to be done in seconds.

He started at the front of the first volume from the work-shop, which discussed methane hydrates and catastrophic release mechanisms. Thermonuclear release was the most eye-catching chapter title. Sam quickly tore out the chapters that seemed most interesting and stuffed them in a bag.

He quickly found what appeared to relate to the science of aging. It focused on cell mitochondria. Fine. He took those pages as well. He had to run, but the question came again to Sam: *What is going on with these people?*

When Rachael finally reached her parents', she slowed down and stood off from the dock about one hundred yards. The water was calm because it was sheltered from the winds and there wasn't much boat traffic at 8:15 on Sunday night. A phone call to her parents' house produced no one. The engines idled comfortably, but loudly, with a deep, throaty gallop, the exhaust blowing forward in the slight breeze, making an acrid smell. Rachael kicked the engines out of neutral and the boat moved ahead. There didn't seem to be anyone about, but there was an eerie feel in the night air and she wondered if she shouldn't go to a marina, instead.

Something moved in the shadows of the channel next to the rocks near her father's dock. Maybe she was imagining things. She spooked, turned a 180, and increased her speed to twenty knots.

She didn't want to be alone with Frick's hired men. As she moved away and was turning the corner into Fidalgo Bay, the boat out of the shadows picked up speed and began following. It was a small runabout. What were the odds on a wintry night?

The runabout increased its speed and kept coming. A wave of panic washed over her. Maybe they had been waiting. Rachael called her father's cell and got no answer. He normally would be out for dinner at this hour on a Sunday night and sometimes he turned off his phone. She couldn't help but wonder if he was all right.

What have I gotten into?

She came hard to the starboard, moving in close to the giant rocky point, sure of the bottom from her days as a teenager. Quickly the runabout changed course as well.

Thinking that she might have to do something drastic, she turned on the forward-looking sonar and increased her speed to forty knots—insanely fast for the tiny channel through the mudflats. In thirty seconds she slowed as she came into a very narrow channel only about 6.6 feet deep. Her props would be stirring mud badly. Abruptly she stopped and turned the large yacht around. She risked running fast aground but didn't. It was precision piloting with the electronics.

Beyond the major marinas with exits off the channel, she turned off all the lights and waited in the dark. The only way someone would come all the way down the channel in a runabout would be if they were looking for her.

Like a bull watching the matador, she considered what she would do. If she were onshore, taking her in secret would be harder for Frick. Out here who would notice? She took out her flare pistol and loaded it. The other boat was warily following her path down the channel. The lights of the gas plants on the far side of the bay to her right shone like pyres on the horizon, like something out of Tolkien.

She got on channel 16 and chose the direct approach.

"What do you want?"

"Just to talk," someone said.

That was amazingly stupid of them, she thought.

A new voice came on the line. "This is the United States Coast Guard. Vessels on channel sixteen, this is an emergency and hailing channel only."

"Coast guard, coast guard, this is the vessel *Inevitable*. I am Rachael Sullivan in Fidalgo Bay, and I am being chased by armed men in a small boat." She idled the throttles and put the shafts in forward and turned on all the lights, including the spot.

"This is coast guard, Bellingham Group, switch and answer twenty-two alpha."

She switched and repeated the message, no doubt to a disbelieving seaman. Still, they would be compelled to send a boat.

According to the line between buoys, as shown on the chart plotter, they were moved over up against the edge of the channel. She stopped. Studying her pursuers' position on the radar chart plotter overlay, they actually appeared to be on the mud. But that wasn't likely. It gave her an idea.

The boat was about two hundred yards distant and she plotted a course to put it right under her bow. She increased speed to fifteen knots. The boat wanted to plane, but she kept it half on the step in the maximum bow-high position. Then she adjusted the trim tabs and brought the bow higher still. She couldn't see over *Inevitable*'s bow now; she had to bring her down so that on the balls of her feet she could see her quarry. *Inevitable,* at sixty-five feet, weighed fifty-four thousand pounds and could walk right over the runabout. They would die if she so desired, and she wouldn't receive a scratch. Bent prop shafts, props, and fiberglass damage were a pain, but they would not kill her.

They were seconds away and dead ahead.

The radio crackled. "Stop, for Christ's sake!"

They fired a flare right at her windshield and it burst bright against the hard plastic.

In seconds she turned off the autopilot, took the wheel, used her eye, and hit the throttle, digging the huge props into the water, sinking the stern and throwing a mammoth wake.

With the precision of a marksman she smacked the small boat a glancing blow. The impact picked the runabout up and tossed it like a chef might flip an omelette. The boat almost ended on its side; her huge wake pushed it high onto the mud; water to the floorboards, no doubt, and grounded.

A thud came against *Inevitable*'s side, followed by a violent lurch. She'd hit the mud. She veered back to starboard and heaved a sigh of relief as *Inevitable* continued on up the channel.

The torrent of curses that came over the radio must have astonished the coast guard.

A coast guard helicopter was coming in close, followed by a coast guard motor lifeboat turning the corner into the bay. The jig was up. She killed the power and waited. This was the beginning of what would be a long night with a lot of paperwork. She hoped the coasties would listen. Thank God her pursuers had shot the flare and shattered the windshield. Given that, and her original call for help, they'd be the focus of the investigation.

Her part of the plan had just begun. Now she could only pray that Sam and Haley would escape Frick long enough for her to get some help.

CHAPTER 24

Frick sprinted down the hall to the other end of the second floor, through the breezeway, and into the Oaks Building. His gun was out and adrenaline pumping. He slowed. Slipping into Ben Anderson's lab with his gun at the ready, he was actually surprised that Robert Chase was nowhere to be seen. He checked the closets and the electron microscope room and other side rooms. Nothing.

Sweat poured off him. Back in Ben Anderson's office he saw a man and drew his gun, then stood down. It was one of the guards, staring openmouthed.

Saying nothing, Frick ran downstairs into the workshop, suddenly feeling sick with worry in his gut.

People made little slips when they did things in a hurry and he had created this particular set piece in a few minutes. When he arrived in the hall at the bottom of the stairs, he could see one regular deputy and one of his men standing in the room with Ranken hanging in the background. So far, so good. It should shock them.

"What happened here?"

"Somebody got in here and Ranken must have found them. They took his gun and his spray."

That shook Frick, but he didn't let on. Could he be that lucky, to have Sam in the building with Ranken's gun?

"It's that Sam—Robert Chase—or whatever he's calling himself at the moment," Frick growled. "He's got to be in the building, and now he's armed. Take a picture. Show all the regular deputies. I want them to see what they're up against. Get Ostrowski down here for the forensics." He turned on his heel and ran back to the Sanker Building and the conference room. Before he went in, he got on the radio and announced Ranken's death and made Chase's guilt a fact as fast as he could. His people would alert the media shortly, as to a new "grisly" killing.

When he entered the conference room, he broke up a conversation between Khan and one of the men.

Khan looked uneasy. That couldn't be good. Frick dismissed the other man.

"They found another body," Khan said, obviously suspicious. "But you look pleased for some reason."

"I'm sure Chase is in the building. This is our chance to get him."

"How do you know?"

"He killed Detective Ranken and took his gun. Or somebody did, and who else would do that?"

"Seriously?" Khan looked unconvinced.

"Absolutely." Frick spoke it like a challenge. "He took Ranken's gun."

"I'll start a search."

"Tell the guys in the boat not to waste any more time hunting bodies."

Khan began calling the security people in the building.

Frick picked up a call from their Vegas man at the Sullivan family dock in Anacortes.

"Rachael Sullivan arrived," the guy said, "or rather she

drove up near the dock, then turned around and ran. We had three men in a boat. They went after her and, I guess, they're stuck in the mud."

"Where's the woman?"

"I don't know. Our guys talked to me on the radio and said they screwed up. They say she radioed the coast guard."

Frick thought for a moment. Staying around was riskier than letting her go at this point. "Just leave, there's nothing to do with her."

"That was smart," Khan said.

"I'm gonna go talk to McStott," Frick said, "see what the greedy little bastard's up to."

Frick found him in a large lab area.

McStott seemed glad to see him.

"I found something weird."

"What?"

"A binder that advocates a recovery method for methane."

Frick sighed. He couldn't help himself; he was impatient.

"Listen," McStott begged. "This is worth a fortune."

The word *fortune* did it.

"I'm listening," Frick said.

"This stuff about mining methane from microbes is not crazy, like I thought," McStott said. "They may have this stuff nailed."

The egghead was almost squeaking with excitement.

"The global reserves for methane are eighty thousand times the global reserves for natural gas. Available U.S. reserves alone are 5.7 trillion cubic meters, and that's enough to meet this country's needs for the next two thousand years."

Frick let out a long, low whistle despite himself.

"So how are we gonna get rich?" he asked.

"There are problems with methane."

"Like what?" Frick asked.

"There are three, actually, aside from the danger of blowing something up. Methane is in two forms: frozen with water in an icelike substance called a hydrate, and beneath the hydrates as a gas. When the hydrate turns into gas, its volume increases by a factor of one hundred sixty."

"Okay. So?"

"The first problem is that the methane diffuses and is hard to collect. To make a long story short, they've found ways to get around that problem, to some extent. They don't specify how the mining is done. They only say it's not cheap or easy, but it is doable. Let's leave it at that."

"Let's," said Frick.

"Problem two is finding exactly the right place to drill. Even though it covers large areas, drill sites are much more rare. That's the key to recovery."

Frick nodded. "And?"

"The third problem is that it's still a fossil fuel. It's the cleanest fossil fuel, but it still makes CO_2. Right?"

"If you say so. I suppose the do-gooders don't like that."

"That's right," said McStott. "So they developed a closed-system way of using it to make electricity. They burn it and use the heat to make steam and the steam drives a turbine that generates electricity. They break down the CO_2 into water and carbon. The carbon goes into the ground, leaving only water vapor."

"Where is all this written down?"

"That's the trouble. They've hidden all the details. So we don't have all the how-to parts," said McStott, "but at least we know what to look for. This is the end of the energy crisis as we know it, man. If somebody does something about it."

Frick grabbed the animated McStott by the shirt, shocking him into silence.

"Get the details. And get the aging technology. That's our priority. Got it?"

"Okay! I know," McStott said, pulling away. "I know you're in a rush. But hear me out. There's something here, it's like a whole thing," McStott blurted quickly, making little or no sense. "Not just aging. But it's all related. See, oxygen-based creatures—"

"What the hell are you talking about? Read my lips. Does Ben Anderson know how to make people live a long time?"

Khan came into the lab in a hurry. "Something's going on. They're about to call me back." On cue Khan's phone beeped and Khan answered.

Frick watched Khan clamp his jaw as an angry shadow crossed his face.

"Where is . . . Hello? Hello?" Khan said. He turned to Frick, his eyes intense. "One of our guards saw a big man in this building. He sprayed our guy with pepper spray and took his clothes."

Sam had to get off the roof but had no good way to do it.

He stared down the peak toward the balcony, holding his bag of papers. Given the murderous drop to the balcony and then the ground, Sam decided to risk going back through the window. He tied the bag to his belt, and as he opened the window, he saw a shadow cross the hallway outside the door of Ben's office.

Immediately he felt he was in bad trouble. He looked at his other option: the jump off the roof to the balcony and then to the ground could paralyze him.

It wouldn't take much to start the swelling, and he had already badly abused his body.

He broke out in a cold sweat as he scrambled up the roof in pain that felt like surgery without anesthesia. When he got his leg almost straight and used two hands and one foot to do the bulk of the locomotion, it hurt less. The far end of the roof was a long way off, but he covered the distance in a few minutes. Approaching the balcony slowly, he peered over the edge. Then the door to the balcony flew open. Somebody was there with a gun making all the right moves.

A trained cop.

His mind did a quick calculation. One possibility remained—jumping to the big fir tree in the dark. Doing his weird three-point crawl and dragging the bad leg, he went down the roof to the fir. It was probably a second-growth tree that the second group of loggers missed.

It would be ironic to die falling out of a tree when the fountain of youth might be hanging from his belt. He made sure it was a fleeting thought. At this time of night it looked like he'd be jumping into a big shadow. A window onto the roof was opening. It was a simple calculation. The fear of pain was daunting. Fear of Frick's murder methods made it seem perfectly acceptable.

It was a good jump, probably ten feet to something really solid. He backed up on the roof and decided to pretend that he had more or less two good legs. It was a ridiculous assumption. In less than five seconds he noticed that he was nearly hyperventilating. Looking at the gulf, the great fall to the ground, he imagined the clean snap of the bones. He really didn't want to jump. He paused.

A few evil men, Ben had warned. Did Ben have any particular evil men in mind?

As someone scrambled up the far side of the roof, he realized he'd have to live if he were ever to find out what was really happening. Taking three giant strides, he leaped from his good leg. Airborne, he reached out with his arms and hit two branches, one near each armpit. The first was flimsy and bent as he grabbed it; the other snapped. Then he was grabbing as things broke and his body fell. Maybe for two seconds branches snapped like toothpicks. Then he slammed into the tree itself, sliding down the trunk, taking off plenty of skin. Everything from his testicles to his chest hurt like hell. His leg throbbed in pain beyond description.

He hung on as a matter of instinct, then sought something solid for his feet. He found it.

Somebody was shouting something on the roof. They would all come. He started sliding down the tree again, burning more skin at the friction points. Then branches thudded against his body like torturers with small clubs. Down he went, never stopping, just trying to control the fall. The last fifteen or twenty feet, he broke his fall only once. Then he hit the ground and pain was screaming in his face, in his ears.

Now he knew who was screaming. He was.

Knowing it was move or die, he rolled and began half-crawling and doing a three-point gallop, happy even to run like a three-legged animal, amazed that he wasn't yet paralyzed.

He hung onto the swinging duffel as he ran. After a few moments he made it to standing upright, and groaned with the terrible, pulsing pain. He grabbed a stick and bit down. His breath came fast. The stick was putrid with rot, and soft, and had an acrid taste. But it stopped the groaning.

Men were coming out of the building and shining flashlights around, but nobody plunged into the thick of it. In seconds he was away from the building and away from them. As he came near the road, he saw flashlights in the distance moving along a path parallel to his. They also were running for the road. He halted at the shoulder and watched them turn down the road, jogging in his direction.

The clouds had opened, allowing the moon to shine down the road, making a fuzzy white worm snaking through the trees. Mustering his will, Sam half-ran, half-stumbled, across the road. Careless shots in the dark sent bullets into the forest, but none found him. Quickly he plunged back into the sopping wet branches of the forest, keeping low like a brush buck. Running wasn't possible, unless one was willing to risk running into a tree trunk. There were no more flashlights and he heard no movement through the trees from down the road. Likely, no one would follow, except in a large group. He began angling just a little west of north, as near as he could figure it, toward the area of the most trees and the fewest people.

He felt nothing now but a raw desire to survive, served by instincts millennia old. Vegas guys in stitched leather shoes, and without a dog, would be hard-pressed to find him, unless some of them were really, like him, country guys living in the city. Of course, as luck would have it, they had one police dog on Orcas Island. No doubt they would bring it over. With a dog they could find him. There were a few tricks he might employ, but with a group of men and a trained dog, they were long shots. If Haley didn't come fast, he was done, cornered on a small portion of a small island. He hoped he would be able to find the needed materials to buy himself a chance. It was either that or try to kill the dog. He didn't want to kill a dog.

Fortunately, the forever-reassembling clouds were disassembling at the right spot. When he had a moment, he intended to figure out an appropriate direction of travel. It was a damnably dense, small-tree forest that, if in northern California, would vaporize like so much confetti at the first forest fire. However, the underbrush was light and there hadn't been any recent windstorms leaving large windfalls that would make passage even more difficult.

He would have preferred the windfalls.

That he used no light would be his strength, and one of the several weaknesses of those who searched for him. They would advertise their presence long before they arrived. To find him in the thickest of the forest, they would have to step on him. It was the tracking dog that would make the difference. To land a seaplane or pick him up in a boat, whichever worked out (either was a long shot), he and Haley would need a rendezvous far away from all the hired help at Sanker. They had a contingency plan if she couldn't make it, but it wasn't good.

As he went, he looked for trails because they might lead him to what he needed.

The warm front was blowing through, opening holes, passing light from the full moon and making a soft glow at the treetops. True to its norm, the weather was changing rapidly. When he came to a break in the trees, he took his bearings by locating the North Star and made an imaginary line running north and south.

He bisected a north-south line with his eye on a bearing that led to the stars of the west in the November sky, and with that he had something of a compass by which to navigate the forest. After taking some precautionary measures he would travel northerly, but west of north, almost paralleling the shoreline until he came to the water. Maintaining a straight line was impossible. It was instead a matter of constant correction and meandering along a route that averaged the desired heading.

The bushes were wet from the rains and his stolen uniform and Top-Siders were now sodden. Above the waist he wasn't much better, although the shirt was wool and tended to be naturally warm even when wet. So far, his parka hadn't completely soaked through.

He did his best to shrug the sharp branches off and slide by; years ago he'd become adept at it. By watching the treetops against the sky, with a nearly full moon, he could tell the thin spots in the forest. By avoiding wet areas and staying as high as he could on the gently sloping terrain, he avoided the brush associated with moist soil.

Every twenty or thirty paces he stopped abruptly and listened so that he could discern if anyone was near. He heard only shouts in the distance from men who wanted an alternative to wandering through a dark forest looking for a mad Scots Indian.

Sam needed to know that Haley was all right; finally he

could afford to find out. He slowed his pace, pulled out his cell, and dialed.

She answered, breathless.

"Are you okay?" he asked.

"Running like crazy," she said. "No time. I'll make it. Are you?"

"Worse for the wear, still at it, running through the woods like we talked about. I think I have fantastic stuff."

"I'm scared for Sarah. Frick's men have her."

"They won't kill her right away because they want information."

"I sure hope so," she said. "I'm feeling desperate for her."

"Then run fast," he said. "We'll find her."

"What did you find?"

He tried to explain that he'd found more than he'd been able to read.

"*You'll* read it. This is no fair," she joked, grunting as she jumped or ducked under something. "You're having all the fun. Please stay safe. Please. I'll be there."

Fun?

Next Sam called the dispatcher.

"Detective Ranken is dead," Sam said baldly. "He was killed by Garth Frick. Frick drained his blood into a barrel." He let that sink in, then explained where to find the evidence. "You might want to let the state and the FBI know."

"We already found the body, and you're wanted for that crime, Mr. Chase."

Sam knew that the dispatcher was not supposed to say that, even if she believed it. Obviously she was shaken and he could only imagine how the rest of the deputies felt.

He needed to call Ernie.

* * *

"He went out Anderson's office window," Khan said. "They're chasing somebody on Warbass, maybe from *Opus Magnum*."

"Give me an earpiece." Frick wanted to be directly connected to the action.

"We think maybe somebody came out of the water near where *Opus* blew up. We followed her. It looked like Haley Walther."

"Stop her. Bring her here."

"Roger that."

"He jumped off the roof and went into the woods," Khan interrupted.

Frick covered the receiver. "How the hell can somebody do that? It's a forty-foot drop, or better."

"Well, he's not lying dead on the ground."

"The men with Sarah James are on the phone," Delia said.

"Where the hell are they? It's been forty-five minutes?" Frick picked up the other line.

"Well, we thought you wanted information," Khan's man said. "Maybe we got a little carried away. We threatened to strip her down, and you know . . ."

"Strip her?" Frick closed his eyes.

"We didn't actually. Just said we had to search. Played with her. Scared her."

"Nothing we couldn't explain or lie about," the man's partner chimed in.

"What happened?" Frick asked.

"She told us Ben's boat was in the bay. You said we could take a look."

"Did you look?"

"There was a boat," the man said. "She says it's his. It had drifted onto the mud near the head of the bay. Harder than hell to get to. We had to wade. That's why it took so damn long."

"Yeah, yeah," Frick said. "So where the hell is Ben Anderson?"

"That's the thing. We don't know. But there's the boat—"

"Why would she lead you to his boat?" Frick interrupted. "Did she want you to think he was on the island?"

"Well, we can't figure it. But he could be on Lopez."

"Bring Sarah James here and let us do the questioning," Frick said.

"Well, there's a problem there."

"What the hell do you mean?"

"You said to soften her up. We thought we could get some more info out of her. And you know she seemed more afraid of the one-eyed monster than anything—well, Shawn was pretending like he was going to get on top of her, just scaring her, not raping her or anything, and she got his gun."

Frick gripped the handset, his knuckles whitening. "Are you saying she got away, or you had to kill her?"

"Got away. Back up to the dock at Lopez. Up the bay."

"That makes no sense," Frick said. "Why wouldn't she take off from the island, head to Anacortes or Orcas or something? Why back to Lopez, where you just caught her?"

"I can only tell you what she did."

"Go find her and bring her here. Think about why she went right back—if thinking is part of your repertoire."

"I'm all wet," the moron said.

Frick hung up in disgust, turning to Khan.

"This Sam character ran into the woods," Khan said.

"And your guys lost Sarah James. Call the dispatcher. Get the damn K-nine, he should have arrived from Orcas in the plane." Frick then said to Delia, "We'll start on Sam with the dog. But send more men to Lopez to help those incompetent bastards find the James woman. I can't believe I paid for this."

Frick thought for a moment. "We have a list of Sarah James's friends. We'll start there."

"We're running low on men."

"I'm sure that's exactly what the Indian bastard intended," Frick said. "Pull some of the men off the search for Sam. The dog will do more than ten men."

McStott showed up looking nervous, no doubt aware of Frick's murderous rage. He mopped the sweat from his brow with a yellowed linen handkerchief.

"Go ahead," Frick finally said.

"We found summaries—abstracts, they're called—referring to papers that analyze the psychological effect of an antiaging regimen. One study proposal apparently deals with the effects on people who don't get the various serums once they learn that it is available. Questions like, would they start a political movement? Would they be violent? And how would the government respond? Would the government control who we give it to and how we give it, that sort of thing?" McStott watched Frick obviously trying to gauge whether he should continue. "I mean, are you going to have a checklist to qualify? Bad grades and you die young? Guys with criminal records or drunks with bad livers? How about guys who are just recognized assholes?"

"You mean like you and me," Frick said.

McStott thought better of responding to that. "You know you have a lot of people standing in line to live a few hundred years and you may have to choose who gets it. Will the government decide that? Will Sanker? What'll be the rules for getting the live-longer-now juice? Would people have an inalienable right to this stuff? Even if Sanker owns it, maybe the government controls it."

"It's a cinch all the politicians will get it," Frick said. "So where are the actual papers discussing these things?"

"Can't find them yet. Just the abstract. There's a whole other proposal on what to do with people who get it. A psychological section to see if it drives them crazy, and then a whole legal section, like for the others. Only this is about whether it's fair for these people to compete in business. For example, do they just keep amassing wealth or do they have to start over? Are they forced into retirement for three hundred years, or can they build fortunes? How about restraints on political power and influence? Would they be seen as icons that would unduly influence the democracy? Would they become the ruling elite?"

"Just how long are they assuming these people will live?" Frick asked, feeling progressively more interested.

"If they start the intervention prior to thirty-five or so, these people will live, they assume, on average, four hundred years."

"So that's confirmed. Not a joke this time."

"It is," said McStott. "I must caution you that it seems incredible, but that is what they're suggesting. You can see that this topic will keep the politicians busy for years."

"Chaos," Frick said. "But as long as I'm rich and can live a long time, I don't give a crap. All of you will come to feel the same way, so keep digging."

McStott remained uncharacteristically quiet for a moment.

"What is it?" Frick asked.

"Something just hit me. I wonder how old that octopus Glaucus is. I'll try to figure that out."

"Think Anderson's been fooling with him?"

"It's possible. Maybe he did it a long time ago. Maybe he's still doing it. It's worth looking into."

"How long will it take?" Frick asked.

"Depends. If we find he did do something genetic and left markers, it could take months to find them. So we need a record."

"Months? I need something fast. And you don't know for

a fact that if he is treating the octopus, the secret's in its genes, right?"

"That's true," McStott allowed.

"That octopus isn't going anywhere," Frick said. "If we can't find something better, we know where to find it."

CHAPTER 25

Haley had pressed her way into a large, leafy hedge near the garage, and once beyond it, she had sensed no one behind her. Heading up through the brush and the neighbor's yard, she went as fast as she could, even if not as quietly. Between Harrison Street, Lattimer's, and a main thoroughfare on the east side of the airport runway, there were forested areas and small neighborhoods. The first twenty feet into the brush had been miserable going as she picked her way through the dense undergrowth. Her eyes were unaccustomed to the dark. Any second she had expected the officer to start shouting for her to stop, but, in fact, she had probably been invisible in the darkness.

The siren from the other patrol car had been sounding closer, though. Then it had been joined by a second, probably a half-mile away.

After only a short distance Haley had broken out into an area with widely spaced trees and a couple buildings. She cut across it and came to a four-way intersection and ran down the street toward a forest. For a block she was completely exposed, but she covered the ground quickly.

Then she was in thick woods with more heavy underbrush. Running, walking, and crawling, she felt like it would go on forever. To her right she knew was a large open field, and to her left a long row of residences that went on for a quarter-mile or more.

Putting her hands in front of her, she tried to feel her way around the tree trunks. In a particularly dark and foreboding thicket, she took several steps and, with one of them, went into a hole that put her in brush up to her waist and skinned her shinbone. She pushed on, vines ripping at her clothing, her skin feeling stings as if from attacking bees; her raw flesh protested the mistreatment. She traveled as fast as she could, holding the bag of clothes, sometimes on three of all fours, desperate to claw her way through.

She crested the top of a gentle hill and moved closer to the houses but remained in the trees and in the backyards that bordered them, stumbling over barbecues and children's toys and all manner of junk.

The two sets of sirens came closer.

She crossed a large street that she knew to be Grover. There were new construction homes on the far side and down a large residential drive. Just as she arrived at a home in the new subdivision, a patrol car came around the corner off Grover, seemingly following her. Fortunately, she was off the street out of the path of the headlights. She hit the ground and the car whizzed past and continued. Quickly she hurried into the shadows alongside the home. It was full of loud-talking teenagers and rock music. There was a light on a back patio and it cast a glimmer into the deep shadows and she tried to avoid the fingers of light that felt their way into the darkness. Careful not to run into anything, she went as fast as she dared. For a good distance she clawed through more brush and trees until she spotted what she knew to be the county fairgrounds, where she encountered a fence.

She reached out. It was chain link. She struggled over it

and ran in the open, fearful that at any moment she would be yelled into halting or, worse yet, a target for a gun.

The silent bleachers of the fairgrounds created a ghostly backdrop and underscored her aloneness in a place designed for happy people living safe, normal lives.

Coming down Argyle, a new patrol car was shining its spotlight to the fairgrounds side of the road. It indicated to her that for some reason they believed she hadn't crossed over Argyle, traveling toward the airport. Instantly she hit the dirt and crawled quickly back away from the street. When she had put the major county buildings between herself and the road, she turned back and began traveling parallel with the main road and the airport runway. There were more trees to the south. She crossed a small street and eventually came to a sizable home.

Hoping she wouldn't be seen in the open, she climbed through a board fence, and went down the driveway toward the house, thinking she should get in the bushes but not wanting to slow down. Eerily, the squad car was coming back up the main street. She remained hunched over, low to the ground. Then the car turned up the side street, where she hid, moving its spotlight. It couldn't be a coincidence, she told herself. Perhaps someone in the house had seen her moving.

Another cruiser was coming up the main street, also using its spotlight. Through the trees she could see yet more flashing lights, indicating that she was slowly being corralled.

When she arrived at the next house, still at least a half-mile from the airport, she saw two police cars out on Argyle. They seemed to have stopped to confer. With all the attention, she had no idea how she'd get to the hangar that housed Ben's plane. It was on the opposite side of the airport complex.

As she came to the back of the house, she slithered through the fence and scratched her back in the process. Looking at the newly constructed home, with its hints of a Victorian lineage, hopeless fear penetrated to her bowels—add a few cobwebs and some faded paint and it could be something out of a Stephen King novel. Go in the house or face Frick's goons—her choice.

One of the officers was exiting the car when a third dark sedan rolled up. A man got out and spoke with the officer and then they both proceeded toward the front of the house.

She looked at the time. When her cell phone rang, it frightened her out of her mind. It was about as subtle as a foghorn in the living room. Sam sounded weary and beat-up.

She listened, casting about for a place to hide.

Sam had mentioned he had papers but no time to talk.

Curiosity burned in her, but she had to find a way to stay alive first.

She switched her cell phone to silent, then quickly looked around for a place to hide before the men started searching behind the house. There was a back door and a flagstone patio. On the patio were two tricycles, a bike, a ball, a bat, some large trucks. The trees were too far distant and there were no bushes that would afford a decent hiding place. She tried the back door and, quite unbelievably, it opened.

By her watch it was 8:32 P.M. Sam needed her now and she was still a long way from flying Ben's plane—even assuming it would fly at all.

All Sam heard was an excited yelp, but he knew it was the dog crossing fresh man scent. That was an amazingly fast response. At about the same moment Sam found a narrow trail through the forest. Because the dog was near, he changed strategy to gain speed. Pulling out his small light, he began walking as fast as his stiffened knee would allow. With any luck this would be the right kind of trail. It wound through salal, huckleberry, some madronas in the understory, and

Douglas fir in the crown. Then it led to the jackpot he was looking for—a fishing spot on the water where people warmed themselves by a large campfire. Or maybe it was teenagers communing in the dark, listening to the gentle lap of the inland sea. Whatever the reason, there were plenty of charred sticks here.

Picking up a good-size stick, with a well-blackened end, he ran it all over his body from the waist down, covering his clothes and skin with the charcoal. Then he walked to the water's edge, backtracked, and ran up the trail for twenty paces before he turned around and ran back to the fire pit. Finally he moved away from the trail, plunging through the brush so that he would not come nose to nose with an aggressive dog. Fortunately, he had gone only about one hundred yards before coming to another trail and a few hundred more yards down the new trail to another small clearing. Again he heard the dog, dangerously close. Apparently the animal was casting about, making an S-shaped search pattern through the woods. The charcoal seemed to have him confused.

They passed each other with only about a fifty-yard gap.

Dogs' noses were so sensitive that they could on occasion distinguish between fires if the combusted wood was of differing species. Sam wanted to smell like every campfire along the edge of the forest, but that wouldn't be possible. He may have found the only one, and even if he hadn't, finding another in the dark was unlikely.

From the clearing he went off into the woods, paralleling the salt water for a couple hundred yards, then dropped down to the steep rocky bank at the water's edge. Hidden behind a badly placed cloud, there was no moon on the darkened wind-ruffled surface and the steep slippery rocks looked ominous. With his bad legs they would be a nightmare.

Without thinking more about the suffering to come, he hobbled down to the water and tried not to scream as the salt water burned into the many cuts and abrasions on his lower leg. He entered the water halfway up to his knees and walked along the rocks, working desperately to keep his already tentative footing. The rocks were uneven and at times he stepped to thigh-deep bone-chilling water when he least expected that result. Salt water on his raw flesh was a new form of hell. But he would use the water to mask the scent of his footsteps, leaving the dog with nothing more than the fire smell at the beach.

He exited the water around the northern side of a blunt-shaped point and stayed very near the steep rock slope that was the beach so as not to spread any scent in the forest. Eventually they would try walking with the dog along the entire beach. By that time Sam needed to be gone.

Surprised, he found a lone house accessed by what looked to be a small private drive. It was set in the forest near the point with a good view of the water. Only one light shone inside, no car was in the driveway. It was an isolated spot. Quickly he checked the garage. No car. He decided to chance staying a few minutes. He was only a little bit amazed when he found the door unlocked. It was probably on university property; here people were casual about locking doors and the like.

It was blessedly warm inside. Sam was still shaking from the cold. He needed to wait for Haley and the plane—at the same time an isolated home was an obvious place to search. He would thumb through the papers.

With shaking hands, he pulled out the note he had taken from Ben's pocket. On it was scribbled: *SJ: Please remind Lattimer to take groceries to Orcas.* That seemed to be the original note; on the back was written: *Haley and Sarah meet Nelson 12:00 A.M. Sunday at M Chef.* Then there was a phone number, perhaps for Nelson. Finally came the notation: *Flowers Sarah*, and a phone number.

Puzzling, he thought. Gibbons to take groceries to Orcas. Ben had no place at Orcas. Or did he?

The other was obviously a reminder note of a meeting with Nelson Gempshorn on a Sunday. But why both Sarah and Haley? Very strange. Haley said nothing about Sarah attending any meeting with Nelson, so perhaps this was a future meeting. *Today?* Sam was anxious to get Haley's take on the note. He decided to wait to call her, and instead to look at the documents he'd taken, then leave.

He hurried. The first volume's content was obvious and shocking. They were calculating the volume of methane hydrates and trapped methane gas beneath a given area of ocean floor and the small temperature changes required to release about half the methane on the planet. Mostly natural causes. One author argued that placement of a nuclear device in the right deep-sea trench would trigger the methane release; that, in turn, would trigger a landslide that would cause a devastating tsunami.

Sam started to see that portions of this volume had been written for laymen, perhaps policy makers, and that was an interesting new wrinkle. In plain English they described how a chain release of methane might start in the Arctic.

Volume two, the Nobeltec bathyscaphic charts, depicted the seafloor off Cape Hatteras, on the eastern seaboard. Apparently the Arcs had been busy off Cape Hatteras; pockmarks and fissures were opening up off the cape, a clear indication of escaping methane.

According to Ben's notes, the most likely result of methane release would be massive underwater landslides, resulting giant tsunamis and catastrophic global warming, methane being a greenhouse gas. Other authors had postulated massive conflagrations in the atmosphere or simple asphyxiation near the coast.

Sam skimmed, always thinking about a hasty exit.

Hurriedly he looked for the fountain of youth. It was all

too complicated. They were searching for some gene. Stranger yet was a notation penned in Ben's hand: *The answer may be found in the Sargasso stew.*

What the heck was that? He had to go. There was much more and it looked the most interesting—more fountain of youth–stuff. Human mitochondria.

The aging stuff fascinated Sam. He was tired of thinking about global catastrophes and the end of the world. He wondered, though, how much of this Ben had already shared with the U.S. government. Any of it? Sam would have Ernie look into the matter. Anything that could become a new terrorist recipe would invoke federal jurisdiction over the entire matter. Probably a long shot.

In his excitement over all the new aging material, Sam decided to call Haley.

She answered, clearly out of breath. Quickly he explained what he had found.

"I couldn't tell, but I thought he might be saying there was some important similarity between Arcs and humans. Maybe in the mitochondria."

"That has me curious as hell," Haley said. Sam caught a set of headlights coming through the trees. Without a word he stepped out the back door and plunged into the pitch-black forest.

CHAPTER 26

Haley slipped inside the house, spooked out of her mind, sure that at any second the owner would materialize with a gun. Her body wanted to sweat despite the shivering cold of wet clothes and she caught herself breathing as if in a race.

"We haven't seen anybody," the lady of the house was saying to Frick's men.

The back door entered into a small vestibule, then into the kitchen. She could see through to the front door.

The man of the house stood with the woman.

"Is she dangerous?" he asked.

"She was with the guy who killed Crew Wentworth," said the officer. "She escaped with the killer. It would pay to be really careful."

"Should we evacuate the house?"

"I doubt that's necessary, ma'am. We'll be checking every inch around here. Keep your doors locked. Someone else thought they might have seen her just down the way, but she's probably not going to crash through a window. She's running."

Then Frick's men were asking about the neighborhood

and who was away for the holidays and how they might get in the neighboring houses. Haley checked her watch and nearly choked. The goal was for her to pick Sam up in thirty minutes and she was stuck in a genteel country house. She resisted panic and the urge to run out the back. It would be suicide until Frick's men were finished with their search.

Quickly she glanced around and noticed two small wooden-slatted doors off the kitchen, probably a small pantry. There was another cubbyhole with a computer, where someone had been working. She had to move or be discovered. Haley proceeded from the vestibule into the kitchen. On the far side of a large counter was a spacious family room done in green leather and fabrics echoing forest themes. No place to hide there.

"Are the neighbors just through the trees there at home?" the officer asked the couple.

"No, they aren't," the husband said. "They went to the sunshine for the holidays."

"We need to get in."

"How about if we give you the key and you bring it back?" the wife offered.

Haley tried the small slatted doors.

Sure enough, it was a tiny pantry, just large enough to hold her and her bag of clothes. The doors had an external latch, so she had to leave them slightly ajar.

The officers left, and Haley heard someone come back down the hall. She peeked to find the woman heading for the computer. Her heart sank. It seemed "Mr. and Mrs. Gentleman Farmer" were going to hang around the kitchen.

"I'm tired," the man said. He was tall and slender, sandy-haired, square-jawed, and had a confident face.

Haley did a double take. The man had caught up with the woman before she reached the computer. Now it seemed as if he were rubbing her backside with his pelvis.

Haley watched, looking for any advantage or opportunity

this bit of romance might offer. The woman, trim and blond, wore an elegant, pale green dress with a judicious application of makeup. Perhaps she'd had something in mind at the start of the evening.

"You're a voyeur, dear," she said.

"What do you mean?" He kept hugging her from behind.

"You were watching me in the shower."

Ugh. Haley wished they would take their growing passion to bed.

"I love you. . . ." Then the man whispered something more.

Haley imagined it was dark and sexy. Then he began planting little kisses on her neck. Maybe he did have some understanding of females. Then he started gently rubbing her shoulder. Prince Charming was obviously working hard at it.

Haley cursed her bad luck.

"Why can't you do this when you haven't been spying on me?" the woman asked, giggling as he kissed her ears.

"I was hardly spying." He tried a kiss on the lips.

Time was crawling. It occurred to Haley that she was carrying her dry clothes. It was risky to change now, but the clammy clothes were making her shiver. Carefully, Haley began undressing. It took less than two minutes, every second more nerve-racking than the last. As fast as she could, she pulled on the dry clothes. She was desperate to leave and get to Sam.

She heard faint rustling sounds.

"Maybe we should wait until bed," Mrs. Gentleman Farmer said. But the woman didn't really sound at all interested in waiting.

Haley glanced back through the crack, unable to deny herself the next installment.

"I guess not." The woman answered her own question.

Haley bit her lip to keep from laughing.

Now they were French-kissing and the man had his wife's

dress unbuttoned. As the soft light played over their bodies, Haley felt the red moving up her neck. For just a second she watched them delving into tender intimacy. When she closed her eyes, images came back to her from thirteen years previous. She was nineteen. It was the Fourth of July. On each day of his three-day visit, she and Sam went to a dock off Brown Island, a friend's pier. They would lie in the sun and talk for hours, and watch the water—the sleek grace of the sailboats, the noisy grind of the powerboats. On the third and final day of his visit, Sam covered her back with suntan lotion. His light touch had given her pleasure. She hadn't known what to think or do, but he was reaching much more than her body.

From his fingers came a longing, almost more than she could bear. Haley recalled his whispers and his promise and the pain of it all. He said he would love her forever. Sam was not a man of idle words. Then came the days of waiting. She switched channels and was back in the closet.

More movements of a chair and the sound of the man's zipper. Heavy fabric hit the floor. His jeans.

"I love you," he whispered over and over.

"You are so good," she said. "So damn good."

It wasn't an original thought, but Haley could tell that Mrs. Gentleman Farmer meant every word. Through some slight miscalculation of her peripheral vision, Haley saw what was happening and made herself look away.

The last time Haley had spied on someone, she'd been watching Sam. They were adults then. It had happened nine months ago, not long after his return to San Juan Island to convalesce. Sam was on a weight bench, his enormous chest expanded, sweat covering his body, his breathing rough, like an old train.

Sam's face looked more intense than Haley had ever seen it. Here, apparently, he let the demon out of him, in the sweat and in the great blasts of air. Fighting the iron, he showed no good manners or signs of culture, he wore no disguise to keep the guttural aspects of the mind from rising to the countenance. At the weight bench Sam was something different.

Back in the closet Haley caught a glimpse of the woman's head flung back as she sat astride the man, her body and soul seemingly in perfect harmony with his. Haley put her fingers in her ears to stop the sounds of their lovemaking.

In her mind Sam's body gleamed, his long, flowing hair tousled. The sweat sheen traced the exquisite contours of muscle and sinew free of fat. He had the proportionality of a ripped gymnast. All her senses had been captive to the image of Sam: the steady rhythm of his breath, the deep groans near the finish, the quivering of muscle as he forced the weights, his arms like spring steel, his chest a beautiful smooth landscape of powerful curves, and the lower abdomen rippled like the rolling tan sands of the Sahara.

Haley removed her fingers from her ears for a moment. From the resonance in Mrs. Gentleman Farmer's voice, she seemed to be in the homestretch. Their rhythm could be heard in the squeaks of the chair.

Sam was laboring under the weights. As she had watched him, something beyond the heat of the sexual wanting, mixed with nervous caution, had stirred inside Haley. It felt like some sort of spiritual event. Nothing massive, nothing like a rebirth or revelation, no burst of hope like spring flowers. It felt subtle and growing, a conviction, at one of the worst periods in her life, that things would start over for her.

The research-theft scandal had been in full bloom. Days before Haley had received a letter so terrible that it had sent her after Sam, desperate that he'd talk to her, reassure her. The letter had come from her dearest college friend and roommate, but it had a cold, distant tone and none of the warmth of their many months together. The worst part was the final line:

For whatever reason, you have chosen to betray a fellow scientist. You disdain academic pursuit. I'm afraid there is no place here for you at the present time. I don't know how, but there must be a way to redeem yourself. For the moment I cannot recommend you to the director.

Her "friend" had signed it, *Trying to understand.*

The letter had shaken her badly. Ben was in Seattle, with no way for her to contact him. For a few moments she had been utterly despondent, but then, as was usually the case with Haley, her sorrow had turned to determination. It was the determination she'd learned as a child, to keep going, keep fighting the curse of her mother's heritage.

On this day she had been in such need of an ear to help keep her from a pit of depression that when she couldn't find Ben, she had gone to find Sam.

Haley had not been with a man in a year. Her mind still swirled with Sam on the weight bench. She opened her eyes and unplugged her ears and saw that her unwitting hosts were moving around. What if they came to the pantry? Now her heart thudded for a different reason. She opened her eyes as the woman stepped into her dress. Standing behind her, naked, her husband wrapped her in his arms as the dress remained draped around her waist. Her mostly nude body was enfolded in his, together a symphony of contours rolling the light.

Dear God, no. Why couldn't they be a typical, bored married couple? For a few moments Mr. Gentleman Farmer looked like he might be interested in a rematch.

"I've got to do the books, honey. Really. If you need more, it's in bed tonight," she said.

Thank God, Haley thought.

But hubby didn't give up, kissing her neck, running his

hands over her bottom. Slowly she started to become pliable
and the woman's resolve melted. The dress dropped to the
floor.

Didn't they realize this was Friday Harbor? Not Paris.
Not Hawaii.

Haley closed her eyes and returned to Sam. As she spied
on him through the crack at the door hinges, she marveled at
the expressions on his face. One of those expressions was
most important. It was not the look as he lifted the weights—
the look she found so sexy that it made her grind her legs together—she would never tell anyone that—it was the look of
Sam at rest.

Sam had a spotter in the room—after all, the weights were
on the order of three hundred pounds, and you didn't lift
weights like that without a partner. It was amazing that a
man with a bad back could bench-press that kind of weight.
The spotter was Jeffrey, Haley's cousin, who worked at the
small gym. When Sam rested, he would sit up on the bench
and Jeffrey would sit beside him, unconsciously mimicking
him.

Sitting there, they looked like two old friends—except
that one of them had the mind of a ten-year-old. There was
nothing about it that was extraordinary except the attention
that Sam gave Jeffrey. To watch from afar, you'd think that
everything Jeffrey said somehow fascinated Sam. Perhaps it
was guile or perhaps in some strange way Sam was able to
remain interested in mundane stories about the tourists, or in
the latest tale about the barber's new chair.

Something about Sam's interest in Jeffrey turned Haley
on even more than the sweat and muscle and the body.

Jeffrey did most of the talking. He wanted to know how
to do certain things with the weights. Haley watched as Sam
explained and invited Jeffrey to give it a try. She found it difficult to put what she witnessed into words. It wasn't enough
to say that Sam was a nice guy or that he cared about other

people. There was a sweetness to this mysterious, wounded man that caught hold of her, that seemed at odds with the great caution that she felt.

There came a moment that day where her shame at spying and her caution about Sam overcame her desire to talk and she quietly left with all her questions still inside her. Safely inside the car, with the motor running, she thought she felt something in her besides her own anger at the Sanker injustice. It was dim, intermittent, and gasping to survive. It lived under the load of stark despair, but it seemed to her like a tiny ember in the dark of the night.

It was hope. At that moment back in February, and only for an instant, she had thought Sam might be worth another try. The thought left as quickly as it had come.

Haley glanced at her unwitting hosts again. She was running out of time. The police must have completed their search. It was now or never. Unbelievably, Mr. and Mrs. Gentleman Farmer were in full swing, starting over. They were in a deep clench. Apparently not everyone was bored with marriage.

Haley slipped out from the pantry as the woman commenced a deep kiss. Three steps and she was at the back door, slowly pulling it open.

It creaked.

"Hey," the woman shouted.

"Oh, my God," said the husband.

Adrenaline shot through Haley. She stepped through the door and was out in the backyard, running with everything she had, watching desperately for the fence. Without thought she high jumped with her hand on a wooden post, the basic moves of her torso and legs left over from high-school track and field. Amazingly, she didn't rip her skin on the top strand of the barbed-wire fence. There was one cop car out on the road. Nobody behind her.

Fortunately, Frick's people had vanished. Unfortunately, they had probably moved toward the airport.

"How's the dog doing?" Frick asked the handler over the radio.

"He's running back and forth. I don't get it. In and out of a fire pit. Never seen anything like it. Darker than hell out here, except when the moon's out from behind a cloud."

"I hope it occurred to you that you're chasing a pro. He's making an ass of you and that dog. He's escaping."

"What should I do?"

"Don't try to follow a trail, just try to use the dog to intercept him along the beach and send cars along the roads in the nearby neighborhoods. Focus on intercepting him until you get a fresh scent."

"Roger that."

"The officers chasing after Haley Walther are calling," Delia announced.

Frick took the phone.

"Have you got her?" he asked.

"Not yet," his man answered.

"What's going on?"

"She was in a house. A couple was home. They didn't know she was there." He went on to explain.

"How long ago did she run?" Frick said.

"Five or ten minutes."

"Damn. She could go a long way," Frick said. "She's in decent shape. Figure a mile radius."

"Maybe the airport."

"Anderson's plane is down," Frick said. "Two men just checked it. Mechanic was there, but it's in pieces. Could be another plane, though, so scour the airport. We'll call in more men, cover the roads. There's a ton of houses in a two-mile circle."

"Roger. She can't have gone that far."

"Oh yeah? Just give her another ten minutes."

Frick knew that something needed to change.

He called McStott on the speaker phone.

"Anything new on your end?"

"Yeah, they found something of interest."

"Who they?" Frick said, annoyed at McStott's habit of starting in the middle of a thought.

"The men searching Lattimer Gibbons's house found some empty vials. The kind you would use for storing organics in a freezer," McStott said. "It looked like stuff we found in Ben's lab. We think he packages whatever he's making with glycerol. That way he can keep it very cold without freezing and he can take out small portions at a time and he doesn't have a thawing problem."

"What's inside these new vials?" asked Frick.

"We're working on that. Probably organics. But frankly there is no way we'll find out quick from a tiny bit of residue. In fact, we need more than a tiny bit. Assuming there *is* residue."

"Well, if you've got it, can't you figure out what it is?"

"Not necessarily," said McStott.

"Call me when you have something." He hung up, disgusted, knowing that at any cost he had to find Ben, Haley, or Sarah.

CHAPTER 27

Although it had floats and was a seaplane, the old aircraft also had wheels built into the floats and therefore could land at a conventional airport for maintenance. Soon Haley would find out if Grant Landon had managed to get it back together right under Frick's nose.

It had taken another twenty minutes of reckless travel in the open, dodging police patrols and goons, to make her way to somewhere around the middle of the airport on the wrong side. Although she had run when she could, the route had been circuitous. She was sopping wet again, covered in various forms of ground scum and mold, and felt filthy and miserable.

It didn't matter.

On this side of the airport, away from the entrances, she felt relatively safe. The place seemed abandoned, but she worried about someone watching the perimeter. Using the drive-through gates for private pilots would probably result in her capture—even assuming she could make it to that side of the runway. She ducked behind a tree and watched for a few minutes, until she realized there was no way she could get the reassurance she was looking for. And she was out of time.

Even if she gained access to the airport, she'd have to cover a lot of open space to get to the rows of hangars. Frick's people seemed already to have finished an initial search of the airport, leaving no men behind. That, at least, was a comfort.

She had an idea. She dialed the mechanic's cell.

"How the hell are you?" Grant greeted her.

"Fine. Just harried. Too much out in the open. Wrong side of the airport."

"Down from the fire station or up?"

"Down. Maybe two or three hundred yards. Don't know for sure how far." Since Haley didn't commonly crawl around near the airport at night, it was hard to recognize landmarks.

"Be right there."

Once, she and Ben had picked wild blackberries near the fire station. There was a chain-link fence with barbed wire atop and she didn't know how she might get through it. No doubt Grant would have a solution, probably in the form of wire cutters. She didn't have long to think about it. In moments Grant's pickup came rolling down the taxiway, then went onto the grass on a large bench below the main runway, right in front of God and anybody else looking. It scared her.

"Down farther," she told him on the cell. "That's good."

After he had killed the engine and gotten out of the truck, she ran out across the road. He carried a hefty pair of cutters and came quite a distance from the runway to the fence. It took sixty seconds or so for him to cut enough chain-link fence to let her through.

Grant wore a graying mustache and hair to match, and plenty of crow's-feet around his eyes. He had a sandpaper voice and a temper, she knew, although he rarely showed it with her.

"Probably violated a bunch of federal laws when I cut an airport fence," he said.

"I won't tell, if you don't."

They climbed in the pickup and drove back toward the hangar. They were very much in the open and she decided it would undoubtedly be proof of God's existence if no one stopped them.

"They came and took some parts," Grant said. "I can't make Ben's plane fly now."

"Oh man. That's bad."

"You can fly a Lake amphibian, can't you?"

"Are you kidding?" Haley said. "Landing those is a trick if you've never done it and I have always flown whatever Ben owned. It would be a miracle if I didn't submarine the nose or drag the tail in."

"Will I go to jail if I fly you someplace?"

"If they think I'm really a criminal, you might."

"You're no damn criminal," Grant said. "Did Sam shoot Crew?"

"No. He didn't shoot Crew," said Haley. "Frick did. Sam wouldn't shoot anybody, except in self-defense."

"You sure about that?"

"I'm sure. And I was there."

"This will help save Ben for sure?"

"And me. Yes," Haley replied.

"That's good enough for me. Where do we pick up Sam?"

"Caution Point."

"Oh, my God," the older man gasped. "At night? With this wind? At least you don't ask for much."

"Is it possible?"

"There's a little indentation, kind of a bay just this side of the point. We could try there, and if we don't make it, we'll probably be dead and we won't have to worry about it. I'm old. Maybe you better let me try it by myself."

"No way are you leaving me," Haley said. "I'd be greatly in your debt if you'd fly. I'm pretty sure I'd crash at night. But I'm going if you're going."

"All right," he said. And that was the end of it.

Haley felt more than a little guilty. "You don't have to do this, you know."

"I prefer to think I'm lucky enough to pull it off." Grant winked. "I've got my skunk tail in my back pocket and everything. Even my copper bracelet. 'Sides, I gotta live long enough to try some of Ben's invention."

That shocked Haley. "What do you mean?"

"You know I been helping Ben?"

"No. What have you been doing? I need to know."

"Well, it's highly confidential and Ben trusts me. I just figured—"

"That I knew?" First Sarah, now Grant. Who else? Haley wondered. "Not a word. Is there anything you *can* tell me?"

"Sometimes we fly people in and out to Orcas. The same people."

"How many people?"

"A lot of people."

"Ten, twenty?"

"More," Grant said. "But there's a dozen that they call project leaders. I see them the most often. But I don't know what they're doing, I swear."

She looked at him sharply.

"Well, I got the idea that it has to do with living a long time."

"What do you know, Grant?"

"There's this manifesto thing."

"A manifesto?"

"They whispered about it once," he said, "and I asked Ben, and he got all stern with me and told me to forget it forever. So I can truthfully say that I don't know where or what. Now I'd appreciate it if you'd leave me with a little self-respect and not ask me any more."

It just keeps growing.

* * *

Rachael sat on the bridge of the Coast Guard Marine Protector–Class, eighty-seven-foot coastal patrol boat called the *Orca*. It was stationed in Bellingham and next to her sat a disbelieving officer by the name of Lieutenant Lew Stutz. He was a lieutenant and apparently it was unusual to get someone of any officer-grade rank on a holiday night at the Bellingham Unit, but this boat had an officer-grade skipper. He had a bit of Kirk Douglas about him and the fresh-faced look of youth. Rachael guessed he had big ambitions, and screwing this up wouldn't help. Her father was a successful local businessman and Rachael well understood life's food chain.

They had tied her uncle's boat in Fidalgo Bay, and she had seen in the young officer the possibility of reaching someone who mattered in the federal government, an opportunity that might not otherwise exist on a holiday weekend in the small town of Anacortes. Using all her persuasive power, she had talked her way onto his boat for what she hoped would be a productive dialogue. Standard operating procedure would be to turn her over to police authorities at the dock, but she had forestalled that and had been talking and waiting for almost an hour.

"These men say you tried to run them down," Stutz said.

"They were following me," Rachael said. "They shot a flare pistol at me. I told you what I was doing. Doesn't it stand to reason someone might attempt to intercept me?"

An enlisted man came onto the bridge with a few papers and handed them to the officer. For at least a minute Stutz studied the papers.

"The one thing you have going for you," he finally said, "is that two of the three men have criminal records. The odds are a little slim that two ex-felons were going with a third man for a boat ride after dark on a fall evening. However, the state police are very clear that your friends over on San Juan are wanted in a murder investigation. They have eyewitnesses to the shooting of two deputy sheriffs. We have a boat theft. Resisting arrest. And the gruesome murder of one Detective Ranken. The list goes on."

"Garth Frick is not a regular deputy."

"You're right, he's a sergeant. And an ex-detective in the big city."

"He's a criminal," she said quickly. "He's the witness, and *he* did the shooting in any gruesome deaths."

"It's not that simple," said Stutz. "The undersheriff is in the hospital alive and he figures he was shot by this stranger who has a driver's license in the name of Robert Chase and calls himself Sam."

"I know the undersheriff and he's a good man," Rachael said. "But Frick's tricked him." She crossed her arms, knowing that she was signaling an end to her cooperation. Hopefully, this would convince him to listen. "I want to see a state police officer or someone from the attorney general's office."

"I'd advise that you get a lawyer."

"I have no time for a lawyer. My friends will be killed."

"By whom?"

"By Frick! You're not listening to what I'm saying. Look, read this." Rachael held out the FBI memo. "Call Special Agent Ernie Sanders."

"I already read it and tried the agent. It's the middle of the night back there and, not surprisingly, he doesn't answer." The lieutenant shook his head, obviously unsure of how he should proceed—probably because he was obviously intrigued by both her and her story. "It's not an arrest record. It's a report." Stutz paused as if thinking.

"Think about this," she said. "If I'm telling you anything like the truth, if the fountain of youth is real, if there *is* a conspiracy, it could be the biggest thing in your career. On the other hand, if I'm a nut or just wrong, it will only be mildly embarrassing and it certainly won't follow you in your file."

"You're saying the upside to believing you could be tremendous, whereas the downside isn't that bad."

Stutz sounded skeptical, but Rachael could tell the argument had hit home. This guy was a no-nonsense, get-ahead career officer.

"All right," he said. "I'll try to get someone from the state police. You'll have to wait here on the boat."

Sam was huddled down in the forest. He heard the dog breathing hard, trampling through the bushes covering more ground in a few minutes than a man could cover in an hour. Although the dog was moving away on his circle that would take him back to the water, on the next swing he would probably run right over him. There wasn't enough charcoal in the forest to block his scent if the dog came too near. Unfortunately, he didn't know what *too near* was.

The dog was concentrating on the portion of the forest that lay between the gravel road and the water. Sam had to move deeper into the forest to the far side of the gravel road, and that would make it difficult for him to respond to the plane. It was a tough choice. If she landed and tarried, these men would come with their guns and it would be all over for Haley unless she fled. If she did that, he would be trapped on foot. None of it seemed good.

When Sam hit the road, he resisted the temptation to run down it. It would be an easy place for Frick's men to lie in wait. Instead, he crossed the road quickly, seeing no one, and walked about fifty yards inland. Then, watching the stars, he did his best to parallel the road. It was rough going. He could see nothing and had to hold his hands out in front of him, guiding himself through the tree trunks. The ground occasionally had holes and rocks protruding from the surface. His body hurt in so many places that at times it seemed one whole leg and his back were an interlocking maze of stabbing pains, muscle knots, and aches.

Lying flat on his back undisturbed became his fantasy.

After checking the stars a dozen times and traveling for fifteen to twenty minutes, he turned back toward the water and came to the edge of the road. Far down around a bend he saw what he figured was the faint cast of a flashlight beam against the trees. He supposed the dog was in that vicinity, working back and forth between road and beach. Nearly dragging his stiff leg, he made it across the road and looked for the trail to the fire pit and found it. In the distance he heard the dog's handler calling the dog; then he heard a woof. Like scalding water on skin the realization came over his mind. The dog was coming closer. No sooner had he thought it, than the dog started whining and barking.

Uh-oh.

This was bad.

He had little time. First he picked up a stick and covered his knees to his shoes with charcoal as fast as he could. It took about thirty seconds. The dog was charging through the woods along the far side of the road, probably on his trail. It sounded as though he were casting about, trying to sift through all the charcoal. It would give Sam a couple minutes. What he was about to do would either save him or kill him. He found a piece of driftwood about the volume of four footballs. He could hide his head behind it; maybe it would help him float.

A large madrona tree stood just up from the rock line. It was nothing but a vague shadow. He felt for the base and, after turning the cell's ringer to silent, placed his phone, watch, and the papers in the bag under the duff right at the base of the tree. Then he found a big rock and put it atop, careful not to put too much weight on the cell phone.

With the first few steps the cold seawater lapped his ankles and immediately set them to aching. It was an ache powerful enough that he very much wanted to step out of the water and find relief. Even worse was the horrible burning from the cuts that he had encountered earlier. Although he tried moving quietly, the dog was coming ever closer, and with his stiff leg some splash was inevitable. It required only seconds to get to deep water. He was still far too close to land. Miserable from the cold boring into his body, probably cooling his vital organs, he winced at the sheer pain of it. He ducked underwater to take off his shoes. It took some fumbling.

The dog's yelps were frantic and the animal was due to break out of the forest.

Sam began swimming with one shoe on the stiff-legged foot and one off. With some effort he stuffed the one shoe into his belt so he could paddle. Placing one hand on the piece of wood, he used the remaining hand to sidestroke and his legs to create a crippled scissors kick. It was tough to swim at all with his sodden clothes. He tried to keep all movement beneath the surface. For some reason, the dog seemed to stop, perhaps running in tight circles, distracted by a scent. Then, after a short time, the dog started running again and soon burst out on the beach, barking. Hopefully, he wouldn't swim.

Sam paddled to keep afloat, knowing the cold would soon kill him. If he ended his life drowning in order not to kill a dog, maybe his decision would count for something, but it would be a dumb decision, nonetheless.

Now the dog was nearly hysterical in his barking. Sam swam into the night, slowly heading toward Shaw Island, knowing the swim was over a mile and that he would never make it. However far he swam from San Juan Island, he would have to swim back. So far that was about sixty yards and growing.

Men arrived on the beach and he guessed he was now probably eighty yards distant. He was too far from shore to see at night with an ordinary flashlight.

"Come on, Roamer."

Sam assumed that was the dog and thought it a good name.

"Maybe the guy went in the water," a second searcher said.

"If he did, he's dead now. That'll freeze your nuts in no time and your brain in just a few minutes longer. He can't survive."

"Not necessarily."

Oh yes, necessarily, thought Sam. *You try it.*

"Go ahead, Larry, jump in," said the dog handler. "Swim out there a quarter-mile and let me know if you see him."

"We could call for the boat," Larry said, chastened.

"Oh yeah. And leave the harbor unguarded on a dumb hunch. Come on, Roamer. Let's go look up here."

Sam hoped they didn't take the dog too near the madrona tree. Roamer would smell his personal items in an instant.

The dog barked and the man kept insisting. Finally the man with the water theory lost.

"Look at Roamer now. He's back in the damn fire pit. That guy's not in the water. See, he's back to circles again."

Sam was getting numb. A nap sounded good. *Just give up and sink and be done with it.* He thought about the *sigh* that *kills,* and about the microbes that live thousands of years and people who do not, and methane disasters and nuclear triggering. One certainly seemed to have nothing to do with the other. If Haley didn't arrive quickly, he might never know. Actually he might never know even if she did.

He went under and had to struggle to get another gasp of air. But there was no air. He took some big strokes and at last he broke the surface. If he died, he would miss the answer to the most incredible riddle of his life. They'd left the beach more confused than the dog. If it hadn't been for the stupidity of the handlers, the dog would have beat him. Now the ocean might beat him.

Sam began swimming toward the beach, thinking only that very few jobs were worth his life.

This one might be.

CHAPTER 28

The Lake amphibian 270 turbo was, in essence, a flying marine hull. Like larger amphibious aircraft, the entire body of the plane landed in the water. It had a single engine that sat up on a pylon on top of the plane. It would carry four people in relative comfort, land on the water or at an airport with equal facility, and was FAA certified.

Haley and Grant looked over the south end of the airport and saw only one deputy pulling through the gate near the fueling station.

"They were all over this place," Grant said, "but I think they've moved on to the houses. They don't know about this amphibian. It belongs to my brother and, to tell you the truth, I haven't flown it all that much."

"Uh-oh," Haley said. "How many water landings?"

"Unassisted?"

"What's that mean, 'unassisted'?"

"Without my brother touching the controls."

"Have you ever flown it alone?"

"No, but I've made unassisted landings," Grant said.

"How many?"

"Well, what difference does it make?" he said. "I'm here and we're going, unless *you* want to fly it."

"Let's just go."

"That's the spirit." Grant went one door down from the end of the hangar row immediately adjacent to the main passenger terminal and quickly unlocked the hangar door while Haley remained hidden inside his shop hangar. Once he had the doors open and the plane out, she ran out and jumped in.

Grant didn't bother with a preflight inspection.

Without hesitation he cranked up the engine, applied full power, and began a takeoff roll with no lights on.

"Can you see?" she asked.

"Not well," he muttered, and hit the lights. They illuminated the cop.

As if someone had jolted the deputy, he hit the gas, spun the tires, and pulled around as if considering whether to drive into them. But he was slightly off center to their left and, in a couple seconds, they would miss him by a few feet. Turning on all his lights and his siren, he waited like the lone bowling pin in the second frame.

"Damn it." Grant kept it at full throttle. They gained speed, aiming for a space between the hangars at the far southern end of the runway.

"You're not going to make it." Haley thought of the cop car, the tethered planes, the hangars, and the chain-link fence at the end of the taxiway.

"The hell I'm not."

They were passing through forty knots; they needed to hit sixty.

"You'll never clear the planes." She gripped her armrests. The cop wasn't moving, probably in love with his life.

"Hope he knows I can't stop," Grant mumbled.

Now it appeared the deputy was backing up. Grant eased back on the yoke, lifting the front wheel. The stall warning went off as their right wing shot over the cop's hood.

"Whew," he said. Then the plane staggered into the sky, missing the cop car and the planes by inches, but the hangar roof by quite a few feet.

Haley's stomach was upset, but she was alive.

Grant's legs were visibly shaking.

"Cop probably pissed his pants."

"I almost did," Haley said.

Immediately they turned over the harbor and were beyond it in seconds, dropping down to two hundred feet.

"Grant?" she shouted. "How did Ben keep this secret with so many people? And why did he keep it from me, when so many others knew?"

Grant glanced at her. She knew it was unwise to be firing questions at him now.

"Only one thing I can figure," he said. "Ben was protecting you."

"They have Sarah James at Lopez," Frick told Khan. "Finally. By Ben's beach house, as it happens. I'm gonna take care of it."

Khan looked dubious, as though he understood Frick's methods and suspected his pleasure in them. Frick didn't have time to be irritated. Khan was pointing.

"What the hell?" Frick looked out the conference room window and saw lights from an aircraft taking off from the airport. Running to the hallway past a bewildered special deputy, he grabbed an M4 from the corner. Out on the patio he started aiming at the plane, a mile distant, and coming in his direction.

Khan came out and stood beside him.

"You're gonna shoot down an airplane, right in front of Friday Harbor?" Khan asked.

"You're damn right. Get her; then get Chase."

"You don't want Haley Walther alive?"

"I want her, unless I can't have her," Frick said. "Then I want her dead. With that plane she gets away and probably beats us to Anderson's research."

Frick now had his finger on the trigger. The plane was approaching almost dead on. He waited.

"Uh, excuse me," McStott said apologetically from behind him. "We found something more."

Sam was kicking and swimming and thinking about whether there was any chance he would live. Fleetingly he decided that next time he might try a full nelson on the dog, temporarily putting it to sleep in lieu of swimming in the North Pacific in the late fall. His limbs were starting to become spastic and it was difficult to swim at all. His leg managed to hurt despite the growing numbness. Occasionally he reached down with his toe, trying to touch the bottom, but got nothing. As he realized that he couldn't swim much longer, that his body would just quit from the cold, he tried to guess how far it was to the beach. His mind was muddled; it wouldn't think right.

Stroke, stroke, stroke, he told himself. It was all he could think to do.

Somewhere he heard his cell phone beep, so he couldn't be too far from the shore. He'd thought he'd turned it to silent. Evidently under the profile "silent," he had inadvertently used a quiet beep for the designation silent. He had done that once before. Big mistake.

It quit beeping. He realized he no longer heard it because he was sinking. Dying in the ocean didn't seem so bad. One good deep breath and he would take in God's ocean.

In that second he realized that he desperately wanted to cleanse himself. It was a wish that lived at the core of his soul and it burned in him. He didn't know why. Probably one swallow of ocean water and ending it wouldn't accomplish his desire. Something about Haley came to mind. She was really not cut out for this.

He decided on a couple hard strokes. There was air and he was coughing, although it seemed like someone else was coughing. The liquid of the ocean felt heavy over him. He took a couple more strokes, or tried, and knew it was over. The arms would not work. Although he could think of the motion, it just didn't happen. It was not a matter of will. The nerves weren't functioning.

So sorry, Haley.

The old pictures in his mind—the torture room, the blood on the walls—taunted him—Anna's screaming worse than he could have imagined. He had to stop it. He had to stop it. The memories went and salt water washed across his face.

A strange thing happened. He touched bottom. Trying to stagger up and stand, he realized he was on a rock. Somehow he managed to flail his arms and take a step that was actually more like falling forward. On the uphill side of the rock, the clifflike slope began, and Sam found himself miraculously in water up to his shoulders. He flailed some more and tried a stepping movement and his legs seemed a little less spastic than his arms. Sudden hope brought determination and he flailed harder, spastic to be sure, yet moving toward higher ground.

Finally he found himself bent over in a strange sort of walking and paddling routine, now in waist-deep water. He fell repeatedly up the steep slope, thankful that the dog was far enough away not to notice.

His cell phone beeped quietly. Haley, he guessed. He fell on his face in knee-deep water and started crawling.

Then he heard the faint drone of an airplane and something inside him radiated brighter hope.

Haley.

He wanted to help her find Ben . . . solve the aging riddle . . . live out the rest of her life. To do that, he needed to discern Ben's plan. At the moment it was like a shredded blueprint. The parts were disjointed and still not quite discernible.

"Let's avoid the Sanker Foundation," Haley said.

"You're right." Grant turned, exposing the underbelly of the airplane as he sought to move away.

She heard a strange *thunk,* and then a much louder smack, accompanied by a very loud whistle. In front of Haley a hole in the windshield appeared. Then another in the side window.

"Oh God," Grant said. "I—"

Many bullets followed. Haley lost count. The only one that really mattered was the one that blew Grant's jaw off just as he was saying something about a leg wound.

Worse than vertigo, the wash of blood disoriented her. Panic set in, but Haley thought enough to switch off the lights.

Grant's body hung against hers, but she suppressed the panic. She let the body hang because she didn't want it leaning on the yoke. She told herself that she was experienced enough at flying Ben's float plane that she could land this one too. She turned her attention to the copilot's yoke and pedals.

Although terribly noisy, the plane seemed to fly fine. She checked the gauges and found nothing amiss. She looked out the window and flipped on a custom-installed ice light.

"Oh no." A fine spray leaked from the wing. One shot had ruptured a fuel tank. A sick feeling came over her and she realized the hopelessness of the situation. Grabbing her cell, she tried calling Sam. Nothing.

She had flown many planes and this wasn't that completely different—except when it came to landing on the water. The whole hull rode the ocean, not just pontoons. Grant had mentioned that waves up to eighteen inches were okay, according to published specifications. Pilots had actually landed in larger waves—she thought wind waves as high as two or three feet depending on how steep. However, even to land in eighteen-inch waves took skill she didn't have. Doing it at night was even more perilous, but Sam needed her. She would have to try to land close to shore, where the water was calmest.

She took a heading toward Point Caution. At 135 knots everything on the ground looked very close. The wind whistled horribly and it was cold, even with the heater pumping full blast.

She didn't want to imagine why Sam wasn't answering.

With her hands shaking in desperation she picked up the phone and tried again.

"Happy to see you." His words were slurred and he sounded bad.

She tried to talk but couldn't.

"Haley? Haley?"

"Grant's dead," she blurted, trying to hold it together.

"Tell me," he said.

"I'm sorry," she managed. "They shot Grant."

"Can you land?"

"I think so. I think so."

"Do your best," Sam said. "Get him off the stick."

"I did."

"I'm well back from Point Caution, toward the UW lab. Had to double back. I'm just beyond the tip of the main point, out of the harbor, where the rocks are steep."

"How will I see you?" she asked.

"I'll see you. Talk you down. Try to act like you're landing way out by Point Caution."

She banked steeply, putting down the flaps. On this airplane they were either up or down. That made it simple.

If only she had asked Grant more questions. Small planes had a lot of things in common, but the differences in this case could be critical. Flying over what she supposed was the landing spot, she could see next to nothing but the outline of the island. Now she made out lights along the beach.

She flew out over San Juan Channel, made two left turns, and lined up on a bay southerly of Point Caution. She slowed the plane down and swooped down to one hundred feet above sea level. According to the fuel gauge she had half a tank. Since she had started with three-quarters, the plane was losing fuel fast.

After she passed by the bay, she gave it power and raised the flaps, simulating a missed approach. Then she turned around and flew way out over Orcas and Jones Islands, turned and lined up once again for a second missed approach.

The stream of fuel coming from the wing continued unabated. Hopefully, she was drawing Frick's band of hunters overland to the vicinity of Point Caution.

She stayed low and held her speed at 120 knots, getting lined up for a controlled descent. Once she reached one hundred feet on the altimeter, she should have set up a descent rate of two hundred feet per minute with an appropriate pitch angle. For the final thirty seconds her eyes would be entirely on her instruments. There would be no looking outside. For that reason she carefully had to gauge the distance to any obstacles, and she had to think way ahead of the plane if she expected to come down anywhere near her target point.

Without a night flight–designed waterway, it was not an exercise for the faint of heart. At 600 feet over the northernmost end of Lopez Island, she had set up the descent. She eased off the power a bit, slowing from 120 knots, raised her nose, lowered the flaps, and watched the rate-of-descent indicator. Two hundred fifty feet per minute . . . too fast . . . 150 feet per minute . . . about right . . . 200 feet per minute, okay . . . ease off the power and trim the nose . . . airspeed 80 knots . . . rate of descent, 180 feet per minute . . . altitude

400 feet. . . . She could see Friday Harbor coming fast . . . 200 feet per minute rate of descent . . . bumpy . . . bumpy . . . hold it . . . altitude 200 feet. . . . She looked out . . . no anchor lights . . . ahead . . . altitude 100 feet . . . eyes locked in the cockpit. It felt like a spook ride at the fair, only much more frightening. She could not see the water or get a sense of it. She played with the stick gently, raising the nose trying to feel the cushion of air that would be compressed between plane and water. Everything was happening in milliseconds, thoughts faster than words. A lot of it was instinct, but it was instinct that had not been intended for this plane and its subtleties.

"I'm coming up on the point right over the water," she said into the cell phone wedged between jaw and shoulder. Her voice was tight. "Any anchor lights? Any anchor lights?"

"None. Fifty feet off the water. Come down, come down. You're too high," he said.

She eased off the power, trying again to feel for the water; she could see nothing.

"Come down, come down."

She lifted the nose.

Where is the damn water?

She was eating up the water and approaching the tip of land just around the corner from Friday Harbor.

"Get down," Sam shouted. "You're here."

She killed the power just before it seemed she would smash into the beach. The plane dropped and hit with a resounding smack, bouncing badly. Then it came back down and hit again. *Porpoising*. Up again, and down, slamming in nose first.

Disoriented and shaken, Haley found herself taxiing slowly with the engine at idle.

"Turn around, turn around," Sam said. She slammed her foot on the rudder.

Wham. The first shot came. She hit the throttle, bringing her in close to the beach.

The shots stopped. Probably the line of sight to Frick's men was impeded. Next would come shooters on the beach to finish them.

"Straight in, straight in."

She slammed her foot on the rudder, powering now right into the beach. She flipped on the landing lights, revealing a big rock. It was low tide.

"Dear God, please . . ." She cut the power and banged onto the rock. Then Sam was there, hobbling, looking terrible, barely able to walk, the water rising fast to his chest.

She opened the wing door.

"They shot him." It was like she had to say it all over again. Saying it once would not be enough.

"I'm sorry," Sam said.

With great effort he gently pulled Grant's limp body into the backseat area of the cabin. He returned to her and took her hands in his own, which trembled and felt freezing cold.

"We need to do the 'focus' thing again," he said. "We have to leave."

Any second there would be a lot more bullets, she realized.

"We're leaking gas."

Sam had no response.

She fired up the engine and used the rudder.

They had drifted out and away from the rock.

Wham, a bullet came. Then another. She looked down and her shirt was crimson. Maybe from a bullet. She couldn't tell.

"You're hit," she heard Sam say.

CHAPTER 29

The voice spoke quietly and had the sound of an obvious disguise. That told Ben that his interrogator was most likely someone he knew.

"Make it easy on yourself," his captor whispered.

"I'd like to take a piss. That would be a real treat, make it very easy on me."

"We're gonna put a wire up there and shoot you full of electricity. How would you like that?"

"First it was my guts in a bowl. Then you were going to do it to Sarah. But there's no Sarah, is there?"

"You're making me angry."

"You're making me bored. We both know that if you haven't done it by now, you're not going to do it. What are you, a government interrogator?"

"You're a smart-ass. But if you're so smart and I'm a dumb fed, then you know that we have agreements with other countries and that those countries lack our scruples."

"The senators and congressmen on Intelligence Oversight say that no such agreement exists."

"First, most of them don't know. Second, the ones who do

know are worried enough about terrorists hurting their friends, family, or constituents that they don't blow the whistle. Third, they want to get reelected. So nobody knows. You follow?"

"You're trying to tell me that the errand-boy orderly that wants to be a surgeon and talks like an Arab butcher is from one of those countries?"

"I'm not telling you anything. You're telling me."

"I gotta take a leak."

"If I let you relieve yourself, will you quit playing games and save yourself?"

"I could think a lot better with an empty bladder."

He could tell that lights were flipped on. Someone played with his manacles and unshackled him. Next he was led blindfolded up some concrete or stone stairs. He heard the sound of a door opening, and then came a new sound. An almost imperceptible mechanical sound, like a refrigerator's, followed by a truck barely audible in the distance. He was led another forty paces or so and into a bathroom. The man put his hand on a toilet and told him to sit to pee. Obviously hitting the bowl would be tough with a blindfold, so it was the only alternative.

As he began relieving himself, he moved the blindfold but did not dislodge it. Looking down at his feet, he could tell that he was in a very expensive bathroom. Marble floors and baseboards were accompanied by ornate wooden wainscoting of light blond bird's-eye maple. It was all he could see, but it was enough to know he must be in one of the most expensive homes on Orcas Island. His mind went to work trying to figure which home.

The man was gone only a minute. Ben finished urinating, pulled up his pants, and was walked back across what looked like a very expensive sandstone floor. They went down some stairs of rough-hewn stone through a very heavy door. He coughed and brought his manacled hands to his face and moved the blindfold up and turned in one motion. For just a second he saw the face of Nelson Gempshorn. A traitor, then, but working for whom? He swung both manacled hands as hard as he could and hit Gempshorn in the jaw hard enough to stagger him. Ben jumped back through the heavy door and closed it. He ripped off the blindfold and found himself in a beautiful entryway. Suddenly he understood the mysterious quiet. He'd been kept in a wine cellar deep in the ground.

Running down a long hall toward the end of the house, he saw a bedroom with a sweeping view of the water, and beyond that a sliding glass door that might lead to freedom. But before he reached the bedroom, the strong arm of Rossitter grabbed him around the waist. An instant later, Len was on him as well. He was done with this escape. Moments later, Nelson Gempshorn came down the hall. A rather large bruise forming on his cheek marred his usual silver-haired, dapper appearance. Although calm, he did appear frustrated and angry.

"You killed all the Arcs," Nelson snapped. "And destroyed all the paperwork."

If they hadn't been putting all manner of shackles on him, he would have knowingly scratched his chin. Things were just starting to become clear. Now they really would kill him when they were finished.

"Rachael Sullivan, this is Sergeant Hershman of the state police."

Lieutenant Stutz introduced her to a man in his late thirties with dark hair. Hershman struck her immediately as the quiet, brooding type.

"What can we do for you?" Hershman asked Stutz.

"You can step in and take over a murder investigation."

"I've heard a little," Hershman said. "Why don't you tell me the whole story."

After laying out the basics, Rachael plunged right into the fountain of youth–tale, even though she could sense mounting skepticism. When she had concluded, the young sergeant looked at his watch.

Not a good sign.

Hershman cleared his throat. "It's a lot easier to believe that your mysterious friend shot two officers in cold blood and stabbed another than to believe what you've been telling me."

"Wait a minute," Stutz said. "You should look at this FBI memo."

The sergeant read it.

"This is the kind of unsubstantiated rumor that ruins the careers of good men," said Hershman. "Classic FBI. It proves nothing."

Rachael took issue with that. "I admit it's not a criminal conviction, but it's hardly what I'd call gossip."

"Yeah, well, where's the agent who wrote it? According to you, the FBI knows all about this. So let them handle it." Hershman paused. "Lieutenant, could I talk to you?"

They adjourned to the officers' quarters, where she could hear all but the whispers. Rachael knew what he'd be saying. After a couple minutes their voices grew louder.

"I'm sorry you feel that way," Stutz said. "Who would be the ranking officer for the Seattle area on duty tonight?"

"For Seattle, I haven't the faintest idea. You'd call main base Seattle to find that out. Do you want me to do anything about Ms. Sullivan here?"

"That's all right. Thanks for coming over," said Stutz.

"I suggest you be careful what you do with her," Hershman said. "She may have been an accessory. This could blow up in your face. The safe thing to do would be to have me get on the phone with San Juan County and find out if there are charges against this woman."

"There's nothing out on her on the wire. All she's done is run her boat a little carelessly. I think it's a civil matter. The sheriff's taken the guys who were chasing her into custody."

"I hope you know what you're doing, Lieutenant."

"So do I, Sergeant. So do I."

Sam thought they still had a slim chance. Haley's arm was bleeding but unbroken.

"Probably metal. Not a bullet. Clean little cut," he shouted above the engine sound. They were heading directly away from the beach.

"Hurts like a bullet hole," she said, tears streaming down her cheeks.

Sam knew that it was the loss of Grant that really hurt.

Fuel still poured from the wings. With power, the engine sounds and the wind tore through the rips in the metal, along with the cold. It was like a deep freeze—the last thing Sam's body needed. Full-blast heat kept them from hypothermia. As they moved away from the point, the chop picked up. They couldn't use the calm water of the inner harbor, now made dangerous by Frick's gunfire.

"Forty," he said, calling out the airspeed.

In the plane's spotlights the whitecaps looked murderous. "Fifty," he said as they suffered a jarring crash.

The plane skipped and Haley played with the stick, then, *wham*, they hit a big wave and were tossed into the air. The airplane came back down and Sam braced for another impact.

"*Pleeeease*," she said, trying to hold it off the wave tops.

"Sixty."

Now they were experiencing the "water effect," feet above the sea, gaining speed.

"Seventy."

She sighed. They were up in the air.

"We nearly bought it," she said. Sam found no response necessary.

The plane climbed, the ride surprisingly smooth.

"Okay," she said. "What did you find?"

"Aside from Detective Ranken hanging upside down and dead, a lot. There's a note Ben wrote: 'A few evil men with the right idea could take us down.' Also, in a hidden room, a freezer with vials. Did you know about it?"

She shook her head.

"Six colors for six groups of tubes. All were full, but the red tubes. I found some kind of a log concerning dosage amounts, I think."

"Wow."

"Ben might have been giving the drug to people—thirty-six of them—though I could be wrong."

"Double wow," Haley said, wincing from renewed pain in her arm.

He summarized what he'd read. As he did so, he noticed that the fuel was down to an eighth and dropping fast.

Haley's eyes followed his. "The question's whether we run out of fuel first or the plane falls apart from the bullet holes."

The original plan had been to fly to Lopez and Ben's beach house. That seemed to be where Haley was taking them.

"We have enough to get there?"

At that, she actually smiled. "We're there."

"Have you ever flown one of these before?" Sam wasn't sure he wanted to know.

"That should have been obvious."

Without warning, they dropped like an elevator. He looked to Haley.

"There's no time to set up a controlled descent. I got one try at landing."

She manhandled the trim, dropped the flaps, and tried to hold a descent of two hundred feet a minute.

"This bay is small at these speeds. I'm gonna just try a visual."

They were passing lights from the first marina on Lopez. The dock lights reflected off the water and made it slightly easier to see the surface.

She turned on the landing light. The inky surface appeared slightly rippled, but distance remained difficult to estimate.

He watched the rate of descent.

"Three hundred feet per minute. We're coming down fast."

"Not compared to a crash," she said, her lips tight.

"Eighty knots," he called out, so she could keep her eyes outside. "Still three hundred feet per minute."

She gave it a little power but was in danger of overshooting.

"Two hundred feet per minute."

"Dear Jesus." She pulled off the power with the shore in her face.

It dropped.

The plane hit, skipped once, then hit a cushion of air. She eased back on the yoke and it settled down on the water.

"Not according to the book," she said, "but we're alive."

Once down, the amphibian drove like a speedboat, turning well at high speed. Haley brought them up to the resort dock and jumped out, her arm bleeding again slightly.

Sam struggled mightily to rise. His limbs hurt more than they had in the ocean, but he could control them better.

On the deck he saw no holes in the plane below the waterline. After some thought they agreed not to put Grant's body out on the dock.

Haley looked at Sam, her face troubled. "I know we've

got to get to Ben's, but first I need to get you warmed up and dry. I know where to do that."

He thought to argue, but his sopping jeans and shirt stuck to his skin and the wind whipped over them, refrigerating his body. He nodded.

The resort appeared nearly abandoned; he hoped she could quickly find someplace warm. Soon he would be incapacitated.

The main building housing the bar, the office, and the restaurant was long, low, and pastel. In late fall the festive-looking outdoor tables and umbrellas were gone. There were no bicycles in the bicycle racks, no badminton nets on the lawn, no canoes or kayaks on the grassy slopes near the beach. It seemed windswept and barren compared to the common jubilation of summer, and it matched the half-dead nature of Sam's own body.

They made it to the door and, thankfully, found it unlocked. Apparently the place was open, after all.

Haley disappeared into the office and returned with a key to a car and some blankets for him to sit on.

"Don't these people have television?" he asked. "Or are the cops on the way?"

"No television, no cops. The tube is in the bar and it's turned off."

"They figure you work in a butcher shop or what?"

Sam nodded at the blood-soaked sleeve of her shirt.

"We know these people. Relatives of Helen's. Our plane had a rough landing after we lost oil pressure. You're soaked. I'm wounded. That's the story. Let's just hope they don't look inside the plane."

"Where are we going?"

"Summer home for a UW faculty member with wealth from way back in his family," Haley said. "Friend of Ben's. Another scientist. The name is Williams. Ellis Williams."

She helped him through the building while they talked.

"This Williams hasn't cut his ties with you after the Sanker flap?" Sam asked.

"Of course, he has, but he doesn't remember—I'm hoping—that he told me where the key is, and I'm equally sure that he never thought I'd have the gall to use it without permission."

They climbed in a ten-year-old Chevy Blazer with leather interior and traces of mold. It had seen better days. She put down the blanket. "Belongs to one of the workers who's gone for the winter. They take turns driving it to keep it running. Tonight we're elected."

He had a spate of shaking from the cold that nearly amounted to a convulsion.

"They said the heat in this old Blazer works well."

"I hope so." He felt unbearably miserable. He forced his mind to work, to continue the conversation. It was difficult to focus on anything but the misery.

"I've got the important papers with me," he said through chattering teeth. "They're wet, but I think we can still use them."

He could feel the heating system start to work as Haley drove. It felt good.

"We may find more at the beach house. Grant told me Ben had used him to fly lots of people to Orcas. A bunch of people knew Ben was up to something big. Even Grant. He said there's some manifesto Ben worked up."

Sam's eyes widened at that.

"They had a big confab at the beach house. Now I see it in a whole new light. Oceanographers discussing the bottom of the sea. I think the papers related to that get-together are in the filing cabinets in the garage. We need to look there."

Sam nodded, still pondering the word *manifesto*.

"Of course, Ben never bothered to give me the slightest hint about any of this." Haley set her jaw in the familiar expression and shook her head.

"I know that hurts," Sam said.

"Wait, don't tell me—it was for my own protection." She shook her head again and kept driving. After a moment she said, "You know what?"

"What?"

"I'm sure now that the beach house meeting had to do with Ben's secrets."

"It means we definitely need to check the beach house." Sam was feeling almost human again with the powerful blast of the Blazer's heat. "So what did these 'few good men' talk about, then? The end of the world in a giant cloud of methane?"

"Something like that, I guess." She saw Sam's look and sighed. "Really, I'm trying not to be upset about Ben keeping me out of it. At least some things are making more sense."

"Do you know anything about a meeting with Nelson Gempshorn and Sarah James together on a Sunday? I found a note in Ben's pants at Sanker."

"Nelson Gempshorn and Sarah James together?"

"That's what the note said."

Haley shook her head. "Nope."

"You're sure. Not on a Sunday?"

"Not on any day."

Sam looked at her.

"Well, not with Sarah and not on Sunday. *I* met with Nelson Gempshorn. It was after that time when I found them with the IV. I didn't mention it expressly because they asked me to pretend the meeting never happened."

"So tell me what *did* happen."

"I feel so stupid now," she said. "I believed the whole thing was about cancer and Nelson wanting to hide it from his family. But he spent half the time telling me what a great man Ben was, in epic terms, as if he were Julius Caesar. I couldn't relate cancer to the epic 'historical figure' stuff. Now, of course, a different possibility is emerging. But still it tells us nothing concrete. That's another reason I didn't mention it."

"I think Ben planned for you and Sarah to meet with Nelson today."

"You're kidding."

He showed her the piece of paper while she was driving. "See the bit about the flowers?"

"That's no surprise. Sarah would be elated, because I don't think Ben's been that overt, but it's hard for the rest of us to miss."

"I have a hunch that had everything unfolded as planned, he would have had you and Sarah go away from here today," Sam said. "We just never got there."

Haley thought about that for a moment.

"I think somebody may be following," Sam said. "Headlights behind us. Douse your lights. Before the next intersection, take the corner hard left and ditch him."

Haley did as he said. They could see almost nothing without the headlights. She turned and found the road, but slowed because of the visibility problem.

Traveling past the intersection, the car following, not a marked police car, turned hard, lost control, and slid off into the forest edge.

"Take off," Sam said.

She turned on the headlights, accelerated, and followed the road to where it made a ninety-degree turn to the right, and then after one more intersection, rejoined Mud Bay Road.

"Not good," Sam said. "They probably have the license number."

"We'll be at the Williamses' place soon. I'm going to take the long way around because the shortest route brings us near Ben's."

It took only about ten minutes to find the private gravel

drive. Sam now had a steady blast of heat on his legs and torso that made it tough to leave.

As they exited the Blazer, lights came on overhead, from a motion detector, Sam assumed.

"That's not helpful," Sam said, hating the light and the signal it would give to anyone who might see the place from around the bay. It was unnerving and that, no doubt, was the purpose.

The Williams home sat on a flat nestled between a few trees to either side and overlooking the quiet bay. A quarter of a mile down the bay, Sam saw a trawler-design yacht riding at anchor. In the light of the full moon, he could see that she was a substantial little ship, maybe seventy feet long and probably a multimillion-dollar vessel.

"Do you know anything about that boat?" Sam asked.

"No. Maybe someone in for Thanksgiving?" She pointed inland. "There's a house up a bank there—you can see the lights behind a couple trees."

"We better hope they don't notice our lights and make phone calls."

"Those people keep to themselves; I doubt they'll be calling anyone."

The Williamses' two-story house had been well-designed and obviously built by a rich man. A lawn sloped toward the beach and above it grew well-groomed gardens fenced in to keep out the deer. A covered porch featured handmade balustrades; copper gutters that reflected gold in the night light. Houses such as this, on the waterfront, were either built long ago or recently by the wealthy.

They walked along the path from the parking area and intermittent shallow steps formed of rock. Haley went to a man-made garden pond, which had a ceramic frog in it. In the bottom of the frog was a key. They opened the door to exquisitely planned, early-American decor. Haley went straight to a thermostat and turned on the heat. Then she went out the back onto the covered porch.

"Hopefully, the caretaker won't come around for the few minutes we're here," she said when she came back in. "We are really in luck. He's left the hot tub on. Either that or the local teenagers have figured out a good thing."

"First get me some bandages to fix your arm. We need antiseptic," Sam observed.

"Fair enough."

She disappeared again.

Haley found a bathroom and switched on the light. As she did so, she realized that anyone near the house might have seen it come on. A momentary glance took in a frightened, bedraggled woman. Her hair was a mess and it got worse from there. She tried to rub some of the dirt from her face as best she could and then used warm water and soap to finish the job. She wished there were time for a shower.

Quickly she looked in the cupboard under the sink and came up with a large first-aid kit. She switched off the light and looked out over a back porch rimmed with forest.

She audibly gasped. Standing five feet from the window and to the side was a shape that looked like a man. She looked closer and in the moonlight saw him back into the shadow of the house.

She ran back to Sam.

"Someone's out back, just standing there."

Immediately Sam seemed to come to life. He slipped out the front door, still sopping wet. For a moment she stood there in shock, wondering if they should flee. Then, determined not to be left behind, she followed him around the front corner of the house. Before she arrived at the back, she heard struggling.

"Stop it!" It was a kid's voice. "Let go!"

Sam appeared, holding the hand of a teenager in some type of fighting hold where the boy's hand was scrunched to his side and behind.

"Tell the lady what you were doing."

"Going for a walk. Ouch!"

"You got one more chance to tell her what you were doing," Sam said. "If you don't, I'm taking you to the sheriff."

"I was looking in the window. I'm sorry."

"Go home," Sam said. "Think about whether you really want to be known as a lizard who sneaks around spying on women in the night. The neighborhood pervert."

Sam let him go and the kid disappeared like a wild trout from the hook.

"He came around the corner and ran right into me, otherwise I never would have caught him," Sam said. "Now we have to decide whether to stay here."

"I don't think he'll be bringing this up at home, but you never know." Haley shivered. "It's a chance I'm willing to take to get warm."

They walked back toward the front door.

"Let's get in the hot tub and then put a bandage on your arm," Sam said.

"I'm not getting in the hot tub."

"Then just let me do your bandage."

"We'll get you out of your wet clothes and in a blanket first," Haley said. "Then we do the bandage."

She was already undoing the buttons on his shirt.

She stripped off his clothes about as fast as a man could peel a banana and she used speed and efficiency to cover for her nervousness. When she got to his undershorts, she hesitated, gave him a towel, and decided she should turn her back. He groaned from the pain of moving as he got the underwear off and the towel on.

"What's bothering you? Surely not a naked man."

"Nothing is bothering me," she said with clipped certainty.

Sam was close and massive and she felt like she very much wanted to put her hands on his body. For her it was an uncommon urge. For a second she thought about just letting go and doing it. There was the matter between them. Some things could not be left to fester unresolved for over a decade.

CHAPTER 30

Sam was amused on an otherwise intense day. Haley, for all her brass, was obviously conservative in some matters. Wrapped in blankets and out of the wet clothes, he felt as though he might actually recover from the hypothermia. His clothes were in the dryer. They found a frozen ham, used the microwave, and ate it half-thawed.

"How many days have you had like this in your life?" she asked. "This is my first."

"I've had days like this. But this one's been exciting enough to suit me."

He watched her as she went through the first-aid kit, pulling out bandage materials.

Her hair came down to her jawline and curled at the ends just below it. There was a slight tautness to her face, so there was a subtle inward curve between her cheekbones and her jaw, making her cheekbones more prominent than soft. It was a strong face; the eyes, reminding him of Sarah, were blue-green and thoughtful; the smile when it came was engaging; her even white teeth gave it confidence. Her brows were neither heavy nor stiletto thin. At the moment she showed no sign of panic or desperation. Being busy with a purpose was a good antidote, he knew from experience.

He was drawn to her face and he knew that under other circumstances he could gaze at it for pleasure. Her arms, he noticed, were firm in the muscle but slender and shapely.

He turned and engaged her eyes and it brought a slight smile.

He tried to handle the bandages but still shook so bad she had to help him. With his knowledge and her hands they went to work. Experienced in emergency medicine, he directed the cleaning of the wound and the slathering on of antiseptic. By the time they reached the bandage stage, he was a little warmer and steady again and he helped her fashion an impressive structure of gauze and tape in just about two minutes. Fortunately, it was an inch-long clean cut that didn't go into the muscle.

Leaning against him with her arm around his waist, she helped him out on the patio and got him to the edge of the tub. They stopped. She ran her hands over his chest and then put her face against it.

"There was a time . . . ," she said, and stopped. Obviously she was displeased with herself for starting down the path.

He understood and in his own mind came to a dead-end wall. It was a large wall and would take some contemplation if he was to scale it. He climbed in the tub sans the blankets in order to get warm, but also to separate her from him.

"Why don't you find a suit and get in," he said.

She just smiled and held up her bandaged upper arm as though the answer to the question was obvious. And he supposed it was, but it had nothing to do with her arm.

"You could keep your arm out of the water."

She nodded but looked unconvinced. "With me friendly-fun hot tubbing is like a prelude at the symphony. You're about to tell me that sharing a tub is not even music. Probably that you don't even *do* music. I don't unpack the instrument if I'm not going to play. And frankly, I'm in a state. And so are you."

"I won't even take a quick look at the program." He made a show of closing his eyes, illustrating that she could enter the tub unobserved.

"I can't," she said.

And he knew she meant it. So he left it alone.

"Sometimes I get the impression that you've become like a priest," Haley said. "Consecrated. I do wish you would explain this consecration."

He could tell this was important to her. Perhaps if he had such a vow, it would make her feel a little less like her mother's daughter. Maybe there was a way for her to escape the shame that haunted her and still leave the memory of her mother with a mother's respect. He would think on it.

It was polite and appropriate that they were both ignoring his sizable erection. One could be consecrated in the heart, if not the body, and obviously that is what she meant.

It was a gutsy suggestion for her and one likely to get turned down. On the other hand, he supposed he could reconsider his decision to hold inside himself the pain and perhaps fear—yes, it was also fear—of the missing memory.

"Think about where I am in life, Sam," she added.

It was an odd remark, but he understood it. There was a lot of self-awareness in Haley. Emotionally she had been through the fire. She'd been stripped of her reputation and struggled with what was left of her dignity. The pain of her mother's humiliation lived inside her. If that weren't enough, everything she valued had been taken from her, except Ben— and now even Ben was threatened. And then there was the summer of '94, Sam's abrupt departure, and the long silence that followed. Probably years. He couldn't remember exactly how many. Haley would not have wanted to be angry when he came back, but Sam knew anger was a common escape from sorrow because anger wasn't as painful. Interestingly, she seemed to understand this about herself. It had happened with Sanker as well. If he honored Haley by telling her what had happened to him, maybe he helped her a little. Maybe he helped himself. If only he knew all of it. But he didn't know the most important part.

Sam had never told anyone, not even his mother, what had happened to Anna and him. He pondered for a few seconds and felt the stress of indecision. It was not a familiar mental state. Normally, he made his decisions crisply and without hesitation, a habit that had kept him alive. But this was not that kind of decision. It was too big and too personal an issue to resolve in the middle of this emergency.

"Relationships come out of good times and bad times. We're having the bad times. Let's get this over with and have some good. Then we can talk."

The disappointment in her eyes pained him.

"We can't stay more than just a few minutes," he added as if to explain. "We should look at the papers I took from Ben's, just in case there is more than one relevant section."

In the end neither her pain nor frustration made him change his mind. In part he decided to tell her because putting it out in front of another human being was a moral challenge. Partly it was because they had just faced death together, and still did face it.

"I was married to Anna Wade—"

"So the stories were true."

"The actress," he finished.

"She was murdered in a robbery."

"It wasn't a robbery. We hushed the torture part for her family. It's been part of my job in life to deceive the press, and we did that. We even deceived the police because they allowed themselves, on an official level, to be deceived. There was no one to prosecute. The assailants died. That's why you can't tell anyone."

"The magazines said it happened at home," Haley said.

"It didn't. We were caught by some very bad people. They wanted revenge and information. They were torturing her while I was required to watch. In the process of torturing her they began on me. It was much worse than if they were just torturing me.

"They were cutting their way up my legs. It was a woman who did the cutting; the man with the grudge watched. I remember Anna being tortured, but I can't remember the end. I do remember that when they were ready to castrate me, they made a mistake. They wanted me to participate in some manner that was . . . not important. They thought they had broken me and that I would do what they wanted. They said I could save my eyesight and they would let Anna live if she could, if I cooperated in their sick game. I didn't believe them. They were just crazy enough to take that chance with me.

"There were four of them, in all. Three men and a woman. Two of the men who were torturing Anna left the room. Anna was screaming, begging to die. The man and woman loosened one of my hands; they were going to make me participate. I know I surprised them, got my fingers into the woman's eyes. That's all I can remember. They found me wandering, semiconscious, I guess. Everyone was dead, with bullets in them, including Anna."

Sam sank a little deeper into the tub water.

"I must have gotten one of their guns and shot them. I tell myself now that I was saving us from the men, but I had to know it was a small, concrete room. Didn't I know Anna might get hit? Maybe I was willing to risk killing her to end her pain. She was pretty far gone already. Or maybe one of them shot her."

Haley had tears in her eyes, and so did Sam.

"Every night I tell myself that I wasn't trying to hit her," he said, "and every night I end the matter not knowing."

Haley put her hand on his.

"How did you escape?" she finally asked.

"We figured that it took me almost twenty-four hours to get my upper body free of the chains. Then I was able to reach one of the captors to find a key to the leg irons. I have a vivid memory re-created in my dreams of the bodies and the blood. I don't remember seeing Anna, although certainly I did see her body."

"Who *were* these people?"

"A man named Trotsky. He had been the right hand of a terrorist who killed people for money. I killed Trotsky. Gaudet, his boss the terrorist, is still in prison in France, where he can't be executed because they don't do the death penalty. He's really messed up physically after what some inmates did to him. There are some badass Muslim terrorists in that jail and he has a problem with them about some money he lost. Trotsky had a brother, who was a killer, and a crazy sister, who was even more vengeful than he was. Together they worked on getting me. I suspect Trotsky's brother took money from some others to kill me as well. The torture was for free."

"I am so sorry," Haley said. "I never could have imagined. I didn't mean to . . ."

Sam managed a smile. "It's okay."

"It's such a horrible story. Especially for your wife."

"It was much worse living it."

Sam felt a little relief, maybe not as much as he'd hoped. He knew that things now made more sense for Haley. It still did not explain the summer of '94 and the following months. He wasn't sure there was an explanation. There was only an excuse.

"Now you've got to get to work on those papers," he said.

While she began carefully sorting through the soggy papers, Sam let the heat soak into him; other than the immense pain of thawing out all the damaged muscle tissue, it felt good to get warm at last.

It had even felt good to tell someone.

"I'm tired of waiting to hear what the fountain of youth will do for me. And how it will do it and what it will cost me," Sam said. "Imagine the lines."

She looked up for just a moment and smiled, obviously getting his dry humor. Then she went back to her reading. He saw the reflection of her in the water. She seemed completely engrossed, observing everything and saying nothing for fear that she might miss some subtlety in the sopping wet papers.

A moment before he had been sure that *he* was the object of her interest. Now it was the papers. It was tough losing out like that, he thought, laughing inwardly at his whimsy.

"I'm really interested in this mitochondria stuff."

"You really don't have time to figure it out."

"I'm a scientist. I read this stuff faster."

"Tell me what you see."

"You know the mitochondria are these tiny little things in your cell, like metabolic furnaces, that burn the oxygen you breathe. Each cell has about five hundred of them and it's how you get your energy. All this health-supplement pap that you read about—antioxidants in the pills, in the wine, in the dark chocolate, in the whatever—is supposed to counter what these little bad boys do when they get old. These furnaces get rusty, to borrow a not inappropriate metaphor, and then they produce the escaped oxygen molecules called free radicals that oxidize your body, in particular your DNA. As you age, your DNA doesn't copy itself quite right because of the oxidation. Hence, everybody wants an antioxidant to stop the deterioration of the DNA."

"I got that."

"Eons ago, mitochondria were actually symbiotic, separate organisms living inside the larger cell of the host. So they've got their own DNA, even though they are inside the cells of our body, and each of our cells has its own human genome."

"So we've really got two sets of DNA. One that is ours and one that belongs to our mitochondria," Sam said.

"Yeah. And get this, Ben tantalizingly suggests in a note that human DNA and mitochondria DNA might have something in common:

> *"We have all read that Arcs are closer to us genetically than are bacteria. What if the Arcs and the mitochondrial DNA and the human genome have something in common?*
>
> *"You should know that human mitochondria use electrical transference and that they operate at about two hundred millivolts. We believe that mitochondria operating at one hundred fifty millivolts do not lose their oxygen-burning efficiency as rapidly. Therefore, they age much more slowly. They also produce fewer free radicals when operating at lower voltage. Therefore, the human that has mitochondria operating at one hundred fifty millivolts may suffer less DNA deterioration and live longer.*
>
> *"We believe that mice on low-calorie diets undergo a change in their mitochondria so that they run at lower voltage. We believe the same is true of mice that have their growth hormone genes suppressed at birth. We all know that these mice live longer than normal mice. Is this making sense? Think this through. I wish I were there to see the light go on behind your eyes. Regrettably, if you're reading this, my presence is obviously impossible. There is so much more."*

"That's pretty fascinating," Sam said.

"It is. The missing link for us now is the nature of the

connection between human mitochondrial DNA and Arc DNA. Arcs don't use oxygen. It would be poison to them, in fact. So one wonders how they could have anything to do with us."

"But they don't suffer the DNA deterioration that we do if they can reproduce themselves after thousands of years. And remember what we found in the other note that they had discovered an Arc gene they called Arc Two."

"You are so right," she said.

"I thought I saw something where they are looking for a gene and he thought the answer might be in the Sargasso stew," Sam said.

"What?" She shuffled through the papers. "Yes. Here it is. Apparently they are looking for a gene or, more correctly, a particular Arc with a certain gene. That's strange. They found one gene Arc Two, but are they looking for its source. How could that be? I don't get the Sargasso stew. I'll have to think about that. Something rings a bell, but I can't remember."

Rossitter had their Judas on the speakerphone. Sanker was listening for more than could be heard, hunched over his bar where the speakerphone was mounted. He normally used it to settle bets and the like, or check the stables before post time at the racetrack, especially on weekends. Sanker owned racehorses and had done rather well at them, like everything else that he undertook. This weekend's particular permutation of corporate life at Sanker was fast becoming a notable exception to his usual success.

"How do you know that Sarah James is in danger from Frick?" Rossitter asked.

There was a pause, as if the Judas were thinking over the answer.

Sanker's mind worked feverishly trying to imagine what

was at risk, whether they might even be taped by the authorities in some sort of sting operation. Not likely, but then again his sons would swear he was over at the stables at this very moment. Hanging it on Rossitter was a last resort, but necessary, in case of disaster.

"Giving you my sources of information," their Judas continued, "won't help me or you. So let's stick with the current events. I believe he has her. If Frick were to torture her, that means he'll have to kill her. Eventually. You see? I'm telling you that this result could be very bad for you. You need to act."

"It should be obvious to you that anyone associated with Sanker Corporation is not going to be kidnapping people," Sanker replied, "and if they were to commit such incomprehensible evil, they certainly are not going to tell us or anyone else about it. Men of this ilk don't go explaining their activities. On the other hand, your allegations are extraordinary, and if you have information, you should do the right thing with it. Tell the state or federal authorities."

"Get off this crap. You're not speaking into a microphone. It's a little late to get paranoid. You're in this too deep. You know there is no way to call the state and stop something that's happening at this very moment at an unknown location."

"We don't know what you're talking about," Rossitter insisted. "You're not telling us anything we can use."

"Well, you better figure it out if you want Ben Anderson's secrets after he's gone. You better get off your ass and stop Frick."

The Judas hung up.

"He's desperate," Sanker said. "This isn't good. He's more concerned about Sarah James than he is about getting us the secrets. I can hear it in his voice. Then again, maybe she is the key to the secret."

"Should we call Frick?"

"Certainly not," Sanker said. "The minute we get involved in the details, we're culpable. We'll just have to trust Frick to extract what we need." The old man thought for a minute. "You know, it may be much better for us if Frick denies any knowledge of her whereabouts. If he has her, he'll never admit it. Never. Without revealing it to Frick, put a private investigator of impeccable reputation on the phone with you and Frick—he'll be a witness to Frick's denial."

Haley worried that Sanker's men would be at Ben's beach house and she worried that Sam was in no shape to fight anybody or even run away. She optimistically argued to herself that maybe there wasn't a lot wrong other than his bad knee and hip and a multitude of cuts, scratches, and near-hypothermia. At times it seemed he could barely walk, and then when he had to move, he somehow managed to hobble along in a sort of spastic lope.

"We've got to get out of here," he said.

"I know, I know, but this is so pertinent."

She was flipping through pages with one ear out for Frick's men, concerned that at any moment they would come knocking at the door, but literally unable to stop reading. She had found some fairly analytic text and proceeded to a page that seemed out of place: *The gene holding the secret to the marvelous paradox between duplication and re-creation and how to control the benefits of each.*

"Here it is. He is talking about the fact that DNA needs to excel at both duplication and re-creation. The incredible beauty of DNA is that it is changeable in sexual reproduction and we make babies. What is more awesome than a baby? A mixing of two people—Nature at Her most creative."

"God at His most creative."

She smiled. The "he vs. she" joke was not lost on her.

"Anyway, this is profound, what he's saying. DNA's strength

in sexual reproduction is also its greatest weakness. It comes apart and changes. But when our body replaces old, worn-out cells, they're supposed to be exact duplicates. In duplication, DNA's changeability is a problem. The copies get blurred, like copies off a bad copy machine. I wonder if Ben's solved that problem somehow. He's hinting at it."

"We really need to go," Sam said. "I'm impressed, but we gotta go."

She took one last look through the papers while Sam gathered his semidry clothes and erased all possible traces of their presence from the Williamses' house.

"Here's another reference to Sargasso stew. I think he's talking about the Sargasso Sea, and I think I know what he means."

Sam had everything together and cleaned up. He was checking the windows for the arrival of any unwanted guests. Or hosts.

"Tell me, but let's get out of here soon."

"We looked at an article at the open-air mausoleum near the old Del Haro Hotel."

"The McMillan family ashes are in the marble seats in this shrine in the forest and old graves mark the path. Hard to forget," Sam said.

"Ben and I had walked there while we were waiting for more dinner guests at the McMillan House restaurant and Ben had gene-sequencing data to go over at dinner. They had used some of Venter's method with help from Venter's lab for analyzing octopuses' genome sequences. It got dark and we were sitting on the family's ashes in the marble seats around the marble table. Anyway, they pulled up on the computer this little article about Venter. Some kind of a voyage on his yacht."

Haley glanced at the computer on the desk in the nearby study.

"I wish I knew the password. We could search for it."

"You probably don't need to. Many home computers don't use a password," Sam said.

Sam turned it on and a password dialogue box came up.

"Oops." Sam fished around in the desk drawer and found the Windows install disk. He put the CD in the computer and then unplugged the computer. Immediately he plugged the computer back in and hit the escape key and F2 key simultaneously.

"What are you doing?"

"Getting into BIOS. We've been here this long, I guess we can gamble on a few more minutes and hope it doesn't kill us."

Another dialogue box came up asking for a password. In about one minute Sam had the back of the computer off and he pulled a pin disconnecting the jumper. Pushing the computer reset button put him into the BIOS. In BIOS configuration he directed the computer to look at the CD before it went to the hard drive, thereby changing the booting sequence.

"I've effectively told the computer to boot off the CD. Voilà. No password needed."

Sam installed the new system and used the new system to access the Internet.

"I'd love to know how you used this in your former life."

"Any computer tech could do this, no problem," Sam said. "It's nothing."

"So passwords are baloney."

"You could say that. Especially on home applications."

They found a number of articles. Then they found the one that discussed the Sargasso Sea:

> *Venter is a pioneer in gene sequencing first on the human genome, when he beat the federal government, and now in beginning to catalog the diversity of the seas. He's on a round-the-world voyage with a yacht*

equipped with gene-sequencing computers. To prove that human genes (some 25,000 of them in all) are a tiny minority among millions of other genes on the planet, Venter pulled up water samples from the Sargasso Sea. It was thought to be a relatively unproductive ocean. Using his advanced gene-searching techniques, Venter isolated 1.2 million genes from no more than a few buckets of seawater. He discovered 1,800 new microbes.

"See that's Sargasso stew. Venter's sequencing methods applied to a random mix," Haley said.

"Why specifically would that be of interest to Ben?"

"You saw something in all these papers about looking for a gene?"

"So I did."

"This is a way to look. Only maybe you look in deep-sea sediment. But I don't think we've figured out the Sargasso stew." Haley sighed. "Maybe the reference is to something else. We'd better go to the beach house. Maybe the rest of his files will tell us something."

CHAPTER 31

She put the papers back into Sam's bag. It was cloth, not designed for papers, and it tended to bend and mix the already damp documents. Thinking about the problem, she went into a study, found a big briefcase, stuffed them all inside, and crammed the lid down. It was a wooden briefcase. A little unusual, but it would work.

"I wonder about driving to Ben's," Sam said. "By now they may have heard about the Blazer and there are liable to be cops on the roads, roadblocks." He paused to let that sink in. "How else can we get to Ben's?"

She thought for a moment. "If we want to try hiking the forest at night, we can walk. It's about a mile through the forest along Aleck Bay. There's forest everywhere on the way, with houses intermixed, especially along the beach." Then she paused again, an idea having obviously crossed her mind. "I think there's a boat here we could use."

"We could hide the Blazer down the way from here and walk back," Sam said.

They walked through the living room, passed the table

where they had eaten a little ham, to the side of the house. Sam watched her smile when she led him right to the boat.

"They have a beautiful dory. We can put it in, row out of the bay, down the coast a bit, and around the point, down the beach, and we're there."

Sam had had enough time in the ocean for one night, but he agreed that the sea approach would be best. It was turning into an unusually calm night, if the present lack of wind was any indication. Earlier, the wind had been building from the southwest but now was calm out of the northwest, unusual for this time of year, so the sea in this area at the southern end of the islands might have calmed outside the bay. If it hadn't, this dory idea would not work.

The Williamses had a well-constructed steel track to get the dory to the beach. Once at the beach they would have to take the boat from its cradle and carry it.

They carefully turned off every light, leaving the place just as they had found it. They needed to get the Blazer well down the road and completely hidden. Haley drove.

They put a blanket between Sam and the wet seat. Haley imagined Sam's hand touching her, rubbing her back in reassurance. She groped for an excuse to touch him over the center console, but wouldn't allow herself.

He turned and looked at her. For a second she switched on the interior light, then turned it off. His eyes were amber and earnest, keeping with the rock-solid nature of him.

"You okay?" he asked.

"Fine." She started the truck.

Frick had ruined or threatened all she knew. Maybe she saw Sam as the human embodiment of desperately needed proof that she really was okay, even desirable. She wanted to believe there was more than that behind her feelings, but life at the moment was such a tumbled turmoil that she couldn't think clear thoughts, much less feel unadulterated emotions.

She still felt the great sense of caution, but now she wanted
to overcome it. Precisely because he seemed unreachable,
because he had gone away, because of the summer of '94,
because he had married Anna Wade, and even more important because her whole life had seemed designed to prove
that she was a born loser—Haley had been angry. Now, at
least, she could look at all that, even if she wasn't over it.
Maybe this thing with Sam was something so boring as having to prove herself, and in this condition, how could she
discern love from desperation? It was a question that she had
begun asking herself.

Abruptly she realized that she was perhaps, on top of
everything else, struggling with falling in love. People who
thought this way got soft in the head and interpreted every
little gesture as proving some great attribute in the beloved.
But history was intervening. Her emotions were twisting in
the wind.

Oh, my God, this is confusing.

Then her mind returned to the problem at hand. "These
people are gone for the entire winter, normally," she said.
"Can't quite think of their names." She pulled into a driveway, drove back past a shed, past the house, and on a narrow
grass strip drove behind a woodshed. They seemed to be
well hidden under a tree.

They were quiet for just a moment, and Sam was acutely
aware of her hand, of her body. He thought about taking her
hand, but didn't. They had to go. Without speaking, they each
hurriedly exited the Blazer. Walking in the dark and talking
were not mutually conducive. They forced themselves to jog
back to the house along the road. Fortunately, they saw no
cars and did not have to jump in the bushes.

The calm in the weather seemed to be holding. Sam was
grateful but still worried about the wind resuming a strong
southerly or blowing in a westerly direction in the midst of
their short voyage. He was acutely aware that they might

have to escape Ben's with papers and the wind could resume during their return and oppose them or create a serious beam sea. On their return they might be required to land on a different part of the shoreline. In places it was steep and hard to make the shore.

When they arrived back at the house, they went inside for a moment to reexamine a chart on the wall and raid the kitchen one more time. The unspoken truth was that they could end up back in the water, and if that happened, they would need great energy. They found a can of tuna and some frozen whole wheat bread.

"We gotta leave, but we have to eat," Sam said.

"I don't want to go back in that ocean," she said, reading his mind.

They waited for the microwave to thaw and ruin the bread, while struggling with impatience. Haley seemed energized, alert, and attentive, especially in her face, and that was strange for such a late hour and such dire circumstances. He imagined her in one of her hats, smiling on the dock, and then he studied her in the softer light and decided she was beautiful everywhere, all the time.

They yanked the bread from the microwave and found some mayonnaise.

Sam didn't usually like watching people eat, but not Haley. Next he knew he would be telling himself that she was unique among women and that there would never be another like her. Finally he would think her worthy of poetry and special gifts. Of course, he knew that this was the beginning of a strange chemical change in his brain that mankind had dubbed love. It could be fed or starved; he could come close or walk away. He had made promises to himself about these sorts of feelings.

There was a look in her eye, even in the soft light.

"We're in the middle of more than a bad tuna sandwich,"

he said. "It's crazy to even think about what we're thinking about. It needs a long talk and we don't have time for one."

"Yes. No one knows that better than I." Then she seemed to agree, or at least relent. They could talk about it later.

"How can we help Sarah?" she said. "I feel so helpless. We're just running around, not really doing anything to help her. It's frustrating."

"Find Ben and his secrets. It's the only reason they have to keep Sarah. Maybe we can feign a bargain. Aside from that, after Ben's we'll try calling her friends and see if she's shown up. We'll call Rachael and tell her to tell the state. But the odds of them letting her go before somebody finds Ben, or brings in the state, are very bad." Sam didn't tell Haley his belief that they would kill Sarah once she was no good to them.

"Why is Ben working on all these topics at once?" she asked. "That's the key question for me. I mean, he seems to give them all equal space and emphasis. This is not all about youth retention."

"You're absolutely right," Sam said, "and there's a reason why we can't put it together. We don't understand his motive."

"Let's get rowing," she said.

Frick drove to Sheriff's Boat 1 in Friday Harbor with Rafe Black. It was dark and swathed in winter quiet, the streets relatively deserted. A few residents scurried into the waterfront pub. There was no one in the marina parking lot, no one coming or going from the public showers at the head of the dock. They were headed to Fisherman's Bay at Lopez Island, and from there they would drive to Ben Anderson's beach house. After walking in silence down the wide main dock to the boat, they climbed in as the deputies cast off.

The big diesels purred, a marvel of mechanical achievement taken for granted like gravity.

They had Sarah James at Ben Anderson's Lopez place. Things were getting organized and starting to work at last.

Frick had a large leather bag in his lap containing his drugs and instruments: tools of his trade. Rafe Black drove.

"We were lucky to catch her so fast," Rafe said.

Frick didn't reply. He was debating how exactly he should squeeze her. He planned to use drugs, which he did not like because she would go off into a sort of stupor. Thinking about having her under his control was like the excitement that a hunter feels when he's very near his quarry, combined with another kind of feeling like a boy on his first date.

"I'd like to be there when you question her," Rafe said.

"Like the last time, when you lost Haley Walther? You and the others will remain outside the house while I question her. I'm in a hurry and I don't have time for games. So shut the hell up about turning this into entertainment. We've got to find Ben Anderson and get out of here before we end up on death row. You got that?"

Rafe sat surly and silent.

Speed in getting the information was everything. Frick ordered them to sail at maximum speed. He was in a hurry to get started on Sarah James.

Sam picked up the boat, which was stout and heavy, and he turned it upside down to put it on his back. When he looked like he would founder because of the bad leg, she got under and helped lift. Haley was strong for a slight woman.

It required great strength to move it to the water and it meant getting cold again. His limp was terrible and so was the pain, but with her help he managed to get it launched. Sam rowed with a steady rhythm, and the pull on his arms and the flex of his muscle was familiar and good. His bad legs only interfered slightly with the movements, and even in his terrible weariness he found the exercise oddly comforting.

As they rowed past the silent yacht he'd spotted before, he listened for the sound of the generator and heard none, which was a clear indication on a yacht this size that there was no one aboard.

He had set into a regular rhythm and knew that his mind could separate from the physical task at hand. He looked at Haley, wondering about her thoughts.

"Nervous stomach, before the battle?" he asked, remembering his own encounters with what amounted to war.

"Uh-huh," she said. There was an understanding between them. They had shared battle.

"A sip of Dewar's about now would really hit the spot," Sam said.

"You don't need Dewar's," she snapped.

The emotional intensity came out of nowhere. He thought about it in the ensuing silence.

"I'm sorry I went off like a cannon," she said.

"Nobody much needs a Dewar's," Sam said.

"Now you're trying to be polite."

"People fly off the handle. Usually a reason."

"My mother drank Dewar's."

"I see."

"Maybe this is just an excuse to talk about it. I don't know."

"I'm officially asking—if that helps."

"Just before she gave me to Ben and Helen, her sister was coming over. Really, it was an inspection. Mother was completely drunk after two o'clock every day at that stage. Gertrude, her sister, wanted to take me. She had boys. No girls. So I try to keep Mom sober, so Gertrude won't go to court. It was a struggle. I clean. I straighten the house out. I do all the old dirty dishes, throw out all the old garbage, haul a ton of bottles out back. I work very hard to make it look normal."

"I think I got the picture. You always were type A."

"She's coming at six. At five forty-five Mom gets the shakes really bad and throws up all over the living-room floor and all over herself. I stick her in the shower and go after the floor.

"At about five fifty-five my mother screams at me. I go in the bathroom. She wants her Dewar's. I went and got it, brought it in the bathroom, and at age nine I defy her and pour it down the toilet. She freaks and stumbles out of the shower. She runs through the house naked and gets another bottle, which she has hid, and starts chugging. About then, Gertrude shows up and she's got my cousin with her. He has a really big mouth. Next day it was all over school. My mother was standing naked in the living room, in the middle of a bunch of vomit, drinking. Everybody looked at me."

Even with the moon, the oars disappeared into water that looked like black silk. On Iceberg Point, the flashing red beacon offended the soft hues of the night while giving Sam a clear bearing by which to row. The water boiled around the boat and the silence made even the oar drips a noticeable part of the water symphony. On the hard pulls the bow dipped slightly, making its own regular *swish*.

"How did your mother get you to Ben?" Sam asked after a moment of peaceful silence.

"The next day I told my mother what happened. Told her the rumors that Aunt Gertrude was going to get a court order. She took me over to Ben and Helen's. She begged them. Helen had already taken care of me, and I think even then she loved me. Ben's love came later, but when it came, it was a torrent. My mother managed to stay sober just long enough for the court proceeding. I said I wanted to be with Ben and Helen and the judge agreed."

Sam let a minute pass.

"So I guess we could say that despite the alcoholism, at the moment you needed it most, your mother overcame the disease and was your champion to give you a good life."

"Funny I never looked at it that way."

"Might try it out for size."

They drove toward the south end of Lopez Island in borrowed automobiles that were being used to supplement the five squad cars in normal use. Frick and Rafe rode in a Yukon lent to the police by a resident anxious to help with the manhunt for the cop killer. Behind them in a borrowed Ford Taurus, which was actually a retired sheriff's vehicle loaned by one of the Lopez officers for this particular occasion, rode four of the Las Vegas men. These were the roughest of the rough.

Frick again looked through his leather satchel containing his tools and his drugs. He was figuring which drugs and how to administer them, hoping that just with the beginnings of physical torture, she would spill her guts and give him what he needed. Then perhaps he could trade her for Ben or his secrets or just go get what he needed. Time was wasting.

His cell phone rang. Irritated and in a hurry, he answered it. It was Nash. The surprise of the call immediately got his attention. This was not like Nash.

"We need to talk."

"Well, I am terribly occupied at the moment trying to solve your problem."

"I need you to go to a public phone and call me now."

"This is interfering with my job."

"I've got to insist unless you are at this moment rescuing Ben Anderson."

"All right." He hung up, seething. "Divert back to the nearest public telephone." He still might need Sanker's money.

* * *

Sam and Haley rowed past Aleck Bay and a small island that was a faint shadow in the night, headed just outside the flashing beacon. Without incident they came around Iceberg Point, the sea calm but for gentle rolling waves a foot or so high. At the point they saw only occasional lights from the residences nestled in the shoreline trees. They were in the homestretch to Ben's.

Frick stood at Fisherman's Bay, at a pay phone. Frustrated. Angry. He was just about to make progress and they insisted on a stupid-ass phone call. He couldn't imagine what could be so important.

"What do you want?" he snapped at Nash. "What is so damn important? Just when I was getting someplace."

"We have a hunch that Sarah James might know something."

"That would be no surprise. She's missing. If I find her, I'll let you know what she says."

"You don't know where she is then?"

"I have a good lead. What about it?" Frick countered.

"You'll tell us if you find her? Tell us what she says?"

"Well, of course. I'm working for you, aren't I? When I'm not chasing murderers. Is that all you wanted?"

"Yes. We want to be informed," Nash replied.

"Why in the hell are you all of a sudden so interested in Sarah James? I thought we were trying to find Ben Anderson."

"She's his assistant. She might know how to find him."

This was a complete waste of Frick's time. "I don't know where she is. All right?"

"Just checking. We want her safe."

"Don't ever call me again about nothing. Ever."

He slammed the phone down. But it was unnerving. They knew something. He wondered who told them and why. Something was amiss. He jumped in the car and drove at top speed. The whole call was strange, as if choreographed. He told himself that they wouldn't be stupid enough to work with the government. And he told himself that he would find out all about what Sarah James knew and didn't know.

He ordered them to drive fast.

Frick knew some would say that he was a psychopath. That was patently untrue. He had feelings of guilt and he overcame them through an act of the will. Pyschopaths were immune to the irritations of the conscience. Sometimes he'd get a case of nerves after a killing, but with Ativan pills it dissipated. Usually it didn't return even after the medication wore off.

Khan had remained at Friday Harbor in the conference room to manage things, but Frick thought the guy had a weak stomach. Rafe was up the road at Anderson's, no doubt frying in his own lust. Having any witnesses to the interrogation was out of the question. Frick would have to kill Sarah James, of course. South America was looking better and better.

After arriving at MacKaye Harbor Frick took a private drive to the Anderson family retreat. It was a large, old New England–style two-story home with blue-gray siding whose charm lay in the studied look of old and weathered. In fact, the seams and finish quality were nearly new. Once in the house he donned a black mask and a voice modulator. He knew that Rafe was trying hard not to give him a strange look. As instructed, Rafe went in the kitchen and sent the other men away. After they had gone, Frick walked straight in and found Sarah James sitting, handcuffed with her hands locked behind a straight-back chair. She looked grim but defiant, and her eyes shone with righteous anger.

Sarah James was gagged, but it scarcely muffled her scream.

It was as if she had peered into the bowels of hell. And indeed she perhaps saw hell in his eyes. Frick knew it was there to find. He would begin by tying her tighter than she had imagined possible. Then he would start with the drugs. And the rest.

They rowed hard down the rocky coast, and it was a sad surprise, though not unexpected, when Sam saw Ben's beach house lit up in the distance. They rowed silently past the house, which was located in the bite of a tiny cove. There were no other houses on this stretch of beach. When they spotted a good landing place, some one hundred yards past Ben's property, they hit the beach with only a whisper of an oar stroke and bumped aground in the fine gravel.

Above the high-tide line the foliage grew densely, as high as a man, between the house and its environs. After pulling the boat in the bushes, they crept slowly down the beach, listening and watching, much like nervous deer.

There was a covered porch, with white posts against the blue gray of the wooden siding. At night only the white of the posts was discernible. Windows were lit like one of those intensive paintings. It was a neatly kept, older two-story structure with three dormers on the second story. Looking through a back window beyond the covered porch, one could see into the kitchen. Sam could see someone in a chair in the middle of the room. A redhead. Sarah. They crept a little closer.

It was obvious that Sarah was somehow tied to the chair. No doubt there would be guards around.

"That's Sarah, isn't it?" Haley asked in a hushed voice.

"Yes, it is," Sam said. "Somehow we've got to get her out of there. If I crash through a window and someone is in there with a gun, they are liable to get me before I get Sarah. And even if I get them, there will be more. Sarah's trapped in a

chair. Getting her without one of us getting shot will probably be very tough."

"What are you gonna do?"

Sam considered the options.

"Oh, my God, Sam. Look."

A man with a weird-looking hood over his face was
putting a blindfold on Sarah.

"Damn," Sam muttered. "Makes it that much harder."

The hooded man approached her with what looked like a
line.

"What's he doing?" Haley asked.

"He's probably binding her. In itself, it inflicts pain."

"We've got to stop him. Look, he's starting with the line."

"I have an idea," Sam said.

"Do something," Haley begged.

Sam input the code to conceal the caller ID on any phone
receiving a call from his cell. He didn't know if it would
work with the sheriff or not.

"I need the name of the people where we left the Blazer,"
he said to Haley.

"I can't remember. Let me think. Let me think. Nisky, I
think. I think it's Nisky."

Sam dialed the sheriff's dispatcher on San Juan.

"You looking for Ben Anderson?" Sam asked the dispatcher.

"We sure are."

"I just saw him on Lopez. I've known him for twenty
years and there is no question. Tall. White hair, dressed like
a farmer. Southern end of the island on Mud Bay Road. End
of the road. Nisky is the name. He's at the Nisky house right
now. Came in a red Blazer. Parked it out in back by the
woodshed. Good luck." Sam hung up. If they could see his
number despite his turning off the caller ID, they would know
it was him and it would have only limited effect. Unless, per-

haps, they were so excited, they got careless. Still, they might know about the Blazer by now and that should intrigue them.

They watched through the window.

"Can't we do something?" Haley moaned. She was beside herself and he knew he would need to act soon or he wouldn't contain her. Frick kept wrapping the line.

"I can't stand this," Haley said. After a couple more wraps of the line, the man in Ben's kitchen went for his cell phone. "Stay here," Sam ordered in his biggest command voice. "Get down." She did as he said. Thank God.

Sam focused like a stalking cat, staying low, watching the man that stood over Sarah. The man was moving, looking impatient, and agitated. He dropped the end of the line. Then he left the room.

Then Sam noticed that Haley was down, but staying right behind him.

"I need to go in alone."

"No."

"You don't want to go in there," he said. "We're going back out and put you on the beach." He turned on her.

"Okay, we're wasting time. I'll go back," she said.

Frick stood in front of Ben Anderson's beach house, speaking on his cell phone in the deep shadows thrown by the moon.

"I can't believe someone just called in to tell us where Ben Anderson is."

"It's detailed," Khan said. "They told us exactly where and they told us he came in that Blazer from the resort. We know Chase and Haley Walther took that vehicle. There's really nobody good over there yet. You better take your guys and go."

"James is going to spill her guts. I was just about to inject her and the mere thought of the chemicals was disintegrating her will. I had the instruments laid out and she was going to become hysterical just looking at them. I can't stop now."

"You do what you want. I understood that what we're doin here is finding Ben Anderson. What does it matter if you can break his assistant."

"Damn it. The timing sucks," Frick said.

"This Nisky place isn't far at all. Down near those three bays."

"Did you give the address to the guys?"

"One of them knows right where it is."

"I'll go over there for two minutes. If it's another wild-goose chase, it's the asshole Chase all over again. Listen, if we jump every time he gives us a false trail, we'll never get anything done."

Frick hung up without giving him a chance to reply. Ripping off his hood, he called for two men out on the road, who were already apprised. "Stay away from that woman," he growled at Rafe Black. "I mean it." Then he realized that he should shoot her up with a pentathol cocktail. He hesitated, then jumped in the truck. He would be fast.

He leaned out the window. "You assholes be sure no one steals her. This could be a trap." They all nodded.

Frick's mind was sinking into a warm, sensuous place and he was enjoying a certain feeling that came over him when he was about to start a job. Odd that the feeling came even when things were going to hell.

Sam kept calm, the only alternative to reckless rage. He had to work fast. Whoever was doing this—no doubt Frick himself—would be back shortly. Sarah was crying, even before the binding had started. She had been cuffed tightly to the chair, feet and hands.

Quickly he unwound the rope, which had been unmercifully tight. There was a weird ball gag in her mouth and he removed that. Then he picked up the entire chair with Sarah in it and walked out the door, down the beach trail, and through the shrubs. Sarah was a svelte woman; so despite his physical limits, he was able to carry her. His pumping adrenaline gave him strength he didn't know he'd had. In fact, he felt no pain at all as he walked out onto the beach, with Haley somewhat amazed at the chair business.

"Be quiet," he said, once on the beach.

Sarah managed to calm herself, at last convincing herself that she was in the middle of a successful rescue.

She was more or less in possession of her faculties. Haley tried to cover her with more clothing, against the cold November air.

"We can't leave without getting those files," Sam said. "Coming back will be impossible. You row down the shore. If I can make it to the beach with files, I'll bring you into the beach. If not, I'll do the best I can."

"Check the garage. I'm thinking those files are in the filing cabinets in the garage. Go right out of the kitchen, into the hall, then into the garage," Haley said.

Sam hobbled back across the beach and into the kitchen, recklessly hoping that Frick would come back so that he could kill him on the spot—or die trying. Quickly he slipped into the garage and, using a penlight, found the cabinets. They were locked. Risking a lot, he flipped on the garage lights and observed metal storage cabinets standing along the wall. He turned the light off, went to the cabinets with a penlight, and began searching. The first had boots and rain gear, but the second had tools. He took out a small pry bar. Against the wall he found a pipe and fit it over the pry bar. With the added leverage he easily snapped the lock bars on the file cabinets.

Two entire file drawers dealt in one way or another with methane. Quickly he took a huge armload of files and ran out the garage's back door. Limping as best he could, he made his way to where Haley had rowed.

From behind he heard shouting at the house. Someone had discovered that Sarah was gone.

CHAPTER 32

Rachael and Lew Stutz sat in a small conference room in the downtown Seattle offices of the Washington State Police. Apparently on a holiday weekend, the best they could do was provide a lieutenant, John Glendale, a blond fellow who did not seem to smile easily. He was young, thirty-five at most, and appeared earnest and sincere. Lew, the coast guard lieutenant, sat in with them. "Do you have any firsthand information about the shootings?"

"No," she said. "But Haley Walther and Sam witnessed it. I trust them completely, and I'm here to ask you to believe these people through me."

"And you want me to accept that an ex–police officer in the employ of the Sanker Corporation is going around killing people for a fountain of youth–pharmaceutical?"

Rachael suspected that was a question best unanswered.

"I'm not trying to be harsh," Glendale said, "but I've got to marshal the cold facts." He turned to Lew. "She really roped you in, huh?" For the first time Glendale smiled at the coast guard officer.

"Right or wrong, I'm a baptized true believer," Lew said.

"Okay," Glendale said. "I'm going to start calling people. Starting with Special Agent Ernie Sanders."

"He's probably on a plane," Rachael said.

"I'll leave messages. I'll call his colleagues. I'll go up the line here and get my ass shot off. I'll even call over to the attorney general and see if there is anybody on call tonight. I'm in. We'll see where this takes us. But no way do I have authority yet to send anybody anywhere or to intervene, uninvited, in the county's case."

Rachael tried hard not to smile. It was more than she'd hoped for.

Frick drove back to Ben's beach house at sixty miles per hour. It had been instantly obvious that no one was around. Yes, the Blazer was there at the Nisky home, but was probably left hours before. They had broken into the house and one man was still poking around. Frick had seen enough after two minutes. Khan had swallowed the bait too easily.

As he ran into the beach house, he realized that he wasn't hearing anything. He pulled his gun, but was reckless in his anger. He forced himself to go more slowly.

In the kitchen the chair was gone and the line was on the floor. His instruments were just where he had laid them, the ball gag on the floor. He charged out onto the back porch, then again thought better of running to the beach and into a bullet. Stepping back inside, he started searching the house while he got on the radio.

"Get in here!" he screamed, not caring who heard him.

A quick run through the downstairs revealed nothing. It seemed unlikely that Sarah's rescuer would have stuck around. By the time he got to the back door, the three men had arrived.

"You"—he pointed at a burly, mustached man—"down

the beach, to the left, patrol back and forth. If you find any-one, you call, check in every five minutes. You, the same to the right. Howell, you come with me. They had to have used the road."

Suddenly Frick stopped. He sent Howell on alone and reentered the house. He had three men here, and more on the way from San Juan to Lopez. His best hope was letting them search in the various directions until they caught a sign of Sam, Haley, and Sarah James. Then he'd join them. More important than getting them was getting the goods. That meant keeping up with McStott, whom he trusted less and less as the night wore on.

He called Khan for an update, realizing that he had to keep a grip, keep moving and not become distracted over a bad turn of events.

"That was a massive screwup," he began. Explaining in some detail how stupid they had been; how it had all been a ploy to rescue Sarah James. Khan listened and said nothing.

"What's our little weasel found?" Frick finally asked.

"Well, Rolf's found a partial draft of some kind of alle-giance document. Like a pledge."

"Belonging to?"

"Anderson was drafting it on his computer," Khan said, "but it reads like a government document." Khan voiced the pledge:

> *"Whereas we have been given by Providence a great discovery that might enhance the life of man and extend his time on earth;*
> *"Whereas we have joined together to use this new knowledge for the good of all, with harm to none;*
> *"Whereas we have enumerated certain goals and the manner of their achievement;*
> *"By this document we commit ourselves. . . ."*

"That's it? Commit ourselves to what?" Frick asked.
"That's all we found."

Haley moved the boat down the beach with the first load of files while Sam returned to the house. Sarah was in considerable pain just from the overtightened cuffs and it was hard on Haley to wait around with Sarah suffering.

Wondering if he was using more guts than brains, Sam emerged from the shrubbery near the door to the garage. He slipped back through the door, grabbed an armload of files, heard whispering, and turned to look back out into the garden. Two men were headed down the path with their guns drawn. Obviously they didn't expect anyone behind them in the house. Putting the files down, he went quietly after them, forcing himself to endure the pain of moving at a trot. They didn't see him coming, intent as they were on the beach.

Sam reminded himself not to strike a lethal blow. Anger over Sarah would make it easy to put a nose cartilage into a brain.

Catching the first man unawares, he delivered a hard blow to the area of the seventh cervical vertebrae. The man spun. Sam slammed a fist into the chin and an elbow hard into the floating ribs. Something snapped and the man dropped. Without stopping his motion Sam kicked at the other man's right arm before he could pull his gun. The kick was a mistake. It hurt and, not surprisingly, it went wide, clipping the man's elbow. The man grunted and swung his firearm up. With one hand Sam clamped the gun while he used the other to deliver a hard, palm-up blow to the chin. The man staggered and Sam landed a harder punch to the point of the chin. It took three strikes and a badly broken jaw to bring the man down, but he would likely stay put for a few minutes.

Sam quickly walked back and grabbed another armload of files that he'd left in the doorway, then reversed toward the beach. His legs were getting worse and he was further degrading them with the kick fighting.

Once at the water he flashed the penlight and waded. In a couple minutes he was in the boat and rowing like his life depended on it.

No doubt it did.

Haley was comforting Sarah, and Sarah seemed in better spirits.

After he had rowed a good half-mile offshore, Sam used his cell phone to call Ernie Sanders. No answer. He left a voice mail message, instead. They tried Rachael. She answered and explained the difficulties she was having with the authorities. They told her about Sarah and she said she would relay it. There was desperation in Rachael's voice and Sam knew she was trying. It was only a matter of time and the government would listen and come.

The two women were now shaking from the cold. Although the temperature was probably about fifty-five degrees, there was a stiff breeze. They had no way to warm themselves out here. Sam was a little better off from rowing hard, and he was naturally hardy when it came to extreme cold. Nevertheless, they were all imagining the luxury of heat.

"Surely the FBI will come now," Haley said.

Sam kept rowing. "Consider that I never saw Frick in the house, nor did I see him with Sarah. Physical evidence takes a lab."

"To investigate, all they need is Sarah's story. True?"

"Jurisdiction. They need jurisdiction, like a kidnap across state lines. Or a civil-rights claim. Civil-rights claims usually move slowly. Otherwise, it's a job for the sheriff or the state police. It's a holiday, in the middle of the night, and there are supposed eyewitnesses to our murderous ways. Obviously Frick didn't steal the *Opus Magnum*. If the state or feds came, they wouldn't know where to come because Frick wouldn't tell them. We can't tell them where we are or what we're doing because it might get back to Frick. It'll get worked out, but maybe not in the middle of the first night."

"So what do we do?" Haley asked.

"We need to leave Sarah with someone. Is there anyone we can trust?"

"I know someone. Sarah knows them. Of all the people on the island they're the ones I would trust. The Harlasens. They've been here for years. They own rental properties on various islands. And they're close friends of Ben and me."

"Let's do it," said Sam. "Where do we go?"

"We can row there. Just past the Williamses', and then into McArdle Bay."

Haley called the Harlasens on her cell and spoke with Eugene Harlasen, explaining the situation in no-nonsense language. Then Haley started answering the obvious questions. People on the islands were accustomed to an orderly world and law enforcement was usually right. The sheriff had been around for years, knew everybody, and nothing ever spun out of control. Haley's tale was disorienting, to say the least.

Haley paused to listen. "We're trying to find Ben before someone else does." Haley spent a few more minutes reiterating with slightly more explanation, then hung up.

"They'll help," she told Sam.

"When we get her there," Sam said, "you take a lot of swab samples. You comb through all Sarah's hair very carefully for any loose hairs that might belong to anyone else."

"Okay." Haley sounded exhausted.

She had her arms around Sarah, encouraging her to hang on and things would get better. Haley promised lots and lots of aspirin.

Sarah actually smiled at that.

Haley took the improvement in Sarah's status to ask a question.

"Sarah, I know you're feeling awful, but we're having a

hard time figuring out some things that Ben left us. He wrote something about Sargasso stew. We think he was trying to lead us to something. Does it mean anything to you?"

Sarah seemed sleepy, and her head was starting to loll. Sleep, Sam knew, was a natural escape from pain and extreme stress.

"Sarah," Haley said again. "Do you know anything about Sargasso stew?"

Sarah's tongue had swollen from the gag and she had a slight slur to her speech. She nodded her head. She moved her tongue, as if trying to clear her mouth, then said: "Look on my laptop."

Sam and Haley stared at one another.

"Where?" Sam asked.

"My computer was in my car at Fisherman's Bay Dock."

"Did you tell Frick's people this?" Sam asked.

"Not at all."

"Do you know what Ben put on there?"

"I don't. It's password protected."

Haley gently took Sarah in her arms and stroked her hair as Sam rowed with renewed strength.

They absolutely had to get the computer.

"I want three cars driving MacKaye Harbor Road, I want one car on Aleck Bay Road, and a couple cars patrolling Mud Bay Road." Frick spoke calmly, having shed the anger. His future depended on doing this right. "If you see anybody suspicious, you check it out. I want another airplane flying this end of the island."

"In the dark?" the dispatcher asked.

"Yes. These people that kidnapped Sarah James are in the water. They left marks from a boat on the beach. The plane's a quick way to sweep the area. Am I clear on all of this?"

"Yes, sir. And I've got the interisland ferry on the dock at

Friday Harbor to make an emergency run," the dispatcher said. "But it will be about forty minutes before it arrives. We've got men coming in boat one, and boat two is leaving in a couple minutes."

"We have no more cars over here, so hurry the ferry."

The dispatcher back at San Juan was excellent and had the latest equipment, so Frick was working through her. More significantly, the dispatcher was convinced that Crew and Ranken were killed by Robert Chase and his accomplice, Haley Walther. With the computer screens in front of him and the sophisticated mapping capability, he could monitor the location of every deputy and every special deputy and all the relevant action. Cars used by regular deputies had GPS locators and transponders, so their position was automatically tracked.

But it didn't matter which men Frick wanted in which location, there weren't enough men on Lopez and there wouldn't be for some time. There were three regular deputies stationed on Lopez Island and one special deputy. The sheriff's boat two, run by Frick's imported men, would be ferrying people and then watching for possible escapes from Fisherman's Bay. Volunteer residents were watching other moorages. Frick had had four cars before asking for volunteer vehicles and now he had nine. The four other men he had already moved to Lopez didn't do much to solve the shortage. So Sam was getting a freebie getaway. Smart of him to go by sea. It would take a lot more men to bottle him up at night.

For a moment Frick wondered how much help he was actually getting from the regular deputies. It was no secret that some of them remained suspicious about Haley Walther's guilt.

He got on the phone and called the local news station in Seattle. "This is Sergeant Garth Frick, of the San Juan Island County Sheriff's Department. We have a new development in the manhunt for Robert Chase and his accomplice, Haley Walther. They have escaped to Lopez Island and have apparently taken a hostage. We're withholding the name of the hostage for the time being, pending the notification of her family, who seem to live off island and are temporarily unavailable."

Next he got Rolf on the line. "Anything more on that written pledge or his fellow scientists?"

"Nothing so far."

"Let's look through his phone records and identify every call to a retired scientist. Look especially at his cell phone bills. Call every number you can. Tell them you're trying to get hold of Ben and you need the number of the place on Orcas. Any numbers you get, call the phone company and get the address. Got it?"

"You're the boss."

Smart-ass.

Frick got back on the radio with the dispatcher.

"How long to get a boat down here to MacKaye Harbor?"

"Boat three, forty-four knots, takes fifteen minutes from Fisherman's Bay in the daytime. At night forty-five," the dispatcher said.

"That's too long. Tell them to get their asses down here with the boat. Get men down along MacKaye Harbor Road."

"They can't run thirty knots at night." Deputy Freeman had picked up the microphone. He was one of the guys who had questions concerning Haley Walther's guilt.

"The hell they can't run thirty knots. They can use a spotlight and keep a sharp eye."

"There're dead heads, logs, that sort of thing," Freeman said, making eminently good sense.

But Frick knew they weren't really arguing about dead heads and logs. They were arguing about the manhunt and murder charges—the rest of the acrimony was a proxy for the real issue. It angered him because in his view of the world he had provided sufficient evidence regardless of its truth or falsity.

"We've got a murderer on this island, Deputy Freeman. He's killed two peace officers and wounded another. He's killed a Sanker employee. Now get this straight. Until we get hold of the Sheriff, I'm Zebra One. It's my job to catch them. Get with the program or go home."

Rachael had been waiting for the Washington State Police captain for about twenty minutes. It was almost 2:30 A.M. and the diligent Lieutenant Glendale had managed to persuade Captain Roy Melrose to come into work. Captain Melrose was a twenty-five-year veteran of the state police and was not accustomed to being up in the wee hours, but he was a nice guy with a sense of humor, the sort who would make a great granddad. And judging from the pictures on his desk, he was a grandfather several times over.

"When Lieutenant Glendale called me," said Melrose, "frankly, I thought he was nuts. Until he told me something. You'd never guess what he told me."

"I won't even try," Lew said.

"Me either," Rachael said.

"He told me that when he saw that paper of Ms. Sullivan's, he decided to call the FBI and so he did. In about twenty-five minutes he was talking to people in Washington, DC. They called back an hour later or so and now they want me to have you at the FBI field office, Third Avenue downtown, at seven in the morning. People are coming from Washington, DC, including Homeland Security."

"That's a long time," Rachael said, not caring about the rest. "People could die while we're sitting here waiting for well-intentioned bureaucrats."

Captain Melrose sat back in his chair. "I suppose we

could take one of our choppers up there and try to find this fellow Frick. We could ask him what he's doing and he'd say he's chasing a murderer. I sure would like to get the sheriff on the phone; he's a good man. But that's not gonna happen. I already tried and he's someplace in the Swiss Alps, and nobody's gonna find him in a few hours. And for the moment there seems to be support among the deputies for what Frick's doing. They think your friend killed their own kind."

"He's told all the deputies that my friends shot two of their own and stabbed another," said Rachael. "What would you expect they'd say?"

But Melrose's mind was moving ahead. "Why the hell would Homeland Security be interested?"

"I don't know," she said. "Couldn't we discuss this on the way to San Juan Island?" Stutz looked willing but uncertain.

"After the FBI, maybe," said Melrose. "And last my people heard, they were on Lopez, anyway."

Lopez Island was good news, Rachael thought. In all likelihood it meant that at least one of them, Sam or Haley or Ben, was still alive. "If you don't do something about Frick now," she said, "heroes will die on your watch and the secret of the century will be stolen. Think about that."

Melrose sighed. "I'll have a chopper at the fed building at seven-thirty and tell the feebies we gotta leave. That's the best I can do. I've told them you think Ben Anderson's in danger from Garth Frick. We'll be up to the San Juans by eight-thirty in the morning. I hope you realize how hard it would be to go up there on a stormy winter night in a chopper and do anything."

Lew patted her shoulder. Rachael bit her lip, wanting to cry in frustration. She knew it would have to be enough because it was all she was going to get.

When she and Lew left, a brief and slightly strained discussion followed about sleeping arrangements. In the little time that they'd been together, Rachael had learned that Lew was a Republican, idolized Ronald Reagan, loved Texans, Texas, barbecue, and catfish. He could smoke a cigar with aplomb, drank Dewar's neat, was confident but not cocky, and treated his mother, kids, and older people well.

In turn, he'd learned that Rachael was a DNA-based Democrat and hated all of the aforementioned aspects of life that he held dear except the part about mother, kids, and older people. She hadn't told him about her penchant for nudism. The one love they shared was for fast boats.

Rachael and Lew went to the Four Seasons, where her father had an account, and with the help of a fastidious night manager, they rented a room with two double beds. One bed was in the east and one the west. She slept in the east but would consider rapprochement with the west. However, she made it clear to Lew that the Berlin Wall didn't come down on the first request. It was insane that they were even having the discussion. On that last point he seemed skeptical about the need for her reluctance and his confidence was troubling. Her growing interest in him, she decided, was a damnable affliction.

As they were rushing from the hotel lobby with their coffees, she decided that she needn't mention about the nudity and that wearing clothes would really not be that big an imposition. Perhaps there was a Liberal Republican group. On further reflection, perhaps there was a Conservative Democrat group. Suddenly working it out seemed very important and she began to see all manner of opportunity for harmony. Some tunes one just didn't need to play around the house.

CHAPTER 33

"Bring her in," said Martha Harlasen in the commanding voice one develops while raising six boys. Sam had carried the chair with Sarah in it, up from the boat.

"Got any big bolt cutters?" Sam asked Eugene Harlasen.

"Out here in the sticks? Of course," he said. He was a strong-looking, graying man who seemed firm in the body and in the mind, with a face that reminded Sam of Abraham Lincoln or at least the likenesses that he had seen.

In minutes they were doing the careful work of breaking off the cuffs. Although a bit painful, because of a slight twisting motion, they came off with the giant cutters and Sarah was loosed from the chair.

Sam picked up Sarah to follow Martha. For just a moment Sam's eyes connected with hers; then he followed her through the doorway exiting the entry area. Martha was a blond woman, maybe forty-five, much younger than her husband. To the right of the entry stood a grand piano in a music room, to the left a living room, and straight ahead the hallway that they entered. He glanced at books on bookshelves and pictures on the wall.

At the end of the hall, near the staircase to the upstairs, was a guest bedroom with a large queen-size bed. Sam laid Sarah down gently. She roused briefly and squeezed his arm. Haley was right behind him and sat with her on the bed.

Sam turned back to Eugene Harlasen, who waited behind them in the hallway. They closed the bedroom door. As he appraised the man and pondered the firm handshake, he liked what he felt and saw, both in the man and in the small things, the pictures, the reading material in the house. Eugene seemed a good man and this seemed a solid family.

"We wouldn't be here if it wasn't an emergency," Sam said. "We appreciate you taking this risk for Sarah and Ben."

"I know that," Harlasen said. "Ben and Haley are good friends."

"We have a very serious problem. Garth Frick is a criminal, and he's temporarily in control of the sheriff's department. He has the Sanker Corporation behind him and all of their resources. That's a formidable combination. It's very dangerous to hide us. And to oppose him."

Not surprisingly, Harlasen's face was dead sober, but as Haley joined them, Sam saw the resolve he was hoping for.

"Evil men win if everyone runs and hides," Harlasen said. "I've heard about Frick."

"Who did you hear from?" Sam asked.

"Lattimer Gibbons."

"What did you hear from him?"

"That, according to Ben Anderson, Frick is crazy."

"Where is Lattimer now?"

"I don't know—at home probably. He's unwell. I don't think he gets around that much."

"Unwell, as in ill?" Sam asked.

"Very. As of a couple of years ago, anyway. Martha and I make a point of calling him now and then, to raise his spirits, you know? He's got some artery disease. And it was pretty much throughout the circulatory system. Already he'd had minor strokes. They were going to try multiple bypasses."

That didn't match Sam's memory of Gibbons. From Haley's expression, she was thinking the same thing. Something had not only cured Lattimer Gibbons's arterial ailment but left him in peak condition.

Sam decided to change the subject. Eugene and his family would be safest if they knew nothing more.

"I need to pick up something really important at Fisherman's Bay, so I need to borrow a vehicle. Secondly, we need a boat. Haley and I may need to leave the island."

Harlasen nodded. "We have a boat. It's down anchored in the bay. It's a Zodiac the kids use for fishing. It'll get you to Friday Harbor, at least."

"First the vehicle."

"Frankly, Sam, you don't look so good. Maybe we should help."

Sam shrugged and smiled, but he felt weary at the mere thought of the task that lay ahead.

"Just let me drive you in the pickup and bring you back," Eugene said.

"It's dangerous," Sam said. "And I'm concerned for your family. I want you out of this. Just let me use the truck. If anybody asks you, claim we stole it. You're already endangering yourselves by hiding Sarah."

Eugene thought for a moment; he seemed uncertain.

"Please," Sam insisted. "You need to stay out of this as best you can. You've already done a great deal."

Eugene reluctantly handed Sam the keys.

"Sam," Martha called out. "Sarah wants to talk with you."

Sam walked from the living room to the bedroom and found Sarah sitting up in bed. She asked to be alone with Haley and him.

"I have to tell you something."

"Yes?" Haley said.

"Ben had someone call before they caught me."

For a few moments Haley had to think about what Sarah had said.

"It was Nelson Gempshorn," Sarah continued. "He said Ben was running but would come to me. He said absolutely not to talk, said the boat would come at eight P.M., at Fisherman's Bay. Then they caught me before I could make the rendezvous. And Nelson said to bring Haley. Ben tried to call her."

"We didn't connect. I went right over to Sanker," Haley explained.

"If I missed them, I was supposed to wait for a call at the Horngraves'," Sarah said.

"But where did Ben want to take you?"

"My guess? President Channel. I was to be ready to dive. You know the experimental area?"

"Did you tell Frick about President Channel?"

"No."

"Nelson was coming in a boat to get you?" Haley asked.

"Yes. That was my understanding."

"You would be diving underwater? At night?"

"That's what I gathered. I can't be sure."

"Is there any other connection between Ben and diving and President Channel or Orcas or Waldron Island across the way?" Haley asked.

Sarah thought for a moment. "I mailed things to West Sound. Just a PO box, no real location. I asked him, but he . . ." She shook her head. "On the phone Nelson referred to the place Ben and I took a picnic."

"Was the picnic at Orcas, along President Channel?"

Sarah nodded.

"Do you know about the other people Ben was working with?"

"Only names—Lattimer, Nelson Gempshorn. I think it's a secret society. They all sign something."

"Where do they meet?" Haley asked.

"I don't know."

Haley thought out loud. "Ben mailed things to West Sound. But that's a fairly big area. Turtle Mountain and such."

Sarah nodded.

"Sarah, was Ben involved with anything? Other people?"

She looked uncertain and deeply conflicted. "I think it was a government secret." She had tears in her eyes, probably torn between a promise made and the exigencies of the moment.

"What do you mean?" Sam broke in at last. "Ben's research?"

Sarah nodded. "Ben has been talking to the government. I don't know who or how or what was said."

CHAPTER 34

Haley and Sam climbed in the Harlasens' truck and Haley started the drive to the marina, where they hoped to find Sarah's car and the laptop computer. The truck was an '80s Chevy that somebody had worked over a bit with a flashy interior. No doubt one of the Harlasen boys had an interest.

"The government . . .," Haley mused. "Could they have Ben? The terrorist angle?"

"It's something we can't answer," Sam said. "Not yet. I'm wondering about Sarah having to dive in the night. An underwater entrance or a secret approach to something, but what?"

"I don't know how Ben thought we'd think to look in Sarah's computer for a stew recipe," Haley said. "Why would I ask Sarah about Sargasso stew? He was gonna pick her up. It was a complete fluke that we figured it out."

"Maybe we didn't figure out about the computer in the way he intended. Also, if he were gone, wouldn't you be talking to Sarah about things you didn't understand, just the way you did?"

"You could be right on both counts," Haley said. "It's just obscure."

Sam looked hard through the trees along a slight bend in the road. "Stop," he said. Haley hit the brakes and they lurched to a stop. "Up ahead it looks like a car stopped in the middle of the road. Just beyond that you see flashing lights—it's a cop stopping traffic."

"I don't see anything," she said.

"Through the trees. It's just visible."

"Oh, I see. Yeah. If they stop traffic in this area, they block off the whole lower part of the island. I'm not sure there's any way around."

"Turn off the headlights quick." Haley did it. "Slide over the top of me. Let me drive."

Sam got behind the wheel of the old, stick-shift Chevy. It was now apparent that somebody had enhanced the power block and power train.

Sam turned around before he flipped on the headlights. After taking a slight turn in the narrow road at fifty, he found a driveway and drove down it, quickly dousing the lights. Within sixty seconds there was a siren and a deputy's car screaming by with all the lights flashing.

"How'd you know to do that?" asked Haley.

"They would have seen the lights approaching and then all of a sudden they disappear. Nothing comes. They're gonna think it was a turnaround."

Sam resumed travel, hurried to the turn, saw no lights, and proceeded to Fisherman's Bay, taking some back roads, trying to avoid as much of the main thoroughfare as possible. They drove the pickup back down along the Fisherman's Bay, the only vehicle on the road, both convinced that at any moment they would be tailed.

They were somewhat surprised when they found Sarah's car unmolested.

"Thank God," she said.

"Amen."

"I think I'd rather shoot myself than let them get me."

"No, you wouldn't."

"I feel so much better knowing Ben is alive and probably safe. Honestly, I can't believe she didn't tell us immediately," she said.

"She was doing as she thought Ben had instructed and, truthfully, she didn't have that much real opportunity. She's been totally traumatized and suffering from stress syndrome. Ben or whoever he's with may have their own security concerns that aren't the same as ours. If you think about it, she told us within a few minutes after she got to the house. She couldn't think clearly."

"You're right. When you say whoever Ben's with, do you mean like the government?" she asked.

"Possibly, but not likely. The feds would never let this go on, even for a few hours. I'm afraid Sarah knows a lot of significant stuff that she doesn't realize is significant. We've got to get that computer back to her and see what jogs her memory. Who knows what's on that thing if Ben used it?"

Sam slid out of the pickup with a big lug nut wrench, broke the window on Sarah's car, and set off the car alarm. He reached in the backseat and grabbed the computer case. In the cradle he noticed her cell phone and took it. Surprising, Frick's men hadn't gotten to her car. They were not a high-IQ group.

Headlights came on just down the road, bathing Sam and the pickup in incandescent light. It occurred to Sam that Frick had left Sarah's car as bait.

"Police! You're under arrest," someone yelled.

Sam jumped in the truck and they didn't shoot.

Must be a real cop.

Sam floored it and headed toward the sheriff's car, but in the right-hand lane. In a split second the sheriff was moving to block him. Sam swerved to the left, got half onto the opposite shoulder, and went around the back of him. As he went around the bend in the road, the cop was turning around to follow.

"Now we've got a problem," Sam said. He put the truck in a slide and waited for the rear tires to hit the gravel on the shoulder of the road. Instantly the truck spun around on the loose rock; now he was going the opposite direction, accelerating full out. He wished he had his Vette, the "Blue Hades."

"What are you doing?" Haley whirled as they passed the flashing lights of the cop car in a blur.

Sam accelerated, quickly getting to one hundred miles per hour. Out of the corner of his eye, he could see Haley's body taut like a bow.

"We're going to take a chance. A big chance. We'll try the plane one more time." When he approached the resort, he noticed there were more cars than before. One was a police cruiser. He slammed on the brakes, anyway; they jumped out and he led the way, carrying the computer, going as best he could toward the dock. Haley actually had to slow her pace to keep next to Sam.

At that, Haley ran on ahead. Sam ran more slowly. Looking back, he saw something that tightened his gut. Frick was in the resort with a tall black man. They had stumbled onto Frick's base of operations.

She ran down the section of the dock spanning the beach, arriving at the long ramp. At the bottom was a wharfinger's booth, which was better lit than the rest of the dock. Then suddenly she was struggling. Someone had grabbed her. Incredibly, they seemed so intent on her that they didn't seem to notice Sam.

Her assailant was facing the water, hanging onto her, saying something Sam couldn't discern. He managed to get the computer flat on the dock. At the last second, before he struck, the man turned and saw him. Shoving Haley away, the man reached inside his coat. Although Sam already had his gun in his right hand, he used it as a club. It was a risk, but he didn't need more bodies.

Sam connected with the man's jaw, but not squarely. It ripped open his skin and angered him. This was a big bruiser of a man, maybe a slight bit fat, but under the fat was a mountain of muscle. Instinctively Sam went for the man's gun hand and dropped his own pistol. The man struggled, shouted for help while trying to free his weapon. With his left hand Sam gripped the man's right wrist. Using his palm, Sam struck upward to the nose.

When the man rocked back on his heels, Sam punched to the solar plexus, doubling the man over. An elbow to the back of the head took the man down completely. Sam took his gun and retrieved his own and the laptop from the edge of the dock.

The squad car had screeched to a halt and another man was coming at them. Haley was cranking the plane's engine. It started. He hobbled the 150 feet or so around the outer rectangles of the dock. Instead of shooting, the deputy was running fast. *Another real deputy,* Sam thought.

The man was gaining.

Sam rounded a large boat at a ninety-degree bend in the dock and climbed in the fisherman's cockpit of a Californian 55. Grabbing a handy boat hook, he waited about two seconds until the deputy came running by. It took some coordination, but he jammed the pike into the dock just ahead of the officer, who tripped and went flying. Sam was on him, got his gun and Mace, and threw them overboard. Then he backed off.

"You're under arrest," the officer said. His shin was bleeding.

"Later. Report Frick and get yourself to safety."

"You're under arrest—now," the man shouted over the din of the plane.

Sam towered over the officer, who seemed determined to

make an effort. The officer tried to get Sam's hand and wrist in a disabling hold. Sam tossed him into the bay.

"I'm sorry," Sam said at a shout. "Can you swim to that ladder?"

"I'm sure I can."

Sam limped over to the plane.

"This whole thing sucks," the officer bellowed in a shout as he was arriving at the ladder. Obviously the man had reservations about Mr. Frick. Perhaps the feeling would grow. Sam managed to push the plane off the dock and get it headed away with a paddle.

Haley gave the engine a shot of throttle, moving the plane forward slowly until Sam was able to flop in the cockpit.

Haley gunned the engine and they were soon hurtling down the rippled bay. Before they took off, at least one bullet thunked into the hull of the plane in the backseat area. Obviously Frick figured out too late what was happening. They flew very low over the sandy spit that formed the bay. They then went down the coast about two hundred feet above the water at half-throttle. They used no lights; they would be virtually invisible. There was no road along the beach, and even if there had been a car inland, it couldn't possibly have traced their path.

"Davis Bay," she said at a sparse ring of residential lights.

They approached a peninsula. "MacKaye Harbor," she said as if documenting her progress.

"Aleck Bay and McArdle Bay." She turned on the landing light.

Sam knew it was dangerous. One miscalculation, an anchored boat or log, and they were dead.

"There's where we're going—that tiny hole in the rocks," she said, dropping down right above the water. She banked to the left. The bay looked like the shadow of a giant outfielder's glove, but with a very narrow opening. It was an area of steep banks, rocky bluffs, and intermittent breezes.

She held the nose high, trying to ease down. They hit the water outside the entrance of the bay and bounced badly about four hundred yards from its mouth. The second time they came down, they stuck. She was giving herself room because once inside the bay, the beach would come up quickly. She flicked off the light and killed the motor.

The dark was eerie and the water sloshed against the hull.

"I think we're just outside the mouth of McArdle Bay."

She lifted open her door, which folded up, wing fashion. There was a slight breeze and the smell of the beach was strong in the air. A bird flopped in the night, just awakened and compelled to flee. Another bird squawked as if encouraged by the neighbor's departure. The largest beach in the small bay lay directly ahead. To either side the rock rose up barren for fifty feet or so, and the shadows of the trees lined up along the divide between earth and rock like spooks on a shelf.

"Shall we use the engine or the paddle?" she asked.

"The bay is maybe two hundred yards," Sam said. "The beach may be another few hundred yards beyond that. Let's use the motor. We'll make noise, but it'll be over with fast."

They heard an outboard motor start.

"Oh no," Haley said, the fear apparent in her voice. "That could be Harlasen or it could be Frick's men."

Sam pulled out the two guns and prepared himself to use them. There was a calm in him that was always there before a fight and he could feel it despite his climbing heart rate. As he watched the white of the boat's wake in the moonlight and judged there were a number of people aboard, he decided what he would do. It was a quiet place, a bowl, and had walls of rock, so the sound was held and then deflected toward the entrance. Sam could hear every change in the motor and the turning of the boat as it made good the course direct to their location. Even the sounds of men talking could be heard, although the words were not plain. The moon passed from behind a cloud and the increase in light made the branches of the trees shine, the figures in the boat starker black silhouettes.

Sam had told himself that it would be unlikely that Frick's men would have been able to move that fast. Wishful thinking, in all likelihood.

As the boat approached, someone in the back flicked on a bright light, illuminating two figures in front. One appeared an angelic apparition in filmy white. He took an involuntary breath.

Sarah.

Something was terribly wrong.

As the boat drew closer, and he began to form an image of what was before him, a horrible feeling of resignation overtook him. In the front of the boat were Sarah and a man standing behind her with her head pulled back, neck exposed, and a knife against her Adam's apple. Pictures of the Harlasen family massacred poured unbidden into his mind. More innocent fellow travelers fallen. He struggled to stay in the moment.

"Surrender or I cut her throat," the man said. He was big and confident.

Sarah's nightgown billowed in the breeze.

"We're unarmed," Sam lied.

"Don't mess with me, Chase. I'll kill her and then the two of you."

Sam recognized the ugly voice of Rafe Black.

Sam believed him. In his right hand Sam had the 10mm SIG-Sauer and in his left he had Ranken's .38.

"Hands on your heads," Black screamed, the knife still furrowing the skin of Sarah's neck.

Sam rose and dived out of the plane into the frigid ocean and disappeared under the sea.

On his way down he put the guns in his belt and used the long, numbing descent to decide exactly how he would get to them.

As he stopped his downward movement into the depths, he turned head up, probably eight feet below the surface, reached down, and slipped off his Top-Siders and crammed them, toe first, into his pants. The pain of the contortion in his bad leg was intense and nearly unbearable. Next he got Eugene's coat off as he was coasting up. Before he broke the surface, he swam for what he believed to be the back of the Zodiac. Glancing up toward the surface, he thought he saw a shadow, but wasn't sure.

Worried about disorientation, he forced himself to remain calm and to take four good strokes. Then he rolled and put his hand in the general direction he thought to be up. He felt the bottom of a boat; he sensed with his fingertips a commotion inside the hull.

Holding his fingers over his head, he bounced along the bottom until the bottom disappeared. He hoped it was the stern. Expecting a gun in his face, he brought his 10mm up and gently broke the surface.

The light shone from the back of the boat. His first glimpse was a split second of hunched-over men below the big man. All were well-illuminated. Sarah remained in front of them, a silhouette.

The big guy was screaming threats, looking around in front and to the side.

"Burial at sea," Sam muttered as he shot.

CHAPTER 35

For a moment Haley was shocked and couldn't comprehend what Sam was planning—only that he'd disappeared into the ocean. In a second she realized that he would attack.

The man with the knife screamed that he was going to cut Sarah. Blood began oozing from her neck.

"Where'd he go?" one of the other men shouted when Sam disappeared.

"He's trying to escape," another said.

"Be careful," the leader shouted.

The men were nearly submerging one of the pontoons, trying to peer over the side. Then a loud bang rang out. Haley saw the man's forehead burst open, spewing its contents all over Sarah. Rafe Black crumpled, leaving Sarah teetering and calling to Haley for help.

More shots. A great rush of air came from the boat's pontoon collar.

Sarah was reaching out into thin air for the airplane. They were drifting apart. Then Sarah and the boat tilted to the side, submerging a pontoon completely.

"We're going under," one man shouted as they rolled over the side and into the freezing water.

Sarah fell and the sight of her white nightgown billowing around her as she went under frightened Haley.

Sarah popped to the surface, screaming in pain.

The scene was chaos—all wild struggling, crying, and splashing.

As Haley removed her shoes to dive in after Sarah, she heard a loud voice from the water, in front of her and to the side.

"Haley, start the plane."

It was Sam, but he couldn't mean it. How could she leave Sarah?

Most of the men were trying to get back into the sinking Zodiac, but one had spotted Sam and had come after him.

When the man reached him, Sam pushed him underwater, moving away. The man came back up and at him, fighting hard and amazingly resilient. He actually got above Sam and shoved him down. Sam went down willingly, deeper than the man expected, then came up the man's pants, quickly disabling the man. Sam could have detached the testicles from their plumbing, but he elected against permanently maiming him.

Sam could hear the screaming even underwater.

When Sam let go, the man was much more interested in swimming in the other direction.

Sam moved toward Sarah.

Even in pain Sarah could swim a little and remained at the surface, floundering next to him.

Then she disappeared. He felt around and found her. He pulled her up, weary, wondering if he could make it.

"I'm trying. I hurt, so tired," Sarah whispered.

"Lie on your back," he said, and she did. "Don't struggle, it makes you colder." Sam knew that struggle circulated the blood and the body acted as a radiator, hence movement equaled lower core temperatures in the body. Her body went limp in the water. "Put your hands on my shoulders." She did that. Instinctively she put her legs to either side of his torso and he began doing the breaststroke, using his healthiest limbs to propel them through the water toward the plane, which had drifted away. As he moved, he could tell Sarah was drifting off; he wasn't sure he could keep her at the surface and breathing.

He heard the amphibian's engine try to start. Haley tried it again and again, but it didn't catch.

"Haley," he called out.

"Yeah," she shouted from a distance.

"Come here, fast."

She kicked the starter twice more before the engine caught. Then she was near them in seconds.

To locate Sam and Sarah she had flicked on the landing light, illuminating a swath at least one hundred yards or more in length. She could see the three men, two appeared headed for a point to her right and the third headed directly at the plane. Sam and Sarah were close by, swimming toward her, Sarah on her back pushed by Sam on his belly. She killed the lights and gunned the throttle, then came up beside them.

Now she flicked on the cockpit lights, giving the area around the hull a soft glow, allowing her to see.

Sarah was floundering and nearly incoherent. Putting a ladder over the side, Haley climbed down and tried to help Sarah up. Sarah was going into shock, from hypothermia probably, and Haley couldn't lift her the couple of feet up and in the plane.

Suddenly it occurred to her that Sam had disappeared.

She had been so intent on Sarah that she didn't see one of the men right near the ladder. He had a gun pointed at her gut.

"Drop her and help me," the man said.

Sam was ten feet away and swimming toward the man from behind.

"I said let her go."

"I can't, she'll die," Haley said. "And if you kill me, I can't help you, anyway."

The man's gun hand was shaking. His lips were blue. He pulled the trigger. Nothing happened. *The safety.* As if telegraphing the thought, the man glanced at the gun. Then the gun boomed. *Missed.*

Sam grabbed the gun and swung it down.

They began to struggle.

"Paddle, Haley."

She knew he was afraid of this man getting to the plane. Desperate, she pulled Sarah up on the edge of the plane, draping her body and putting her hands on the seat where Sarah could grip. Grabbing a paddle, Haley pulled on each stroke trying to move the plane away. She hoped the plane was moving fast enough. Haley could hardly think with Sarah's terrible groaning in her ear and Sarah about to fall back in.

Sam and the man had disappeared. Pain squeezed Haley's heart as she imagined that Sam might die.

"Hold on, Sarah," she said through gritted teeth.

She heard screaming from the man fighting with Sam.

"Let go, let go," the man yelled; then he went under again. Sam was still nowhere to be seen. They both surfaced. "Oh God, my fingers," the man shrieked.

Sam hit him in the jaw and he disappeared. Then Sam was pulling something, no doubt the man.

Haley stopped paddling and turned around, keeping a strong hand on Sarah's arm. "Let him sink."

"Maybe in a minute," Sam said. "Right now I'm busy trying to save him."

In one of the strangest moments of her life, Haley smiled at Sam's joke.

He drew the guy to the side of the boat. Sarah was still groaning, but more quietly now.

For a moment Sam let go of the man and helped shove Sarah in the plane. Quickly he grabbed his assailant, who was starting to sink.

Sam wedged the unconscious man's head and shoulder through the ladder rungs until he could climb up and into the plane. Then he took the plane's dock line, wrapped it under the man's arms, crawled out on the wing, and tied the man under the wing to a tie-down eye.

Haley was exasperated that they were saving this killer, while Sarah was suffering and hypothermia was menacing the three of them. Then she felt ashamed and knew Sam was right. They were not like Frick and never would be.

Sam was shaking badly. His stamina had left him.

Sarah curled in a ball from the sting of the salt and shivered from the cold. She could not endure much more.

Haley revved the plane's engine. *Still a little gas left,* she guessed.

Frick pulled up to the Harlasens' and found a man named "Philly" Duggan in the front yard. The first name was a handle reflecting his choice of baseball teams.

"What's going on?"

"Residents are in the house, except for two of their boys. We have the boys cuffed in a car."

"Where's Sarah James?" Frick asked.

"Out on the water. All hell broke loose out there. I've heard shots and screams, but I can't see a thing. We made the Harlasen lady talk when we threatened a kid. They had Sarah James hid pretty good. Chase and Haley Walther went off in a car, then the Lake airplane. Rafe's team jumped in one of the family boats and went out, figuring the plane would land. I guess they came back for the James woman.

Besides, the plane is full of holes, so they ain't goin' far. We know that."

"You're holding two kids hostage?" Frick knew he shouldn't have been surprised. "You threatened them in front of their mother?"

The man nodded.

"Why didn't you call me or Khan?"

"We did, but you didn't answer," Philly said. "And it all happened so fast, I mean we heard the plane. It was seconds."

Frick was shocked but displayed utter calm, as was his habit before killing. There would be no means of explaining this on Monday morning unless he created one. There was still the slim possibility that he would be around giving explanations.

"I heard a lot of shooting and hollering out there on the water," the guy said, hoping for redemption. "Rafe's got 'em. I'm sure of it."

"All right," Frick said. "You take this gun and come with me. You shoot this family. We'll say Chase did it."

"Hey. Wait a minute. I've killed people, you know. But not kids. Not a family."

"Fine." Frick shot Duggan between the eyes before the man could think to protest. Strangely, he didn't drop immediately. It was as if he were staring out from either side of the bullet hole before realizing that he couldn't stand.

Frick walked toward the house, knowing that he had no choice but to kill them all and blame Sam.

Sarah, barely conscious, clearly suffered hypothermia. Sam dug a coat out of the amphib's storage compartment and covered her.

"Now what?" Haley asked.

"Those men are poor swimmers, but they'll probably make those rock walls and crawl out," Sam said.

"I'm not worried about them," Haley said. "I'm worried about the Harlasens. More'll be coming. You know it."

"Take us to that big yacht. Just taxi us there, on the water. I'll go back to the Harlasens, once we get Sarah taken care of."

Halfway to the yacht, Sam signaled Haley to approach the shore. In a couple minutes they had motored to a sloping rock face on the westerly point and then paddled the plane in until they bumped rocks, which were like granite shark's teeth in the thigh-deep water. Sam pulled the unconscious gunman onto the rocks and left him. He had a police radio, and they left it on; the GPS in the radio would send a location signal to the dispatcher and a deputy would eventually show up to save him.

The man had a pen, which was surprisingly serviceable, and they had a piece of paper in the cockpit. Sam scribbled on the paper: *I am a killer and a criminal brought here from Las Vegas by Garth Frick, of the Sanker Corporation.*

"As if they'll believe you," Haley said.

"It's a start, whether they believe me or not."

"Now what? We're going to die of exposure."

"I know," Sam said, his body already shaking. "Let's get to the yacht."

"We'll wake the dead with this motor," Haley pointed out.

"She may die of exposure if we don't." Sam nodded toward Sarah, huddled under the light summer coat.

"Pulling up that anchor with the windlass will be too noisy. I don't think we can take the whole yacht."

"Agreed. We'll warm up and take the big inflatable to Orcas."

They pushed off the plane and Haley tried to start the engine. She hit it a dozen times, but it wouldn't engage.

"This time we're really out of fuel," Haley said. "Now what?"

Inside the Harlasen home, in the living room, Frick found rope and tape on the floor. Duggan had tried to bind them after a fashion and was counting on keeping them under control, with the two younger boys as hostages. Now the entire family was gone, this after having freed the two young boys.

Frick kicked in a large-screen TV set. He was dealing with morons. The minute Duggan had walked out of the house, they finished loosening their bonds and found the two boys and headed into the thick forest. There was plenty of *that* around. The area was covered in second-growth trees and the Harlasens apparently had been here for a generation or two, so they had to know the whole forest and its ridges, thickets, and swales.

Frick ran out of the house, toward the beach, where Rafe Black and his guys had allegedly trapped Sam and Haley Walther. On the shore he strained to discern something on the black water, but could see only the shadow of the hills. The water had calmed after the front and was quietly lapping at the shore, largely undisturbed by wind or swell. It was near high tide, so the air smelled clean and salty, the herring in the bay making little splats as they jumped to avoid some hungry predator.

Frick did not like the quiet. With the near-silence ringing in his ears, he walked out toward the easternmost point of McArdle Bay. Given the steep rock near the water, he had to stay high and in the trees, and it was difficult to see through the heavy forest. He told himself he could not be diverted from his main targets and his new goal. This was no longer a job. He wouldn't stick around, trying to explain all the bodies. Ben Anderson's discoveries were all that he needed; then he could flee and begin planning their sale. The notion was somewhat freeing.

He put in a call to dispatch and said there were cars at the Harlasens', but no men. Robert Chase, aka Sam, had terrorized the family, which had escaped, then shot Special Deputy Duggan right between the eyes and left him dead. He was concerned that Chase had slaughtered the remainder of the men as they pursued his plane in the bay.

Stories remained necessary in the near term, and Frick thought he'd just told a good one.

As best he could, he walked parallel to the beach, just inside the tree line. There was no answer on any radio, and that was not good. He had most of the men on the island coming, but it was difficult to reconstruct what might have happened. They had heard a plane, but they really didn't know where it landed. Rafe hadn't had the good sense to report on progress, so there was no telling where that Zodiac had gone. Even full of men, it would go twenty knots easily. They might be around the point, but if they were there, they should still answer the radio. More likely, Chase had taken down Rafe and three men and gotten away.

But to where?

On instinct he looked to the sky. No plane there. None on the water, at least within view.

He cursed in his head in long, rhythmic phrases with such guttural texture that his invective made poetry.

This was another waste of his time.

He dialed McStott.

"What are we finding? We're running out of time."

"We've torn apart Ben's home place," McStott said. "Your guys are over there tearing apart the beach house, and we've gone through the Gibbons residence. I'm convinced he does have something amazing—beyond the methane mining. But exactly what, I don't know."

"And why do we conclude that he has something amazing?"

"Because he's been talking to the government and to American Bayou Technologies, and everybody is imploring him to tell them what he knows. Although I'm not at all sure that the requests pertain to the same subject. Or maybe they do and I just don't see the connection."

"Doomsday, energy crisis, and living several life-spans," Frick said. "Could there be something else?"

"Maybe."

"Are you nuts, McStott? What else could there be?"

"Maybe no other technology, but there's a storehouse, some sort of off-site lab. Best I can tell, it's a large house or building, where he meets with other scientists."

"Where in the hell is it?" Frick asked.

"I think Orcas Island, near West Sound, maybe Deer Harbor. I'm working on it."

"That's one big area, so work faster. I'm tired of all your notions. I want results."

Frick heard the sound of the engine on the amphibian. "Damn," he muttered.

It stopped.

He wondered if they were headed to Orcas Island.

CHAPTER 36

Studying the plane, Haley had found a fuel tank switch that sucked from the dregs of a second ruptured tank. For just a second she had fired it up and got them started in the right direction away from the unconscious officer and then shut it down, wincing at the horrible racket.

"To paddle this plane, it's too far and will take too much time," Sam said. "That leaves walking or the motor. If we motor, we wake people and arouse curious eyes."

"Some people get up at this hour. It's all dangerous. I'll leave it up to you. I'm worried about Sarah," Haley said.

"Use the motor to get near; then we paddle."

They both silently cringed at the noise of the big Lycoming engine and, of course, its sound was magnified greatly by their worry. It reverberated off the rocky bluffs and probably caused Haley to shut it down early. It would be a long paddle.

Fortunately, they found a second paddle behind the rear seat. With both Sam and Haley paddling, they reached the yacht in twenty minutes. The hard work had one side benefit: neither felt hypothermic. In fact, they were cold but breathing strongly as they approached the yacht from the stern, then climbed out on the fantail.

It was a large, beautifully constructed north-sea trawler design. Once on the stern, teak steps rose to the aft deck. Sam tried the aft main-deck door and found it locked. It was beefy and the glass heavy, so breaking in was a poor option.

He climbed to the wheelhouse and found it locked as well. Normally yachtsmen would hide a key. He climbed back up to the wheelhouse and looked for a hiding place.

Using his fingers to hunt every nook and cranny around the wheelhouse, he found nothing. He studied the far back corner of the upper deck and saw a large round canister that held an emergency life raft. He felt underneath it and all around it. Nothing there.

He went up on the outdoor bridge above the pilothouse and took the canvas off the controls and the wheel. It was too obvious a place to hide a key, but he looked, anyway. After opening every storage locker door, he found nothing.

The situation was getting serious. They hadn't the time to move Sarah again.

There was a door on the front deck that would be rarely used and he tried that as well. Of course, it was locked. There was a second tender on the yacht, a large Avon hard-bottom inflatable. The owners had taken the other ashore. He took off the cover, begging the Great Spirit for a break. He didn't claim to deserve it, but he thought Sarah might.

He found a box in it, which he opened. It revealed a very large crank handle, apparently the anchor winch handle for the fiberglass tender boat. It wasn't a key, but it might do to smash one of the heavy windows.

He went to the rear window of the pilothouse on the starboard side next to the ladder to the upper bridge. As he drew the handle back, he stopped short, thinking he ought to look under each stair leading to the flybridge. He went down to his knees and felt under the first stair: there, velcroed underneath, was a key; it opened the pilothouse.

He stepped inside, his eyes looking for an alarm box. Immediately he saw the keypad and knew they were finished. Then he saw the small green light, not blinking or flashing. It was too good to be true. He shone his flashlight on the control box. The word *Unarmed* appeared. He could not recall being so lucky, or a wealthy owner so foolish—blessedly foolish.

One pleasant feature of this floating castle was the very large moat surrounding it. Even at the poky ten knots that was the vessel's top speed, there was no way to come on the boat easily, except over the stern, and Sam could hold off an army there in the short term.

As quick as he could, he took Haley and Sarah below to the master stateroom, which he knew would be amidships. Using the ship's flashlights, he covered the windows with blackout curtains.

It was just over twenty-one feet across the stateroom and it had a large king-size bed on one side and a small study area and library on the other. On the side opposite the bed in the master suite stood a section of wall with floor-to-ceiling bookcases and cabinets, along with a built-in desk.

The two women went in the marble-tiled bathroom and climbed in the shower. From the sound of it they were greeted with a powerful spray of water. Sam stripped and found pants and a shirt that fit him and then found clothes that looked like they might fit the women. He tossed them through the bathroom door.

In about three minutes Haley was out of the shower and helping Sarah into the bed. Sarah was still shaking and beyond exhausted. Sam and Haley sat on the bed and opened the laptop. It took sixty seconds to find the recipe for Sargasso stew. Below it they found information about sorting through

Arc genes using Venter's computer technology. At the bottom of the page was a stand-alone notation: *Archaea—closer than you know*.

Haley put her chin on her fist, deep in thought.

"What do you see?" he asked after what seemed a reasonable time.

"Archaea is an organism that makes methane—or consumes it—that lives almost forever and for whom oxygen is poison. So he says they are closer to me than I know. But their DNA is circular, I believe. It's primitive even if it's closer to ours than, say, a five-thousand-gene bacteria. But none of that leads me anywhere. It's just a bunch of facts. For some reason Ben's sorting through a bunch of different Arc genes from different Arc species. If only I knew why. This is a stew, for sure. I see why Ben likened it to the Sargasso stew."

"Sarah, where are Ben's files on this computer?"

"Look under 'Ben,' in My Documents." Her tongue's swelling had reduced enough to make her easier to understand.

"These are password-protected documents," Sam said. "What's the password?"

"Don't know," Sarah said. "I never looked at 'em."

Sam tried the word *Haley* and got nothing. Then he tried *ARCLES* and they opened. There were five documents and they were all blank.

"Damn it," Sam said.

"He thought I'd be opening them," said Haley. "So what do I know that would help?"

"Nothing if they're blank," Sam said. "Unless they are specially programmed to look blank when they aren't. Like a program within a program."

"I have a wild idea," Haley said. "Ben has a code for the burglar alarm in his house. It's 2872, my birth date. When he wants a longer password for something, like the Internet, it becomes 42872Haley. He uses it on the Internet and everyplace he needs a long password. It's way too obvious, but why not try?"

"But who else knows it?" Sam said.

"I think only Ben, Sarah, and I know it."

Sam closed the blank document and typed in the code. This time the document opened to another dialogue box, which asked for another password. He typed *ARCLES*. This time the actual document opened.

Before them lay a map of the North American continent with red dots around it. Sam guessed these represented all the known methane hydrate deposits. Below were calculations and some text, which Haley studied.

"They start out telling where methane is, et cetera. Like an executive summary. I'm guessing these are elaborate mining techniques, here." She pointed at the relevant pages. "Look at all these sketches: giant anchored ships and barges. It's like what I saw Ben and Nelson looking at."

She pointed.

"They say here that using their methods . . . God, get this. . . . One 50- by 150-kilometer area off the coast of North and South Carolina is estimated to hold enough methane to supply the needs of the United States for over seventy years. Can that be true? That's unbelievable."

"So they think they know how to mine it," Sam said. "No more energy crisis and worth a fortune, if they can pull it off."

"Let's open another file," he said.

They opened the second. Once again Haley started reading, then scrolled through pages of calculations.

"We're back to aging again." She paused and a look of shock came over her face. "Oh, my God. He *is* giving it to people."

Sam looked over her shoulder and read Ben's notation: *I have interviewed all thirty-six men and the two women on the life-extension regime denominated Arc for short.*

"Interesting that there are only two women."

"He's got some general material about how they chose these people for the program," Haley offered. She pointed to the text:

> *Of paramount importance, however, are the psychological impacts, which are as yet only partially understood and documented.*

"Then he's got some comments about other reports that are related, and then he goes on some more."

> *A more surprising development is the complex of psychic issues that arise from taking the regimen and reorienting one's thinking to an extended life span. None of those currently on the regimen can be expected to add more than fifty years to their lives because much of the genetic damage and transformation of age was accomplished before they began the regimen and, hence, the outlook is much different for the late middle-aged and elderly participants than for those who in the future will begin the regimen before age thirty-five.*
>
> *I have not yet personally begun the more robust portions of the regimen because I did not want any altered state of consciousness that might be associated with the regimen while I was evaluating its effects on my colleagues.*
>
> *I am sorry to report that there seem to be significant changes in mental orientation from the onset of the regimen. However, they seem much more pronounced in the men than in the women.*
>
> *First, there is a great sense of well-being that seems to be experienced by all those on Arc, including the two women.*
>
> *Second, they seem to have developed a strong emo-*

tional focus on continuing self-supply—similar to that of an addict, although this seems much less pronounced in the women.

Third, one cannot overstate the universal sentiment among participants. Perhaps belief is a better word. They view themselves as a distinct group, distinct from the rest of the human race. It is a bit disconcerting that they have such a strong us/them consciousness. I am finding that, because I am not on the regimen, I am not considered one of them.

Haley and Sam looked up at the same time, searching each other's eyes. Sarah lay asleep beside them. They continued silently reading:

On the positive side the regimen seems to foster great energy and optimism that is prevalent, unless one gets on the subject of scarcity—medication scarcity.

Unfortunately, the treatment for aging is expensive, never ending, and complex. Any hint that there might be a problem with supply seems to arouse anxiety and a mental state bordering on paranoia, particularly in males. To this group, the paramount value seems to be securing continuing availability of Arc.

An expert in the field might be able to counter some of these mental effects with drugs, but for the present I have to deal with it psychoanalytically to the best of my ability.

Members of the group seem to have retained their sense of humor and self-awareness and they are often able to laugh about their seeming paranoia over losing the supply of regimen drugs.

In all other regards mental performance of subjects remains as high, if not higher, than it ever had been.

Lately, however, they've become extremely concerned

*when they do not know my precise whereabouts. In the
beginning I kept the various recipes for the various
portions of the regimen in a vault at the foundation,
but recently I destroyed the hard copies and then had
only the copies on my computer and on Sarah's computer. Recently I also destroyed critical portions of the
electronic documents on both computers so that I now
possess the critical information only in my memory. (I
was able to access the escrow and did the same.) My
mistrust of Sanker necessitated these actions. I tested
Sanker's integrity and, unfortunately, it failed, thus
giving me reason to thwart the escrow. I am concerned
about the reaction of the male subjects when they
learn what I've done.*

*For specific interviews and psychological test re-
sults, see the main body of this report.*

Sam took another look at Haley. She seemed taken aback
to the point of shock.

"I can't believe he's done this," she said.

"It's bold to the point of recklessness, I agree. It should
make you feel better, though."

"How?" she said.

"You can see now why he kept you out of this," Sam said.
"Right? I'm sure he was afraid of your reaction. In addition
to your safety. Interesting that women don't seem to have the
level of paranoia."

"Two women is too small a sample. It's anecdotal."

"Spoken like a scientist."

She closed her eyes and nodded, as if clearing her mind
for the work to come.

"Let's open another."

There were three left. Haley typed in the codes this time.
The third popped up a third dialogue box, asking for another
code.

THE BLACK SILENT 387

"Uh-oh," Sam said. "He hasn't made this one easy and we don't have a code breaker."

They tried a dozen words and then the computer flashed a sign that said no more opportunities to open were available.

"We're cooked," Sam said. "We'll never get in without help. And maybe not then. I'll try for the help, but it's a long shot."

Frick was wondering whether McStott was worth a 1 percent offer, let alone the 20 percent of the take he and Khan had discussed. At Khan's insistence Frick took a call from Rolf.

Rolf spoke first: "Hello?"

"Talk quick," Frick said.

"Okay. Two things: Ben Anderson has been corresponding with people from Homeland Security and various other branches of government. We just have indications of the discussions and meetings, not the substance of them. I'm sure he destroyed any notes. The bulk of this activity started months ago. It's real," Rolf added unnecessarily.

"What else?"

"I'm closing in on Anderson's meeting place. You know, hideout, or lab, or whatever."

"Enlighten me quickly."

"This first part could be trivial, but we read everything coming in from the field. We asked the deputies to put out an APB for Ben and they threw in his old boat, the *Mallard*. Someone saw divers going in over the side off a forty-something-foot boat that sounds from the description like it might have been Ben's old boat. But they said its name was *Alice B.*"

"Why the hell didn't you tell me?"

"I'm telling you now," Rolf said.

Frick's cursing pounded in his head. He wanted to break

something. Then he spoke in patronizingly measured tones. "Then let's have a deputy call the people who saw this boat and get a precise location."

"We told Khan about it."

Khan answered immediately. "The boat was between what they call the old lime kiln and Turtle Mountain in a sparsely populated area. There's several different roads in that vicinity. We have some Anderson photos that also help."

"Is there anything in there that might be a laboratory?" Frick asked.

"Yep. That's why I got Rolf on the line with you. They're not done yet, but they've got this preliminary indication."

"I say we go there," Frick said. "Full force. Now."

"That's putting our eggs in one basket," Khan said. "It's a huge gamble, but I'm with you. I have one suggestion, though."

"Keep the real deputies on Lopez? Take our guys to Orcas?"

Khan chuckled. "I *like* how you think, my brother. But I'd change that just a tad. We keep the deputies on the roads going through this whole area, but we send our guys the last half-mile down all the roads."

"Then do it."

Frick hung up on Rolf.

It was time to go.

CHAPTER 37

"I found another file that's not even protected," Sam said. "It's in a CAD program and it's huge. There's a floor plan, and there's a photo."

He showed Haley and Sarah.

"I know that place," Sarah said, sitting up in bed. "We went on picnics. Waldron Island is across the way." She pointed.

"Yes, it is," Haley said. "I wonder if that's the place?"

"Deer Harbor Road, near Turtle Mountain—Orcas Nob. No Trespassing signs."

Sam and Haley listened carefully as Sarah explained how to get there.

"You know things that don't seem significant," Sam said to Sarah. "That's often the way we find something that nobody wants found."

Haley jumped off the bed. "I need to check on the Harlasens."

"The men took me, but they didn't hurt them," Sarah said, finally wearing out. She looked groggy.

"When you were there, they didn't hurt them," Sam said.

"We need to make sure they're safe now before we run over to Orcas. I'll take the ship's tender," Sam said. "It's fast and will get me close in a hurry."

"On the water you'll be a sitting duck. Not to mention, you're crippled when you get ashore," Haley said. "It's getting worse. I can see it. You won't be able to run, so you'll fight. Outnumbered. Don't go by yourself."

Sam's cell rang, but the signal was bad and the caller disappeared. The phone recorded the number. Using the yacht's satellite phone, he called back.

"This is Eugene."

Harlasen, Sam mouthed to Sarah and Haley.

"Where you at?" Sam asked.

"Out in the forest, up on a hill. I didn't want you to come looking."

"You got away?"

"Yep, and we'll be a little trigger-happy here, I'm afraid. We've got guns. In this forest at night, I think we can take them down."

"I'm sorry about all this, Eugene. Stay put and good luck. Do you know where we get a boat to head to Orcas? I'd like something really fast and a little bigger than a Zodiac tender."

"Neighbor over there on Aleck Bay has a big Boston Whaler anchored out," Harlasen said. "He's really a hobbyist and not a fisherman, but he has some crab pots and runs a couple long lines. Sometimes when he's away, I check them. He's normally got a key under the driver's seat, right-hand side. It's on a ledge and hard to get to. Sometimes I have to put another key in the crack to get it out. If you wreck it, we'll have to replace it."

"Understand." Sam wished him well again, hung up, and called Ernie, who would be craving his sleep by this time. Ernie answered on the first ring; Sam began by explaining what had happened in the meantime. He emphasized the torture: more civil-rights violations for Ernie to pursue.

"My boss wants me to call the Washington State attorney general first thing this morning. He probably won't be home. I don't know what to tell you."

"We have got to get some independent law enforcement in here," Sam began. "You would be good."

"With no official jurisdiction and against orders?"

"Uh-huh. This is so egregious, somebody is bound to do something. You might as well be here, Ernie, and get the glory. We are talking big things, Ernie, very big."

"Like what?" asked Ernie.

"Like terrorists blowing up the ocean."

"Are you out of your mind? It sounds hokey."

"Maybe."

Sam proceeded to give Ernie a breakdown of all Ben's discoveries, with an emphasis on the methane angle.

There was a very long pause.

Sam could imagine Ernie with his chin in his hand, squeezing it so tight his knuckles were turning white.

"This is serious."

"This involves the most important secrets to overcoming aging. And it's not just the future we're concerned about. We have people *killing* for Ben Anderson's knowledge," Sam said.

"All right. Hell. I'll probably get fired. Actually, I'm already in San Francisco. It automatically rings through to my cell. I hope my career survives this. Friday Harbor on San Juan Island, is that where I go?"

"Come there and I'll call you on the cell and tell you where we are. But if something goes wrong, we're going to Orcas Island, around Lime Kiln Road, or the Sawmill Road. Somewhere in there is an unmarked road. It has a couple branches. Follow the biggest No Trespassing signs."

"What I don't do for you." Ernie sighed. "Out of my jurisdiction, out of my mind—I tell you."

"Well, there is one more thing."

"Of course. There always is."

Sam knew he wouldn't like the next part.

"I'm on the Internet with a laptop through a satellite uplink. I need Grogg, wherever he is, to remote control Big Brain and then use Big Brain to remote control this PC and download the contents of this PC and break into some files."

"Are you kidding me? They'll have my ass."

"Don't go through channels; just call Grogg. It'll be on us."

"I'll tell Grogg what you need," Ernie said. "And let's be clear: I am not authorizing it."

"Perfect; that will insure Grogg's full commitment to the job," Sam joked. Another pause followed; then Sam explained how to get to the files and Ernie took notes.

Sam set up the computer online through the ship's satellite network so that it would be ready for a Grogg job.

From the resort on Lopez, Khan launched Sheriff's Boats 1 and 2 with sixteen of the hired men and made for Orcas. Others took vehicles on the morning interisland ferry. Frick sent Khan ahead without him, wanting to stay at a command center until somebody found something.

Orcas already had four deputies and five patrol cars. The sergeant remained drugged in a basement. They would keep the real deputies on the roads and checking leads. They'd use the special deputies for assaults on suspicious properties.

The cold air chilled Frick's skin as he stood on the back deck of the resort, sipping coffee, anxious for the caffeine to take hold. On the eastern horizon the black night sky was giving way to morning and he could see the first signs of light off in the west.

His radio crackled. Delia had McStott for him.

Frick tried not to sigh audibly.

"What is it?"

"I still don't know what Anderson's been making here in the lab, but I'm beginning to think I know what he's using it on."

"Yeah?"

"People." McStott let that sink in.

Big surprise. Frick almost laughed. "Is that so?"

McStott missed the sarcasm. "I think so. I mean, I'm pretty sure."

"If it turns out it's true and this stuff works, you'll be a rich man, McStott. If not, you may be a dead one."

Frick let McStott think on that. Once an egghead, always an egghead. McStott still didn't understand that he was dead meat either way.

The motors made an even slick hum as the boat rode over the flat obsidian smooth sea. The Boston Whaler was like a thoroughbred whose owner had fitted it to a plow. Mechanically, it was excellent transportation, traveling comfortably along at twenty-five knots at a little over half-throttle.

They pulled into Brown Island at Friday Harbor before daylight. There were some people that lived there year-round—the Milfords—but they were traveling in Europe. The dock was old but serviceable. They had dressed Sarah's neck wounds and various other abrasions left courtesy of Rafe Black. Her muscles were giving her trouble left over from Frick's tight bindings, but she was tough.

They went to the back door of the Milford place, a lovely well-maintained cottage, and Sarah found the key in its place.

"Are you sure you're okay by yourself?" Haley asked.

"I'm sure," Sarah said. With big hugs they parted.

"God, I hope she's safe," Haley said as they climbed back in the Boston Whaler. Without more words they shoved off and headed for Orcas.

They were in a hurry but had almost been killed enough times for one night so that they kept the boat at a reasonable speed. It was twilight Monday morning and using the spotlight was perhaps a little risky from the detection standpoint. They snapped it on occasionally through the tide rips, where wood collected. By the time they were well into Upright Channel, it was approaching sunrise and they could see well enough without the artificial light. As the gray morning painted the sky, they increased the speed to forty knots.

On the gunnels and the floorboards the evening dew vibrated in a soft glistening and that, together with the spray, made it a very wet place outside the fiberglass and canvas enclosure. For the Pacific Northwest's fall and winter, the boat had a hard fiberglass top. Inside, a vigorous diesel heater blew hot air, a hypothermic's dream.

Sam could not remember when he had been so tired. As he sat in the captain's chair and sagged, Haley watched him. In three or four more hours it would be about twenty-four hours since the nightmare had begun.

"Sleep," she said, and put her hand on his arm and took the wheel.

"Why don't you sleep," he said. "I've got to end this thing before I sleep."

"Me too," she said. "Me too."

They skimmed along in silence, dislodging the occasional seabird, a gull, a marbled murrelet, and a spoonbill duck. The usual tangles of kelp, driftwood, and sea grasses floated along, like small islands, sometimes a resting place for the sandpipers. They were going too fast to see the jellyfish, but the jumping bait fish were visible as a wrinkling on the surface and occasional miniature splashes. Sam spied plumes of white mist from a pod of orcas, followed by their black humps and large dorsals as they traveled San Juan Channel, past Shaw.

Sam glanced at Haley as she smoothed her hair back the way women tend to do when they know that a certain man is watching. He could not help enjoying the look of her and the angles of her face, and the look of the eyes that even now did not completely hide some mirth and tender guile.

In the end he couldn't stand the waiting. Frick was coming in from West Sound, having decided to take Sheriff's Boat 3, when Rolf finally got more specific in his clues. He relayed them to Khan and expected at any moment to hear Khan call in from a big, lodgelike place out in the forest on a bluff overlooking the water. Just as he was growing impatient, the call came through.

"It's right on President Channel."

Frick listened as Khan described what he and his men had found. "It's high up on the rocks. I'm down the road here, where the reception's better."

"What did you see?"

"The place looks like it was occupied very recently. We found a pipe burning in an ashtray. Hot coffee in a big multi-gallon dispenser. Suitcases in the rooms, shaving gear and toiletries out. It looks like they all just ran out of the house, but where—I don't know. They don't seem to be hiding in the bushes."

"Tell your guys to tear the place apart," Frick said.

"Give me credit," Khan replied. "I already did. They'll call me the minute they find something. Just so you know, the sign outside is for an Astrology Research Center. A local told us that several different astrology groups come here regularly. In theory, we could be breaking in on a bunch of zodiac buffs."

"Suddenly disappearing astrology buffs. That sound likely to you?"

"I hear you."

"Look, Khan, we're way too far gone to worry about who gets hurt. Keep all your men inside, unless they find something to chase outside. First sign of anything, call me and I'm there."

If anything went wrong, he didn't want to be there. The feebies had been asking a lot of questions of dispatch; it was hard enough just dodging them.

"You said we would leave by seven-thirty; that was half an hour ago," Rachael told the people around the table.

Lew put his hand on hers, obviously trying to calm her and keep her cooperating with the authorities. It was very Republican of him; she would have to explain the virtues of rebellion as the Founding Fathers understood it.

"We are going to leave in just a few minutes," good old Melrose said for the benefit of the FBI and Homeland Security people around the table.

"First we want your personal assessment of Ben Anderson," the Special Agent in Charge, a woman who had told Rachael to call her Gayle, asked Rachael. "Is he honorable? Does he have a plan? Is he stable?"

The dozen-plus other people listened with very serious faces. Gayle Killingsworth was the Special Agent in Charge of the downtown Seattle field office. Apparently she was married to a federal judge, if the banter at the coffee urn was to be believed. It disgusted Rachael that on this morning there was a coffee urn and that there was banter. People could be dying.

"I've answered all of these questions" was Rachael's response.

"But we keep learning things every time you explain," Gayle said with a *Good Morning America* smile.

"I have been at parties and social gatherings with Ben Anderson probably more than twenty times. I have dined with him more than a dozen times . . .," she started again. After five more minutes of how she knew what she knew, and questions about Haley and her near lifelong relationship with Haley—and her utter conviction that Haley had stolen nothing, Rachael slammed her hand on the table without warning.

Lew winced; she regretted his discomfort. Dating him after this was going to be difficult.

"I cannot sit here and answer the same questions while the lives of my friends are at stake," she said.

Gayle leaned forward and brushed back her short, well-coiffed hair.

"As we speak, we have agents moving into the area. We are on the phones. We have not located Garth Frick or the men you describe. It will do us no good to start flying around the San Juans."

"Actually, it might. I know the islands. Your people know nothing." Rachael's voice was intense, and Lew winced again. "Now let's get off our butts and talk while we travel."

Gayle sat back. "Get me Agent Willinsky."

A young male agent nodded and dialed a phone.

"How are we doing?" she asked when the phone was handed to her. "I don't understand why it isn't a simple matter of asking the dispatcher." There was another pause. "If the dispatcher refers us to Frick and says they're moving about, I want to talk with Officer Frick then. I want to know where they are so that we can render assistance." Another long pause. "Insist that you speak with him. Do you understand?" She hung up, disgusted, but tried to show a more hopeful demeanor. "I've changed my mind. We go now. I don't like what I'm hearing. At Port Angeles we can use a coast guard helicopter. From the reports Lopez is the latest hot spot. We'll go there. It's civil rights and potential terrorist activity." She trained her eyes on Rachael. "Satisfied?"

"Thank you so much," Rachael said, Lew's hand death-gripped in her own.

At last they were leaving; now maybe they could do some good.

CHAPTER 38

Sam and Haley came ashore at Deer Harbor, on an expansive modern dock attached to a substantial pier. It was nearly as close to Lime Quarry Road as the town of West Sound, but less traveled and less populated. Sarah's best memory had been that the mystery structure was on an unmarked access road, near Lime Stone Quarry, that rounded Turtle Mountain on a lower shoulder. Once they landed, they had no vehicle and there were none for rent this time of year, except at Rosario Resort, which was some distance away and risked alerting Frick's people.

Modern condos stood around the harbor proper; real estate here came at a premium. It was overcast and felt like temperatures were in the high forties, and Sam could feel the drizzle coming on. Even in the gray, the greens still managed to be vivid. The feathery tree needles had a translucence to them that lightened their color and made them seem more ethereal and at home in the ghostlike shrouds of floating mist that were not all that common even in winter. The lower foliage glistened with moisture like a well-tended grocer's aisle.

With Sam in the lead, they hurried past more than one set of prying eyes and hoped that none of them would be connected to Garth Frick. Once up the short hill and away from the harbor, they faded into the forest-covered hills and avoided the neighborhoods. The landscape was spacious and unencumbered with the trappings of high-density living; in the fall and winter quiet patches of morning fog hanging in the trees swallowed the sound before it could find a listening ear.

The invigorating chill made walking easy and gave an escape from sleepy lethargy. With the daylight it was not difficult traveling in the mostly open forest. Finally they crossed Saw Mill Road, then Lime Quarry Road, and turned parallel to an unnamed road. They remained in the forest, keeping Turtle Mountain to their right and heading toward President Channel.

The turnoff for the private road with the signs came very close to the end of the larger private road, and a little farther along than Sarah had remembered. They crept across the larger, more traveled road and followed along the private drive that took them ever closer to the inland sea and the channel. With the trees limbed up, the forest was especially open and they would be readily visible. As Sam motioned to slow their pace, they saw the lodgelike structure some distance away. From the water's edge a thick layer of fog climbed the hillside, looking like a giant wool carpet that had been pulled over the edge of the island.

Closer to the bluff, the cedar structure looked imposing. Sam estimated that it covered at least five thousand square feet on the footprint alone. It was two stories high, and the side closest the access drive appeared much more open because of the large parking area, circular drive, and covered entry.

Evidently the building site had been carved right out of the hillside and the forest, and a portion of the back side of the structure fell within fifty feet of the forest edge. As they got a better view of the high, rocky bluff, Sam guessed that the building stood some 150 feet above the water.

A closer glimpse revealed their worst fears. There were a number of cars, four of them deputy sheriffs' vehicles, parked in the large circular drive. A sign said *ARC Foundation* and in smaller letters beneath: *Astrology Research Center.*

Sam chuckled, knowing that someone must have thought long and hard to disguise Arc as an acronym rather than an abbreviation.

"What do we do now?" Haley said.

Sam's cell phone beeped and he answered.

"Hey," shouted one of the most irreverent and welcome voices Sam knew. "How goes it in the island paradise?"

"It's a little tough at the moment, Grogg."

"Ernie tells me you're back doing a job when you're supposed to be chasing babes or fishing or something."

"That seems to be what I'm doing, although there is a babe here." That got a sidelong glance from Haley.

"I opened one of the files," Grogg said. "One's a bitch and I haven't been able to open it yet, even with all the horsepower of the Brain and all her links. But I'll tell you what I did open."

"Let's hear it."

"According to this document, Ben Anderson is giving the magic antiaging stuff to a bunch of people. I could read you certain portions of the introduction to this report and you'd get the idea."

"Go ahead."

Sam motioned for Haley to hunker down with him; she brought her ear close enough to the phone to hear what Grogg said.

"Okay," Grogg began, "it starts with a bunch of letters to the government. They all address at least three different parties: Homeland Security, the FBI, and Health and Human

Resources. A few are copied to NOAA. Anderson lays out a program called ARCLES, and then he refers to certain meetings they've had and conference calls . . . okay . . . and then he says that he'll deliver the information—ARCLES, the secrets of the Archaea—that the government wants if the government agrees to do certain things in certain different, um, arenas. Anderson wants promises, commitments, even legislation. Oh, and funding. It goes on for pages—antiaging, undersea mining, climate programs, energy programs, protection from terrorism and natural disasters. Not surprisingly, it costs a hell of a lot of money. He wants the government to spend megabillions."

"Is there a government response?" Sam asked.

"Lots of them. But I don't see anywhere that the government says they'll do what he wants. I just went to the most recent correspondence and they aren't saying they'll comply. And he says that he won't cooperate until they reach an agreement on every item."

"The disasters? They involve methane?"

"Yeah. But the climate-change thing seems to be Anderson's main focus."

"And the mining is for methane?"

"Yeah."

"And what about the aging treatment?" asked Sam.

"There's a ton on that," said Grogg. "Here, let me read you something.

"The government must commit to a set of immutable principles regarding allocation of the Arc regimen for aging before impaneling any commission. The goal of the commission would be to develop regulations based on the principles, and to interpret the principles in regard to particular situations, and to make specific allocation decisions. Scientific achievement and contributions to humanity are to be the seminal principles

controlling allocation. Wealth can neither be an allocation criterion nor a disqualifier."

Grogg snorted. "No wonder the government's not game." Then he went on reading:

"The second prerequisite for the release of all information is that the government agree to comply with the manifesto. There must be an honest, binding commitment and a commensurate dedicated budget to the following three endeavors: (1) implementing serious experimental methane recovery from the deep ocean and coal deposits and alternative-energy development with a plan to make the United States foreign-petroleum independent within two decades; (2) an honest evaluation of the risks of methane escapement either through natural means or terrorist acts and a commensurate public education program which we see as crucial to mustering the national will; and (3) research into controlling greenhouse gases by farming the ocean for plankton and related research into long-term climate control."

"God," Sam said. "Ben has been busy."

Haley just shook her head, still stunned at how little Ben had shared with her.

"Okay," Grogg resumed, "that's the last of what Ben says to the government." He then launched into the government reply:

"It is premature to set forth principles of allocation regarding your Arc regimen. Before anything is done, appropriate, FDA-monitored trials must be conducted first with animals, then with people. After trials the next step must be to undertake a study, incorporating

*the research trials, that can be provided to appropri-
ate committees of the Congress so that they may for-
mulate legislation, if appropriate.*

*"Obviously the government cannot authorize the
immediate use of the Arc regimen on human subjects.
Please know that any such subjects will run the risk of
an interruption in the treatments.*

*"Though the government can make no assurances,
the FDA would be likely to expedite your application
for experimental trials, providing you agree to a full
and open disclosure of the science involved.*

*"As to the other matters, you will need to submit
your impressive body of theoretical work for peer review; once that is complete, your suggestions regarding methane mining, energy policy, safety, and climate
control can be presented to the legislature.*

"Then the government drones on about constitutional
democracies, the rule of law, and the like," Grogg said. "I'll
take some time with this stuff and try to figure out what's really going on."

"Do that. In the meantime we'll try not to get shot."

"Please be careful," Grogg said in a moment of utter so-
briety.

In his gut Sam dreaded the situation in the lodge. Frick
had beaten him to the building, which, in all likelihood,
housed the majority of Ben Anderson's secrets, if not Ben
Anderson himself.

"I can't believe that all this was going on and I never
knew it. I just don't get why he wouldn't tell me," Haley
said. "I know I said he was trying to protect me, but this is so
big. . . . Who did he think would protect him?"

"I understand how you feel," Sam said, hoping he wouldn't
sound too blunt. "Let's hope there's still time to get to Ben
and talk it over with him."

"Still, though—"

Sam turned and took her gently by the shoulders. "Haley, I don't mean to dismiss your feelings, but I don't want you dead either. It would help me a great deal if you would go back a few hundred yards into the woods and sit down and not move." Before she could protest, he continued. "Call Grogg if I don't come back. He can try to call Ernie in transit."

She didn't blink. "Not a chance."

"You're going no matter what I say?"

"Absolutely. Unless you have something even more dangerous that needs doing."

Sam shook his head, wondering at this woman.

"Sam, this is my problem as much as yours."

He stood, and motioned for her to follow.

"If you don't stay right behind me," he said, "I'll tie you to a tree."

Sam picked the spot closest to the forest, which was the back of the lodge, and crept toward a window. Haley followed like she was his shadow.

The longer the silence in the building continued, the greater his concern, and he'd told Haley as much.

The first window was a back bedroom with no one inside. There was, however, an open suitcase, clothes hanging in an open closet, and shoes in the corner. An open book lay facedown on the nightstand.

They crouched and moved to the next window, that of a corner bedroom, its inner door open. Through the door Sam could see into a large living area with a ceiling that appeared to rise for two stories all the way to the roof. Peering for another ten or twenty seconds, Sam was sure he saw the foot of a man lying down, probably on his side, in the living area. His arm went around Haley's shoulder before he realized he was holding her. He hurried with her back the way they had come and beyond the first bedroom window to the next bedroom. Once again the door was open and this time Sam could see through to the great room, where at least two bodies lay on the floor.

"It's time to go inside."

"Let's go," she said.

"I wish you'd stay out here."

"One of us is hard of hearing," Haley whispered. "And it's not me because I'm staying right behind you. As instructed."

They circled to the front, saw no one around the parked vehicles, and tried the front door. Sam opened it and immediately he felt light-headed. They pushed the door all the way open and stepped back. Two men, both in the uniform of the San Juan Sheriff's Department, lay sprawled on the floor, unconscious.

"Gas," Sam said. "But I don't know what kind of gas would knock someone out this way and keep them down."

Nelson Gempshorn and American Bayou came to mind. The company manufactured all sorts of medical equipment and could easily administer a heavy sedative. But to take out this many men?

They waited and watched for a moment; then Sam hurried in and opened windows around the first floor, holding his breath the entire time. He returned, and this time they waited for three or four minutes on the front doorstep.

They went back in. As they walked through the first floor of the lodge, they found a back bedroom with four more men on the floor. The men looked rough and ready, even in repose: definitely Frick men.

"It's odd that four men were all right here," Sam said. "I wonder what they were looking at?"

Sam looked around, searching the walls and the floor. Haley followed, doing the same. The men lay near a heavy large trunk. Closer inspection of the men and the floor revealed that they probably were gassed, shot by a Taser, and then anesthetized with a hypodermic in the neck. It was elaborate.

Haley pointed at the trunk, and Sam nodded in agreement. Together they pushed on the trunk, but it wouldn't move. It took a moment to realize that it was affixed firmly to the floor. They tried opening it, but it was locked.

"This trunk is curious," Sam said.

"Yes, it is," a voice said. It seemed to come from inside the trunk.

Sam smiled. Such incredible surprises amused him.

"Would it be . . . ?"

"Ben Anderson and company."

The trunk slowly began to open. Sam and Haley stepped back in disbelief. Ben Anderson stuck his head out. Oddly, he wore handcuffs.

Without another thought Haley leaned forward and hugged him long and hard.

"Oh, thank God you're all right," she said.

After they had hugged again, and reproclaimed their joy at seeing one another, Sam cocked his head and pointed at Ben's handcuffs.

"Oh. Yes. If you want to come down, you'll have to put these on. My friends are the anxious sort. Very anxious, actually."

"Where would we be going?" For some reason Sam felt less anxious than he knew he ought to.

"Under this lodge is a very large hollowed-out vault in the rock, and below that an exit out to the sea, as well as tunnels leading to other exits above ground. It's a big place down here."

"These islands are all glacial till," Haley said. "You taught me that yourself. How can there be a cavern?"

In place of an answer Ben held out two sets of cuffs. "I know I haven't been . . . truthful with you." He was directing his comments at Haley, but he glanced at Sam as well. "You can trust me, if that's what you're wondering."

Sam wondered about Ben's "friends," but he didn't see a choice in the matter. First he moved the bodies away from the trunk in hopes of keeping the trunk's secret a secret. Then he accepted the cuffs, along with Haley.

Ben led them down a long set of stairs. Sam closed the trunk over their heads and latched the strong but simple lock.

"Miners around the turn of the century made part of this," Ben said, belatedly answering Haley. "So in that sense it's not truly a cavern. For some reason there's limestone in this granite and that's a riddle that the geologists can debate. Now you'll get an idea just how giant these rocks can get. One of them had a hollow in it, as you'll see below."

Sam shook his head silently. This had become surreal, a sort of mix of *Alice in Wonderland* and *Charlie and the Chocolate Factory*, with Ben playing the role either of the white rabbit or the chocolatier, take your choice.

There were stairs and lots of them, a new test for Sam's legs. For twenty feet or so the steps had been carved in the rock; after that, they were made of wood, going down in a square-edged spiral. Twenty to thirty men stood at the bottom, all gazing upward as they descended. One of them was Lattimer Gibbons. Two were younger men armed with no-nonsense Uzis, both bulky, with backs straight and shoulders squared, obviously the sort whose business was protection. Sam didn't see the two women mentioned in the documents.

As they reached the cavern floor, Sam noted a silver-haired man with a mustache and a bruise on his cheek, who seemed to be calling the shots. He had a perpetual slight smile as a regular part of his expression, as if none of the ironies of life were ever lost on him. Of the group he seemed the most confident, speaking in short, clipped sentences when he wanted one of the Uzi fellows to move.

"Nelson Gempshorn," Ben said.

Sam and Gempshorn nodded at one another.

As Sam and Haley stood for introductions, they took in the whole of the cavern, which was larger than Sam had expected, and carved from gray stones with occasional white streaks in the walls. In the middle of the man-made cave, and nearly filling it, stood a structure that looked like a typical upper-middle-class house, complete with siding and windows—except that the roof angles were shallow and the shape was rather boxlike. The floor around the building was stamped concrete that Sam recognized from one area of the Sanker lab complex. Coming from the top of the building, and disappearing into the side of the cave, ran a very large duct pipe.

Another extraordinary feature of the place was a giant copper tank, the size of a two-car garage, in the shape of an ellipse, with all manner of tubes and wire about it. With its hand-crafted look, the contraption appeared to be something out of a nineteenth-century science-fiction story.

"What on earth is that?" Haley asked. "Don't tell me, let me guess. You grow Arcs under pressure and with no oxygen in it."

"Very good," Ben said, stepping closer to hold her hand. He indicated the general space. "We imported labor to do the rock work and build the lab. Most of the workers, I'm embarrassed to say, were in the country legally but working illegally. We took the best of some Mexican crews building condos for Americans in Baja. When they were down here, they didn't even know where they were. We built the whole thing in ten weeks. No one left the compound during underground construction. It was a phenomenal effort. Of course, the copper vat was built by some very curious metalworkers in a metal-fab shop three states away."

Sam looked around, wondering at both the physical plant

and the well-preserved, older gentlemen standing around him.

"We have a great shaft down to the base of the cliffs that comes out in the sea. Originally we used it to house a large conveyor that moved some of the broken-up rock out to the sea bottom. It also served as an underwater test bed for our research ideas. That was, and is, its most important function. Today its third and final use comes into play: it's a useful hidden entry to the lab, and an emergency exit."

"How did you fund this project?" Sam asked.

"All courtesy of American Bayou Technologies."

Haley and Sam shared a look, wondering how that worked. "I'm astounded," Haley said. "All those times you said you were going to Seattle, you were coming here, weren't you?"

Ben looked a little sheepish and Sam knew that Haley was getting heated up.

"I don't see how you could do this . . .," she began.

"Haley, there is a special calling for you. It is a very important position of leadership. In the coming days you will understand why I had to tell you nothing."

To Sam, Ben's words were a great illumination of the twilight that surrounded the grand plan. But his attention returned to Ben's wrists. Of all the scientists in the cavern, Ben was the only one wearing handcuffs.

Ben anticipated Sam's question.

"Nelson is the president of our little club at the moment," Ben said. "He speaks for the group. We had a very big misunderstanding, which we've mostly straightened out."

"I see," Sam said. "And I gather you're not part of the group."

"He is one of us," Nelson said. "We're just cautious about Ben."

"Why is that?" Sam asked quickly before Haley could protest.

"Because he is an idealist and we are dealing with hard,

practical realities." Nelson said it without derision and Ben seemed to accept it that way.

"It's also because they are slightly paranoid from the Arc regimen and don't really know it," Ben said in a stage whisper.

"That's your view," said Nelson good-naturedly.

From above came the sound of an electrical motor and two large metal plates moved to cover the entry hole, one immediately under the trunk, the other just above the spiral wooden staircase. It would take hours or days to break through the metal plates. Going around them would entail burrowing through solid granite.

As the plates settled into place, one of the beefy security men unlocked Sam's handcuffs. Before Sam could comment, the guard refastened them behind Sam's back.

"I'm Sam and I'm pleased to meet you," he said to the beefcake.

The man nodded, but his face didn't change expressions. "I've heard from Ben that you're a guy who knows his way around."

The other guard never moved his Uzi from Sam's midriff.

"Let's go to the conference room," Ben said, seeming to pay no attention to the Uzis or the handcuffs.

Inside, the house-cum-laboratory was crammed with equipment; in the middle stood a large workbench with a vent over its top. To the right, before entering the lab, was a conference room as spartan and functional as the lab itself.

"The amenities stay topside," Ben said, as if to explain as the group squeezed into the room.

No one responded.

"This thing with the guns and cuffs is silly," Ben said.

"When the whole world will soon be plotting against you," said Nelson, "it is normal to be paranoid." He smiled slightly.

"All right," Ben said. "Everyone here but me, Len, and

Stu is on what we call the Arc regimen. Nelson is on a modified lesser form. Hence, he's a little less paranoid."

Nelson didn't smile this time.

"We've read about it," Haley said.

"What have you read?"

Haley explained quickly and very succinctly.

"You got into Sarah's computer," Ben said. "Good for
you."

"How were we supposed to know to look there?" Haley
asked.

"You got your birthday pearls?"

"Yes," Haley said.

"There was a line drawing in there. It was of a watercolor
at Sarah's place. Back of the watercolor."

"Oh," Haley said.

"You must have had your hands full," Sam said, looking
at Nelson Gempshorn when he said it.

"I have, for some time," Ben said. "And given the situation above us, it's time the counsel voted."

Sam and Haley shared another glance, wondering what
this could mean.

Nelson looked uncertain; the rest of the group appeared
to be concerned, but no one spoke.

Ben turned to Sam. "I believe I have persuaded them that
we need to completely cloak the secrets of longevity. Destroying files and notes is one thing. You and Frick probably
have all that's left, in the way of documentation. To finish the
job we need to release Glaucus into the sea. He has genetic
markers that could be reverse-engineered to reveal part of
the regimen."

"But he could reproduce," Haley said.

"No. He can't," Ben said. "I'll explain, but first we need
the vote." He addressed his next comment to the group of
scientists: "I have to be freed along with Sam and Haley to
go release Glaucus."

As Nelson rose and left to discuss the matter with an apparent American Bayou fellow executive, Ben told the other men, "I would like to talk in private."

Without argument the others left and closed the conference room door.

Haley started to speak, but Ben interrupted her, a grave look on his face.

"Let me explain, sweetie. I kept you out of this because we were breaking the law. If you have an unapproved pharmaceutical and you give it to someone in order to stop them from dying, you are breaking the law. Maybe not a moral law but some regulation or other of the federal government. I knew eventually I'd need someone completely clean and uninvolved to be a leader and an intermediary with the government. I hoped you would be one of those people. I was going to bring you in, once we made a deal in principle with the government."

"It makes sense to me," Sam said, but he could tell that Haley didn't completely buy it. In time she would.

"What was the big misunderstanding you had with Nelson?" Sam asked.

Ben lowered his voice. "For a long time I've been sure that Sanker would do anything to get sole ownership of the regimen. So I created an imaginary persona—I called him Judas—to contact Sanker. Judas was a turncoat, someone close to me, who told them a lot and offered to sell me out."

Sam couldn't help but smile at the crafty counterintelligence plan that Ben had concocted.

"When Judas contacted them," Ben said, "instead of calling me, Sanker worked with Judas against me, including hiring Frick."

Sam had a guess. "Did Lattimer Gibbons play 'Judas' for you?"

Ben nodded. "When I knew Sanker was bad, I did some things. I was also worried about my colleagues." He nodded in the direction of Nelson and the group. "The regimen affected their mental condition."

"We read about that," Haley said.

"So are you and the Arc regimen scientists on the same side, seeing eye to eye? With handcuffs?" Sam said wryly.

"You have to understand that they are slightly paranoid, anyway, and a couple days ago they discovered that all the Arcs in that vat had been deliberately exposed to oxygen by yours truly and the Arc DNA destroyed. The Arcs in the vat died in the microbial sense. Although I saved some Arcs in a special container, the other scientists did not know that, and this misunderstanding was critical in their thinking. I destroyed all the documentation in the vault beneath this building. That's a pretty outrageous thing to do. Nelson and the others didn't know I'd saved a batch of Arcs in a special portable container. To reassure them, I had left a note saying that I kept some of the Arc regimen in Seattle and I saved some Arcs as well. They didn't find the note, though, and . . . Well, they went nuts. As a result they did things they shouldn't have done. Like they kidnapped me and brutalized me terribly in a mental sense, although they never intended to hurt me physically.

"Once I explained that I hadn't destroyed all the Arcs—that I had written some things down in Sarah's computer—they became somewhat mollified."

"But not completely," Sam said.

In response Ben held up the cuffs.

"But could they create the Arc regimen without you?"

"Between you and me, probably not. Don't forget, various of them know most of the parts. I think maybe all the parts, generally, if you put all of their knowledge together. But I actually created it and there are many details. And there is another problem that we can discuss, and that is whether we should keep this technology. But as far as it goes, we are mostly on the same side, they and I. Maybe completely. If they can't stay on Arc, though, we may not be on the same side."

"We hope they are with us," Sam said. "Clearly Frick is against us."

"No doubt about that."

"And Sanker."

"No doubt about that, although Frick and Sanker may not be together."

Sam and Haley nodded their understanding.

"There clearly was more to Lattimer than met the eye," Sam said.

Ben laughed at that. "He sent you to my study in the workshop at Sanker because, until recently, I kept plans for this place there. If you found the plans, you could find this place. He figured your leaving would free him up, and it would also lead you here, eventually. He wanted you to find me, but he didn't want to betray his brethren or lie to them. It's a little odd, but that was Lattimer's way of having it both ways."

"What about the call to Sarah?" Haley asked.

"That was Nelson trying to get to her computer and, to be fair, to save her as well. He believed Frick had her. Lattimer called Sanker and even suggested that the way for Sanker to get what they wanted was to let Sarah go and follow her to Ben. Lattimer was doing his best as Judas to get Sanker to call Frick off Sarah."

"What I don't get," Haley said, "is how you afforded all this. I mean, did Nelson do all this through American Bayou, out in the open?"

"Yep," Ben said. "Maybe not completely out in the open, but to answer your question, American Bayou Technologies is running the energy part of this show. Initially they were investing in the methane-mining part of the equation. In fact, we've been testing certain mining precepts out through the underwater tunnel here. Sanker has no legal interest in that aspect, but they would have made a fortune on the aging discovery if they hadn't tried to steal it. In the end Sanker probably would have controlled American Bayou. Instead, old Sanker himself tried to have Frick kill me and steal Arc."

"So what do you want to do now?" Haley asked.

"I'm still trying to decide if the world is ready for this."

"And?"

"I don't know." Ben looked crestfallen. And uncertain. "I don't know," he repeated. "Right now the genie's not back in the bottle until Glaucus is set free." He paused. "It's a terrible decision to make. I'm responsible for the renewed lives of more than thirty people."

Before he could continue, Nelson and one of the security men entered the conference room. Nelson looked as wild-eyed as any of the other scientists now, but he kept the tone of his voice even.

"They have broken out all the windows up above and now they are tearing the place apart, board by board. They have pulled all the unconscious men outside on the lawn. It is only a matter of time until they discover the steel door."

Ben rose.

"We can't put these men down safely like we did the first group," Nelson said as Ben followed him out.

"Are they going to let us go?" Haley called after Ben.

"We're about to find out," Ben said.

CHAPTER 39

Frick stood in the great room of the Astrology Research Center, trying to calculate whether they could tear it apart fast enough. Burning the place was an option that presented as many difficulties as benefits. Any paperwork hidden away in a wall would likely be destroyed.

Khan's men were emptying cupboards and tearing through walls and furniture, and even examining the giant brick fireplace.

Khan stuck his head out of a bedroom door. "We got something."

Frick walked into the bedroom and saw a trunk that had been torn to shreds with a pry bar. Underneath it was a large opening that could only be an entrance. And underneath it, a solid steel sheet.

"Get through it," Frick said.

There was a man standing near Khan who looked like he understood something about such things. "Its edges are fit into the rock. We have no idea how thick the steel is. It will be very tough to jackhammer the rock and get around the edge. Not in a few minutes, anyhow."

"There must be another exit," Frick said. He nodded toward the men around him and Khan began organizing them. "We aren't going to use a jackhammer," Frick said. "I have something much better."

Frick went to the Suburban with tinted glass, which he'd had brought from San Juan Island. In the back lay several wooden boxes. Combined together, they contained a phenomenal arsenal.

Frick brought out five automatic weapons and chose one. "Hopefully, you men are familiar. This is the P90. Be careful on the trigger. Take a few minutes and get used to it. You may need to use it."

The men walked off toward the house.

Next he grabbed a handheld M136 AT4 88mm antitank rocket launcher with six rockets. A second lay beside it.

"What you got there?" Khan asked.

"It's an antitank rocket," Frick said. "Should bore right through steel. Then it'll explode and blow the hell out of everything. Help me with these."

Khan motioned two men over; the three of them carried the boxes back to the house.

Khan seemed amused. "What else you got?"

"Claymore mines and good old-fashioned TNT."

Khan's cell rang as they got to the house.

Frick took the antitank weapon into the room and stared at the steel plate. Firing it in close quarters was a problem, but if he stood outside, it would strike only a glancing blow. The men would mutiny if he tried to sacrifice one of them, likewise the sheriff's deputies. Quickly he took the P90 upstairs and shot a circular hole in the floor. It wasn't easy and required several clips, but he didn't want to use up a Claymore just yet.

After he made sure all of the men were away from the house, he found a volunteer who wanted to make $10,000.

The man stood on the second floor and aimed the rocket directly down on the steel door. Frick went outside.

Everyone waited. There were seventeen men ringing the house, not counting those unconscious on the lawn.

"Well, fire," Frick shouted. "We're in a hurry."

"I'm not sure about this," the man called out.

The men muttered about Heinz being a chicken. Frick went back inside, climbed the stairs, and looked at the fear-filled face of a thirty-five-year-old bodybuilder. His hair was cropped close and blond and his eyes were blue. With that physique he certainly hadn't seemed like a coward.

"Heinz is your name, right?"

"Yeah."

"Well, Heinz, would you hand me the rocket launcher?"

The man looked uncertain, so Frick took it.

"I'll do it. I'm just trying to figure . . ." Heinz faltered.

Frick aimed the weapon and hid his face in the crook of his arm. He fired while Heinz was still talking and had turned his face toward the hole, unprotected. The shot and the massive explosion from the impact were simultaneous. It threw Frick backward, along with the big fellow.

"I can't see!" Heinz screamed from the floor.

"Should've covered your eyes," Frick muttered. His own forearm was bleeding; it would have been his face, had he not covered it.

"Let me help you," he said to Heinz. He took Heinz's hand and, after getting him on his feet, pushed him in the direction of the hole. Heinz fell through and landed head down. He made a small noise and his body shook. It smelled like he'd defecated.

"Terrible tragedy," Frick said when Khan met him in the room.

"We can't afford to lose men," Khan said.

"He was no man."

The explosive rocket had opened a large, jagged hole in the steel plate. Frick held his breath against all the dust and lowered himself through the ripped metal.

"I need a light."

"Light," Khan called out.

"I need the damn Claymores and a stick of that TNT."

Even with the light, it was hard to see. He took a few steps down what felt like a stone stairwell. As the dust settled, he discerned what appeared to be another slab of steel about twenty feet below.

Khan joined him with the Claymores and TNT. When Frick armed the Claymores, Khan looked nervous.

"Nothing to worry about," Frick said. "If one of these babies go off, you won't even have time to think about it. You'll just be gone. You hold one, have Jake hold the other. I'll blow a hole with the rocket. Then I'll throw down the TNT. Then we'll send some men down. If anybody wants to fight you, get down in there and see if there's an opening to toss a Claymore. Now, if there isn't, you be very careful until we get the mines disarmed. You got that?"

"It all sounds good," Khan said, "except the part where I go down in there."

Frick stuck the rocket launcher over the lip and made sure it was aimed down the stairwell at the door. He got his men with the automatic weapons ready to go. He pulled the trigger and the rocket detonated with an earthshaking roar. Frick fell onto his back, his arm burned but functional.

Looking down the hole, he saw that the plate had been breached. Next he threw the TNT. This explosion equaled the rocket's.

"Now," said Frick, "we'll see if anybody wants to fight."

Outside the conference room Nelson whispered in Ben's ear.

"The counsel is uncertain about letting you go," Ben said when he returned. "No one has broken in yet."

The "counsel" members looked like nervous cats. Sam thought that drugs might indeed be in order if you were on the regimen; he didn't fancy spending a very long middle age fidgeting like that.

"I hope they know," Haley said, "just how bad Frick is. He's right above us now, and believe me, you don't want to find out. He'll torture us and then kill us to get what he wants."

"And presumably he wants," said a slim, white-haired gentleman, "the Arc regimen. Correct?"

Ben and Haley both nodded.

"If we gave it to him, would he let us go?" the man asked.

"Of course not," Nelson said. "They need to steal it without witnesses."

"That's right," Sam said. "Doesn't matter if Frick's still working for Sanker or himself. No witnesses."

Ben closed his eyes. Haley unconsciously moved closer to Sam.

"We're not only dealing with a greedy criminal," Sam said. "Frick's also a desperate man. His old plan, framing Haley and me, won't work now. He's gone too far. He'll keep coming until we stop him."

All at once, everyone involuntarily ducked as a massive reverberation coursed through the rock, followed by an ear-splitting boom.

"It sounds like they might be making progress," Ben said.

"That was heavy military stuff," Sam said. "Now who's going to let me out of these?" He indicated his hands cuffed behind him.

"I think we should unlock them," the guard Len said. "We may need them."

Nelson unlocked Sam's handcuffs first, then Haley's and Ben's.

"I'd like to make use of one of those Uzis," Sam said.

Len obliged him without hesitation.

"Everybody needs to get out of here," Sam said.

"There are other tunnels," Ben said, "but the three of us and a couple of others will take a boat. It's standing by. We'll go the underwater route."

As Ben spoke, the other scientists hurried out of the chamber, using a small, steel portal hidden near the back.

"That's great. You and Haley go. I'll stay with Len and we'll give everybody a head start. I'll catch you if I can. But don't wait. I'd suggest the other big fellow here go with you."

"I'm Stu," he said.

"Get going, and keep her safe, Stu."

"Count on it," he said.

"I can shoot," Haley said. "I'm staying."

Sam knew that she meant every word of it, and he stared at the ceiling for a moment, as if seeking inspiration. "I could argue the greater good, and that would be true," he said, turning and looking into her eyes. "Or that Ben needs you, and that would also be true. But what if I simply don't want to deal with it if you die? How about I've had enough people die? You've taken enough chances." He could tell his words were rolling off her like water. "Let me talk to you."

He glanced at the others, who moved away as if distracted by their upcoming exit.

"Right now," Sam said, "in a way, I'm like your mother. This is a critical moment for me, for us. Letting you go— *making* you go—is the only smart decision, no matter how I feel, no matter how you feel. Think about your mom. You were the only really precious thing she had. You were her caretaker, her dream, her reason for living. And still she gave you up so you could live, thrive. Survive. And right now I need to do the right thing, just like your mom. And so do you."

Haley bit her lower lip. She was looking in his eyes, engaging him in a mutual soul search that neither fully understood.

"Okay," she said at last. "Okay." She kissed him on the cheek.

Thank the Great Spirit, he thought.

"Take the left-hand fork," Ben said as they moved to the back of the cavern.

Sam kissed Haley back; then she followed Ben to the same small, steel portal with Nelson and Stu.

"Pleased to meet you, Len," he said. Since they might die together, Sam figured a proper introduction was in order.

"Likewise," Len said, arming himself with another Uzi.

They had just taken cover behind folds in the rock wall when another massive explosion came from above the staircase. An avalanche of dust poured out of the ceiling.

The last of the older men had disappeared down a side tunnel. It was all happening too fast.

Because of the narrow entry they could hold off a small army, unless Frick had enough military firepower to kill everyone in the vault.

Sam was counting the seconds, estimating that he needed to give the others a five-minute head start.

"Cover your ears," Sam told Len.

There was then a huge explosion that blew the wooden stairs in every direction.

Sam held the Uzis between his legs, plugging his ears. Then he saw something else falling and pulled back as tight as he could against the rock. The explosion was incredible and he felt the shock wave in his body.

In his mind he saw another explosion of white. He was in the room, Anna was screaming.

Another explosion rocked the cavern. The shock wave slammed him against the rock.

This time he could see Anna screaming, begging to die.

In front of him, his female captor taunted him. She had loosened one of his hands.

Another explosion slammed into him.

Her lips were forming obscene words. Faster than she could see, Sam drove his fingers into her eyes and felt the membranes give as he pushed deep into the sockets, enough to put out the light forever. He hit the man with his elbow before he could react, the distance between them perfect for achieving maximum force. The blow went to the point of his nose, shattering bone and cartilage, driving it into the brain, dropping him to the floor like a sack of cement.

The woman was clutching her face, screaming. Sam grabbed her gun from the holster at her waist. The other two men had heard the ruckus and ran back into the room with guns drawn. A glance to the side showed a dim, final light in Anna's eyes; she was begging Sam to shoot her, the words and tone pure and without a hint of doubt. Then her head rocked to the side, shattered by another man's bullet. Something broke inside Sam, blurring the actions that followed.

But here, near the end of his life, huddling in a rock cavern under assault, Sam felt a great release inside him that he could not explain with words.

Once again his eyes saw what lay before him. The small building was full of bullet puncture and other, jagged holes. In the space of a few seconds, the laboratory had been ruined.

For a moment nothing happened. It was dead quiet. Sam looked around at what little was left of the wooden stairs, also blown apart. It didn't appear that the remaining fragments of the stairway would hold a man; Frick may have outsmarted himself.

Sam looked over at Len. He groaned at what he saw and tried not to second-guess himself. Len lay on the floor bleeding from the head. If he weren't dead already, he soon would succumb. Sam looked again just in time to see the green blur

of the next falling weapon. Once again he covered and again
came a terrific explosion.

He looked at his watch. Three minutes had passed. A man
on a rope descended quickly with a rappelling device alongside the stairs. Scooping up Len's Uzi, Sam fired a burst. The
man on the rope appeared dead when he hit the ground.
Within sixty seconds a rocket came down the hole and there
was another fiery explosion near the base of the stairs.

The next time a rocket launcher appeared out of the ceiling, it was pointed nearly parallel to the ceiling. When it was
released, a blinding explosion appeared across the cave,
some fifty feet in front of Sam. Even though he was behind
solid rock, the shock wave traveled around the vault and hit
Sam like a fist. But for his hands over his ears, he knew he
would be deaf. Another man rappelled against the destroyed
stairs, only this time the rocket launcher appeared simultaneously. Sam didn't want to lose his ears, so he covered. His
eyes were closed just long enough to avoid being blinded by
the flash. The man hit the ground, shooting an automatic
weapon at him. It was probably a P90, a superior weapon to
the Uzi.

Sam fired back, hitting the man, but to no immediate effect. *Flak jacket.* He glanced around the cavern. Instead of
watching the man on the ground, he looked to the ceiling.
The moment he saw the rocket launcher come down, he released a burst at the opening. A hail of bullets poured in
from the man on the ground. Sam flattened himself against
the rock, but not before he saw the rocket launcher fall. He
had wounded the man who held it.

Sam heard sounds of gunfire from a new direction, in the
distance, and he imagined a firefight wherever the extra exit
tunnels emerged. He wondered how many of the old men
would be slaughtered by Frick. It renewed his determination.
Taking a terrible chance, he tossed his coat out from the
rock, drawing a hail of bullets. He took the moment to focus

on the fallen rocket launcher and to fire at it. With a near blinding flash it exploded a few yards from the shooter. As he ran for the small, steel portal, Sam could see the mangled body.

This wasn't going the way he had planned.

As quickly as possible, Haley, Ben, Nelson, and Stu donned bulky diving suits, known as dry suits, designed to keep the moisture out and warmth in. Haley, like many marine biologists, was an experienced diver, and they were ready in a third of the time that might normally be required by the inexperienced. They pulled the dry suits over their clothes, while more explosions came from above. All Haley could think about was Sam. She cursed herself for letting him stay.

When ready, they dropped the sea sleds in the sea and did a large scissor step into the water, which Haley discovered was at least twenty feet deep. They each grabbed a sled, pulled the triggerlike throttle, and started down into a round rock bowl, cored by a corrugated pipe of at least ten feet in diameter. The pipe was the only exit.

Haley and the others had gone through the same steel portal at the rear of a cave and into a rough tunnel carved from the rock. Fortunately, the lights still worked. Sam didn't want to be stuck feeling his way around in the blackness with no light. Behind the steel door he looked for a crossbar and found it. A stout board slipped through two steel holders affixing the door in the closed position. It was a common but brilliant idea. If they had no more antitank rockets, they might be stymied for long enough to enable Haley and Ben to escape.

When Sam came to a fork in the tunnel, he took the left,

as Ben had said. The right-hand fork probably had led the others to the surface.

Sam climbed down a circular stairwell of cut stone that seemed endless. When he got to the bottom, he found another much smaller vault carved in the rock, its floor primarily seawater.

Off the main vault was a side vault, housing a closetlike chamber. Just in front of the chamber they had laid out two sets of dive gear and a couple torpedo-shaped sleds. He had seen but had never personally used the latter. Another explosion rocked the stone around him, its blast forcing air and debris into the vault.

So much for his head start.

Without warning Sam was plunged into darkness, able to see nothing, neither the gear nor even the water. He could not hope to don the intricate dive gear.

He was trapped.

CHAPTER 40

Each sea sled had a bright light that lit the inside of the pipe, the bottom of which was covered with a sprinkling of sand, which stirred from the quiet whir of the propellers as they skimmed over the rippled surface, their chests just inches from the sand. It was claustrophobic and the thought that you couldn't just rise and burst from the surface into the clean salt air was never far from consciousness.

The divers entered single-file and continued for about three minutes, then broke into open water at a depth of about sixty feet.

Ben turned parallel to the beach, obviously intending to come up a good distance from the lodge. Would they be shot like fish in a barrel? Haley worried about that, and she worried even more about Sam.

Based on his memory, Sam felt for the pile of dive gear and turned on the air to one tank. Pushing the purge valve, he verified that it had some air and hoped it was full. Feeling the second tank, he unscrewed the regulator and opened the valve, creating an eerie, very loud hissing sound as the tank began to empty.

The shoulder straps on the buoyancy compensator doubled as a backpack. Sam slipped it on over his pants and shirt and managed to find the mask by the tank and some fins. Once he had the tank, mask, and fins on, he fired the Uzis in the direction of the water, hoping to scare someone with the sound.

"We need more lights," he heard someone shout from above. All his diving had been for sport, and usually in the tropics, and no one had ever shown him how to turn on a sled. Given that he had as little as a minute or two, he knew he had to get in the water and get out of sight. He pulled on the fins, sucked the mask tight to his face to make sure he had a seal, and sat on the edge of the rocks. In the water with the sled he tried the trigger throttle. Nothing. There was no time to grope in the darkness and guess at where the switch might be. Going into the cold ocean with no dive suit and no light was foolish, but it was his only choice. He kicked in a direction he thought was down, until he hit the bottom, then swam with his hands touching the bottom, until he hit a rock sidewall. It was pitch black and he could see nothing. The cold felt worse than he had imagined; he didn't know how long he could stay conscious this time around.

Feeling along the rock, he hoped for an opening. The rock disappeared and it felt like metal. As his fingers ran along the corrugated metal wall, he thought about meeting his Maker. Even if he made it out to the sea, he wasn't at all sure he would be able to remain down long enough. Without doubt the cliffs would be rimmed with shooters.

Frick and Khan had remained in the lodge by the shattered trunk.

"Maybe we should go down," Khan said.

"Anderson had months or years to prepare security here," Frick said. "There have to be other exits, some on land, some in the sea. I think they'll come up in the ocean and a boat will come. That's why we heard about boats and divers on President Channel. It's the reason nobody notices large groups driving vehicles in and out. It's why I sent men to the bluff. Let's get a report first."

When the report came, Frick didn't like what he heard. No live bodies and apparently no significant research materials—written or otherwise—anywhere in the cavern that they could find. The search was continuing.

"So where the hell did they go?" he asked his man.

"Down into a stone stairway," the man radioed back, breathless. "It goes to a pool, looks like the sea. There's no usable diving equipment. There are tanks, but the valves are all open and they're empty. We can't pursue. Repeat, we—"

"I heard you," Frick growled. It was just as he'd thought, although he hoped his men would catch up before they completed their exit. "Khan?"

"Yo."

"Get men down the bluff. If anybody comes to the surface in front of the bluffs, cut 'em to pieces—unless it's Ben Anderson. Him we have to swim for."

"At this late date, what good will shooting divers do us?" Khan asked.

"It'll make me feel a hell of a lot better. I want Chase dead. He won't forget."

"All right. But then we take what we have and we leave," Khan said.

"I'll take the sheriff's boat around from West Sound. You go by land. We should get them one way or the other."

"After that, I've had enough," Khan said. "If the men find something, I'll bring it." He paused. "There's one other thing. McStott's back on the octopus. Said he told you about it before, but now he has proof that it's got the genetic markers. Could be at least part of the formula."

"He also said it could take a long time to learn anything from it," Frick said.

"Look where we're at," Khan said. "You wanna leave it behind?"

"So what do we need? Just a good-size piece of that ugly bastard?"

"That's what he says."

Frick snapped his fingers. "Wait a minute. You suppose *that's* where they're going?" He thought for a second. "I bet they are. Kill the octopus and hide the carcass, and the secret's safe. Call the foundation and tell them to stop anybody from getting near Glaucus."

"All we got's McStott, Rolf, and a couple broken-down old night watchmen."

Frick realized he was right. His radio crackled: "There's men coming out a hole in the ground."

Now Frick could hear the shots.

"Big bastard's in the rear and shooting an automatic."

"Let's go," Frick said.

They ran about twenty-five yards into some trees and came to three of their men hunkered down. Almost immediately they jumped flat on the ground as automatic fire whacked the trees, throwing wood about like a buzz saw.

The radio crackled again: "There's a boat."

"Follow the guys on foot," Frick said to Khan. They called for more men and Frick ran back toward the lodge.

Breaking out of the trees, Frick ran across the plateau through green grass grown high by fall rains. When they made the edge, they saw two divers in the back of a large yacht. A third was climbing up the ladder. His men were down the bluff somewhere and obviously weren't seeing the boat.

The dive tanks were in the back in the cockpit of the yacht, and even as he watched, a man at the helm gave it power and the boat pulled out. Frick looked for a man with an automatic weapon but found none. He grabbed his semi-automatic pistol and aimed, thinking he might shoot the dive tanks; he emptied the pistol.

"Too far away," one man, who had just come from his car, said. "We need one of those rifles in the Suburban or one of the automatics. And you don't even know who you're shooting at."

The man was a regular deputy and Frick wished he hadn't come in from the road.

"It couldn't possibly be the people shooting at the other men down underground. They haven't had time to get out."

"It's their accomplices, I'm sure of it," Frick said.

Khan came running up. "There was a road, they got in cars. I didn't see it, but a couple men came back and said it was useless. It was obviously a planned escape route."

"Put men to work searching the entire place underground. We're going after that boat. It's big and not very fast. The sheriff's boat will eat it up."

"Look, the yacht stopped," Frick said, looking way down the coastline. "Let's grab the rifles quick." Frick and Khan ran to the truck, looked in the back, grabbed four M4s, dropped two on the ground, and ran with two.

"You men get the rifles!" Khan shouted. "And start firing!"

They went back to the cliff edge, ready to cut the big yacht to pieces, but it had disappeared, probably behind the rocks that made a small point close to shore.

Frick noticed that Khan seemed to have forgotten all about protocol—the sheriff's men weren't supposed to be killing people.

"I want you to work the land," he told Khan. "I'll go to the water. I'll be on the phone and radio. I think I can get them in that slow boat. I got one more rocket launcher."

Sam felt his way along, using the big fins to propel himself, his right hand touching the steel of the pipe and his left wrapped around one of the Uzis. It was the spookiest thing he had ever tried. It was utterly dark and utterly cold and the temperature bored in on him, getting down to his muscles in moments. Because he had no weight, he had to swim in a slightly head-down position, his body having some tendency to float to the tunnel ceiling. It was probably related to his BC, but he didn't have time to figure it out in a pitch-black pipe.

The cold was so pervasive it became a form of pain. That was the first stage. Soon he knew he would start becoming spastic again, like a hamstrung animal in a pack of wolves, only here he would be eaten slowly, a tiny piece at a time.

He kept looking for light, thinking somehow it would help him fight the cold. If he could just see something, anything, it might not seem so hopeless. No one had told him the length of the pipe. Surely he would be able to sense the light, twenty or thirty feet off, at the very least.

If he made it, he'd have to contend with the men on the rocks. He didn't know if his Uzi would still shoot. If he survived the cold, he guessed he'd need to worry about such things.

Time was hard to measure in the cold and he didn't know how many minutes he had been in the pipe when he finally could see light ahead. It was dim, he supposed he was very deep—probably below sixty feet, near a hundred. As soon as he came out from the pipe, he angled down the beach, while moving up slope to shallower water. As he rose, he realized he had overestimated his depth because of the great cold and the darkness of the water on a late-fall morning.

He felt the weakening first in his legs and knew that if he didn't get out soon, he wouldn't get out at all. He was moving with the current, at perhaps a knot or two, and his buoyancy became welcome now. He fought through a patch of kelp and headed for the rocks finally visible at the shoreline.

The trick was to break the surface unobserved and avoid being instantly shot. Hopefully, the kelp would provide cover and make his bubbles less noticeable.

He slipped the mask down around his neck and came up under some broad kelp leaves. Quickly looking around, he saw no one on shore. It was rocky and steep and a sniper would have no easy route down to the beach.

Studying the bluffs carefully, he finally saw what he hoped he wouldn't: five men, four with automatic weapons, making their way down a slash in the rock overgrown with alders. Turning, he saw the yacht in the distance, waiting. He knew that Haley would be nearly hysterical with worry. If they came for him, the boat would be shot to pieces and perhaps even disintegrated by a rocket if they had any left.

With the cold he knew he couldn't stay in the water, so he crawled out on the rocks into some nearby bushes, which grew at the base of the bluff. His clothing stuck to him and the denim of his jeans created a murderous cold in the wind. The wool of the shirt was better, but not much. Crawling next to the bank, he slipped off his tank and stood with his back to the rock. The gunmen wouldn't be able to see him here, but he hoped that with binoculars his friends might spot him from the boat.

In minutes the men would reach the water and they would find him. He had to move. Forcing his body, he made his way along the steep rocky slopes, stumbling frequently as the

cramped muscles and shot nerves sent all manner of pain
through to his brain.

He'd hoped he wouldn't have to use his Uzi.

Frick drove back Deer Harbor Road to West Sound, where
his boat was moored. If the yacht remained behind Orcas, he
would intercept and destroy it. And if Ben Anderson were
found, he would fish him out of the water. Spurred on by his
proximity to the prize, he floored it and went eighty miles an
hour, except where the curves were too much.

He called McStott.

"Did you get a piece of that octopus?"

"It's harder than you think," McStott said. "We don't have
any of the technicians and none of us dive. We don't know
what they do to get him to come up."

"Get food. Put it over the side, entice him."

"Where's the food?"

"In the house, there on the dock, I would think." *This guy
had a Ph.D.?* "If not, it would be in the storage areas."

"All right, we'll try."

"Do better than try."

Evidently the gunmen saw Sam just as he was disappearing around a large rock. He heard shouts of "cop killer" that
bore the excitement of blood sport, a sound he would never
get used to. Given the nature of the hired thugs, it was an
ironic rallying cry and a tribute to Frick's ability to control
the message.

Knowing that they wouldn't be able to see the beach
down the way without coming quite some distance, Sam signaled madly at the yacht. He tried to run down the shoreline
on the rocks. From the cold his already suffering muscles

had become so incapacitated they didn't want to function. Even if they spotted him, bringing the yacht in tight to the beach risked running it onto the rocks.

By coming down the rock face on a series of ledges, the gunmen had lost their line of sight down the beach rendering their weapons useless at certain target angles. As the yacht moved, this condition wouldn't last. Well down the beach from the gunmen, Sam went to a large rock and leaped into the ocean, swimming frantically with his last few calories. As the yacht approached, a barrage of automatic shots rang out and he could see the superstructure of the yacht begin to dissolve. Apparently the gunmen could see only the uppermost portion of the yacht, to a level just below the flybridge. He hoped no one was on the upper bridge because they could not have survived. The shots continued to eat away at the bridge, sending bits of fiberglass flying and opening up long lines in the fiberglass that became jagged slices.

Sam held up his arm as a signal, as best he could, when a shot hit the water directly in front of him. He went under, waiting for the boat. More shots hit the water around him, but not many. When the boat was almost atop him, he bobbed up. Stu stood on the fantail of the boat. Nelson and Ben held him as he leaned over. They would have one try. After that, the boat would be shot to pieces as the gunmen got closer and improved their line of sight.

Sam grabbed Stu's forearm as it passed and they struggled to hold him.

CHAPTER 41

Ignoring the five-knot speed limit, Frick drove the sheriff's boat forty-eight knots through Poll Pass. It was the most direct and therefore the fastest route if one ignored all safety considerations, as well as the no-wake zones and the speed limit. At least one man on a small dock shook his fist.

Instead of the roiling waters, the bobbing seabirds, diving eagles, and splashing harbor seals, Frick's mind was on the yacht and the best way to sink it quickly. The victory, if he could achieve it, would be sweet.

Frick got on the cell phone, slightly irritated that Khan hadn't called him with a report.

"He's down by the water and it's rocky," Khan said. "Can't get a clear shot. The guys are going down the rock face. May be a mistake, but it's too late now."

"Where's that yacht?"

"It's in close now. As soon as we get a clear shot, we'll pick 'em apart."

"Sink it, but don't kill Anderson or Walther, unless you have to."

"We'll see. The guys are shooting right now. From up

here it looks like . . . yeah . . . that's Chase in the water and the boat's coming fast."

"Kill him," Frick shouted into the phone. "Kill him!"

Stu gave a massive pull and got Sam half out of the water with his legs dragging in the wake. Spray flew everywhere as Sam tried to get his leaden lower body clear of the water. Suddenly, as they turned seaward, Stu clenched his own leg, now pressed beside Sam's chest. The blood sprung red from his pants, but Stu kept on. At last they got Sam aboard.

Haley was steering belowdecks in the main salon. He saw no blood on her. Amid a new flurry of bullets they all hit the deck.

Too close to shore to turn in toward the beach, Haley continued an outbound turn and immediately the bullets ate their way along the hull as more snipers had better lines of sight. They all stayed down, and Sam saw Haley sitting on the salon floor trying to steer blind.

The bullets made a horrible racket as they shredded the yacht. Sam expected at any second to see Haley's body explode in crimson. She completed a 180-degree turn and then reached up to shove the throttles forward. A line of bullets blew up the steering console and Sam could see sparks shooting down from under the destroyed woodwork. He crawled forward into the main salon, throwing himself at the cabinet containing the main breaker switch. He broke the glass, dousing the main breaker.

Then he saw something chilling. A man he didn't recognize—no doubt the captain, who had brought the boat to pick them up—lay dead with the top of his skull half-blown away. He had pitched headfirst into the bullet-riddled galley.

"The shore," Sam shouted, seeing that they could get closer to the steep granite wall. Haley turned the wheel as more bullets poured into the boat. A bilge alarm sounded.

"Oh, my God," Ben said. A bullet had gotten below the waterline.

Then there was a horrible impact shaking the boat and tilting it. More shots blew through the boat and everybody stayed down. A damn rock! There was a gut-wrenching grinding sound forward. As bullets poured through the superstructure topside, it literally started to collapse. Haley threw the slowly turning engines in reverse, resulting in more grinding. She increased the power and the grinding got worse. They came off the rock. More shots. Haley turned the boat slightly outward and it seemed to run without shaking.

They must have stopped before the rock hit the shafts, Sam thought, as another swarm of bullets tore through the boat. Haley applied more throttle. The bullets began missing the boat and sprays of water leaped around the yacht as it accelerated to top speed.

Sam rose, marveling that the shredded boat still floated. Engines and steering system were intact, but little else. Nelson came up from below, stepping over the body. Ben came to Haley's side. Miraculously, everyone but Stu and the dead captain had escaped injury. Nelson went to work on Stu's leg.

The raucous bilge alarm continued, assaulting their ears and putting fear in their heads. The alarm ran off batteries and could not easily be silenced.

"I'm wondering if they've gone for their boat. It's probably in West Sound," Sam said.

"We can't outrun them then," Haley said. "They'll just board us, unless we resist. Then they'll sink us. Assuming that by some miracle we're still afloat."

The alarm continued unabated, reminding them that their bilges were filling.

"The hole is forward," Ben shouted above the din. "When the boat rises with speed, the hole must be above the waterline."

"I've got it floored," Haley shouted back.

"Head south," Sam said, "back toward Friday Harbor. Stay right near the beach."

Haley looked skeptical. "But that's the way they'll be coming."

"I have an idea."

"All right," Haley said. "It'd better be good. Their boat goes about fifty knots; ours goes about fourteen."

Frick tried to get Khan to talk to him, but Khan was too busy shooting.

"I think I may have hit Chase right when he was being picked up," Khan said. "I'm sure I saw blood on the back of the boat. Quite a bit of blood."

The reports slowed, then stopped.

"They're out of range," Khan said, his voice less animated. "Boat's still afloat, but I'm sure I punctured the hull at least once. Probably hit some of them. Headed your way."

"Good." Frick rounded the tip of Orcas and headed into the channel between Orcas and Jones Islands, knowing that around the next point he would find a crippled yacht and the people he desperately needed.

More clouds were moving in and the wind was rising. There would soon be small-craft advisories in the open water if there weren't already. Off to his port, dolphins were cruising along, but they were just humps in the water, disappearing and reappearing. Frick felt not even a flicker of interest. It took two minutes to round the point. They'd have to be there.

At first the yacht appeared as a white blob on the horizon. It wasn't moving. Perhaps Khan and his men had disabled it, after all. With their combined firepower it was certainly possible.

He glanced down at the rocket launcher, waiting to get within fifty yards. Then he'd blow the bow off and pick off the survivors as the yacht sank. He'd keep Anderson and Haley Walther alive long enough to extract the real meat of the scientist's research. And in a way he would have his revenge on Mr. Chase, because as the guy went lights out, there would be no doubt in his mind as to what would happen to Haley Walther.

At fifty yards he cut the throttle and studied the craft, staying low so as not to take a bullet. They could have a rifle on board. He saw no sign of life. That told him he was facing an ambush. They might not anticipate a rocket launcher, though.

He shouldered the green tube and used the laser sight to put the red dot three feet in from the tip of the bow. He blinked sweat from his eyes despite the chill; he didn't like the quiet. There should be some sign, a gun barrel over the edge, anything. He saw nothing.

Curious, Frick lowered the launcher and glassed the boat. They remained well hidden.

"Damn," he muttered, and pulled the trigger. It was almost instantaneous. The whole boat exploded. In front of his eyes it disintegrated. Had he been closer, he would have been injured.

He saw no swimmers; no one could have survived the blast. The blast was unnatural. Chase had turned on propane or the like. Then it struck him. This was no ambush. It was misdirection. They had gone ashore and he was wasting time. Frick cursed his mother, his father, God, and, most of all, Robert Chase.

He got on the cell phone.

"Khan."

"Get the men down Deer Harbor Road. They've gone

ashore. I'll meet you at the dock. If we don't find them quick, we'll get the octopus, McStott, and his papers and run."

"I figured they might do that," Khan said. "I already have men on Deer Harbor Road and the back lanes."

Khan was a smart man. They might get them yet.

CHAPTER 42

The Sinclairs were good people, Midwestern stock whose ancestors had been covered-wagon settlers. Retired, they lived year-round on Cormorant Bay Road. It was an idyllic setting, the house painted in pastels from the era of Elvis Presley and a sweeping water view. All they needed was an Edsel. Without a doubt, the Sinclairs were with their children in Seattle for Thanksgiving. Nobody was going to check.

Haley showed Sam the large new RV parked by their home.

"Could be tough to hot-wire," Sam said.

"I don't think you'll have to," Haley said. "They loaned it to us a while back so we could put up some visiting scientists. I know where they have a key inside it, I think. All you gotta do is break in through the side window."

"Oh, my God," Ben groaned. "Have we sunk this low?"

"Some of us have," Haley said. Sam figured she was still a bit pissed about the experimenting on people.

It worked just the way Haley said it would. There was a horn alarm and Sam yanked the wires on the horn. Now they'd stolen an RV, if they couldn't convince somebody that it was borrowed.

They drove the Sinclairs' RV to the end of Deer Harbor Road into a large cul-de-sac. When they parked at the bottom of the street, the deputies were just arriving and starting to screen people.

Sam and Nelson had gotten the bleeding stopped on Stu's leg and applied a dressing, but Stu was in no condition to go anywhere. Sam took a moment to look out through the RV's curtained windows. Attracted by motion, his eye went to the outer docks, and in the distance he saw someone standing behind a piling. It was Frick, gesticulating and talking with a tall man. Sam recalled the guards at Sanker talking about a second-in-command. Khan, if he remembered correctly.

Luckily, the RV remained on the far side of the deputies' search wave. A deputy was still a hundred feet off and approaching when Sam, Haley, and Ben made for the boat. The RV started up and headed out. The deputy made no attempt to stop either the RV or Sam's group.

When Sam had almost reached the Whaler, Frick realized what was happening and began screaming, the phone to his ear.

Once in the Whaler, they wasted no time. After casting off, they applied the power, pulling away from the docks and heading to the far side of the bay. Sam saw Frick and Khan each raise a pistol and fire repeatedly. Several bullets hit their craft above the waterline, but none connected with flesh.

Sam turned sharply and headed right for Frick and the sheriff's boat.

"Get down," he shouted at Haley and Ben.

Khan seemed to have reloaded quickly. As he took aim, Sam raised the Uzi, hoping it wouldn't misfire. The man's rapid fire drove Sam to the floor and peppered the foredeck of the Whaler, but not before Sam had put a burst under the bow of the San Juan sheriff's boat.

The opposing fire stopped. Reloading, Sam thought.

Swinging the Whaler in a partial turn, Sam put another burst into the Orcas Island deputy's boat as well. It was almost painful to imagine the bullets popping through the aluminum hull.

Sam was almost certain that the Lopez boat was at West Sound Harbor.

Now they had the head start they needed.

Succumbing to exhaustion and the extreme cold of still-sodden clothes, Sam gave Ben the helm and retreated to the Whaler's tiny cabin, where a diesel forced-air heater created momentary nirvana. The others still wore dry clothes, having stepped off the boat and onto shore. After they had lifted the dead captain's body to the beach, Sam had forced himself to take the *Alice B.* away from the shore and swim one last time.

Sam got naked and dried off; then he lucked out when he found a pair of swimming trunks. No doubt the owner used them when he had to go under the boat and cut a fouled line on the prop. Sam knew he was right about the trunks when he found a diving mask in the next drawer down. He put on the swimsuit, and after he had wrung the water from his clothes, he hung them in front of the heater outlet. He kept the cabin door open so that he could hear Haley and Ben. The size of the boat was such that he sat only two feet away from the helm.

Haley had clearly gotten over the hurt of Ben's keeping secrets from her. She nuzzled against Ben while he touched her hair. As if reading Sam's mind, she told Ben, "I forgive you."

Ben's craggy face broke into a half-smile. "But I haven't asked for forgiveness."

She punched his thigh. "I'll give it to you just the same."

Ben put his hand on hers, and she unclenched the fist, hugging him harder.

"I've always been a bit of a renegade. In the end the government won't care that I bought these men more time than their genetics had ordained. The bureaucrats will huff and puff and then want the secret. It's the way things are."

"Can't you tell me how you did it?" Haley said.

"Did what?"

"Don't be coy." She pulled away and looked in Ben's eyes. "Used Arcs to lengthen human life. Everything."

"Essentially," Ben said, "we looked at the problems that humans have and that Arcs don't. We then tried to think of ways to emulate the DNA protection that Arcs enjoy. It's counterintuitive because we burn oxygen, and oxidation destroys our DNA. Arcs don't use oxygen."

"People rust. Arcs don't. Right?"

"Exactly." Ben smiled. "But it gets complicated quickly when you try to understand why."

While Sam listened, he glanced at the nearly flat wake as they passed Reef Island in the Wasp group. Even the small islands had trees and one a resident hawk, another an eagle. There was no sign of any boat following yet. Sam imagined Frick cursing two leaking sheriff's boats and a third coming all the way around from West Sound. Though the leaking boats would still float, they'd be slowed significantly; each bullet hole would be a fountain—at speed, a geyser.

"The simple answer is that we activated a gene," Ben was saying. "Human mitochondria, it turns out, have an extra crumb of DNA that's not functional. In the Arc it *is* functional. We activated it in humans with an Arc peptide that controls the production of the Arc protein. Kind of like a hormone—which is just how it acts in humans."

"Is that what you were doing with the vat?" Haley asked. "Making Arc hormone?"

"Mm-hmm. We found this unusual gene in a deep-mud/deep-ocean Arc. At least we think so. I'll get to that in a moment. There was no point in trying to grow those particular

Arcs, because they live under tremendous pressure and they reproduce very slowly."

"So you used a related Arc species and changed its genetic makeup to include the Arc gene you wanted?" Haley guessed.

"Very good. The Arc we used reproduces much faster. That's why we have the vat in the cave. It grows Arcs in an oxygen-free environment in three atmospheres of pressure—the equivalent of one hundred feet underwater."

Haley leaned forward for more, the eager protégée completely absorbed in the scientific process.

"Part of the joke there is that we had thousands and thousands of Arc genes from numerous drilling rigs, all brought up under pressure. Through an unfortunate string of circumstances we don't know exactly where the magic gene came from."

"You mean you have the Arc, but you don't know where to find more?"

"It's not even that good. Now all we have is yet another Arc species that has been genetically modified to contain the original special Arc gene."

"These would be the Arcs you kept a sample of?"

"Right," Ben said. "Unlike their deep-sea cousins, these Arcs can be mass-produced somewhat quickly, and I do have a supply of the necessary peptide in a Seattle lab. But that's just the product. The only place I have the gene that produces the peptide is in the genetically engineered Arc."

Sam wondered whether Ben had hidden the flask of the genetically engineered Arcs on his person or elsewhere. As if reading his mind, Haley asked that very question of Ben.

Ben smiled and opened his coat and removed what looked to be a custom-made flask. It was roughly two inches thick, flat in appearance, and a little larger in surface area than a phone book. It could be strapped to Ben's chest using shoulder straps.

"Of course, having this on me," Ben said, "leaves me with an obvious problem. I can't have Frick catching us and somehow getting these." He patted the flask. "That's the first problem. Frick aside, I have no place to multiply them at the moment. And no idea where to find the original Arc that naturally carries the gene."

"But you found them once," Haley said.

"Yes, and I'm sure someone will find them again," Ben said. "Most of the Arcs were in the North Sea, but others came from off South America, southern California, and even from below stagnant freshwater ponds."

Haley didn't look like she wanted to believe in the enormity of the task. "There must be some way to trace . . . I mean forensics . . . mud . . . ?"

"All long gone, and nothing saved. Everything's gone now, except what's in the flask," Ben said, "and if for any reason we can't mass-produce it, we could spend the next one hundred years looking for the special Arc, the original, and still never find it."

Haley groaned. "The Sargasso stew. That's why you want a Venter-like system, to sort through gazillions of Arc genes."

"You got it."

Carefully Ben handed the heavy flask to Haley. After she had examined it for a moment, Ben spoke again, his tone different. "Maybe I *should* lose these Arcs."

Haley cradled the container in her hands. "You don't think the world's ready for it."

"Look at us. Look at Frick, willing to murder. Look at the subjects, moved to kidnapping by their paranoia. Who can you trust? The government?"

"What are you going to do?" she asked.

"I don't know."

Sam knew there was an underlying, damnable truth. Humankind could sometimes only take so much good stuff;

hen it had to digest it before it could advance. Like nuclear
nergy, for example. During the digestion, just about any-
hing could happen, and it usually wasn't good.

"We discovered antibiotics without murder and may-
hem," Haley said as if reading Sam's mind.

"I'm afraid the fountain of youth has a lot more food for
greed and the lust to live, than do ordinary discoveries.
Antibiotics only cure a disease until the next resistant disease or aging gets you."

Haley remained silent, as did Ben. The Whaler was now
just south of the Wasp Islands. Sam stepped out of the cabin
and scanned the horizon for a moment. Still no sign of a
heriff's boat. There were breaks in the overcast and with
hem came a little sun.

"We read about the manifesto," Sam said, breaking the si-
ence. "No surprise that the government wouldn't play ball,
but I'm curious about the thinking behind your manifesto."

Ben sighed and sat back in his seat, looking as if he'd
suddenly aged a bit.

"Nelson called me an idealist. I suppose he's right. It was
beautiful, at least to me."

"What?" Haley asked, turning to face him and putting her
hand on his knee.

Ben shrugged and snorted a small laugh. "Everything.
Nothing. You read about methane mining, other alternative-
energy sources, energy potential, and the risks involved.
Yes?"

They both nodded. "Some of it, we tried to learn; there's
a lot of material," Haley said.

"Did you read about the other alternative-energy sources,
ike tidal, methane from coal mines, and solar?"

They shook their heads.

"Well, you couldn't be expected to find it all in twenty-
four hours. It's an extensive and grand scheme. For me, it

was a beautiful integration, like the symmetry of a snowflake. The secrets of the Archaea. ARCLES means abundance, replenishment, climate, longevity, energy, and security. It's a global cycle, and it begins with mining the methane and other alternative-energy sources. You do that in a planned way, with government oversight, and you not only get massive energy benefits, but you reduce the long-term risk of methane eruptions. Everybody agrees that greenhouse effect is going to materialize if you put enough junk in the air; it's just a question of whether it has started yet to cause global warming. To me, that's not the issue.

"Anyway, back to the point. Greenhouse gases will be an issue if we keep emitting volumes of CO_2. If methane escapes in abundance, the CO_2 will be a bigger issue. We need to learn to cope with it.

"We must get over the notion that if it's natural, it's good. Polio is natural; cancer is natural; tsunamis, volcanoes, earthquakes and forest fires are natural; ice ages are natural. We're moving into the age where humankind must begin to act as the custodian of its environment. It requires thoughtful leaders. Probably an oxymoron."

"We read about possible thermonuclear methane release."

Ben waved his hand as if to dismiss it.

"Good political talk to stimulate methane research. Some of the guys calculated that one well-placed nuclear device in the right deep-sea trench could start a chain reaction of methane release, but in the end I didn't think this was the key risk for our planet. After all, it's hard to heat enough water or change enough water pressure or salinity even with an atomic weapon. No . . . the risk is elsewhere."

"We read about asphyxiation, conflagrations," Haley said.

"I'm not a big believer in the instantaneous, all-at-once methane release theory. Although I believe it happens, and could theoretically happen perhaps from deep-sea events like volcanoes or the giant hot-vent system under the ocean undergoing a change, as it has in the past. These natural furnaces can really heat water and it only takes a few degrees and the changing of ocean currents and the like—not many realize it, but a five-degree change in ocean temperatures could release half the methane on the planet. Startling.

"But more likely than quick release in a matter of days, I think—given our knowledge of history and prehistory—is that the methane will be released more gradually. *Is being* released gradually. Global warming has already started or will start if our emissions continue. We have cars running all over the planet, and at some point . . ." Ben shrugged. "So the methane release would only exacerbate it. Once atmospheric warming starts, it triggers more methane release. It's a potentially bad cycle.

"I think the real catastrophe is climate change, though it will happen over time—slowly, in human time."

"Will mining the methane help?" Haley asked.

"A little. But my vision is this: you finish the cycle by growing plankton or scrubbing the air in other ways. We know how to take CO_2, make water vapor, and dispose of the carbon in the ground."

Ben appeared transported by this grand scheme of his. This dream. ARCLES. Sam nodded, although he knew the devil was in the details.

"Did your colleagues buy the whole ARCLES vision?" Haley asked.

"We were all excited about it. We saw the longevity benefit as the reward for humankind's improved stewardship of the planet. It was ambitious, I know, but—"

"Longevity's also the biggest problem," Sam said.

"True," Ben said. "When you make old age a disease, you create mind-bending, psychological, political, and social issues."

"I can see that," Sam said.

"There's always hope," Haley said. "But then there's always wrinkles too."

Sam and Ben chuckled, despite the difficult truth.

Then Ben paused, giving her a look of Santa-like reassurance. In that moment only the two of them existed in their universe.

"Helen told me why my discovery would captivate so many. And really it's why we are here today being chased by crazy people."

Haley put her hand on Ben's and waited.

"Well, it's not that profound," he said. "It is because we get older faster than we think." Ben waited to let that sink in. "When I was a little boy, ten years old, standing by a big old madrona over by the old lime kiln, on Orcas, I thought about time. I think it was my first virginal experience with the subject. I reasoned that I could only remember back a few years and yet it seemed quite a while that I had been around. To my way of thinking at ten, getting to thirty would be many multiples of my conscious life remembered. And so I concluded that as a practical matter I just didn't have to worry about getting old. After that time by the lime kiln, there were many such good days; many winters of fireside reading, summers of sun and blue water, many happy years with Helen and you. I was still surprised. I got older faster than I thought and, so in a way, I felt I needed to make some bargain for more. It is the bane of conscious life that it wants to hear the cry of another grandchild, taste next season's wine, watch the latest meteor shower, listen to one more *Messiah*. Even such banal things as next year's Super Bowl sound good. But there's no one to bargain with. It was my dream to find a way to make that bargain—not just for me, but for millions. Now I may dump that dream overboard in San Juan Channel because living with the rotting carcass of selfish humanity seems worse, for the moment, than dying. Or maybe

I shouldn't be such a pessimist. Maybe a democracy can handle it."

No one said anything for a long moment.

"So now we have to deal with Glaucus," Ben said, his eyes clear and purposeful again. "Other than the flask of Arcs, and what I have stored in my brain, he's the clearest existing path to the Arc regimen."

"But aren't you going to tell me how the aging formula works?" Haley asked. "For God's sake, I've earned it. Spit it out!"

Ben smiled as if it really didn't matter how it all worked. "Well, for God's sake, I might be doing you something of a disservice. But you're a young scientist. I remember what that's like. So a quick explanation. We do five things, or work on five systems, if you will. Mostly it's rooted in protecting your DNA and stimulating cellular regeneration without causing cancer. We first limit a primary source of damage to human DNA by limiting free radicals; we then make the DNA itself less susceptible to damage; we then slow the cellular clock that controls the number of times a cell can divide; we give powerful mitogens, which some people call growth hormones; and we influence cardiovascular health by making lipo protein molecules larger, and bad cholesterol lower and good cholesterol higher."

"How does it work?" she prodded.

"We know the result of activating the gene, we've been discussing. We're getting the additional un-coupler protein molecule that does indeed limit free radicals by altering the mitochondrial cell wall. With the treatment the mitochondria leak much less unused oxygen. It is the ultimate antioxidant supplement, and it really works.

"This Arc peptide hormone superactivates yet another apparently silent gene in your genome. I say *apparently* because we don't know what else it might do. This gene we call Arc Two, even though it's not known in Arcs, and we call the hormone that activates it 'Arc stimulator' or 'AS.' AS induces the gene Arc Two to express a protein that creates a sort of shield for your DNA. You could think of it as a toughening agent or genome copy insurance."

Sam wasn't following the science anymore, but he was interested in the bottom line, which he sensed was coming. Haley, on the other hand, was obviously transported, so he didn't dare interrupt with basic questions.

"In scientific terms," Ben said, "AS causes alternative splicing of the Arc Two RNA, giving rise to a molecule that stops meiosis and greatly reduces abnormal recombinations in human DNA. It significantly affects the nuclear chromatin structures into which DNA is packaged, although we haven't finished analyzing how it does that. So the tightly packed DNA in the reorganized chromatin will not replicate for purposes of sexual reproduction and it pretty much won't allow the abnormal recombinations of DNA that often result in cancer. Cancer is still possible, but unlikely. But here's the good part: recombinations run by the immune system are largely unaffected."

"You can't make babies, then, once the AS hormone's induced the Arc Two gene?" Haley said.

"Yes. That's right."

"Glaucus was your first subject, then, and can't reproduce."

"Yes. We've given Glaucus the effect of the Arc gene by in vitro gene infusion. That's not the important thing about Glaucus. There's a homologous gene in humans that stimulates cell growth. But it's much more active in octopuses."

"Don't tell me you used an octopus hormone to stimulate a human gene?"

"Oh no. A combination of other human hormones that we discovered by studying octopuses. They exist in humans in infinitesimal quantities and are related to the common growth hormones already used by physicians. We produce the super-hormone in transgenic bacteria."

"That's part of what the bacteria were making in the lab," Haley said.

The motors throbbed on a calm sea. Over the stern, Sam watched as a bald eagle dragged its talons across the water but missed its prey.

"Yes, exactly," Ben continued. "Glaucus and his huge size are a good example of a different part of the regimen attributable to the growth hormones. Octopuses in the wild have gotten five hundred pounds in four years and started at the size of a rice grain. Compare that to people. The hormones we use in the Arc regimen have the advantage they don't lose their effectiveness over time and they are self-limiting. On the regimen you won't develop endless muscle, for example. No cancer, because we altered the chromatin. Big muscles—light workouts."

"Oh, so you don't lose muscle mass as you age."

"Bingo," Ben said. "Except, actually, you hardly age in any usual sense for a long time."

"Okay. Then?"

"Another reason we age is because telomeres in each cell of our body get shorter with time."

"So you're about to tell me you can slow the shortening of telomeres by activating telomerase without getting cancer," Haley said. "You can use powerful cell reproduction stimulators without inducing cancer?"

"Exactly."

Sam saw that they were approaching their destination. He moved to the wheel.

"What's next?"

"Next is pedestrian, but necessary. Even thirty-five-year-olds have arteriosclerosis resulting in damage to the arteries. We learned how to increase the size of lipo protein molecules in your blood and lower bad cholesterol while raising good cholesterol."

"And that's the end of it?"

"That's it, dear—except for a few thousand details."

Haley thought a moment. "We can release Glaucus because he can't reproduce."

"Bingo," Ben said.

As they entered Friday Harbor, Sam saw no boats about they were safe, for the moment.

Now all they had to do was dump an impotent octopus into the Pacific and stop a money-mad, crooked cop from hurting anyone else. The first sounded simple enough. The second, not so much.

Sam looked at Haley. She was actually caressing the flask. If they succeeded with Glaucus and Frick, then they could decide what to do about the Arcs.

CHAPTER 43

As they approached the dock surrounding Glaucus's pen, they saw two men bent over the edge of the dock.

"That's McStott," Ben said. "Probably wants a hunk of Glaucus."

McStott and the other man stood and stared at them as they approached. Neither Sam nor Ben made any attempt to disguise himself, and McStott ran back up the dock toward the Oaks Building. Sam could see McStott going for his cell phone.

"Quick," Ben said. "Let me out."

Ben hopped off the Whaler and onto the dock. He tried to lift a wooden section that spanned the main concrete sections.

Haley tied a line to a cleat as Sam crawled off the boat to help Ben. They lifted up the section of dock, exposing the cable that held fast the top of the net over the pen.

"I'll get some squid," Haley said, running for the small house that held Glaucus's food. She returned with a large bucket and a strange-looking megaphone and set them down. Then, stopping to think for a moment, she changed direc-

tions and ran down the dock to a large aluminum workboat
Its main feature was a large circulating-saltwater tank amid
ships. The huge tank took up most of the boat's interior. I
had to measure six feet across, ten feet long, and five fee
deep. Because the boat, known as the *Venture Too,* was line
with ventilated wooden stripping over a thick layer of Styro
foam, with all the benches along the gunnels made of wood
cored with Styrofoam, the boat was unsinkable. But for the
huge cost and some upkeep requirements, it was pure prag
matism for a biologist.

It was a roomy and open vessel with an eleven-foot beam
and benches running along most of its length, even beside
the tank. If needed, it could accommodate easily twenty stu
dents or visiting biologists.

"Give me the whooper," Ben said.

Sam presumed he meant the megaphone and bait. He
complied.

"They obviously didn't know to use it." Ben ruffled the
water with his hand, dumped over a few squid, and put the
metal horn of the whooper in the water.

Sam looked over the edge and observed what could only
be described as a giant creature coming up the sidewall of
the net. The head of the creature was enormous—the size of
a garbage can—and coming out of it were eight tentacles
larger than a big man's thighs. They were long and graceful
and the span of the creature was too large to determine, with
suctioned arms going in every direction. An orange brown
color was apparent.

The whooper made a low sound, something like the bass
pedal on an organ. As the creature came inexorably upward,
Sam was in awe of its smooth grace and obvious strength.
He told himself that the creature's mass was 25 percent smaller
than it appeared in the water because of the water's lense effect. In about a minute a tentacle came up and Ben ran the

food up and down the creature's suction cups, teasing him, then let a tentacle tip slop around in the bucket.

Sam marveled at the length of Glaucus's arms, at least fifteen feet; the span of him now appeared over thirty.

"He can taste with his suction cups," Ben murmured.

Soon the mammoth octopus hovered just below the surface and Ben could see the large gills blowing the water in through the creature's huge mantle. Ben talked with the creature as though it could understand Ben's voice, and he kept rubbing up and down his suction cups. At Haley's instruction Sam retrieved more buckets of food and put them along the inside of the workboat. With the circulating-saltwater tank pumps turned on, Haley pulled the boat across the opening and parallel to the dock.

"I've done this before on the dock and with this boat," Ben said. "He'll be pissed, but he'll probably let us coax him in. These guys can stay out of the water for thirty minutes or so. Glaucus doesn't like it much, although one time he walked across the dock and tried to get in the shed. After that, we built the overhang."

"We've only got minutes," Sam said, thinking about Frick and the boat that would be coming behind them. Sam and Haley stood along the side of the boat and began gently pulling the creature, while Ben continued to encourage him by rubbing the squid along his suction cups.

Sam was watching the dock when he saw McStott creeping around with a gun in his hand. Sam fired two shots just over his head. McStott turned and ran as fast as his considerable girth would allow.

Slowly they raised the unruly creature until they managed to get a tentacle into the saltwater tank, now baited with hundreds of squid. Sam hoped Glaucus would like what he tasted. Haley grabbed a hose hooked to a saltwater pump and began spraying the parts of Glaucus that were exposed. Finally they had his massive brown-looking head up to the gunnel. His eyes were the size of half-dollars. Ben got a large tarp from the dock, put it under Glaucus, and they used it like a hammock. With several back-wrenching lifts, which to the creature were just good nudges, they got Glaucus over the edge and he eagerly joined the food in the tank. Glaucus used his tentacles to move the food to his beak, but only for a few moments. Glaucus quickly became unhappy, flashed red, and tried to climb out of the tank.

"Get the tarp over him," Ben said.

Ben and Haley jumped on Glaucus, while Sam got the tarp over the tank. Sam threw off the dock lines, started the motors, and gave the boat full throttle.

Glaucus put a tentacle out from under the tarp, still flashing red in a pulsating rhythm. Ben spoke gently and Haley climbed on top of the giant lump under the tarp, trying to hold the seven-hundred-pound mass of muscle in his cage.

"This is not a happy octopus," Ben shouted. "He'll be leaving when he really wants to."

Frick had the throttles of the thirty-two-foot Donzi wide open before he was out of Deer Harbor. The use of the boat for a day had cost San Juan County $5,000, but he wouldn't be around to pay it. Powered by three 250-hp Mercury outboards, it was a fast boat designed to get rich fishermen to the fishing grounds in a hurry.

As they passed out of the harbor, McStott called. His voice shook in panic. "They're here. I tried to call you. They've about got the octopus in the workboat."

"Shoot the bastards."

"Chase just shot at me," McStott said, breathless. "I've never shot a gun and don't want to."

"You little prick. It has a trigger. Point and pull."

"I can't."

"Get the guards," Frick shouted into the phone.

"They saw Ranken, man," McStott said, almost crying. "They're long gone."

"Do something, McStott," Frick said, "or you're gonna end up like Ranken."

Frick hung up. "It's useless," he said to Khan. "It won't matter. We'll catch them. That boat is slower than hell. I'll take them all out with this." He patted the antitank rocket.

Khan just nodded, but looked grim.

They were past Wasp Islands in minutes, traveling at forty-five knots.

As they neared Friday Harbor, just north of the point of San Juan, McStott called again.

"They have Glaucus and they've gone."

"Which way?" Frick asked.

"Toward the Straits of Juan de Fuca. Glaucus is in a tank under a blue tarp."

Frick stopped the boat in San Juan Channel and looked with glasses. He sighted the workboat moving down San Juan channel, ahead of them, toward the straits.

"We got 'em now," he said to Khan. "Get the rocket launcher ready."

"Head toward the straits, but stay in the middle of the channel," Ben said. Sam flipped on the bilge pump because Glaucus was sloshing gallons of water out of his tank as he struggled.

Haley's phone rang.

"Answer it," Sam said, thinking it might be a cop.

Haley was bouncing around on Glaucus and held up her phone. Ben took it and answered.

"It's Ernie," he said to Sam.

"Yo," Sam replied.

"I'm at the docks at Friday Harbor. Where are you?"

"Get a boat and follow us. We're just pulling out of Friday Harbor. Forty-foot aluminum boat. Wheelhouse on the back."

"I see you. Can't you come and get me?" Ernie said.

"No time. Get a boat and follow."

"How the hell . . . Okay . . . I got cash. There're some guys here. Bye."

By dangling his tentacles, Ben said, Glaucus knew that the wide blue sea wasn't far. He obviously thought he could crawl there pronto.

Haley tried again to get the tarp down all around the huge beast and keep all his tentacles in the tank, but she was losing the battle. A set of massive suckers felt her back and played with her shirt. It was almost comical. Then the creature erupted and Haley was on a wild ride, trying to hold it down and keep herself in the boat. Ben took the wheel and Sam tried to keep the tarp down, but the creature was strong enough to throw the new intruder off its back.

Haley managed to stay mostly in place, bouncing up and down, constantly fondled by Glaucus's tentacles.

Sam crept up beside Haley, then grabbed as much of Glaucus's bulk as possible, giving him a mighty squeeze. For some reason the bear hug calmed Glaucus, or distracted him, much like pinching a horse's upper lip. Gradually Sam worked him back over the edge of the tank.

When Glaucus moved again, Sam squeezed harder. It was a standoff.

Sam looked at Ben, wondering how long he'd have to remain engaged with the wily invertebrate.

"When octopuses make love, they get in a hug with all eight tentacles," Ben shouted, laughing. "They'll do it for hours."

"Great."

"Behind us," Haley called out. A boat was approaching a quarter-mile off.

The boat was obviously a fast one, closing the distance quickly. The bilge pumps were still pumping, but the aluminum workboat carried too much weight and too little power to make it a race.

A new noise joined the clamor. Sam looked behind them, then upward. It appeared to be a coast guard helicopter.

"It seems we have both the good guys and the bad guys converging," Sam yelled.

"They can't see us drop Glaucus in the straits. They can't find him," said Ben. "Let's keep going."

Sam nodded. The big orange-and-white helicopter swooped low; the men inside obviously wanted them to stop.

"Can't trust anyone," Ben said over the whine of the chopper's jet engine.

Silently Sam agreed. Ben kept the outboards running at max throttle. Haley pumped water from the tank and bilges to lighten the boat. Sam kept Glaucus in an octopus embrace. He guessed they were cruising at just under thirty miles per hour. Frick was in a very fast boat and gaining on them.

Haley's phone rang again. It was Ernie.

"My boat is slow," Ernie said.

"So's ours. Keep coming," Sam said.

"Frick will catch us long before we get to the Straits of Juan de Fuca," Sam said after he had hung up.

"That's apparent," Ben said. "You would think he wouldn't do anything with a coast guard helicopter standing by. . . ."

It was overcast all around, with a low, soft, undefined ceiling. To the right lay Griffin Bay, a broad expanse of water in the large hook of San Juan Island. Where San Juan Island and Lopez Island nearly converged, they created a narrower passage to the Straits of Juan de Fuca, replete with tide rips and bad seas on heavy wind days.

"*Venture Too, Venture Too*, this is United States Coast

Guard helicopter Lima, Papa, Bravo, Alpha, Tango. How do you copy?"

Ben said nothing. Sam tried putting a line around Glaucus, and pulling it tight as a substitute for the bear hug. The creature moved about like a simmering stew, but stayed put. Sam moved to the wheelhouse and picked up the mike.

"This is *Venture Too*," Sam said.

"Switch and answer twenty-two alpha."

"Roger that, twenty-two alpha."

Sam changed the channel.

"This is *Venture Too*."

"*Venture Too,* please return to Friday Harbor. We have some government officials and your friend Rachael Sullivan, who would like to speak with you."

"Copy that," said Sam. "We have a seven-hundred-pound octopus in the tank that we'll be delivering to the straits."

"Negative on that, *Venture Too*. Please return to Friday Harbor."

"We believe the boat right behind us is driven by Garth Frick," Sam said. "He's the murderer that law enforcement will soon be looking for. He's going to try to kill us."

"This is Special Agent Gayle Killingsworth; that doesn't seem very likely, so long as we are here."

"Get your guns ready," Sam said. "Last we saw, Frick has a rocket launcher."

"Say again. Rocket launcher?"

"Give me that," Ben said. "This is Ben Anderson, formerly of the Sanker Foundation. Garth Frick is behind us and most certainly has been trying to kill us and won't hesitate to blow your ass out of the sky. Is that plain enough? I need to deliver this creature to deep water. It's a matter of life and death—he can only live out of the water for thirty minutes maximum—and I'm afraid we can't comply until we're done."

"The octopus will die if you turn around?" Killingsworth asked.

"Yes."

Haley had come up and was listening. She and Sam shared a glance at Ben's lie.

The coast guard's silence spoke volumes. Sam assumed that Rachael Sullivan had something to do with their arrival. If so, he could imagine Rachael pleading their case.

Ben gave the wheel to Sam, took the flask from Haley, stepped to the stern of the boat, and put it in a locker.

"I'll tell you if I decide to dump it," Ben said.

"Are you sure?" Haley said. The scientist inside her was no doubt screaming. They watched Frick's boat pull up behind and then swerve to the side, accelerate, and then come in close.

Frick waved a gun, motioning for them to stop.

Rachael and Lew sat, side by side, on a bench seat in the coast guard helicopter; Gayle Killingsworth sat to the far side of Rachael. Behind them sat two more FBI agents and one state police officer. Ahead and to the right was one airman and near a large open door another airman. In the front of the cockpit sat a pilot and a copilot.

They had been to San Juan, Lopez, then Orcas, and were returning to Sanker when Rachael saw what looked to her like the Sanker workboat in the distance, so they followed after to check it out. Gayle's attitude toward the mission had improved. The obvious evasions had convinced her that something was wrong under Garth Frick's command. After catching the workboat they had tried to turn them around, but Ben Anderson was a stubborn man. For his part, Frick insisted he was in hot pursuit of a murder suspect.

Gayle held a police radio provided by the sheriff's department. It crackled, the sheriff's dispatcher putting her in touch with the long-awaited county sheriff himself.

"Tiger One," the dispatcher said, using Gayle's chosen moniker. "I have Sheriff Larson, patched in on a landline."

"Go ahead." Killingsworth waited.

"Tiger One," said the sheriff, "this is Sheriff Larson. I'm gone for two days and all hell breaks loose."

"That's affirmative. What is your position on Garth Frick?"

"I never intended for him to be in the chain of command. I don't believe that two-oh-one would have put him in command. There must be a mix-up."

"What now?" she asked.

"I've got one-oh-one coming back from vacation and he is, as of this moment, in charge. He can be reached on his cell phone and will arrive on the ferry within the hour."

"May I communicate this to Officer Frick and the other officers?" Killingsworth asked.

"If you can find Frick, you can tell him."

Gayle clicked off and nodded at Rachael.

"Seems we should have moved faster," she said. "I'll give you that. This is a massive mess."

They looked down at *Venture Too* and Frick right behind.

A new voice came on the radio frequency.

"This is Special Agent Ernie Sanders."

"Huh?" Killingsworth seemed taken aback.

Rachael cheered silently.

"I'm in a boat about two miles back," Ernie said, "and having a hard time catching the pack. My yacht's a little slow."

Killingsworth identified herself. "Where are you from?"

"Washington, DC, but as I mentioned, I'm offering my services. Seems I'm the only public servant down here with a boat."

Other than Frick, Rachael thought.

The pilot interrupted.

"I'm not liking what I'm seeing down in that chase boat."

At that moment the world for Rachael instantaneously went upside down—she heard a huge explosion and in an instant the chopper was violently spinning. She was thrown into Lew and felt herself still grabbing him when they hit the water with an unbelievable jolt. Green seawater poured from every direction, worse than a nightmare. Lew was frantically pulling off her shoes and yelling at Gayle to get hers off. They all wore inflatable life jackets.

Vaguely Rachael recalled being told not to inflate the vest until she was clear of the copter.

"Wait until it fills and you're out," Lew yelled.

Rachael grabbed Lew's hand with one of hers and his belt with the other.

It was torture watching the cabin fill. Brief torture—for it was full in seconds. Cold water hit her face and the world disappeared in an ugly green haze.

CHAPTER 44

Ben pointed a finger at the coast guard helicopter—a message for Frick to back off. Instead, Frick motioned for them to stop. Without warning, Sam fired a shot into one of the three big outboards on Frick's boat. For a second it raced; then, with an ugly clunk, it died.

Now Frick's boat was crippled. Frick shoved the throttles on the two remaining engines forward and peeled off to the side. Sam saw the left-hand motor tip forward and the idle prop come out of the water. This made the two boats more equal in speed, but Frick's still had more horsepower and a more hydrodynamic hull form with less weight.

Sam turned sharply away, but Frick followed—and with slightly more speed, he was able to stay right on his tail.

Frick lifted what looked like a green tube. Sam knew it was a rocket launcher.

"Duck!" Sam shouted, turning the boat so abruptly that it almost spilled Glaucus's tank.

He heard a rushing sound, but Frick's rocket passed above them. Before their eyes the tail boom of the helicopter exploded and the copter whirled crazily, dropping abruptly into the ocean.

"Oh, my God," Haley breathily observed.

Sam reduced the throttles and turned the boat hard again, attempting a 180-degree turn back to the copter. There was another *whoosh*. A muffled, wet explosion sent Sam flying, and he realized that a rocket had struck just beneath the water, blowing the motors off the stern of the boat and exploding the structure beneath the pilothouse.

His body, lying over the gunnel and half out of the boat, screamed in pain. Something in his shoulder and something in his leg burned. Haley, just forward of the helm superstructure, looked dazed. He rolled to her, holding her for dear life. Behind him, Ben was groaning and barely conscious. He would be out of commission.

Frick's boat roared up close. Maybe thirty yards off, Sam raised his eyes above the gunnel. Frick looked like a hungry animal, rocket launcher at the ready. The tall man rose with a pistol. Sam fired four times, hitting him square, once in the side of the neck, and Khan went down, probably for good.

There was a second explosion. It was hell, packed into a moment, a blinding fireball rolling over him at the same time the concussive shock wave seemingly flattened his head and nearly punctured his eardrums. For a second his mind was like an empty neighborhood—quiet, lifeless, suspended. Then sound and color returned: Haley was screaming about Ben. The bang of a bullet puncturing the aluminum hull. Sam took a hit to the shoulder. It was a flesh wound, but he played dead because his gun was empty. Haley struggled beneath him to get to Ben.

Venture Too bobbed about, mangled, burned, and listing badly.

"Be still," he whispered in Haley's ear. For once, she didn't argue.

Frick rammed the *Venture Too,* putting the sharp bow of his craft right on top of the workboat. Frick's boat stalled and he leaped aboard like a pirate, a side arm in his hand.

He met the boat's largest occupant head-on. Glaucus was out of the tank; his grasping red tentacles were everywhere.

Frick stopped for a moment, his mouth and eyes wide. Sam quit playing dead and grabbed Frick's gun hand. Pulling himself up Frick's arm, Sam swung his gun hand into Frick's jaw.

The wound in his right shoulder impeded Sam, rendering the punch indecisive, but Frick lost his footing. Sam wrenched the gun free, throwing it overboard.

Frick wheeled, a long knife in his hand. Sam feinted a left-hand punch as Frick slashed with the knife. The blade caught only air. Sam followed the slashing motion, getting behind the knife, driving it into Frick's own leg. Frick screamed and Sam turned the knife in the man's flesh. Frick went crazy with the pain.

Sam felt wet tentacles feeling his legs, moving around him. Frick was in Glaucus's grip as well, suction cups over his bloody leg—tasting.

Almost too late, Sam saw a new gun, attached to a shaking, bloody hand in the boat above them. A deafening shot and barrel blast rocked Sam as the bullet slammed into the meat outside his right clavicle.

Khan rolled his eyes and fell.

Frick pulled the knife out of his leg, grabbed Haley by the hair, and put it to her neck. She sank her teeth into his hand in desperation. The blade parted skin on her throat as Sam lunged, using his left hand to get at the knife. The three of them struggled, blood running down Haley's neck as she ducked and pulled out of the scrum.

Sam found himself eye to eye with Frick, blood-slippery hands competing for the knife. With a sudden motion Sam used his head for a massive butt to Frick's forehead. It staggered Frick. The knife clattered to the deck and Sam sank hardened fingers into Frick's neck.

Frick gouged for Sam's eyes. Sam ducked and dug deeper into the neck. He found the Adam's apple and closed his fist.

When Frick couldn't find Sam's eyes, both hands went around Sam's neck and squeezed. Sam felt light-headed, but Frick was making a wheezing sound, weakening as Sam's hand assumed a death grip on Frick's trachea. Sam felt cartilage pop. Frick screamed and squeezed, then released Sam, who shook Frick like a rag doll.

Sam felt himself falling.

The shock of hitting the wet deck brought him back to semiconsciousness. His neck still felt as if Frick's hands clenched it. But that was impossible—Frick lay next to him, fish eyes opening and closing as the man tried to draw oxygen through his ruined windpipe.

Frick's hand spidered across the floorboards and grasped the knife. To Sam's surprise, he drew the blade to the base of his own throat.

Sam had just enough energy to stop him. He knew what Frick feared and it wasn't death.

"They'll put you in a cage," Sam said as he pulled the knife away. Frick passed out, probably imagining the headlines announcing that a discredited female scientist had taken him down.

Sam felt fingers pressing down on the wound at his shoulder. It was Haley, blood seeping from the wound in her neck. Ben lay beside them on the deck, two bullet holes in him. He struggled to breathe, and it didn't look promising.

Haley sobbed as the last of Glaucus's tentacles slipped noiselessly over the side.

"Don't worry," Ben said. "I've lived a very good life."

"You're not going to die," she sobbed.

"Haley," Ben whispered.

She put Sam's fingers in the hole under his clavicle an moved to Ben, taking his head in her lap.

"I loved you more than my dream. That's why I kept yo out of it," he said. "The world isn't ready, but maybe it's lik a new mother . . . never ready."

"Stop talking," she said.

"You understand I love you more?" he asked.

She nodded.

"Hide it from all the Fricks and Sankers of the world. . . .

"No. No. No," she said, trying to quiet him, unintereste in the Arcs for the moment.

Ben rested a moment, catching his breath.

"Save your energy," she whispered, trying desperately t somehow hold the blood in his body. Sam understood he desperation.

"The flask," he gasped.

"It's gone," she said. "Blown away over the side." Sh cradled his head. "We don't get to choose." She kissed hi forehead and smoothed his hair.

Ben managed the slightest smile. Then he sighed an looked up at the sky, his face growing peaceful, content.

"I want you to have babies," Ben told Haley, his min clearly wandering. "And if some fishermen catch a giant oc topus, tell them it's not Glaucus and let them make sushi."

"I said quiet, old man," Haley chided, tears in her eyes.

Ben managed another smile. "I have loved you as muc as I could love anyone," he said. "And if I could, I would se your children."

Ben closed his eyes and Sam's heart shrank within him The weariness of death was overtaking him as Haley's rack ing sobs filled his ears. He'd lost another fellow traveler.

EPILOGUE

Sam sat on the veranda above the ferry, with the turquoise of the water against the blue of the sky and the breeze washing over his mind like the waves on the rocks. The orcas made their rounds, looking for foolish seals, the salmon having mostly passed to the rivers. Food was already a bit sparse for the bald eagles and they were flying about hunting and generally looking magnificent.

After all the hysteria about youth retention, Sam occasionally found himself looking in the mirror, wondering about the coming of the age spots and wrinkles. He was too young to think about such things, about which kind of bypass surgery worked best, what diet might keep his prostate reasonably small and his hemorrhoids under control. Despite the aches and pains of aging and not-so-old injuries, he felt better than ever. Felt comfortable with getting older (unless Haley could make him a deal). Felt happy to take his place in the order of things, content to breathe the sea air and listen to the blow of the whales. Life brimmed inside him, and, for the first time since his wife, Anna, had died, his joy was unmitigated. He hadn't yet decided why the fullness of his spirit had returned, but he thought the reason might have been buried in a conversation with Haley about measuring life by whom you loved and who loved you—and not by what you thought you did or did not do. Anna was a terrible loss, but now he knew that they had agreed in a moment that she should go on ahead.

Ben had been right. The older Sam got, the more surprised he was by the shortness of his days on earth. It was important to get to wherever you were going before you went out of this life. Anna had done that.

Haley had her own lab at the university compound and was desperately trying to figure how she might extract microbes and mud from the deep parts of the sea and keep it under pressure. Sam had been there when they gave her an award and had reveled in the gleam in her eye when her shame became just a memory.

Finding the magic Arc was a grail quest she undertook willingly—largely, Sam thought, because she thought humankind was meant to have it, to use it, despite men like Garth Frick. Frick himself awaited a death sentence or, if unlucky, life in prison.

Sanker and Rossitter were fighting charges of conspiracy to commit murder, and Sanker had the largest criminal team ever assembled. Sam figured having to deal with all the lawyers was in itself some punishment. Of course, Sanker and Rossitter had turned on each other. Everybody figured they'd both end up with life terms, which in Sanker's case wouldn't be long.

Frick's rocket had melted the Arc container, effectively disintegrating it. Whatever was left of the genetically engineered Arcs had been blown over the side by the explosion. The obstacles to rediscovery, given the luck of the first find, were turning out to be enormous. Somewhere down in the depths of the sea, under the mud—maybe a thousand feet down into the earth or even deeper, or perhaps under a brackish freshwater pond—lived a particular Arc with a particular gene with a certain codon. No one knew exactly where and no one knew how many of this Arc subspecies existed.

Perhaps people could handle the prize, given a second chance and armed with the knowledge of the mistakes of the past. It was a decidedly optimistic view. Haley slipped up behind Sam, but not unnoticed. She came around him and sat across the table, a little short of breath. She must have been running to keep from being late. One of the many things Sam had learned about her was that Haley considered lateness a subtle form of arrogance.

She looked at his sling and then at his eyes, and she seemed to enjoy the way they held hers.

"You're not going. You aren't better yet—you've had holes blown through you. Don't tell me you called me here to say good-bye."

"The muscle's knitting well enough. Besides, I'm just supervising."

"You're going into a war zone."

"Not technically. We're just gonna get some food and some medicine to people who need it."

"We're not discussing this. I'll fight you."

It was hard not to chuckle, but she wasn't having any of it. Haley was angry, determined, and utterly sincere.

"I more than appreciate your concern."

Her face softened and she stood, came back around the table, and sat in a chair close beside him. It was rather pleasant.

"I'll sit on you until your flight leaves," she said matter-of-factly.

"I'll be back."

"How would I know that? You've been all over the world. The rest of your family is from California."

"Ernie is going with me. I don't have to stay for the whole thing."

"Ernie, of the FBI?"

It had surprised Sam too. "Yeah. He's taking a little leave from the FBI to celebrate his hero status and he wants something worthwhile to do. I won't be doing it all myself, Haley. As soon as Ernie gets the hang of this private contractor work, I'll leave. They just need someone to follow."

"You really have to go, all broken up like this?"

"I gotta go."

"You're a wonderful idiot." She kissed him on the forehead.

He paused, working up his courage.

"I let you down all those years ago. I let you down bad." The words came from his soul.

In her eyes he saw the flood of pain. Then tears poured. It was almost more than he could handle. She said nothing, waiting.

"The day on the dock when I was touching you, we both know I was trying to say that I loved you. Of course, we both knew I did. I whispered it so quietly you weren't sure what I said." He waited, wishing there was an easy way to do this. "If you want, you can say you don't know what I'm talking about." Judging from the increased flow of tears—she knew what he was talking about. "I promised you I would call you. I said I'd call you the next day. We both figured that on the phone I might be able to say more about how I was feeling. But I didn't call. Not that day, not the next. You probably went the first week, making excuses for me, telling yourself there would be a letter or something. I know this sounds ridiculous. It does to me. We talked so little about our feelings."

"It's not ridiculous," she said, sniffing and coughing through the tears.

"I'm sure you called yourself foolish for even imagining that we were in love," Sam said, choking up himself. "That's maybe the worst part. You thought you were a fool, and then you figured that I never cared, or if I did, I was some kind of weird guy with a personality disorder."

Haley laughed despite herself.

"*Then*, to add insult to injury, I never even brought it up. I pretended that it hadn't happened, that it was the folly of youth. We had cousinly love or something of the sort."

"And then you married Anna Wade and said nothing," she said. "Not a word."

"I need you to forgive me, for not calling the day after we sat on the dock."

"Why?"

"I was going to save the world from some very bad people. I was pumped up. The next day I was going underground, to Europe, to try to break a big case. It was for a government and a corporation. It just possessed me and I knew I could never do right by you. Your life with me would have been hell. But I should have said something. I should have given you a chance."

"So now what do you want?"

"Another chance. I want you to open yourself and give me a chance. Run the rock pile. Take a risk."

"You know that I loved you ever since that day," she said.

"I know that."

She looked sheepish for a second. "I even practiced how I'd tell you off if this ever came up. In my head, at least."

He chuckled, and she laughed too.

"You wouldn't seduce me," she said. "I hated you for not even trying. Of course, I really wanted you to mean what you said, you jerk."

"I am sorry," he said, meaning it.

"That's it?" she said.

"I didn't know exactly how much I loved you in the let's get-married sense until I saw you in your tam-o'-shanter hat the day all this started."

"You didn't tell me that either."

"We were a little busy," he joked. "And I did have that thing about people I cared about dying all the time." He grew slightly more serious. "I couldn't remember about Anna, and I guess I couldn't be at peace."

"Are you over that?"

"Enough to run the rock pile one more time," he said.

"How are things with your mother?"

"Much better. And with the part of me that is my mother. We're in the game, she and I. There is no rule that says we can't succeed."

"Amen. Or Pacna, if you're Tilok."

"My life with Ben and Helen is a testament to the fact that my mother's gift worked."

He kissed her then, hoping to end the dialogue and begin the peace. She climbed in his lap and they continued until he realized it might be a breach of the public's peace. Then they talked, and he said all the things he might have said thirteen years previous. Sometime, he knew, she might ask about the other women and how he could have fallen in love with them. Then again, Haley was a big person and she might never get around to that one.

"Ben call today?" he finally asked.

By some quirk of the Great Spirit, Ben had been alive when Ernie's boat arrived. Ben and Sarah were recuperating together at an exclusive place in Switzerland, with Ben holding court for the scientists of the world. Each visitor thought he would successfully ply the old man and separate fact from fiction. The idea of retirement to a small island with a little laboratory had come up.

The passengers in the coast guard helicopter had also survived, with varying degrees of injury. Ernie had rescued them

ll. Rachael and Lew were together and beaming, though
am hadn't seen either of them on San Juan Island in the last
ouple days. Sam had given them a bottle of champagne and
week's reservation at the most romantic spot he knew.
They took it and went. That boded well, he guessed.

"Ben wants me to come to Switzerland at Christmas. He
aid he'd love it if you would come too. And after what you
ust said, you better not hesitate for one lousy second."

"I will," he said.

Her mouth dropped open.

"Not hesitate," he clarified.

"Wow," Haley said, "just like that! The mysterious Sam
vill go with me to Switzerland at Christmas?"

Sam's mind weighed the pros and cons, still feeling the
leuth, the spy, the nameless man who doesn't draw atten-
ion, eyes shifting to see who might be watching. Then the
noment caught him and he gave way, locking his mind and
pirit with hers.

It was a rhetorical question.

BOOK YOUR PLACE ON OUR WEBSITE AND MAKE THE READING CONNECTION!

We've created a customized website just for our very special readers, where you can get the inside scoop on everything that's going on with Zebra, Pinnacle and Kensington books.

When you come online, you'll have the exciting opportunity to:

- View covers of upcoming books
- Read sample chapters
- Learn about our future publishing schedule (listed by publication month *and author*)
- Find out when your favorite authors will be visiting a city near you
- Search for and order backlist books from our online catalog
- Check out author bios and background information
- Send e-mail to your favorite authors
- Meet the Kensington staff online
- Join us in weekly chats with authors, readers and other guests
- Get writing guidelines
- AND MUCH MORE!

Visit our website at
http://www.kensingtonbooks.com